novel populated with characters who are in every way larger than life: opium warlords of the Shan highlands, aging Mafia dons who rarely emerge from their Staten Island compounds, soulless hit men and equally soulless yuppie financiers, and a lawman who's so far out of his league he doesn't even know it. And at its heart is Johnny Di Pietro, who after sixteen years of nickel-and-diming for the mob—running numbers and taking action; handling jukebox routes; dealing stolen guns, booze, and cars; working as purseman in two precincts; handling the Teamsters' dirty paperwork; dispatching legbreakers—is annointed by his uncle Giuseppe to lead their kind, men of the old ways, back to their rightful place of power.

Never before have the worlds of Asian drug traffickers and the Italian Mafia been portrayed with such deadly fidelity and insight. Written in lyrical, incandescent prose, **TRINITIES** takes us further into these worlds—incendiary, malevolent, and vicious—than any novel has before.

TRINITIES

TRINITIES

✠

NICK TOSCHES

DOUBLEDAY
NEW YORK ▲ LONDON ▲ TORONTO ▲ SYDNEY ▲ AUCKLAND

PUBLISHED BY DOUBLEDAY
a division of Bantam Doubleday Dell Publishing Group, Inc.
1540 Broadway, New York, New York 10036

DOUBLEDAY and the portrayal of an anchor with a dolphin
are trademarks of Doubleday, a division of
Bantam Doubleday Dell Publishing Group, Inc.

Book design by Julie Duquet

This novel is a work of fiction. Any references to real people, events, establishments, organizations, or locales are intended only to give the fiction a sense of reality and authenticity. Other names, characters, and incidents are either the product of the author's imagination or are used fictitiously, as are those fictionalized events and incidents that involve real persons.

We gratefully acknowledge permission to reprint the following:

"Land of a Thousand Dances" by Chris Kenner. Copyright © 1963 by Thursday Music Corp. Copyright renewed and assigned to Windswept Pacific Entertainment Co. d/b/a Longitude Music Co. All rights reserved. Used by permission.

"Cool Jerk" by Donald Storball. Copyright © 1966 by Trio Music Co., Inc. & Alley Music Corp. All rights reserved. Used by permisson.

"Suck or Die" by W. Jones. Copyright © 1994 by W. Jones. All rights reserved.

Library of Congress Cataloging-in-Publication Data
Tosches, Nick.
　　Trinities / Nick Tosches. — 1st ed.
　　　　　p.　　　cm.
　　1. Imaginary wars and battles—Fiction.　2. Organized crime—Fiction.
　　3. Drug trade—Fiction.　4. Mafia—Fiction.　I. Title.
　　PS3570.O74T75　1994
　　813'.54—dc20　　　　　　　　　　　　　　　　　　94-16083
　　　　　　　　　　　　　　　　　　　　　　　　　　　CIP

ISBN 0-385-47003-7
Copyright © 1994 by Nick Tosches, Inc.
All Rights Reserved
Printed in the United States of America
October 1994
First Edition

10　8　6　4　2　1　3　5　7　9

For her,
physician and destroyer,
thrice-damned, thrice-blest,
our lady of the gust,
inspiratrix.

All things come alike to all: there is one event to the righteous, and to the wicked; to the good and to the clean, and to the unclean; to him that sacrificeth, and to him that sacrificeth not: as is the good, so is the sinner; and he that sweareth, as he that feareth an oath.

This is an evil among all things that are done under the sun, that there is one event unto all: yea, also the heart of the sons of men is full of evil, and madness is in their heart while they live, and after that they go to the dead.

—Ecclesiastes 9: 2–3

Can it be that what man regards as evil, God regards as good?

—Liu Chi, *Yü-li tzu*

ONE

He stood there like the lesser part of his own shadow; stood there, as he did every night, on Second Avenue near the bodega at the southwest corner of 115th Street, a vaguely unsettling spectral presence in a fake-leather jacket. He was barely twenty-five years old, but all youth had been drained from him, and he had the sallow expressionless face of a corpse. Even the sparse scraggly hairs of his mustache were like those of postmortem growth.

In his left hand, he held a torn-open cellophane bag of Rolets barbecue-flavored fried pork rinds. Raking through it with the fingers of his right hand, he brought its remains to his mouth. He tossed the greasy bag to the pavement and with his fake-leather sleeve wiped the oil and crumbs from his mouth and mustache. He looked abstractedly at the back of the hand he had raised to his face. *"Mierda,"* he muttered. He was turning yellow again. He shook away the thought. No, he told himself, it was just the ugly light from the bodega. He looked up at the moon that rose in the darkening sky and saw that it too cast an ugly light.

"El Jockey es vuelto," he muttered to those who passed: *los toxi-*

cómanos, the wretched ones like himself, and the young roving ones that moved in loud gathering packs.

He had picked up too soon after rehab this time, he told himself. Tomorrow he would kick. If he chilled out now, he could do it on his own. No Thorazine, no detox, none of that shit. He still had some Trexan. He'd get him some methadone, some Librium. There was a meeting at Our Lady Queen of Angels. He'd be all right. *Mañana*. He cursed himself, but the curse was washed away by the gentle eddying tow within his veins of death's sweet tidal flow. He scratched through the fake leather at the sclerotic skin of his left arm and almost smiled as his eyes began to close.

"*El Jockey es vuelto, el Jockey es vuelto.*"

He had a taker, then another. It would be a good night, an early one.

Not far from where he stood, two men from Brooklyn sat at a table in the small dining-room of a tavern on the corner of First Avenue and 116th Street. The two men were in their mid-thirties. One, whom men knew as Willie Gloves, was overweight but not quite fat. His dark thinning hair, held stiffly in place by a glazed mist of styling spray, was already graying and receding at his temples. The other, Johnny Di Pietro by name, was lean and wiry, with his hair brushed back in chestnut-colored waves. The heavy man wore a long-sleeved floral rayon shirt and a gold bracelet; the other, a navy blue pullover and a black kid-mohair suit. They ate in easy silence, pouring occasionally from the bottle of wine that had been placed between them. Now and then, the lean man, who drank more sparingly and more slowly than the other, turned to look through the window at the shabby Chrysler that was parked outside.

Only two of the other seven tables were occupied. Beyond the latticed partition, men sat at the bar in hushed groups or alone in quiet drunkenness. Here, where the ominous Hispanic breezes of East Harlem did not enter, here, where the must and gloom of older and more ominous breezes lingered, even the jukebox seemed to whisper. At minimum volume, the crescendos of Jimmy Roselli's "Mala Femmina" drifted through the room like faint wisps of some distant angry sorrow. The two men from Brooklyn who sat eating with the bottle of wine between them had known this place since they were boys, and to them, the old man who ran the place and cooked the food had always seemed to be old. Now, with the passing of years, he had become more like a ghost than a man, and the joint itself, once bright with color, was now a somber chiaroscuro of brown and faded ocher hues, subtly ever darkening beneath a patina of nicotine and age. No, this was not so much a bar or a restaurant anymore, but a haunted sanctuary, and the old man was its sentinel, guarding something that was no longer there, preserving times and honoring ways that long ago had ceased to be except as a memory to him and the dwindling few, strangers now in their own streets, who continued to gather here.

But there was something about the squid in this joint that brought the two men from Brooklyn here again and again. It wasn't the sauce, thick and garlicky and wine-rich and good as it was. No. It was the squid itself. The old man's squid was not the bland white rubbery stuff that other joints served. He used only *calamaretti*, the smallest baby squid; and the flesh of their sacs and tentacles possessed a rare tenderness and a faint sweet taste of the sea. The *calamaretti* must be *freschissimi*, the old man never tired of explaining, using the Sicilian words *calamaricchi* and *frischissimi*. After two days of death, he said, their true succulence and flavor were lost. As a boy in Sciacca, he had learned to make squid from his uncle. He had learned to let the little ones die slowly on ice, for the cold, slow death relaxed their flesh and made them tender. He had learned to pull the tentacles from the sacs so the guts came out in one clean clot. Their tiny bulging eyes would still be clear and lucent as he cut above them. Their flesh was always sweetest in the spring, the old man said. And this was the spring.

Yes, there was something about the squid in this joint. It was the reason the two men from Brooklyn returned here Friday after Friday, year in and year out. And the fact that the old man served squid only on Friday was the sole reason that the sallow-faced figure in the fake-leather jacket had been allowed to live out the week.

The two men swabbed their bowls with crusts of bread and drank the last of their wine. One of them placed a fifty-dollar bill on the table, and, still unspeaking, they rose. From amid his hanging pots and pans, framed by the kitchen doorway, the old man raised one arm and waved it in a slow, slight arc. They returned the gesture, then made their way to the door, nodding their taciturn regards in passing to those at the bar who acknowledged their exit.

They walked to the shabby Chrysler, and the wiry man got behind the wheel. From the glove compartment, the other removed a Colt Woodsman .22-caliber pistol and a long, fat Gold Star silencer, and he married them. He rolled down the car window and extended his elbow from it, letting the weight of his arm rest in a natural position on the door. With his left arm across his midsection, he held the gun flush against the interior door panel, the snout of the silencer nuzzled near the crook of his armpit. The driver waited until the man with the gun was settled and still, and then he backed up to pull out. As he switched gears from neutral to reverse, a deep muffled clunking sound, like heavy objects thudding in a metal drum, issued from the underbelly of the car. Neither of them responded to it; they both looked straight ahead.

The car moved slowly west on 116th Street, then turned slowly south on Second Avenue.

"There he is," the driver said. "My new transmission."

The Chrysler came to a casual idling halt near where the young man stood. The young man peered at them for a moment, then approached the car.

He spoke softly in English to the one whose arm rested in the window: "The Jockey's back."

The elbow of the resting arm rose slightly, suddenly, and from beneath it there were three fast hollow pops of muted, rushing light. In the moment before he lurched backward and fell, the young man's eyes closed and his mouth opened, and he made a strange sort of sound. To the man in the floral shirt, he looked in that moment like a broad who was taking it up the ass and just starting to like it.

They were halfway across the George Washington Bridge before either of them spoke.

"Fuckin' spic looked like he was about ready to croak on his own," the gunman said. He lighted a cigarette. "You still got no idea what the fuck that was all about?"

The driver grimaced nonchalantly and shrugged. "Just some piece of shit sellin' dope to feed his own jones," he said. "Maybe he got too big for his Reeboks, stuck his chuchufritos where they don't belong. Who the fuck knows."

"Shit, he's the first fuckin' spic over the age of sixteen I seen sellin' dimes on the street since fuckin' God knows when. Besides, it must've been somethin' important, or they wouldn't have got us in on it."

The driver was silent, and then he spoke, and there was a grim resignation in his voice. "Nothin' we do is important," he said. "By now I got that much figured out."

The gunman looked out the window, and he nodded slowly, as if making a show of weighing the driver's words.

"Ah, you know your uncle's groomin' ya," he said.

"Yeah. To trim the weeds on his fuckin' grave. He's on his way out. They're just waitin'."

The driver drew a deep breath, and his eyes narrowed. He thought of all the nickel-and-diming he had been through in the last sixteen years. He knew more of this life than men twice his age. He had done most of what there was to do. He had run numbers and taken action, had handled jukebox routes and video slots. He had been a purse-man in two precincts, had handled the Teamsters' dirtiest paperwork in three different locals. He had turned stolen bonds and guns, booze and cars. He had dispatched legbreakers, overseen gambling operations, dealt everything from counterfeit fifties to swag Mass cards. He had seen the inner beast of this world laid out before him in gross vivisection. And still there had been no passage from the realm of nickels and dimes; no green light, not from his uncle, not from anyone.

They were in Jersey now, heading toward Bayonne: the long, slow way back to Brooklyn. The driver's mood lightened, and he glanced with a smile at the gunman. "What the fuck was that he said to you?"

"Who?"

"My new transmission. That island nigger back there."

"Oh. Him." The gunman uttered a sardonic guttural sound, a chuckle of casual derision. " 'The Jockey's back.' "

The driver repeated the words: a quizzical mumble ending in a snort of low laughter. The gunman laughed then as well, in his own low way, and they drove on like that for a while, shaking their heads and grinning. The gunman sucked the last morsel of squid from between his teeth and spat it into the night.

TWO

Those who were arriving to mourn moved aside, and some lowered their heads, as old Giuseppe Di Pietro, his right hand firm on the railing and his left hand firm on his cane, slowly and laboriously descended the steps of the Scarpaci Funeral Home. His legs and back were weak with pain, but he did not allow his countenance to betray that weakness or that pain. Beneath the cocked brim of his Milano fedora, his eyes through the thick glass of his horn-rimmed bifocals stared straight ahead, as if Eighty-sixth Street, and indeed all of Brooklyn, were not there. His face, cold and expressionless in denial of his pain, was like a weathered tombstone carving. The wind and attrition of the better part of a century had worn it down, but no emotion had ever etched the slightest trace upon it.

At his left, adjusting his stride to accommodate old Giuseppe's pace, was Louie Bones, a younger man of sixty years, who wore Ray-Ban sunglasses and carried his black hat in his hand, letting the warm afternoon breeze tousle the thick silver waves of his vanity's preening. He knew not to brace the older man's arm with his hand, or to assist him in any way; for this was how Giuseppe Di Pietro wanted it.

A man in a dark gray shadow-stripe suit and dark gray tinted glasses opened the curbside rear door of the black Mercedes 600 SEL that was parked in front of the funeral parlor. With some difficulty, old Giuseppe settled himself into the soft leather seat. The man in the shadow-stripe suit closed the door gently, then walked around to open the other rear door for Louie Bones.

" 'A cummari secca," the old man intoned as the car moved smoothly, silently down Eighty-sixth Street: the dry mistress. He said these words whenever death was near, and when he said them, his voice lent them an august dignity that he seemed to reserve for them alone. As if observing some tacit ritual protocol, Louie Bones waited until Giuseppe pronounced these words before he himself spoke.

"Did you hear that fuckin' undertaker?" he said. His words were uttered absently, softly. " 'I'll see you soon,' he says to me. 'Fuck you,' I told him, 'I'll see *you.*' "

A hint of something like laughter rippled through the older man's thorax. He removed his hat. The lining of its crown was yellowed with age, like the cuffs and collar of his white-on-white shirt. He watched the other man flick lint from his Stefano Ricci necktie and adjust the flourish of the matching silk foulard in his breast pocket.

"He's right, that *beccamort'*. He'll have us all soon enough." The old man stared through the window as they made their way west through Brooklyn. "*Brucculin',*" he whispered to himself: a curse, an exorcism, an obscure and tenebrous judgment. He cleared his throat. "Look at me. I seen better carcasses hangin' from hooks. I'll be eighty-one next Christmas. That piece of shit in that box back there was only seventy-five. Every morning, I wake up, I thank God."

"You'll outlive us all, Joe."

"Yeah. That's what I used to tell that piece of shit in that box."

The old man took a pack of DeNobilis from his pocket. He placed one of the gnarled little cigars between his teeth, and Louie Bones held the flame of a gold lighter to it. They crossed the Verrazano-Narrows Bridge to Staten Island.

They rode in silence. Then old Giuseppe said it again: " 'A cummari secca." He said it more slowly this time; he said it as if he had not said it before.

The Mercedes pulled into the driveway of Louie Bones's house, on Castleton Avenue.

"There's coffee in the kitchen," Louie told the man in the shadow-stripe suit. "Tell my wife we're out back. Have her put the game on for ya."

The old man followed Louie to an open flagstone patio that looked out onto a broad lawn bordered by neatly trimmed hedges. There were rosebushes, and an old concrete birdbath in the shade of a big blooming Norway maple. Two pairs of pin-striped Zimmerli boxer shorts, some socks, and an old girdle flapped from a clothesline that ran between the house and a pulley set into the big maple's trunk. The men sat on cushioned wrought-iron chairs at a large wrought-iron, glass-topped table. Louie's wife appeared: a fat woman in a brightly colored house-dress. Her hair, dyed platinum and tinted with streaks of silver, was spray-cast into a frigid grotesquerie of bouffant insouciance. She bent and kissed the old man on the cheek.

"Did you see the garden, Joe?"

Old Giuseppe looked in the direction of the rosebushes.

"Eggplants this year," the fat lady said.

"Nice."

"The white ones," she chirped.

"Ah."

"Oh, well, let me get the demitasse," she said, as if excusing herself reluctantly from a conversation whose pleasures had distracted her from the pressing duties at hand. The men sat silently until she returned with a silver tray, from which she set out fancy little china saucers and cups of steaming espresso, little silver spoons and linen napkins, sugar and a small plate of cookies.

There was the sound of a car pulling into the drive. "Here's Tonio," Louie said to the old man. He lighted a cigarette and sipped his coffee. "Bring another demitasse," he told his wife. "And a bottle of—what's that shit he drinks?"

"He don't drink no shit no more. He quit."

The voice was that of another old man, whose appearance followed his words. He was Antonio Pazienza, older even than old Giuseppe, and more bent in the back, dressed in a dark plaid shirt buttoned to the collar and loose gabardine trousers gathered round the waist with a frayed belt that was several sizes too large.

"Yeah," he said. "I broke down and bought it. Miracle Ear. Micro-Elite. Top of the line. Makes me wonder what else you been sayin' all these years."

He put his arms around the fat lady and returned her kiss in kind. "Why don't you dump this bum here. You and me, we'll go to Niagara Falls." The eyes beneath his perpetual scowl brightened somewhat as he made his little joke, the same little joke he had been making for many years.

"We'll let Louie carry the bags." She giggled, meeting his little joke with the same playful response with which she had been meeting it those many years.

"Go, already. I'll buy the tickets," Louie Bones said, as he had been saying for years. He avoided her gaze, as if she were a spray-frosted Medusa.

"See how he is," she said, tsking. She withdrew and returned with a third cup of coffee, and when she went back into the house this time, she closed the sliding glass door behind her. With a sound that was lost between a growl and a groan, old Tonio eased himself into a chair.

"So," he said. The obsidian coldness had returned to his eyes, restoring his scowl to its true nature. "Here we are."

Old Giuseppe snorted. Louie Bones nodded slowly. The three men sat, still and quiet, as the lengthening afternoon shadows lapped, gently trembling, toward them.

"They might as well put our names along with his on that tombstone," Giuseppe said. "They gave us our last rites when we gave them our blessing."

Old Tonio's eyes were lost in the encroaching, horripilating shadows, which seemed to contain the glimmering of things that were long lost to memory.

"It's our own fault," Louie Bones said. "Our blessing, our fault. All them punks with the fancy talk. All them college joes with the degrees and the computers. Spreadsheets, venture capital, statutory mergers, cash-conversion cycles—this, that, the other thing. They gave us this line of shit and we bought it. It makes me laugh. Leveraged buyouts. We got more leverage out of a fuckin' lead pipe than them and all their fuckin' mumbo-jumbo put together. But we bought it. We gave 'em the world on a fuckin' silver platter. It was us, not them. We're the ones who cut off our own fuckin' balls."

Tonio turned from the shadows, and he spoke. "What Louie says is true. Our bellies were full, and we were getting old. We wanted to wash the blood from our hands. We wanted a new kind of respect. And we did what fools do: we trusted."

"And now," Giuseppe said, "they've lost what we gave them. The spics, the niggers—they've run our own kind off our own streets. Look at this shit up in Harlem. They go to the spics for the *bubbonia* now, just like with the cocaine. My own nephew, my brother's son, he had to go up there. And for what? For nothing. They step on a cockroach, and nothing changes. *Tutto è marruni scuru.*

"Kids like him, my nephew, they're lost. Look at that *guaglion'* the feds made a big deal out of, that Gotti boy here that Cherry Hill had dancing on a chain for a while. There's nothing for them. We got ours, but they won't get theirs. We betrayed them. We're the end of the fucking line. These punks we gave our world to, they're wheeling and dealing and playing big shot, and this other scum is laughing, taking what once belonged to us."

"It still belongs to us," old Tonio said.

"No," Giuseppe said. "It belongs to who seizes it. It belongs to who holds it."

His words were spoken as much to the shadows as to the other men. Like Tonio, he too felt their obscure beguilement. For a moment, there were the mingled imagined scents of lemon blossom and the sea, the remembrance of an ancient threnody, of the blood's mysteries darkening a young boy's flowering senses with the slow fatal dance of eros and death.

"And those we gave it to are weak," said Louie Bones. "All greed and no *cughiuni.*"

"We wanted to be legitimate," Tonio said. "So now we're legitimate.

Like a bunch of dick-faced politicians and lawyers. We're legitimate shit."

"What we gave them, we can take back," Louie Bones said. "Fuck this legitimate shit."

The cold eyes in Tonio's scowl brightened once again, but with a different, deeper radiance than they had before, a radiance that seemed to bear something of the unspeakable insinuations of the quivering shadows that were now upon him, flickering across his leathery skin, enlacing him.

"Look," Giuseppe said, leaning forward, studying Tonio and then Louie Bones. "We are different from this new blood."

"*Siamu siciliani veri*," old Tonio declared, nodding once in stern agreement.

"We are different," Giuseppe repeated, "and there are few of us left. Like Tonio says, we are true Sicilians. Louie, you were born in this country, but your blood is Sicilian—"

"*Sì, u sangu viru.*" Tonio looked at the younger man as he spoke, but the shadows now obscured his eyes. He seemed now to be of the shadows: shadow-breath and shadow-words.

"And you are like us," old Giuseppe continued. He paused and drank the last of his coffee, which was bitter and cold. "There is not much strength among the three of us who sit here," he said, "not in the back or in the fist. Those days are gone. But"—he brought his forefinger lightly to his temple—"there is still strength here."

"*Sì. 'A forza di vuluntà*," Tonio said.

"And we still have the loyalty of those who understand the true blood, men who yet possess the strength of youth that we have lost."

Tonio mentioned names; Louie Bones mentioned others.

"And that is an alloy more powerful than any other: the wisdom of age and the strength of youth. While there is still time, before it is lost forever, we can take back all that once was ours. And more."

"These spics are bad, Giuseppe. And this other shit, these *schiavi* that do their dirty work—*i cubani, i dominicani, i giamaicani, gli hai-*

tiani, i nigeriani, cacata di tutte le tinte—there are more of them every time you turn around."

"They're bad?" Tonio spat. "And what are we, towel-boys? Fuck them. Fuck them where they breathe."

Louie snorted laconically and looked at Giuseppe.

"You're right, Louie," his padrone conceded. "But Tonio is right as well. And I think I am right when I say that if we do not move now, we will die in a world we no longer know." From the drooping clusters of the maple branches there came the sudden soft lilting of birds. "Besides," Giuseppe continued, "it's not the spics and the niggers. They're just *'a feccia*, the scum on the surface."

Tonio leaned back and spoke with slow deliberation. "Giuseppe, my friend," he said, "your words are like a beautiful cloud in the sky. *Ma*" —his tone became less placid—"*unni è 'a sustanza?*"

Giuseppe once again brought the crooked forefinger of his right hand lightly to his temple. "*Ecculu*," he said softly, with an open expression revealing nothing. "Here," he said, "the substance is here." He drew gentle breath. His nostrils flared, and when he spoke again, the words rushed forward in a violent hush. "*Eccu, è nella putenzia che sta tra noi e il nostru calcagnu nelle culline e i sue sciavazz' delle cosche siciliane.*"

Louie Bones, whose Italian and Sicilian were good, but whose *baccàgghiu—la lingua della mala*, they defined it in Sicily: the language of evil—was poor, let the words unravel in his mind. "Here," the old man had said, "here, and in the power that lies between us and our friend in the hills and his"—*sciavazz' delle cosche siciliane*; there was no unraveling that phrase into English within his mind, nor any need to. It lay coiled, chill and venomous, as the old man had invoked it.

Tonio and Louie Bones stared at Giuseppe and were silent. And when old Giuseppe spoke again, all he said was "*Avimu a fari comu San Giorgio. Avimu a fari muriri u dragu.*" He said the words slowly and pronounced them finely, and even Louie Bones's grasp of them was fast and clear. "We must be like Saint George," the old man had said. "We must slay the dragon."

They were all in the shadows now, and nothing remained of the spring day's warmth. They heard the sound of the glass door sliding open; they saw the cotton-candy Gorgon, the painted gargoyle mouth of delusion smiling wide.

"You boys want some more cookies?"

THREE

The teacup, which bore the Qing Dynasty mark of the emperor Tao-kuang, was perhaps a century older than Chen Fang himself. The white porcelain surfaces of its bowl and lid were decorated on the outside with scenes of romance and on the inside with scenes of lust. Standing at his kitchen sink in baggy gray trousers and a shabby undershirt, Fang half filled the cup with warm water, then brought it from the kitchen, which was bright with sunlight and loud with the sounds that rose from Baxter Street below, to the bedroom, which was quieter and dim with the shadows of late afternoon; and he set it down on the little mahogany table near the window.

Everything else he needed was already there. He sat and removed the plastic orange cap from the needle of the B-D Ultra-Fine 1-cc syringe and dipped its fine siliconized point into the cup. Slowly he drew from the warm water, watching until it reached the fifty-unit calibration. The five glassine bags sealed with the printed stamp of the racing horseman had already been opened, and the white powder from them lay brimming in the hollow of a bent silver spoon. He released the warm water from the syringe to mix with the white powder in the spoon, then raised the spoon to the flame of the devotional candle that burned in a bronze tray before him. He held the spoon steady, careful not to let the milky liquid boil as he cooked it. Laying down the heated spoon, he pinched off a piece of a cotton ball and placed it atop the mixture in the spoon. He brought the point of the needle to the soaked cotton, and he drew the liquor through it into the syringe. Cocking the needle upward, he tapped gently on the syringe with his forefinger, dispersing the few tiny bubbles of air he saw within. He pushed the plunger softly, damming the solution upward to the needle's neck. With his right hand and teeth, he wound and laced a length of black quarter-inch sponge tubing above the elbow of the arm that held the syringe, tightening it until the long blue median vein in his wizened forearm bulged. Taking the syringe in his right hand, he slipped the cool, gleaming needle through his thin skin and into the vein. With two crooked fingers, he drew back slightly on the plunger and watched the rosy plume of his blood rise in delicate aspiration amid the paler fluid. Then, pushing full on the plunger, he emptied the warm blood-darkened junk into himself.

Xūwú, nothingness. *Fangfú*, ecstasy. *Shiiwu* and *guǎngshi*, as they said in the tongue of his native Shanghai.

Chen Fang had come to know Mandarin and Cantonese in the many ten-years since Chinatown had become his home. But even now, as an old man, he still thought and dreamed in the Shanghainese of his youth. He attributed this to the fact that he had been one of sparse talk his whole adult life. He understood the sounds of Mandarin, Cantonese, and English, but he did not much voice them, and thus they had never overtaken the sounds of his imagination.

But nothingness and ecstasy possessed for Chen Fang no inner sound as in this silent, placid moment he walked between the two, wading in them.

The young Malaysian girl in his bed drew back the covers for him as he sat and removed his trousers. She was perhaps twelve or thirteen years old, and her expression belied what she saw: a skeletal apparition with skin like translucent parchment and glassy yellow eyes set deep in ashen sockets. He lay down beside her, and soon he felt her lips and tongue and fingers lightly upon him; and he drifted.

He saw himself then, a small boy in Shanghai, in the moments before the twilight of the first day of May of the year 1929. The *gwailou* his grandfather had sent him to fetch was a *Jidò*-man, a Christ-man, a tall, dour Jesuit whose cassock was like a monstrous black moth flapping against the boy as they walked together, the little schoolboy and the pale *zengvü* ghost-moth, down the stately granite steps of the Palace Hotel. There was an awaiting rickshawman, slight and misshapen, dressed in dirty khaki kneebritches and a ragged blue smoking-jacket. He bowed, grinned, and crossed himself with sycophantic extravagance. The priest nodded.

Lifting the hem of his cassock and settling onto the carriage's worn red velvet seat, the moth-priest noticed with uneasiness that the rickshawman was staring at the carpetbag he held in his lap. He moved two of his fingers with calculated suddenness, and the runner diverted his gaze from the satchel to the crucifix that dangled above it from a golden chain around the priest's neck. The little man crossed himself again, smiling blankly at the ivory Christ on its cross of black onyx. Chen Fang saw that his eyes were opalescent, like a blind man's.

The runner began to raise the oiled-paper hood over the carriage seat, but the priest extended his arm to stop him. The runner rubbed his eyes and pretended to cough in vigorous pantomime. Young Chen Fang found it amusing, but the priest's sternness did not waver as he restated with his arm that the hood should remain lowered.

"*Dza!*" the priest commanded impatiently. It sounded like the only Shanghainese he knew.

The runner bowed, then squatted to grasp the rope-wrapped helves of the rickshaw's bamboo shafts. He rose and heaved, and the rickshaw lurched forward, gaining speed as the runner broke into a lugubrious trot down the cobblestones of Mao Ming Road.

The priest removed his biretta and ran his hand through his thin black hair. He looked then at the palm of that hand as if it were a stranger's, staring at the sweat that glistened in its lines. The stench of raw sewage in the gutters and the sweet smell of sea broths steaming in the makeshift stalls and lean-tos that crowded those gutters overtook them in waves, and the din of the people grew louder and more threatening the farther the rickshaw advanced into the sulfurous dusk. The priest gazed at the domes and glimmering spires of the great buildings in the distance, the clearinghouses and ashlar seats of empire, near the mouth of the Huangpu. The darkening sky above them was shot through with burnt gold and silvering grays, and the gulls, like the mournful weavers of those colors, coursed higher and higher, toward the flushed shades of rose, and higher, toward the vast melancholy sigh of falling night. The last rays of the red sun presented the priest with the sight of his long shadow rippling silently across the heathen tide in dark benediction.

The din ebbed and the multitude dwindled. The cobblestones came to an end as the runner steered from Mao Ming Road onto the rutted dirt thoroughfare that led to the old Waibaidu Bridge. Coming to the other side of Suzhou Creek, the runner halted before crossing the railway tracks. Near a clump of tall weeds, a woman crouched with an infant child and two woven-frond bushels. She looked beseechingly at the priest as he glanced down into the bushels. One was filled with small iridescent fish, quivering vainly in the cool spring air of their death. The other held a writhing, muddy cluster of black snakes. As the rickshaw began to move, the woman hurried to it with the child in her arms. She raised the baby toward the priest, and with his thumb he made the sign of the cross above its brow. He extended his thumb toward the forehead of the woman, but she withdrew. The rickshaw trundled onward.

Entering Yanan Road, the priest began whisking with his fingertips at the dust that had collected on his cassock. The little runner, seeming now in the gloaming to be more piteously misshapen than he had appeared barely an hour ago, slowed to a stop near a willow tree, a yard or so from a narrow but imposing doorway. It was one of Tu Yueh-sheng's properties: a place where ledgers were kept, where the revenues of the endless vast ladings of opium and heroin that passed through the Green Gang's waterfront hongs were registered and tallied en route to the Bank of China, Tu's own Ching Wai Bank in the French Concession, T. V. Soong's new Central Bank of China; to the recesses of the Mokanshan monastery in the Wuling Mountains; to other black accounts in Nanjing, Canton, Hong Kong, Hanoi, Singapore, Bangkok, Paris, London, Amsterdam, Zurich, New York. It was to this place among willows in a quiet crook of Yanan Road that the compradors and taipans of the International Settlement came and went. It was here that Chen's grandfather waited upon the men whose dominion encompassed the thousand miles of the Yangtze Valley, from Shanghai deep into the poppy-growing lands of the far interior: Pockmarked Huang, boss of the old Red Gang and chief of detectives for the French Sûreté; Chang Ching-chang, the lame financier, Republican shadow-boss, and dealer in rare antiquities whom the Western taipans called Curio Chang; and the man who twenty years before had brought the Red Gang and the Blue Gang into the fold of his now-almighty Green Gang, grotesque Big-eared Tu himself. It was here that young Chen had not long ago been brought to bow before Big-eared Tu's acolyte and partner, Chiang Kai-shek. It was just last fall, soon after Generalissimo Chiang's Guomindang government in Nanjing had become the government of all of China.

There was a stone lintel above the door, and carved into it, in a single stylized ideogram, were the merged symbols of *ji* and *shou*, good fortune and longevity. Standing beneath it, in the gloom between two small scagliola columns, was Chen Fang's grandfather, an elderly man robed in long blue silk. He approached the rickshaw and said something —fast, imperious words of Wu-dialect Shanghainese—to the runner. Then, bowing his head perfunctorily, he turned to the priest.

"*Buona sera, Padre. Come sta?*"

The priest stepped down from the rickshaw and nodded.

"*Sta aspettando,*" Chen Fang's grandfather said.

The priest followed him through the doorway into an electrically lighted foyer paneled in rich brocade. They came to a room where candles provided the only light, and the old man, bowing his head once again, turned and walked away. Chen Fang saw all this from a distance; then, when his grandfather had retreated, he crept to where he could spy through the breach in the door.

Sitting at a great desk in the candle-lighted room was a fat man whose dark, tanned scalp gleamed through sparse brown and silver locks. Grandfather and the others called him *Kěsà*, Caesar. Wispy shadows rippled slowly, rhythmically across the front of his collarless white shirt, and the soft candlelight illuminated the rising and falling of his every breath. There was nothing on the desk but a bottle of Thorne's Scotch and three small ceramic tumblers. On the wall behind the fat man, hanging crookedly in a cheap gilt frame, was a painting of Jezebel being devoured by the dogs of the Lord. The priest's eyes seemed to fix on the long teeth sunk into the pale breast. Then, stepping forward, he looked down at the fat man.

"*Salute, Satana. S'accomodi,*" the fat man said, grinning. The priest stood motionless, and the fat man changed the tone of his voice. "*Dunque,*" he exhaled. He gestured then with his chin toward the priest's carpetbag. He patted the desktop, and the priest placed the bag before him. The fat man withdrew from the satchel a heavy parcel wrapped in chamois. He removed this covering, revealing a large book bound in reddish brown sheepskin, tooled in blind, and bossed with brass corner-plates and clasps. Its thick vellum pages were warped and tawny with age. The fat man tried the clasps, which opened easily, but he did not further examine the book. He raised his eyebrows and nodded his head slowly; then he drew the chamois around the book and put it back in the sack.

"*Il denaro, Signore. Dov'è il denaro?*" the priest said, breaking his silence.

"*Calma, eh?*" The fat man rose and smiled. He walked toward a rear door. "*L'ho nella cassaforte sopra. Prego,*" he said, opening the door and allowing the priest to precede him.

In the darkening twilight beyond the door, the priest glimpsed a luxuriance of broad green leaves and salver-shaped blossoms, lush blue vines and wild mulberry, and nameless orange-petaled things that drank the light of the moon. For a moment he must have been as a child, lost in a fairy-tale garden of sunless enchantment. In that moment, the fat man raised a large black revolver to the back of his head and blew him forward to hell.

"*Ti scomunico, prete,*" the fat man said. "*Ti scomunico.*"

The sudden blast of Chen Fang's heartbeat was like thunder in his ears, and he emerged from his haunted dream with a start. He became conscious of the warm willowy breath and slender body beside him. He opened his eyes to the little girl's drowsing face. Drifting, inhaling her young breath, he let reverie take him as he beheld her. He imagined slitting her throat and satisfying himself within the throes of her spirit's black flight. He remembered those days of the gleaming *ti-doa* and thick rubber sheeting, the sweet terror in the eyes and the low howlings of his own deep slaking. But those days were gone. The body, like the soul, was now withered and dry.

FOUR

Johnny Di Pietro drew a breath of idle disgust, threw the *TV Guide* down beside him on the couch, and, exhaling that same dismal breath, took up this morning's *Newsday* instead. Walking past with her green-triggered Spray Pal in hand, Diane Di Pietro glanced warily toward him at the sound of his breath, then continued on her way to the spider plant that hung by the window.

The dead spic had not made the paper. Good. He tossed the folded *Newsday* onto the *TV Guide* and looked across the room at his wife's ass. He had not fucked her in over a year.

"Anything good on tonight?" she asked.

The blowjobs had been first to go, then the other shit. A couple of years ago, she had got some sort of throat infection and attributed it to his semen, which she said—screamed—had been contaminated by the hygienic horrors of his drunkenness and filthy infidelities. His seed, she railed, was a toxic distillation of the diseases of barroom toilets and barroom sluts. Not long after she swore off swallowing his spratz, she accused him of infecting her cunt as well. He could no longer remember the name of the venereal malady her dyke gynecologist had armed her with, or the name of the antibiotic she had prescribed; but he still had it in for that dyke, who did not have the class or savoir faire to tell Diane it was a yeast infection. Then, one night when he was loaded, he had smacked her; and that was it. The months had passed. He had quit drinking, except for a glass of wine now and then behind her back, and he had sweetened up to her. But by the time she had allowed herself to get close to him again, it was too late. Too much cold, unsettling distance lay between them. And now that cold, unsettling distance was the tie that bound as well as estranged them. Their marriage, as he had known it, was over. She spoke of wanting to work things out, of resolving things, of getting back to where they once had been—the babble of dissolution. He knew there was no getting back. But inertia kept him from moving forward. Something in him found comfort in the dead stillness beneath the unsettling surface of estrangement. It was always Willie's finger, never his own, that pulled the trigger, that served as the intercessor between himself and the truth of himself. In the estrangement that lay between his wife and him, he found that same tenuous reprieve from the ravings and cravings of will and soul. It was the only kind of peace he had ever known. And he was beginning to grow to hate it.

"No," he answered.

"How was the meeting last night?"

Which meeting had he told her he was going to? AA? The union?

"Same old shit," he said. That covered it.

"Give it a chance. You're doing so good. I'm so proud of you."

AA. He actually did go to AA once in a while, though he never told her the real reason why. He made out like a bandit there. All those lonely broads, all that desperate dysfunctional pussy wandering lost in the stairwell of those twelve steps. But God, could they talk.

The telephone rang. He answered it with a tone of uninviting indifference. He immediately recognized the voice that greeted his, but he was momentarily taken aback at hearing it. Diane watched him curiously as he shifted his posture, leaned forward and straightened his back.

"Uncle Joe," he said.

Rather than satisfying Diane's curiosity, this only increased it. The old man both repelled and beguiled her. She was naive, but she was not stupid. It was true that she believed there was a legitimate aspect to Johnny's position in the sanitation union, that he did more than pick up an inflated paycheck and serve occasionally as a middleman in straightening out the territorial disputes of carters sharing the same streets. But it was also true that she was aware of the nature of the forces that Johnny represented in the sanitation union. In her mind, however, the legitimacy of his occupation, as perceived by her, distinguished him somewhat from those forces to which he was beholden. While it was plain, she knew, that Pete Seeger would never sing about Jimmy Black the way he sang about Joe Hill, it was also plain that unions were considered the salvation of the working man, the backbone of America. Her husband's place, as she believed it to be—a relatively innocent, relatively respectable position in the ingrained American scheme of necessary evil—was one that could be comfortably rationalized.

The figure of his uncle, however, and the nature of his works and days, afforded no such comfort, no such explaining away. The old man had set Johnny up in the union, as he had set his own kid brother, Johnny's father, up before him. Johnny's father had ended up drinking his way out of life, leaving behind nothing but the ambivalent grief of a brother and a son and the gambling debts that had enslaved him and betrayed them. To Diane, the worst aspect of Johnny's place in that rationalized scheme of necessary evil was that it lay in the suffocating shadows of his father's doom, and she could not help but wonder what Johnny might have become were it not for his uncle, whom she viewed as more of a curse than a blessing. And yet there was that beguilement. Uncle Joe was like an air of dark romance, carrying with him the intrigue of mysterious powers. But it was the idea of him, not the reality of his presence, that her imagination savored. Lately, he had all but evanesced from her consciousness, and from their lives. Now here he was, in a wholly new and sudden emanation. He had never called before. Never.

The old man asked Johnny what he was doing on Monday.

"Nothing," his nephew answered.

"Meet me at the club."

"Hester Street?"

"Yeah. Eleven o'clock. I want to talk to you."

"Is something wrong?"

"No. I just want to talk to you, see how you feel about something. After that, if things work out, we'll take a ride down to see somebody. One way or the other, we'll have a nice lunch."

"Sure. Sounds good."

"Eleven o'clock Monday, then, at the club."

"See you there."

Johnny returned the receiver gently to its cradle.

"What's up?" Diane asked.

"Nothing."

She repeated the word to herself: a weary, inaudible mutter that barely stirred her lips. Her cold look grazed him in passing as she retreated to the kitchen. A cabinet door slammed, then another, then the refrigerator. A pot came down heavy on the stove, hitting the grate like a gong. The cutting-board slammed with a ringing thud upon the drainboard. The sounds of slicing and chopping were violent at first, then grew calmer. Soon Johnny could smell the fragrance of the garlic and onions, the parsley and basil, the oregano and thyme sizzling in the oil.

"Do you want me to get a video?" she asked from the kitchen. There was a weary serenity now in her voice.

"Sure."

"What are you in the mood for?" A ray of optimism flickered in her voice.

"Tits. Blood. Monsters. The usual shit."

FIVE

Johnny got off the B train at Grand Street, walked the few short blocks to Mulberry Street, then south a block, turning right on Hester. It was a beautiful morning, and three men, the usual Central Casting sort of *cafon*'s, were gathered outside, sitting on the tattered vinyl seats of rusted chrome-frame chairs they had brought out of the club into the warm spring sun. Johnny recognized his uncle's black Mercedes, parked down the street in one of the spaces that men such as these kept reserved for men such as he.

"You go all the way to fuckin' Spring Street to get a fuckin' haircut?" one of them was saying to another.

"What fuckin' 'all the way'? A few fuckin' blocks, a nice walk," the other said.

"You're fuckin' nuts. You got fuckin' Sal right here aroun' the corner, and you go all the way the fuck up there."

"This guy Rocco there, he gives a nice haircut. What the fuck would you know, anyway? You got that fuckin' *tizzun'* hair, that fuckin' Brillo."

"Ah, you could never have hair like me."

As he approached them, Johnny observed that their hair was virtually identical, including that of the third man, who said nothing. They looked at him inquisitively as he ascended the three steps to the club's open door, recognizing him but unable to place him; and he could hear their hushed talking behind him as he passed through the open door from sunlight into gloom. Two figures sat at a small table drinking coffee and saying nothing. Johnny knew one of them: Frankie Blue, his uncle's chauffeur and *guardia del corpo*. He was a few years older than Johnny, and he held out his hand to grasp Johnny's own as he passed. Behind the bar, a man alternately patted his pockets absently and peered and poked intently between and behind bottles, looking for something. Uncle Joe sat alone, at a table by the wall, entwined in *toscanello* smoke and shadows. Johnny patted his back affectionately, then sat across from him. Giuseppe raised a crooked forefinger and beckoned the man behind the bar. As he did so, he turned to Johnny.

"You're still taking it easy with the booze?"

Johnny nodded resolutely, and Uncle Joe nodded resolutely in turn. The subtleties of the old man's stony expression were indiscernible to most, but his nephew read them fluently, and he could see in the cast of his face not only approval but understanding and admiration as well.

"*Due?*" the man called from behind the bar.

Giuseppe did not immediately respond, but spoke instead to his nephew. "That's good," he said. "It's good for you, and it's good for us." Then he raised his eyes and answered, "*Sì.*"

"How you feeling?" Johnny asked.

"I can't complain," the old man said. "Some days good, some days bad. It comes and it goes. There's a lot of guys my age would want to trade what they got for what I got."

"You still tell people it's the gout?" Johnny grinned.

"Yeah. You say rheumatoid arthritis, they figure you're over the hill."

The man brought two cups of espresso and set them down, then returned to his search behind the bar.

"So," Johnny said, "what's on your mind?"

"I'll tell you," the old man said. His voice was low and calm and direct. "But first let me ask you something." He sipped at his coffee. "How do you feel about dope?"

"What do you mean?"

"What I mean is, how do you feel about dope? Do you think dope is a good thing? Do you think dope is a bad thing? How do you feel about dope?"

"I think dope is a bad thing. I think it's a plague. I think it's turned this goddamn city into a fuckin' jungle overrun with scum. I think dope-dealers are worse shit than lawyers. I think together they're doin' a good fuckin' job of ruinin' the world."

"So you would never get involved in it?"

Two men entered the club, one of them speaking loudly. Johnny could see Frankie Blue saying something to them, gesturing with a tilt of his head toward the back of the room, where Johnny and his uncle sat. The eyes of the two men followed the direction of Frankie Blue's gesture. Both nodded with vague, tacit comprehension, then turned and left.

"It's like this," Johnny said. "I see some filthy fuckin' illegal-alien piece of shit with two or three pounds of ratty fuckin' dreadlocks stuffed into a high-rise pea-cap the size of a fuckin' duffel bag, and he's struttin' down the street talkin' that jive-ass shit with some fat ugly fuckin' acne-faced *ammazzacrista*, and he's sellin' dope and the fuckin' cops are doin' fuckin' nothing—as long as it's right there, here to stay, out in the open, with none of these fuckin' half-a-*ricchion'* cops doin' a fuckin' thing, as long as they want this shit in the streets, well, then, fuck 'em. Yeah, I'd get involved in it. On aesthetic grounds alone." He smirked. "I mean, I'd rather see me than a fuckin' eyesore Rasta strollin' down the street. I'd cut a far more striking figure."

The old man was grinning, actually grinning. Then he raised his cup to his lips, and when he lowered it, his face had once again turned to stone.

"I'm not talking about the street. That shit on the street is there for good. It'll be there until they've raped this country for all they can, then they'll move on."

Johnny looked at him.

"I'm talking about the world, not the street."

"As goes the street, so goes the world. Those are your words."

"And they're still true. The world will follow the streets to hell. It's happening now. And no one man, and no army of men, will turn the tide. The question I'm asking you is this. Does your morality—call it whatever you want, your code, your principles, your sense of right and wrong, that scrap of something in your heart or your soul that separates you from the beasts—does it allow you to make money from the business of hell? Given the . . ." He searched for a phrase that he knew but had never used, then settled for more familiar words. "Given that there is no end to this plague, does whatever wisdom you possess lead you to side with your principles or your self-interest? I know you're no altar-boy, but I'm talking here about . . ." He raised his right hand slowly, upturned and grasping, in a gesture that took the place of words; and he lowered it just as slowly, and he drew breath.

"When I was a young boy, when I first came to this country, back before your father was born, I'll never forget, I saw a horse go mad on Cornelia Street. It was the dead of summer. A big black horse with big wild eyes, foaming at the mouth and galloping crazy through the street. Finally it crashed through a big glass storefront. Blood and glass everywhere. The horse was down and bloody and whinnying and kicking, and somebody put a revolver to its head and put it out of its misery. That dead horse stayed there for days, all bloated and stiff. The stomach blew up to twice its normal size. Finally the DSC came to try to haul it away, and one of them took a crowbar and ripped open the belly. Pus gushed out like a torrent, and you could smell the stink a block away, on Bleecker Street.

"I think of this world now as a black horse running wild to hell, its body filled with disease. I think of seizing that horse for one terrible moment as it gallops toward those flames, riding it and looting all that is in the path of its destruction, then jumping off before being thrown and broken. Just that one moment. That one terrible moment. Then I'll watch that doomed horse continue on its way. Nothing will have changed. The world will be no better and no worse. The only difference will be, as you say, *estetica*." He pronounced the word clearly and finely. When speaking to his nephew, he eschewed Sicilian for Italian. Johnny's Italian was faltering and fair at best, but his understanding of Sicilian was for the most part confined to its crudest and most common elements.

"How big a deal are we talking about here?"

"As I said. The world."

"What does that mean in terms of money?"

"For you? Or for me? Or for all of us?"

"For all of us," he said.

"Many billions of dollars."

"And for you."

"Two, maybe three billion."

"And me."

"A few hundred million. Maybe more."

The sum was beyond the ken of Johnny's reality. He had never had more than ten thousand dollars at one time in his life. If his uncle had spoken of a few hundred grand rather than this fantastical few hundred million, the lesser figure, in its greater plausibility and comprehensibility, would have hastened his pulse and excited his greed. The idea of a few hundred million fell to the bottom of his consciousness like a dead and meaningless abstraction. It did not seem to him like a vast amount of money—it was beyond his sense of vastness. It seemed more like a vast amount of imponderable darkness. It seemed both unreal and deadly at once.

"How dangerous is this?"

"We win or we lose. We got one way to win. We got three ways to lose. One of those ways doesn't affect you, because you're not putting up any money. So for you, danger has two faces, death or prison. Those are short odds. Two to one. A chalk bet. But the stakes are high. At my age, death doesn't mean what it means to you. But then again, neither does the money."

"Why, then? I mean, at your age. Don't you have enough by now? Money, I mean. Is it worth it?"

"I'm an old man and I'm well off. I could turn my back on everything and live out my days in the sun without a care. But those days would not be peaceful, any more than they are right now. It was my mistake to think that they could be. In my own way, Johnny—and don't misunderstand me here—I want to save the world: *my* world, the world as I knew it. I'm not talking about saving it from evil. I'm talking about something else. I'm talking about something in here." He brought two fingers to his heart. "An old man's dream, maybe. One way or the other, wisdom or folly, my reasons should have nothing to do with your decision."

"You mention you, you mention me, you mention 'all of us.' Who are 'all of us'?"

"Other old men like me. You know some of them. Tonio Pazienza. Louie Bones. And others. Men who believe as we do and think as we think."

"Why me? I have no money. You've been good to me, but we've never done any business together beyond the union. What do you want me for?"

"I want you because I trust you."

"You trust me?"

"Yeah."

"I didn't think you believed in that shit."

"Sure I do." The expression on the old man's face was one that even Johnny could not read. "Trust. Love. All that shit. I believe in it like I believe in dope. I've dealt in it all my life." He drank down the last of his coffee. "But I'm talking something else here. A different sort of trust. Same word, different shit.

"You are my godson and my only living blood. That counts for something, even in these times. You also have a brain. Since you were a boy, with your books and your chemistry set, you've always had a brain. That you've chosen to sit on it, well, that's something else. In any case, you're not stupid. You can think. And you can get around. You have the strength that I lack. I want you because I need arms and legs and backbone and brains that I can trust. It's as simple as that. And I would rather see you prosper than another."

And would you just as soon see me die? It was a question that Johnny let pass through his mind unsaid. Instead, he gave voice to another: "What, exactly, is involved?"

"The control of the heroin industry at its source, at the morphine level, and through to its production and its primary and secondary distribution levels. That's as exact as I can be right now. If you come in with me, you'll learn all you need to know."

"When do you need my answer?"

"Now."

"I'm in."

The old man nodded once in affirmation of his nephew's decisiveness, and his open hand came softly down upon the table.

"So," he said. "Let's go eat. After that, we'll take a ride downtown. From here on in, we move together."

Old Giuseppe rose, and when he did, Frankie Blue across the room rose as well. The man who had served them had quit his search behind the bar and was leaning in the doorway. As they approached, he straightened his stance and stepped aside. "*Grazie tanto, Signor Giuseppe,*" he said, "*e grazie a Lei, Signore,*" he added to Johnny, as if in afterthought. The man who had been sitting with Frankie stood, and Giuseppe took his hand between his own.

"My nephew," he said, with a trace of pride.

"My pleasure," said the man, nodding as if in understanding of some greater implication in those words, extending his hand in turn to Johnny.

The tonsorial academy fell silent in their chrome-framed chairs as Giuseppe emerged into the sunlight among them. Only when he threw them a bone of recognition—"Enjoy the day, boys"—did they burst from their obeisant stillness, expressing their effusive thanks and best wishes.

Frankie turned left at the corner, drove down Baxter Street to White Street, then west on White to the southeast corner of Church Street, where he slowed to a halt against the light.

"Give us about an hour and a half, Frank. And call down there to that monkey at 67 Wall, remind him we're coming." The old man allowed his nephew to help him from the car. "You'll like this place," he said, moving forward, using the shaft of his cane as well as Johnny's arm to guide his balance as he rose from the car. "It's something different."

He mumbled the name of the restaurant as they entered it. "Arquà." He snorted. "Know what that means in Italian?" Johnny shook his head, and his uncle snorted again, a sound like the ghost of stillborn laughter. "It don't mean shit."

Johnny looked around. It was a small joint, but the layout of the tables, the high ceiling, pale yellow walls, and soft lighting gave it a comfortable, spacious atmosphere. Standing at the bar to the right, one of the young, dark-haired, white-aproned waiters smiled.

"*Buon giorno, Signor Joe.*" He, like Johnny, followed rather than led the old man to a table for four against the wall near the back of the room.

"Tell him what Arquà means," Giuseppe said to the waiter.

"A little town in the Veneto," the waiter explained to Johnny as he drew back two chairs for them. His smile turned wry. "When I first come to work here, I ask them, and that is what they say to me."

"I told you," Giuseppe said. "It don't mean shit."

"*Acqua e vino?*"

The old man nodded, and the waiter left them with menus. When he returned, he set down a liter of San Bernardo mineral water and a bottle of Barbaresco Santo Stefano 1986.

"*Ecco. I santi,*" the waiter said happily as he uncorked the wine. Then, turning to Johnny, "My friend here, he likes the two saints." He poured. His voice trailed off into a whisper: "Always the two saints. *I due santi. Molto religioso.*"

Johnny studied the menu. It all looked good: sautéed polenta with grilled mushrooms, homemade *salsiccia*, cold stuffed roasted rabbit, *osso-buco*, venison stew. Even baby *calamari*.

"The risotto is good," his uncle told him, "but they make it the right way, from scratch, so it takes a while. The lasagna's nice too."

Johnny ordered the *calamaretti* and the lasagna. The old man ordered a roasted baby artichoke and *pappardelle* with sausage, mushrooms, and tomato sauce. Johnny thought of 116th Street, and he felt the distance between this joint and that: not the stretch of blocks or miles that separated them, but the incorporeal span between the pervasive haunted darkness of that somber sanctuary and the light breath of this place. Here, just as the tender squid, showered subtly in lemon and oil, possessed a delicacy that the old man's sauce uptown, fine as it was, did not, so the ocher walls were rich and bright with light rather than dull and gloomy with the accrued patina of nicotine and age and dying breath. He looked through the window. Across the dingy street, on the opposite corner, a crude sign proclaimed the entrance to the Baby Doll Lounge. Red and blue neon advertised TOPLESS GO-GO GIRLS. Beneath the neon was a hand-lettered placard: ALL BEERS $3 ON WEDNESDAYS. That distance, that contrast, the Janus face of being, was everywhere. His uncle seemed to bridge the shores. He cast a certain aura in this room of well-dressed businessmen, imbuing its sunny, simple elegance with a darker, cooler aura of old, unchanging ways as surely as he had brought a vague but undeniable dignity and grace, a simple elegance of his own, to that chamber of cheap malfeasant dreams on Hester Street.

Johnny liked the *calamari* of both shores—truth be told, he favored the old man's up in East Harlem—but he preferred the view, the sunlight and sense of buoyant illimitableness, here.

"Do you tell your business to your wife?" his uncle asked him.

"No."

"Good. What about that *cafùn'* you gallivant with, that Willie Gloves?"

"We've known each other since we were kids."

"Well, from here on, you don't know each other so well. You mention nothing of this to anyone. Nothing."

"I'm not stupid," Johnny demurred.

"We're all stupid, Johnny. We're born that way and we stay that way. The trick is to never lose sight of that, to never allow ourselves to be blinded to that by whatever little wisdom we have."

The old man ate his pasta with an air of rapt and sensuous finality, as if there were nothing in this world but himself and the food that lay before him.

"This Willie, he's your *amico* and he's not work-shy. Don't worry, I'll put in a word, I'll keep him busy. Just keep our business to yourself, that's all."

He drank some wine, and he nodded slowly, as if in oblique conspiracy with that sensuous finality.

"I've still got the place uptown. I haven't used it since your aunt died. You can take it over if you want."

These words stunned Johnny more than the "few hundred million" his uncle had spoken of, stunned him more because it was imaginable. Johnny knew the place. It was an entire floor in a fancy brownstone on East Sixty-seventh Street, between Central Park and Madison. It was where Uncle Joe had kept his *comare* while his wife, Johnny's aunt—Matilda; Joe had named his carting company for her—was still alive. Upon the death of his wife, Giuseppe, who had been unfaithful in marriage, became faithful to her, as if some perverse sense of piety prevented him from defiling the sanctity of her memory with the felicity with which he had defiled the sanctity of their marriage, as if extreme unction rather than marriage was the sacrament that bound. So it seemed. The truth of the matter had been summed up by his uncle long ago: "*Solo pisciare!*" His cock was no longer good for anything but pissing. Johnny knew that his uncle preferred to live, with his ghosts and his memories, in the old apartment on Sullivan Street where he had lived for more than half a century. He did not know that his uncle owned the entire brownstone uptown, that he was its landlord. Until now, he had not even known that his uncle had held on to that uptown place.

"Jesus. How much?"

"We'll work something out," Giuseppe said, dismissing the question with a slight backhand wave.

Frankie had managed to double-park in front of a truck that was backed up to a loading platform down the street, and he was there and ready when they came out of the restaurant. They turned right on Church, right again on Walker, then drove straight down Broadway to Wall Street. The car stopped at the corner of Wall and Pearl.

"This shouldn't take long," the old man said.

They took the elevator to the seventeenth floor, and Johnny followed his uncle's steps to a numbered door that bore the words NOVARCA MANAGEMENT GROUP.

"Novarca," Giuseppe muttered. "That don't mean shit either. New-ark in Latin, some shit like that." That ghost of stillborn laughter came again. "Words."

The reception area was painted a pale blue, which neglect was now turning gray. The cheap blue nylon pile carpeting that covered the floor was worn and ragged and had been patched here and there with vinyl duct tape whose color did not quite match. There was a cheap black Naugahyde couch. It too was patched, but with black electrical tape, which brought less attention to itself. Beside the couch was a tall rubber tree, whose drooping leaves were covered with dust and brown and brittle at the edges, and next to it, set at a right angle to the couch, was a particleboard desk unit with a dull, scratched wood-grain finish, on which there was a telephone console, a computer keyboard and monitor, and an ashtray full of lipstick-stained cigarette butts. At the desk, beneath an assembly-line painting of the city skyline at sunset, sat Uncle Joe's old *comare*, a woman named Rose, who was now about fifty and wore too much makeup.

"Good afternoon, Mr. Di Pietro."

"Two," he said to her. "Two Mr. Di Pietros. You don't remember my nephew."

"Of course. Johnny," she said awkwardly.

Without any further words, Giuseppe walked down the hall, past two closed doors, to an open office that was furnished not much better than the reception area but was brightened by a glimpse of the East River between the buildings that dominated the view from a single large window. The man who stood to greet Giuseppe was younger than Johnny. He was dressed in a white shirt and an expensive-looking tie with matching braces whose leather straps were buttoned into pleated olive-colored trousers. He looked like he worked out, took a haircut every week, and would be lost without the Living Section of the *New York Times*.

Giuseppe waved away an offer of coffee. He sat down and motioned to Johnny to do the same. He put a DeNobili between his teeth and lighted it, then held out the spent match, prompting the man behind the desk to fetch an ashtray.

"Bill, this is my nephew, John." He turned to his nephew. "Bill works for us. Paperwork," he said. Then he turned again to Bill, just in time to catch the twitch of umbrage in the lines of his mouth and his eyes. "Draw up some power-of-attorney papers for Johnny here. Make him a general agent of my principal interest in that new company, that —what is it again?"

"R.P. Corp."

"And from now on, when you talk to John here, anything having to do with R.P., you're talking to me. Unless I say otherwise."

Bill nodded in understanding, an understanding not so much of reason as of resignation.

"And I want you to draw up a loan from Lupino to R.P. for a hundred million dollars. Transfer the money through our fiduciary in the islands to the bearer-share company in Holland, then deposit it at the Banca Masini in Milan."

Bill looked at him blankly. "That's going to be a problem. The Lupino Corporation is a thirty-percent partner in a joint venture that's just been awarded a major contract by the city's Department of Environmental Protection. Lupino's share will net a profit of over fifty million, but it's a capital-intensive investment, involving a lot of new technology. We'll go into asset financing as soon as the contract takes effect, on the first of July, but until then, Lupino's not going to have that kind of money to throw around."

"What the fuck are you talking about?" Giuseppe demanded. "A contract for what?"

"Sludge removal. Lupino will be involved in removing the sludge from the city's waste-treatment plants."

"Sludge removal." Giuseppe snorted. Johnny could hear anger this time. "And what do we do with this sludge?"

"Dump it in Jersey, like everything else, I guess." Bill grinned uneasily.

"Who the fuck's bright idea was this?"

"Your chairman."

"Get him on the fuckin' phone. Now."

Bill lifted the receiver, and his forefinger danced nervously on the button pad. He rocked back and forth, eyes raised to the ceiling, then leaned forward. "Mr. Krauss, please." He leaned back. "Dolores, this is Bill Raymond. I need to talk to Stanley." He leaned forward. "Well, where is he? Do you have that number?" He leaned back. "Trust me. This is very important. I have Mr. Di Pietro here." He leaned forward, grabbed a pen, and wrote. "Thank you, Dolores." He turned to Giuseppe and dialed anew. "He's having lunch at Bouley with the director of the Environmental Control Board."

Giuseppe grimaced, turned the palms of his hands upward, and shrugged.

"Stanley, this is Bill. I'm sorry to—"

"Gimme the fuckin' phone."

Bill did as he was told.

"What the fuck is this sludge-removal shit?" Giuseppe growled into the receiver. His eyes widened. "What the fuck do you mean, 'Who is this?' This is your fuckin' boss. This is the guy that owns your fuckin' pink perfumed ass. Right. That's better. Now shut the fuck up and answer me. Who gave you the go-ahead on this? I don't want to hear about my best interests. Fuck my best interests. Rosario! Fuck Rosario. Who? Jimmy Guarino? Fuck Jimmy Guarino. Fuck all those punks. They're like you, Stanley. They work for me. Don't start with my fuckin' best interests again, Stanley. Yeah, they love me, you love me, everybody fuckin' loves me. Let's just cut the shit before my cunt gets wet, huh? Now, you listen. I told Bill here, I want a hundred fuckin' million from Lupino moved to Milan. I want it moved right away. Today, tomorrow, this week. And I want another two, three hundred free and ready to move at my say-so. Stanley, I don't care. I don't give a fuck what you have to do, just do it. I don't want to hear about collateralized obligations. I don't want to hear about any of that shit. Fuck that shit, and fuck you too. Just figure out what you have to do and do it. Right. Yeah. Choke on it. Him too."

Handling the receiver with distaste, as if it were a foul and unclean thing, Giuseppe returned it to Bill.

"That's that. Draw up those power-of-attorney papers. Lose that hundred million to the Banca Masini."

As they left, Johnny saw that Rose had freshened her makeup and fixed her hair. Her lips were now a different shade of red.

The breeze was growing cooler, and the shadows were lengthening in the pale midafternoon light.

"Sludge," the old man whispered in a low, derisive voice.

SIX

The three dark-suited men who stood bowed in prayer at the red-and-gold-draped altar of the Queen of Heaven could hear the plucked notes of mourning that drifted through the temple like sighs of spring from far away. The light of the long tapering candles seemed to dance to the lilt and sway of those faint mourning sighs.

Green-eyed Shang Wing-fu, the Shan warlord whom men had come to know as Asim Sau, "the Lord of Radiant Power," stood tallest and eldest among them. As general of the Shan United Army and underground ruler of the vast poppy-growing highlands of the Shan Plateau, sixty-year-old Asim Sau controlled the source of almost three-quarters of the world's opium supply. The two men, both in their fifties, who flanked him were his partners in the dozen great heroin refineries that snaked along the wilderness border separating Myanmar from China, Laos, and Thailand, and in the smaller heroin factories that lay hidden among the mists of Hong Kong's two hundred and thirty-five islands: the Thai shadow-boss Tuan Ching-kuo, who served as the liaison between their domain and the Guomindang of Taiwan, who were their biggest buyers, and Ng Tai-hei, the leader of the 14K Ngai Triad, which controlled the international heroin market here at its center, in Hong Kong.

Besides the Tai-Shan language of his homeland in the Shan State of Myanmar, Asim Sau spoke Burmese, some Thai, some French, and some Yunnanese, the language of his father, who had been a Guomindang general. Tuan Ching-kuo was fluent in Thai and Swatow Cantonese and spoke the Minnan Fujianese dialect of China and Taiwan as well. Ng Tai-hei spoke Cantonese. Though they could understand smatterings of one another's natural tongues, English was the language they shared when gathering on rare occasions such as this.

"It was best, I thought, that we meet alone before joining the others," said Ng Tai-hei as the three men walked slowly from the Tin Hau temple past the scattered groups of old men gambling in the courtyard. They stood together on a knoll of grass and trees that lay like a buffer between the serenity of the ancient holy place and the mad rushing noise of Nathan Road, which cut through the heart of the Yaumatei District of Kowloon. A chauffeur stood some yards away beside a black Rolls-Royce limousine, awaiting them. The breeze blew open the unbuttoned jacket of his black Baromon suit, revealing the strap of a black calfskin shoulder holster.

"Is there anything to discuss, really?" said Asim Sau. "A crazy old man named Chen Fang, long ago washed up and left for dead, crawls from beneath his dank stone and comes to us with a dream entrusted to him by other old and crazy men. *Gwailou* men, no less."

Tuan Ching-kuo smiled at Asim Sau's words. "I have heard stories of Chen Fang from old men in Taipei. They say that things die wherever he goes."

"Chen Fang is only a carrier pigeon to these men," said Ng Tai-hei. "And I think there is much to discuss. Look at us. Ah Fu, you who are known as the lord of this world, have been under the indictment of the United States of America for some years now. Since February of 1990, to be exact. In itself, that perhaps is a matter deserving more of laughter than of concern. But there are forces in your own land who would stop at nothing to renew the rich flow of American aid to which your continued freedom and power have brought an end.

"Ah Kuo here faces a similar situation with so-called pro-democracy forces in Thailand, where his regime's policy of gunning down those forces in the streets of Bangkok is increasingly attracting the ire and distaste of other nations as well as the concern of many of his countrymen, and the long rule of the generals seems to be drawing to a close. Furthermore, the Taiwanese, whom he represents in our dealings with them, have been forming an ever greater alliance in trade with the mainland Fujianese, who in turn have become the clandestine suppliers of the Vietnamese in America and elsewhere—a source of growing anger and trouble among other Chinese factions here and abroad. And can there be any doubt that the days of the Guomindang's power in Taiwan are numbered?

"Then there is me. I, who rose to take the place of old Dai Bei-tang upon his death, have inherited an empire whose throne now rests in a quaking place. This city of Hong Kong will soon revert to Chinese rule, and there is no soothsayer, be he British or Chinese, who has yet convinced me of what this shall truly mean for the future.

"Together we represent what is perhaps the most lucrative industry on earth. But it is also the most dangerous of industries. And there are now stormclouds. So, yes, I say there is much to discuss."

"And at the heart of that discussion," said Asim Sau, "no doubt lies your proposal that we withdraw from this world as we know it and retreat to a life of monastic tranquillity."

"Have you ever paused to weigh your riches?" Ng Tai-hei asked him, then spoke past him to Tuan Ching-kuo: "And you?" Neither man answered, and Ng Tai-hei continued. "Among us we have the wealth of nations. Not a cent earned among us from this day until we die will we ever live to count or touch or spend. The well of our gold is already too deep to fathom. And yet we go on."

"There is more than gold involved," said Tuan Ching-kuo.

"Yes," Ng Tai-hei answered him. "We enjoy this view that we have come to share with the gods."

"Who, precisely, are these men who have raised old Chen Fang from the dead to whisper in our ears?"

"Men in America and men in Italy. Men who, like ourselves, share ways and desires of their own. And I would not dismiss old Chen Fang so quickly or so broadly. He was once a man of power and of wiles who enjoyed for a glimpse this view that now is ours."

"It was the white powder, the dragon in his own garden, that felled him," said Tuan Ching-kuo. "That is what they say."

"And what, precisely, is the proposal that they make, these *gwailou* men so like ourselves?" pressed Asim Sau.

"They propose an arrangement whereby they become in effect our partners. In exchange for their participation at the source, they offer us a great deal of money and other considerations of a less quantifiable, but no less appealing, nature."

Asim Sau laughed aloud and lit a cigarette.

"You speak in one breath of a well of gold too deep to fathom," said Tuan Ching-kuo, "and in the next breath you speak of adding to it."

"To call upon your own words, there is more than gold involved."

"We know these men," Asim Sau declared. "By different names perhaps, by different faces. But we know them. They are a dying breed. Forty years ago and more, these men had power on earth not unlike our own. In those days when the cowboys of the Central Intelligence Agency first became a presence in my country, our poppy fields were nothing compared to those of Turkey, and these men, through their alliance with the Corsicans of Marseilles, controlled the world that has since passed to us. Now, for almost a quarter of a century, they have been little more to us than important clientele."

"*Yōu shèng, liê bài,*" interjected Tuan Ching-kuo. An ancient saying: the superior win, the inferior lose.

"Even in their own American cities," continued Asim Sau, "they have been reduced to impotence, serving only as fodder for the aspirations of bumbling government prosecutors, lingering on only as quaint and fabulous figures of romance in the comic-book imagination of a nation whose true capital is Hollywood. *Cán zhá yú niè,*" he snapped: evil dregs of a dead society. With the flick of his middle finger, he sent the butt of his cigarette flying in a long, low arc. "Why make partners of customers?"

"Because of the stormclouds. And because those who thirst for our blood may be satisfied with theirs. Because the season is drawing near when we will need a beast of sacrifice, and because they are willing to pay to be led blind to that altar of stone."

His companions looked at him, said nothing for a while. Then Asim Sau spoke.

"Perhaps you are right," he said. "Perhaps there is much to discuss."

The long black limousine carried the three men south to Austin Road, then left to the broad swerve of Austin Avenue. It came to a stop at the mouth of a narrow alley near number 16, where a retinue of three black-suited bodyguards met and accompanied them to a steel door set into the wall near the alley's dead end. One of the guards rapped hard on the door. An elderly man opened it and lowered his skull of sparse snowy hair as the guard stepped past him, followed by Ng Tai-hei, Asim Sau, Tuan Ching-kuo, and the other guards. They walked in single file through a long, brown-painted corridor, then through another door and down a flight of stairs to a wine cellar. The three guards went no farther, joining the other retainers, who milled about or sat talking on benches at a long plank table that ran the length of the room. Ng Tai-hei, Asim Sau, and Tuan Ching-kuo passed through a final door, a door through which no *gwailou* had ever stepped.

The door opened to a large underground chamber of imperial splendor: the secret banquet hall beneath the Tian Zi restaurant. It was a room of rich teak walls on which were displayed, amid the soft light of silk-shaded, brass-mounted lamps, the delicate ink-and-watercolor paradises of dynasties that spanned the centuries. On the far wall hung a black silk banner embroidered in gold with the image of two lions resting their forepaws on a globe: the symbol of the triumvirate's Uoglobe number-four heroin. Covering most of the polished stone floor was a wine-red carpet, around the black border of which eight dragons of woven gold converged, two at each corner, to devour the orbs of heaven and earth. The ornately carved cabriole legs of the great circular mahogany table set upon it, as well as the legs of the twelve leather-upholstered chairs around it, echoed that motif of voracity, each leg tapering to an ivory-inlaid claw and ball.

Nine of the twelve chairs were occupied by men of various Asian nationalities. They ranged in age from young Phoumi Ma of Laos, who was barely forty, to silent old Li Kwang-chih of Shanghai, who was but seven years younger than the century itself, and whom many referred to in Cantonese as *suksùk*, uncle. Upon the entrance of Ng Tai-hei, Asim Sau, and Tuan Ching-kuo, the nine men, except for ancient Li Kwang-chih, rose and stood bowing before them, in much the same manner as the three themselves had stood before the deity Tin Hau.

Two servants in formal attire moved forward from their positions at either side of a rosewood sideboard that was set against the far wall, beneath the Uoglobe banner. They drew back the three vacant chairs and lowered their heads as Asim Sau and Tuan Ching-kuo sat. Ng remained standing between them, and the attendants withdrew silently to their positions at the far wall.

"Please," Ng said, gesturing with a slow, graceful sweep of his hand for the others to take their seats. Before each man, on a tablecloth of rose-colored linen, there was a setting of Aynsley blue cobalt and twenty-two-karat gold bone china, engraved ivory chopsticks with gold trim, crystal stemware, and a small porcelain cup. At the center of the table, surrounded by white jade ashtrays and bathed in the pale light of a chandelier that hung from the vaulted stone ceiling above, sprays of cherry blossoms were arranged in a tall Kangxi vase atop the stationary hub of a large hardwood *zhuàn taí*, the rotating tray central to every banquet.

"Once again, my friends, we gather to celebrate the birth of the Queen of Heaven. It has been a good year. Owing to the downward trend of the Nikkei, the continued stagnancy of the commercial real-estate market in America, and other circumstances detailed in your copies of our annual report, our little Tin Hau Fund has not fared so well as in recent years. Still, its ratio of income to average net assets, a more than respectable twenty-one point seven percent, remains well above that of most openly traded funds. And the overall performance of its various international investments once again surpassed any of the world's major established stock indexes for the same period, including the Hang Seng, which rose an impressive twenty-six percent." He gestured with a dignified flourish of the hand toward one of the men who sat across from him. "The esteemed Guo Chow, who oversees the management of our fund, continues to humble and delight us with his expertise."

There were smiles, then a stirring around the table of subdued applause and murmurs in several tongues—Burmese, Cantonese, Mandarin, Taiwanese, Lao, and Thai. Ng nodded once in the direction of the servants, and each of them removed a magnum of Krug Private Cuvée 1982 from the ice of a silver basin on the sideboard, swathed it in white linen, and with a strong, expert twist, quietly uncorked it.

"Of course," continued Ng Tai-hei, "our little fund is only the symbol of the greater bond among us. It is a bond of brotherhood as much as of business. We at this table—men of finance, men of the triads, men of government, men of industry—are but disparate rays of a common sun, whose power we share as the source of our own. And as we know, that golden sun shines brighter and more powerfully than ever before." The servants made their way around the table, pouring chilled champagne into the tall crystal flutes. "For this we must be thankful, not only to fortune, not only to our Queen of the Heavens, but to the one in whose rich fields our prosperity has its roots." Ng Tai-hei raised his glass and turned to Asim Sau. "To the prince of our world. May the gods forever love him as we do."

These words were met by a gladdening salute of tongues, and all save Asim Sau, who gracefully nodded, drank. Ng Tai-hei bowed and took his seat, and Asim Sau rose in turn with glass in hand.

"To you, my friends," he said, then emptied his glass in one long swallow. Those around the table cheered his gesture, and he held out his glass for more. "Let the feast begin."

One servant tended to Asim Sau's glass, then to the orders of the others as they called for more champagne, Scotch, mineral water, beer, or *chiu*. The other servant left the room and soon returned with a cadre of waiters in white. An array of *choi* dishes were placed on the revolving tray. There were silver platters of braised shark's fin, chilled gingered jellyfish, sea perch roe, pig's-foot jelly; peppered ham, and sausages of cured meat and rose-flavored vodka; bowls of quail broth, ceramic tureens of green-crab and bird's nest soup; brine-boiled prawns and crabs with cold dipping sauces of vinegar, red Szechuan oil, and chili and soy; kettles of steaming chrysanthemum tea. Each man was served a *fan* bowl of eight-precious rice, sweet with lotus and almond seeds, candied fruits, and sliced red dates. The cadre vanished and returned again and again as the afternoon passed and night fell unnoticed in that chamber beneath the earth. There was nine-course Peking duck: tender sweet flesh and crackling skin; sautéed liver, kidney, and intestine of duck; deep-fried duck's tongue and salt-fried duck's pancreas; smoked duck's brain and egg steamed with duck fat. There was the golden roast pig known as *kam tsu siu iuk*, and silver carp steamed in lotus leaves; bottles of Château Haut-Brion Blanc 1989; dim sum of shrimp in black seaweed, razor clams, and squid; camphor-and-tea-smoked goose and country stew of forest mushrooms, bamboo shoots, wild roots, and hare; a magnum of Château Pétrus 1947, which had arrived as the latest token of entreaty from Cali; dried beef in brown-pepper sauce, raw oysters, fried whelk; garlicked mustard greens, cabbage sautéed with star anise and daylily buds; poached sea snake and roast venison; Château Margaux 1900; sun-dried chestnuts; wild pears and mandarin oranges; pine nuts and yew; Château d'Yquem 1921; sweet water-chestnut cakes, candied mint leaves, and melon; Armagnacs and Madeiras from the century past; chicory coffee, Nine Dragon tea, and a stoneware jar of wolfthorn brandy bearing until this moment an unbroken seal marked with the symbol of the Qing.

Through the hours of the feasting, there was much talk of the spring harvest; of transport routes, tariffs, and price-fixing agreements with the leaders of the Hmong and other poppy-growing tribes. Individual and consortium orders for opium tar, morphine base, and ninety-nine-per-cent-pure number-four heroin were discussed in terms of tons and kilo-grams. There was much interest in what triad leaders from Guangzhou and Shanghai had to report concerning the logistics of ongoing negotia-tions with Hashemi Rafsanjani to barter ballistic missiles for the bulk of Iran's annual two-hundred-ton opium crop. Arguments were heard for and against lifting the long-standing ban on direct dealings with the Nigerians and the Vietnamese. By the time the brandies were poured, many of the twelve at the table were, as the classical poets often described themselves, *zui*: at the blissful threshold of the perfumed garden of drunkenness. The formal terms of address, such as *seng* and *xian-sheng*, gave way to the friendly intimacies of *ah* and *gau* and *xiao* and *lao*. Tuan Ching-kuo, for one, had begun the feast hailed as Tuan Seng, and had become, as the wine and liquor flowed, Ah Kuo. From Li Xiansheng, the elderly Li Kwang-chih had come to be embraced as Lao Li, Old Li. There was singing, laughter, and many good-natured cries of *"Diu nei!"*—"Fuck you!"—and *"Diu nei loumou!"*—"Fuck your mother!" As was their custom, none of what was said would possess true meaning until attested with clear eyes in the light of the days to come.

The festivities continued at the penthouse suite of the Regent Hotel, on Salisbury Road. The eighteen whores, Asian and European, had been selected for their beauty and grace by one of Ng Tai-hei's vassals, a man named Kung who ran the 14K Triad's Hong Kong prostitution ring. There were several young men attired in black trousers, formal onyx-studded white shirts, and black waiter's jackets. One of them tended the bar; the others circulated with trays bearing an ever-changing array of dim sum. It was understood that they as well as the women were there to accommodate any imagining or desire.

Sitting solitary in a corner divan was an adolescent girl with eyes like those of a sad and frightened fawn. Ten years ago, three years after her birth in a poor village in Yunnan Province, her parents had sold her for fifty thousand yuan to an emissary of silent old Li Kwang-chih. The child had been removed to the household of a more remote village, and there the two ancient spinster sisters of that household began to work upon her the long footbinding process of the lotus tradition, which had been outlawed in their youth. On the twenty-fourth day of the eighth lunar month, during the feast of the goddess known as the Little-footed Miss, the four lesser toes of each young, supple foot had been bent under and held tightly in position by long bandages of silk, which were then bound around the instep, heel, and ankle in a manner that forced the foot into an unnatural downward arch. Twice a week the bandages were unraveled and the feet washed in a bain of hot water, balsam powder, and alum. New bandages, drawn ever more tightly, replaced the old after every ritual washing, and every two weeks the feet were forced into a new pair of tiny shoes, each pair slightly smaller than the last. The putrescent flesh of the transformation was sloughed off at each washing, and pus oozed through the silken bandages, but no toes fell off. After two years, the cries of the little girl's burning pain had ended, and her eyes had begun to take on that sad look of the fawn which was with her still. By then her feet had become true lotus hooks. The four lesser toes of each dead foot were permanently bent beneath the metatarsal, the plantar cavity of the sole was crushed into a gruesome clench, and the altered bone structure of the small stunted feet transformed them into narrow triangular appendages, hooves of rotten flesh, that hung almost vertically. In time, when the lotus transformation was complete, the girl tended herself to the maintenance of her bandages and took pleasure in concocting perfumed rinses of various flowers to loosen the crusted smegma and sebacious mold that gathered in the deep folds and fissures, though the old spinsters assured her that the stench she sought to banish was to true lotus-lovers the very scent of ambrosia itself.

The young girl's education was cursory. Crippled by her transformation, she rarely strayed from the spinsters' house, and then only in a wheelchair with a blanket to conceal the true nature of her infirmity. Last year, on the twenty-fourth day of the eighth lunar month, Li Kwang-chih's emissary had brought the girl her first pair of fancy bowed lotus slippers and a pair of red silk sleeping-shoes. Now, having delivered her from the little village of the spinsters to meet her true master and owner, the emissary had dressed her in the dark satin *chángpáo* of a fairy-tale empress and shod her white-stockinged lotus hooks in rich blue silk embroidered with black pearls and golden thread. The eyes of the men in the room were drawn again and again to her, mesmerized by the demure young girl in an imperial dragon robe gazing sadly down at her feet, which were like errant emanations of a dream, or a nightmare, made real. Calling her Li Kwang-chih's blossomed treasure, the emissary, who stood beside her, presented her to the old man as the rarest flower of her generation. For Lao Li, it was a moment of great face.

Ostensibly as part of the city's Tin Hau festivities, Ng Tai-hei had arranged for a fireworks display to be held this evening in Victoria

Harbour, of which the Regent suite offered a panoramic view. Ng stood on the terrace of the suite, gazing out abstractedly across the harbor to the lights of Hong Kong's Central District.

From the suite's master bedroom, where Asim Sau leaned with his back to the wall, drawing deeply on a cigarette, there came a faint, sudden sound, like the cracking of kindling. The blonde on her knees before him whimpered, and Asim Sau gently patted and caressed the reddened skin of her cheek with his fingertips. He zippered his trousers and ambled from the room.

Ng Tai-hei did not turn as Asim Sau joined him, nor did Asim Sau speak. The two men merely stood together awhile in the night spring air. Then Asim Sau, in a voice that was almost a whisper, spoke in words of Cantonese.

"Your speech today at the banquet, Ah Hei, evinced a love of poetry I never knew you had."

Ng Tai-hei looked at him but said nothing.

"You spoke beautifully of a golden sun that shines brightly. But not a word of those stormclouds you see."

Ng Tai-hei sighed, and Asim Sau could see the shadow of a slight smile.

"I will meet soon with these—" Ng Tai-hei seemed to search for a word, or words, and in the end settled for the plainest. "—men. Then we shall talk. Of sun, of storm, of many things."

The first rocket shot from the barge in a soaring arc of showering light and smoke, and the black sky filled with an enormous bursting chrysanthemum of red and gold. Then there were rocketing salutes and flashing comets throughout the sky, each blast bursting into a wild-willowing rainbow of its own. The others joined Ng Tai-hei and Asim Sau on the terrace, the whores as wide-eyed as children. The lotus girl came forth slowly, aided by the support of the blonde whore on her left and old Kwang-chih's emissary on her right; and even she opened her mouth in innocent wonder, in something not unlike happiness, as if the monstrous marvels in the night were the comforting revelation of something somehow kindred to that sense of her own monstrosity that lay at the heart of her sadness.

SEVEN

Johnny used to run with an *albanese* shylock named Lou. Once, in the weakness of his drunkenness, Johnny had confided to him the deepening woes of his marriage. "I don't know what to do," he had confessed. The advice of the sympathetic *albanese* was heartfelt, softly spoken, and straightforward: "Kill the cunt." Johnny could hear that calm voice and those words of guidance now, like an inner incantation that followed the rhythm of his pounding pulse, as Diane stood there above him screaming while he sat on the edge of the bed putting on his socks.

"I'm going to ask you one last time," she yelled, "and I want a straight answer: what the fuck is going on here?"

"Nothing," he told her, battening his voice, reaching for his shoes.

"You sonofabitch."

"That's enough."

"Fuck you," she hissed. "You come to me after seven years of fucking marriage, and you say you need some room to breathe awhile? Well, fuck you and fuck your breath."

"Seven years of marriage," he sneered. "You call this a fucking marriage?"

"It was until you ruined it, goddamnit." Her voice broke, and her

tears welled, and she began to sob. Her tears, as always, melted whatever ice and anger was in him. There was something about her way of
crying, the way it revealed the lost and sweet and vulnerable and all-
alone little girl inside her, that never failed to subdue the monster,
never failed to touch the heart of and summon forth whatever goodness
cowered in the shadows of that monster. It was not so much the tears
that affected him. It was the inarguable truth that flowed in them, the
truth of her hurt, the revelation and reminder of those things—love and
trust and all the defenseless indwelling tender purlings of the soul—that
had fled or died or been destroyed within himself, those things that still
suffered and cried for light within her; and of the lake of sadness
between that loss within him and that suffering sorrow in her. He could
watch men die before him of his own evil and theirs, and he could spit
on them and feel nothing but some vague disquieting uncleanness. But
he could not bear to see her cry. He stood and he reached out to touch
her, and she drew away and wept all the more. Then, overcome by an
anguish that overthrew all reason and all right, she let herself be taken
in his arms.

"Everything's going to be all right," he told her, soothing her, pressing his lips gently to her head, feeling the emptiness of his own deceit.

"Oh God, Johnny, what happened to us?" Her voice was a whisper,
like a forlorn breeze in the aftermath of a gale that had laid all hope and
illusion to waste.

He knew the answer to her question: *I happened to us*. But he said
instead, "We'll be all right."

Her crying had drained her, and there was nothing in her voice or
her eyes but soft disarming melancholy.

"What do you want, Johnny? What do you want?"

"I want you. I want what we used to have. I want for us to be happy."

It was true. He wanted her. He wanted to be lost again in the waves
of her gathering love. He wanted everything, the world. He wanted all of
her—and the flesh as well of every bitch that caught his eye—without
offering up a glimmer of himself, just as he craved wealth without
deigning to work for it, just as he wished to draw all the happiness and
joy in the world into the dead vortex of his being without giving forth any

in return. As he killed through another's hands, so he wanted Diane—
and the world—to serve as the handmaiden and vessel of his well-being
and soul's salvation. He wanted what he would not abide, endure, sanc-
tion, or forgive in her or anyone else: truth in return for deception, fealty
in return for infidelity, love in return for coldness, devotion in return for
indifference, honor in return for contempt, prosperity in return for sloth,
right in return for wrong. He saw the iniquity and the inequity in this,
and yet he persevered in his ways, as if somehow believing in some
elusive demonic dispensation and birthright, a certain *droit du mal*, that
was his and his alone.

"It's just a bad time," he said. "Things will work out. As long as we
love each other, things will work out."

"We do love each other, don't we, Johnny?"

"I think we always have and we always will. We've had good times,
we've had bad times. We never got that kid we wanted. I did a lot of
things to hurt you. We drifted apart. But we still have each other, and we
always will."

He meant what he said, but he said these things not so much to
express and commit himself to the truth of them, but rather to avail
himself of their temporizing effect on her. Eternal love could wait. Uncle
Joe and Tony Pazienza would not. He needed to get out of here, and he
wanted to leave with a kiss rather than a slam.

His plan to move into his uncle's townhouse had brought on this
mess. He had figured it best to broach the matter by presenting it in the
guise of a constructive measure, as a brief separation that, by giving
them both room to breathe, would help eventually to bring them closer
together and restore them to harmony.

"We need to rediscover each other," he said. "We need to learn to
appreciate the things about each other that we've been taking for
granted." He paused, saving his best line for last. Those sweet believing
eyes of hers were lost in his, and he delivered: "We need to fall in love
all over again."

"Do you really think we can, Johnny?"

"I know we can." *Damn*, he was good. There was nothing like an
undercurrent of truth to imbue a good line of shit with the sincerity and

poignancy that neither truth nor sincerity alone possessed. He could see it in her eyes. She was looking at him and seeing fucking Trevor Howard. "I feel a lot of responsibility right now," he said, "responsibility that I've been dodging. Most of all, responsibility to you. To us, really. And I know how you feel about my uncle"—Diane's head moved in a subtle expression of ambiguity, a qualm of conscience: beautiful—"but I'm all the family he's got, and he's not well. He's old and he's sicker than I thought, and I can't turn my back on him."

She hugged him, and they stood, swaying slightly in a long silent embrace. She remembered how they used to slow-dance to "You Belong to Me."

"Do you really have to go out tonight?"

"I wish I didn't," he said, sighing.

"I love you," she said to him, or to the fantasy of his weaving.

"I love you too," he said, and he meant it, not knowing in that moment who or what he was, seeing a young boy whose soul had been filled with the exhilaration of the illimitable world that lay before him, who had wanted to paint pictures and write poetry and sail the seas, and at the same time seeing a man whose soul had become a stain without meaning, whose pictures were dark and inward, from whom poetry and passion had fled, leaving only the unarticulated and rhymeless rhythms of a heartbeat banging out the cadence of its own dirge, a man whose moorings in Brooklyn and the few bleak miles beyond had never slipped from sight. And it was as if, in that moment, the two strangers grasped in the air, like fools, at the mystery that lay between them.

Uncle Joe was sitting in his easy chair watching a *National Geographic* program on television. Johnny watched as a pack of hyenas tore apart a zebra.

"I like these animal pictures," the old man said.

Johnny glanced from the hyenas' nocturnal feasting to the baseball bat that leaned beside the doorjamb. It had been there for as long as he could remember. He wondered idly if his uncle still had the strength to swing it.

"Where's Tony?"

"He'll be here. I wanted to talk to you first, just you and me." The old man sat still and silent, the feast of the hyenas flickering dimly on the surface of his eyeglasses. When the feast was done, he rose slowly from his chair, and Johnny followed him into the kitchen, to an old linoleum-topped table that, like the bat, had been there for as long as Johnny could remember. On the table, beside a black plastic ashtray advertising a long-gone joint called Dario's, there was an envelope, and the old man pushed it toward Johnny as he sat.

"Get yourself a new suit, a few shirts," he said. "Nothing flashy."

Johnny opened the envelope and saw that it was thick with hundred-dollar bills. The old man waved away his stunned, awkward thanks.

"Tonio's going to want to draw some blood," he said. "Play along with him. It's no big deal."

"What do you mean, draw some blood?"

"Some blood," Joe repeated, snapping the nail of his right middle finger in a demonstrative clip across the soft side of his left middle finger. "It's like a"—he churned the air absently with his hand, indicating so much nonsense—"like an oath. The blood seals the oath, some bullshit like that. He's an old-timer, he goes in for this mumbo-jumbo. Just humor him."

"What do you mean, oath?"

"Honor. Loyalty. That sort of shit. It's like the Boy Scouts for *cafùn*'s. Guys like him and me, when we were coming up, it was a big thing. We all did it. Tonio, he still likes the old ways. He's the kind of guy, he still wears a carnation on Mother's Day. Like I say, just go along with it. Make him happy."

"Is that what you wanted to tell me before he got here?"

"No. I wanted to talk to you about that spic you whacked the other night. Did you smooch him or did your buddy do it?"

"I drove."

"You drove." The old man snorted. "Did you ever actually get your own shirt dirty with this shit?"

Johnny shook his head and muttered.

"That makes me feel good in a way," Giuseppe said. "See, to me, you'll always be a godson first. I look at you and I still see that kid with the books and the chemistry set. So in a way, I'm glad to hear what you tell me. But in a way, it makes me wonder. It makes me wonder if it's a matter of brains or balls. I mean, a matter of your having the one or lacking the other."

Johnny averted his eyes for a moment, then looked straight at him, not knowing what to say.

"You get involved in this shit with us, you're gonna need both. There's more than a deal involved here. That spic uptown, he was nothing. He was somebody's junkie brother. That Rosario, that's the way he does things. He beats around the bush, hits one brother as a warning to the other. Me, I never went that way. The best route between two points is a direct line. That's my way. This beating-around-the-bush shit is over and done with. That's how Rosario and the others, and the rest of us along with them, ended up with hind tit. See, that spic's brother is a big shot up there. Thinks he is, anyway. He used to buy a lot of *bubbonia* from our boys. Then he went to the Gum Sing, the Vietnamese. This was Rosario's way of bringing him back around. All he did in the end probably was do the guy a favor, get his fucking junkie brother out of his hair.

"What it comes down to, Johnny, is this. The *bubbonia* comes from the Chinese. We buy from them. They will not sell to the Vietnamese. They hate the fucking Vietnamese. But there's one group of Chinese who've begun to sell bulk to the Vietnamese. They're the Fukienese. The Fujianese. Whatever you want to call them, they're here to stay, and they're bad motherfuckers, and the other Chinese are afraid to mess with them. They're the ones, them and their Vietnamese friends, that are taking over what the Italians once had, and the other Chinks are following their lead. They're selling directly to the spics, the shines, everybody. The spics are more important to us than the niggers, because the niggers only sell to each other, but the spics sell to everybody—whites, niggers, other spics. Don't get me wrong. The niggers are money too, but the spics are better hustlers. Anyway, all of them, the spics, the niggers, they always got their *bubbonia* from us. Now that's changed.

"We want to restore order. And the only way to do that is a direct line. You're going to Milan in a week or so. You and Louie Bones, you're going to meet a friend of ours, of Tonio's and mine, from Sicily. He'll be meeting there with a man from Hong Kong. You, Johnny, are to be my eyes and ears at that meeting. Before you leave, you'll meet with our Chinese friends here. This guy Billy Sing, he'll lay everything out for you. In the meantime, me and Tonio and Louie Bones are gonna hand out a few dance cards around here. Some things are going to happen. Some warnings that have nothing to do with two-bit junkies up in Harlem. And they won't have anything to do with you, either. But like I say, it's your balls that hang between your brains and your ass. Remember that. And don't wear any shirts you don't mind getting dirty."

"Well," Johnny said, smiling uneasily, trying to lighten the mood, "should I make sure my will is in order here, or what?"

The old man tapped a thick gray crust of *toscanello* ash into the black plastic tray. "Fuck wills." He laughed. "They just give people a reason to want to see you dead."

The howling of the hyenas had ceased by the time Tonio arrived. After some small talk, Tonio reached into his pocket and placed on the table an old bone-handled pocketknife and a small folded scrap of what at first glimpse appeared to be newspaper. Upon closer look, Johnny saw that it was a page torn from an Italian Bible.

"Give me your hand," Tonio said, holding out his own hand in a manner that brought to Johnny's mind Michelangelo's Sistine ceiling. Johnny did as he was told, and old Tonio spoke again:

"Do you swear with open heart and eyes upon your life and soul and all that you hold holy that you will never betray in word or in deed those who sit with you on this night?"

Johnny glanced at his uncle, who sat as if his mind were far away, his eyes occluded by smoke and the thick glass of his spectacles. From the other room there came a lilting of saccharine song—"Groovy Kind of Love"—and a reminder that "*Magic Moments*, the music you love, is not available in stores. Save COD charges by sending check or money order." Johnny looked down at the blade that Tonio held to his forefinger.

"Sure."

The blade cut sharply across his skin, and Tonio twisted the bleeding finger downward and began mumbling in Sicilian as the blood drizzled onto the torn Scripture. Johnny watched Tonio's eyes, which never wandered from the bloodletting as he spoke, and he followed the strange ritual sound of the rising and falling phrases: ". . . *d'u sangu unu e medesimu . . . un onuri luntanu da chiddu degl'autri 'omini . . .*"

—and, from the other room, a bright sisterly chirping: "You better sit down for this. The tampon you use was probably designed by a man"—

". . . *non tradiri questu duviri sacru . . . avribbi far muriri terribilmenti e suffriri nu focu d'infernu eternu . . .*"

"O.B. You can stand up for it."

". . . *non duviri dimenticarlu . . .*"

Tonio crumpled the bloody paper and put it in the ashtray, then struck a match and set it aflame. He looked at Johnny and, grinning, smacked him gently on the back of his head. The last lacy embers died, and the little burnt mass in the ashtray looked like a tiny dried black flower.

"All right," Tonio said with satisfaction. "*Novu sangu, novu viguri.*"

Johnny walked a long way alone that night, wandered hours without thinking, feeling nothing but a faint lapping at the edge of his awareness, the lapping of something like an indistinct incoming tidal darkness, a foreboding. He ended up at a small table in a café on Mulberry Street, staring blankly through plate glass at the city of night. The joint was almost empty, and so was the street. Raising a cup of coffee to his lips, he paused as the dark-stained Band-Aid on his forefinger captured his gaze, eclipsing both the emptiness within and the emptiness without.

EIGHT

Special Agent Robert J. Marshall stood on the third-floor balcony
porch of the Hewitt Wellington looking out over the breadth of the lake
and the blossoming trees beyond, watching the aureus planchet of the
morning sun rise above the sea. He closed his eyes for a moment,
luxuriating in the glow of daybreak and the balmy caress of the spring
sea breezes.

God, he loved this place. He had been born barely fifty miles from
here, but in another world. Growing up in the decaying hell of Newark,
he had come south to the Jersey coast summer after summer. He had
thought he knew every rundown shore town and dirty beach from Keans-
burg to Asbury Park to Atlantic City. But here it had been all along,
unknown to him, nestled just south of tawdry Belmar: paradise, the
idyllic little town of Spring Lake, a community of Victorian mansions
and quiet tree-lined streets and the most beautiful, unspoiled stretch of
beach on the entire coast. It was a wealthy town, predominantly Irish
and Italian, and for over a century that wealth had protected it from the
common fate of the other towns that lined the Jersey shore. There were
no nightclubs here, no food or drink allowed on the beach. There was no
crime, no litter, no graffiti. Even the cars seemed to move quietly, as if

humbled by the strange majesty of a place where birdsong and the sounds of the sea held sway, where the dominion of nature rather than civil ordinance precluded the blaring, vibrating Grand Am sound and fury of man's cheap and ugly impotence. The moment he had first laid eyes on this place, making a wayward turn one afternoon on Highway 524, he had fallen in love with it.

That was seven years ago, the year he had risen from detective sergeant in the New York Police Department's Narcotics Division to join the New York Field Division of the Drug Enforcement Administration; the year he had met Mary, just days before leaving for the DEA Academy at Quantico. There, for fifteen weeks, in the classrooms and conference rooms, in Hogan's Alley and Combat Village, in the dormitory and cafeteria, in the rolling woodlands that surrounded the training complex, he had dwelt as much on her as on clandestine laboratory investigations and constitutional law, had found himself as possessed by romance as by raid practical exercise and federal rules of criminal procedure. Qualifying with twelve-gauge pump shotgun, M16 carbine, submachine gun, SIG-Sauer, and Colt, practicing night after night for the redhandle test —forty consecutive double-action trigger pulls with each hand—until his forearms and wrists ached, working his way up to twenty pull-ups, seventy-one pushups, a hundred sit-ups, cutting his time in the hundred-and-twenty-yard shuttle run to twenty-one flat, the two-mile run to under twelve minutes, through maneuvers, physical and psychological examinations, and seventeen written tests—through it all, in every rare lull, he could see her eyes and feel her lips. Two years later, he and Mary had honeymooned here. Over soft-shell-crab sandwiches and beer at Eggiman's, they had decided that this was where they would someday live, that this was where they would bring up their children and share their love.

Now the first of those children was on its way, the hint of a swelling upon her girlish belly, and their dream seemed to be coming true. His latest promotion had brought his salary up to GS-15. With twenty-five-percent overtime, he was already taking down close to seventy grand a year. Between that and what he and Mary had managed to save, they would be able to swing a decent mortgage. Their meetings with the realtor had passed from the realm of vague fancyings to that of dollars and details. Houses here were expensive, but property taxes were low and the market was down. For three hundred grand, the realtor said, they should be able to find something nice. Nothing big, nothing fancy, nothing quite close to the sea, but their own little piece of paradise all the same.

The morning sky began to turn a rich lustrous blue. By now there would be coffee brewing downstairs in the hotel dining-room, but Robert decided to walk round the lake to a café on Main Street. He stepped from the porch into their room, where Mary was still asleep in the dwindling darkness where daylight had not yet reached. He stood awhile, silently watching her slumber. She was beautiful. She belonged here, he thought. As for himself, he was merely blessed. Benevolent fate had led him from the streets of Newark to the New York Police Academy and the John Jay College of Criminal Justice, had raised him to become the youngest detective sergeant in the history of the Fifth Precinct, had overseen his rapid ascent through the New York Drug Enforcement Task Force to the DEA. And that same benevolent fate had blessed him with Mary.

He bent and gently kissed her temple, nuzzling the hairs that sleep had freed like windblown corn silk from her long blond waves. She purred and smiled, lost and drifting in the limbo bliss between sleep and waking. She was thirty-two now, five years younger than he, and she still looked like a goddess to him. He loved her. He loved this place. He loved this morning. The job and the bad guys and the evil of the world that accrued day in and day out like grime on his soul and his mind—he was free of it, if only for a moment. The sound of the surf and the exundant rays of sun and love had borne it all away, and every breath he drew was like a whisper of sweet exhilaration.

Old Chen Fang knelt naked with his bony arms draped around the yellowed porcelain rim of the commode, his head bowed, retching, and his frail groveling body quivering like that of a wounded nestling. From deep within him, in a rush of bitter bile and fetid liquid, there exploded from his mouth several thick, heavy globules of black coagulated blood.

He wheezed desperately, gasping for breath, until, finally, the quaking of his body subsided.

He was dying. It was as simple and plain as that. He had felt it coming. Death, the westward horseman, the harvester. Now it had announced itself. Neither the fancy doctors of Memorial Sloan-Kettering nor the root-men of the older ways, neither prayer nor oblation, would save him now. It was here, beside him.

He raised himself weakly and washed the deathly drool from his face. Beholding himself in the cracked mirror above the sink, he muttered words of Shanghainese in judgment of what he saw: *"Gua sa zu za,"* a man reduced to nothing, wasting away to shadow and bones. He made his way unsteadily to the little mahogany table in the other room. He prepared his white powder, cursing all the while the tremor in his right hand, and hissing breathlessly through clenched rotten teeth, shot it like venom into his blood.

An hour or so later, stirring from his daydream of death to the reality of its presence, he boiled water and made a steaming broth of the concoction the herb doctor had given him: bulrush pollen, to stanch internal bleeding and bloody vomit; sponge gourd and mimosa bark, to reduce cancerous swellings; ginseng root, to arrest cancer cells and remedy the weakness that followed the vomiting of blood; privet fruit, to prolong life. He dressed himself and ventured forth into the light of day. He did not feel fear, and his pain was slight, but his melancholy was as vast as the sky. It was as if all that had come before had been nothing but an idle dream, *tzi shing mǒng shìang*, a meaningless reverie that had lasted but for a breath, only to end in darkness.

Then again, it had been dark all along. He walked slowly east on Bayard Street, and it was as if each step took him further into the memory of that idle dream, that lost reverie without meaning. He passed Winnie's Bar. Two young men standing in the doorway nodded respectfully to him, addressing him as Chen Xinseng, employing the formal Cantonese salutation of deference. They were not too young to know, Chen Fang reflected. Not too young to know that this old scarecrow who walked among them had given them their place within the greater scheme of things.

More than a quarter of a century ago, when the Immigration and Naturalization Act of 1965 had brought great waves of Chinese to New York for the first time since the quota laws of the twenties, the teenage boys of new immigrant families had banded together to protect themselves from the *ha ju* and *shibenga ju*, the black ghosts and the brown ghosts, who then outnumbered them by far in the public schools near Chinatown. Even the *tzo gang*, the American-born Chinese youths, were against them, branding them as *tzo nga*. It had not taken these *tzo-nga* outcasts long to turn from protecting themselves to victimizing others. Knowing that the Chinese community both feared and ignored the *gwailou* authorities, these new gangs had begun shaking down shopkeepers, taking the place of the Continentals, the older, tamer gang of American-born Chinese. In time, they had dared to stick up the dongs' gambling-dens.

The dongs at first had decided to kill these boys. It was Chen Fang himself, a shadow power in the On Leong Dong, who advised against this. It would be far wiser, he had said, to hire them instead, to train and cultivate them to do the On Leong's bidding like so many dogs, to have them protect the On Leong's interests in the streets from others like themselves. Thus the young gang known as the White Eagles had come into being, under the aegis of the dong's martial-arts group, the On Leong Youth Club. Some of the White Eagles had splintered off to become the Black Eagles. The On Leong had watched as the Black Eagles and other gangs challenged the White Eagles: first the Chung Yee, then, from Henry Street, the Quen Ying, which evolved into the Liang Shan. Meanwhile, the Hip Sing Dong had cultivated its own youth gang, the Flying Dragons. In the end, letting the weak perish and the strong prevail, the On Leong had accepted the allegiance of the Liang Shan, from which the Ghost Shadows since had grown, while the White Eagles and the Black Eagles in the end had been subsumed by the Flying Dragons of the Hip Sing.

Fang wondered if the two Ghost Shadows in the doorway would come to anything. It was true that many of them had risen to the ranks of the dong itself—"I'm not a Ghost Shadow, I'm an On Leong now," Fang had heard one young man exclaim not long ago—and in fact, the current president of the New York chapter of the On Leong was a former Ghost Shadow. But for the most part, they merely perished in senseless confrontations over face, or they faded away to become cabdrivers, junkies, petty thieves, or grocers. On the street they were *jŏ ling*, big shots, great and dark-swaggering princes, but to the dong that fed and used them, they were nothing more than yapping dogs to guard the peace of a garden whose recesses they would never know.

Chen Fang continued on, past the On Leong gambling-joint at number 85, past the Coffee House, where more Ghost Shadows gathered, past the entrance at number 63 to the secret cellar of the Chinese Masons. What secrets could those old fools offer him?

He crossed the Bowery, to Tung On Dong territory. Although he was On Leong, he walked without fear, for he was yet esteemed as *dzeng ning jüng dzi*, a man of honor in all domains. Venturing farther east, he passed to the East Broadway stronghold of the Fujianese. With their two impenetrable dialects and death-dealing ways, these were the Chinese who had become the most aggressive of the white-powder forces. The pair of stone dragons that stood as if guarding the entrance to their dong headquarters, the Fuk Ching Association at 125 East Broadway, had always struck Chen as indicative of their ways: a violent reminder of an evil past in a day when other, older dongs strove to affect a façade of social benevolence.

Pausing by habit to examine the fish at Hing Hing on the corner of Market Street, he wandered back around, past the Tung On gambling-joint at the corner of Division and Catherine, then across the Bowery again to narrow, winding Pell Street, the territory of the Hip Sing Dong.

Passing the Hip Sing gambling-joint at number 9, he paused a moment where number 13 once had been. He remembered the opium den that had been here long ago, remembered the thick smoky perfume of the place, the mingling odors of the various opiums: Ti Yuen and Ti Sin, Wing Chong and Quan Kai, glorious creamy Fook Yuen and fruity Li Yuen. To his mind came the soft little flames of the opium lamps flickering like fireflies amid the shadows of an eternal forbidden night, the long slender steel needle held over that flickering, the sweet *yapiyia* tar upon it bubbling and swelling, turning in hue from pitch to golden copper, the swirling of the needle within the bowl of the *yia chiang*, the taste of the ivory mouthpiece, the first deep swallowing of the sweet white smoke. When Chen Fang had first come to Chinatown, this joint had been here longer than anyone could remember. In the old century, it was said, when *yapiyia* was legal, men could buy women as well as smoke here at number 13, and in Chen Fang's day there still were women, old and widowed, who bragged of having been bought for great sums by men of stature and means. Chen Fang himself had long ago found women here, but they were *gwailou*, degraded white women, slaves whose master was *yapiyia*; and they were few, because the age of white powder, great *héloying*, had by then come. Now number 13, like the smoke itself, had vanished, its space taken over by the new Hip Sing Federal Credit Union next door, at number 15, where the old Hip Sing Dong headquarters had been. From the doorway of number 16, the Hip Sing Association's present address, an old man waved idly across the street to Chen. It was a man whom Chen had thought to be dead for years. He returned the wave, one ghost acknowledging another.

Where Pell Street ended, he roved north on Mott Street. Number 53 was now a nameless trinket shop. Chen could still discern the faded, peeling sign in the corner of the window: N.Y. STATE LIQUOR LICENSE L-1262. Here for many years had stood Tai Pei Liquors, the shop of Peter Woo. It was not liquor, however, that was old Woo's true trade. Woo had made a great deal of money overseeing gambling for the dong, but he had wanted more, and so, with Chen's assistance, he had been introduced to men of the 14K Triad and had become *ba feng ka*, a broker of white powder. As such, he had grown wealthy beyond the dreams even of gamblers. Woo was in his seventy-second year, and greed still drove him, when federal agents seized him with eight hundred and twenty pounds of Uoglobe number-four heroin in the winter of 1989. Now these grubby trinket-sellers were freer men than he, whom only that westward horseman common to all would deliver from his cage.

Chen passed number 57, a nondescript door that led to a roof where the Ghost Shadows hid their guns; number 63, where an On Leong gambling-joint occupied the basement of the Hong Fat restaurant. Chen saw that the cops had padlocked it, but across the street, at number 66, below the Western Villa restaurant, the other On Leong gambling-joint on this stretch of Mott Street seemed to be going strong. A few doors farther along, in another basement, was the Mayfair Tea Room, another Ghost Shadows hangout. Passing the dong headquarters, which lettering on plate glass identified as the On Leong Merchants Association, he crossed Canal Street, whose northern side was now the realm of Vietnamese peddlers and the Vietnamese gangs who preyed on them.

He walked round to Mulberry Street and paused to stare at an old brown-painted steel door, number 163. It was here that young Chen, barely twelve, had been brought by those to whom his grandfather had entrusted him.

Here it had all begun. Here, in the basement of this address, in the years before Chen's arrival, *yídalíning*—Italians; *hasar do*, black-hand men, from Sicily—and men from Shanghai had formed a partnership in white powder. Here, for both, America truly had been found. The man who had arranged that partnership, the Jewish gambler Arnold Rothstein, had been murdered by the time young Chen came to know this place. But Chen had known his protégés well: Salvatore Lucania, the one known as Lucky Luciano, and Tommaso Pennacchio, the one known as Tommy the Bull. From the Green Gang's waterfront hongs in Shanghai, across the sea to the docks of America, to this basement it had come, the fortune of a few and the plague of many. Chen remembered Pennacchio's apartment, right down the street, at number 89, where the Siu Cheong Meat Market now was; remembered how the men would gather there, Chinese men and *gwailou*—the one who in Shanghai had been known as *Kěsà*, Caesar, was at least once among them; remembered the counting out of money into tightly bound bundles the size of bricks; remembered the great Crucifixion effigy on the wall, the plaster eyes of the *gwailou* Christ transfixed in sadness upon them.

Chen was still a teenager when Luciano and Pennacchio were sent to prison. Pennacchio's wife, Mary, and his brother Vito, who sought to inherit the white-powder kingdom, had been seized soon after, along with many Chinese. But the partnership had continued. Other crucifixes, other men. Only when the flow of heroin was reduced to a trickle by the blockades and waterfront security of World War II did the partnership dissolve. With the end of Chinese opium production under Communist rule, the poppy fields of the Middle East had taken China's place as the heartland of the heroin trade, and Marseilles had taken over from Shanghai and Hong Kong as its primary source of export. Forgetting the Chinese, the crucifix men, under the one named Vito Genovese, had formed an alliance with the Corsicans of Marseilles. By 1970, however, the tide had turned. Burma had overtaken Iran as the world's greatest opium-producer, and Hong Kong had regained for the Chinese control of the international market. To obtain their white powder, the crucifix men now had to stand in line like any other *gwailou*. They had made their fortunes, but not as partners, and the counting out of money into tightly bound bundles was done now beneath the symbol of the triad, far from the sad plaster eyes of the *gwailou* Christ.

Yes. Here it had all begun. And, thought Chen, not far from here, beneath crucifix or triad, perhaps it all would end.

NINE

Looking around the third-floor apartment of Uncle Joe's brownstone on East Sixty-seventh Street, Johnny wondered when the old man had last been there. As he wandered from one large room to another, it seemed to him that dust was the only presence the place had known for many years.

The rooms seemed to have been decorated by a woman, or a faggot. His uncle's old *comare*, Rose, perhaps? Or, more likely, a professional chosen by her. The *Better Homes and Gardens* effect was thrown off here and there by incongruous traces of the old man's own artless aesthetic. There was the big bronze crucifix over the walnut headboard in the bedroom. In the living-room, a modern flowery blue sofa bore an old crocheted antimacassar, and beside the couch was a Mosler safe with a doily and an ashtray atop it. On a shelf there were a few old books: *Dodici Cesari*; a crumbling three-volume set bearing the title *La Guerra del Vespro Siciliano*; a brittle 1949 paperback, *Lucky to Be a Yankee*, by Joe DiMaggio. He opened the paperback and found stamped on the inside cover the words LIBRARY • GREEN HAVEN CORRECTIONAL FACILITY • STORMVILLE, N.Y. On the kitchen wall there was a faded religious print of Saint George on his white steed, his lance piercing the winged dragon beneath him, the Virgin Mary kneeling in prayerful observance nearby. When Johnny looked at the rearing, wild-eyed steed, he thought of the story the old man had told him about the horse going crazy on Cornelia Street, the *equus mundi*, doomward bound, that his uncle wanted to ride. Johnny read the words at the bottom of the print: S. GIORGIO, PROTEGGI LA NOSTRA CASA DALL'INSIDIA DEL MALE. Odd, he thought, that a man such as his uncle should call upon a saint to protect his home from the treachery of evil.

In the living-room, he drew apart the curtains and threw open the heavy Palladian windows that overlooked the street. There seemed to be a thirst in the rooms that lapped up the airy sunlight and set the stale stillness aswirl with the exhilaration of breezy reprieve. He stood there in that sunny breeze, and he smiled. All he needed, he told himself, was to have the telephone turned on and get a cleaning lady in to give the joint a once-over.

Slowly, he began to realize that the breezy exhilaration that he sensed to be at play about him really was within him. Standing there in those new, unthinkable surroundings, he felt the tinge of a new beginning. The dead vortex in his guts gave way for a moment to a sudden sanguine current, and the familiar dirgelike rhythm of his heart began to lighten.

He still felt good as he emerged from the subway in Brooklyn. As he neared home, he stopped at a Korean grocer's and bought a bouquet of flowers and a pack of scumbags.

The meaningful-dialogue-and-sensitivity shit the other night had softened Diane. She too felt the glimmer of a new beginning, born not of a breeze through an open window but of something even less palpable: words whose dazzling magic had obscured the cathode and anode of deceit and truth from which they had danced forth.

She used to hang around the apartment in her underwear. In the past year or so, after she had cut him off and the distance between them had grown colder and more unsettling, the sight of her flesh in cotton, Antron, and Lycra had given way to the chaste armor of her trousers. He could still remember when their love and heat were unbridled. He could remember her shy, lascivious whispering in the dark, the sighs from deep inside her as he tied her wrists and ankles to the bedposts with nylons and scarves. He had blindfolded her like that one night, let her draw from a cigarette that he brought to her mouth, replaced the cigarette with his forefinger, then his cock, and on and on like that, watching her loosen and drift in luxuriant trance. She had liked him to fuck her mouth while she masturbated, keeping her head still and passive and deeply drawing, then hurrying him to fuck her cunt as she neared orgasm. She had liked to lean against the bedroom wall, a pillow propped behind her back, the knees of her open legs raised toward her breasts, massaging her clitoris with her electric Panabrator as he, lying on his side, fucked her, endlessly, it seemed, as she came again and again until she could take no more.

Those days were long gone. When he was still drinking, there had been blowjobs from the broads in the barrooms. And occasionally, in the long months since then, there had been Bill's girls, the not-so-anonymous lonelyhearts of AA. But these twelve-step trysts had become fewer and fewer, for to him, fortuitous sex and sobriety were oil and water. Alcohol was his aphrodisiac, his lubricator and liberator. Many men he knew, most of whom drank far less than he, complained of liquor's deadening effect. But for him the effect always had been different. Liquor served to render sufferable, even enjoyable, the fatuous, vaporous follies exacted by the race of women as the conditional prelude to dropping their drawers for a stranger, that tribute of hollow talk demanded by the womb troll of all who sought passage, as if the vain, foolish words and bleatings of any man differed from those of any other. Liquor served to transfigure homeliness into beauty, obliterating through bleary eyes and benumbed fingers the variegated imperfections of those he had led like fatted calves to the sacrificial pallet.

But for him, no woman had ever held a candle to Diane as she was in those long-gone days, those days that he could neither forget nor hope to bring back. Tonight, however, the air was auspicious with the conspiring confluence of their moods, and her sisterly denim was laid aside. Nuzzling him on the couch in her peach-colored camisole and tap pants, she seemed once again the woman whose soul he had adored and whose flesh he had cherished. Seeing the inside of her thigh and the soft, loose line of her panties, he realized that only the lingering chill of the distance that lay between them prevented him from falling to his knees and putting his mouth to her crotch then and there. Unlike Willie Gloves and others he knew, he had never bought that old-timers' line of shit about eating out. To them, and to the *vecchioni* they got it from, going down on a broad was *proibito*, the equivalent of kissing a nigger. It was as if a faceful of *succo di figa* expunged one's manhood and was but the first fatal step toward a shot in the shorts. No, he liked eating pussy —Diane's pussy, anyway—liked the feeling it gave him of power in drawing her out of her senses in febrile waves, the feeling it gave him of immersion and communion within her. But that too was part of those long-gone days.

In bed that night, when he brought his lips to hers, her mouth opened warmly, as if gently to swallow his breath. He nibbled at the cleft of her upper lip, and at the groove of the philtrum above it. Her nostrils flared and her breathing grew lusher. He lowered his mouth to her breast, circled her nipple with his tongue until it hardened, then drew it into his mouth and sucked. She coaxed his head upward, opening her mouth again to his. Drawing her closer, pressing himself against the flesh beneath her left hip, he could feel the down of her skin rise in response to the tremors of his rising cock. She lowered her fingertips, let the tremors grow finally violent at the faint tracings of her touch, then clutched the pulse of its still strength in her hand. His own fingers slipped beneath the satiny veil of her panties, moving from the hollow of her thigh to the tendon of her groin. Her labia parted deliciously. He slid his fingers upward from the drench of her wet heat to the cowl of her clitoris. She sighed from her guts and held him tighter. He felt as if he would come in her hand, soak her fancy panties and trembling hip. But that would not do, not tonight, not after all this time. He needed conse-cration, renewal, redemption.

The scumbags had been stashed in the drawer of the night table beside the bed. With a parting stroke—a reassuring gesture of *ar-rivederci*, not farewell, to the little man in the boat—he rolled over and opened the drawer. He placed the plastic packet in her hand, and she opened it with her teeth and brought the scumbag to his cock. The rolling motions of her hand worked the taut, lubricated latex sheath downward. He shuddered, feeling once again as if he might not be able to control himself. He returned his fingers to the wet heat between her legs and kissed her cheek, her mouth, her neck. She raised her right leg slightly, a movement he remembered as her sign that she wanted him to get on top.

He was almost inside her. His cock felt like a length of galvanized steel drainpipe. He was invincible. Consecration, redemption, renewal, were at hand. It wasn't a blowjob, but it was a start.

"Johnny," she whispered.

He loved the sound of her voice. He pressed his cock to her mons veneris, then raised his pelvis higher, letting his engorged glans find the warm, wet folds of her labia.

"Johnny." Her voice was different. "I need to ask you something."

"What?" His heart sank.

"Don't be upset."

The galvanized steel turned to copper.

"I'm not."

The copper became an elbow joint.

"I can hear it in your voice."

The elbow joint drooped and shrank into a scrap of flexible tubing.

"What do you want?"

The flexible tubing melted.

"I just need to be reassured."

There was nothing down there, nothing.

"What do you mean?" He knew what she meant.

"I love you, Johnny, I just need to feel right."

"You seemed all right a few minutes ago."

"I was. I am. I'm just afraid. I'm afraid that if I get my hopes up, I'll just set myself up to be hurt again. I want to be sure, but I'm not. This whole business of us being apart for a while. I just don't know. All I know is I don't want to be hurt anymore."

"Nobody's gonna hurt you, babe."

"Johnny." She said his name slowly, sadly, a trochee of forlorn exasperation. "You just don't understand."

"I understand that I want things to be right between us."

"And that's what I want."

"So what the fuck was tonight all about?"

"There you go again."

"No, babe, *here* I go again." He got out of bed and pulled his shorts on.

"What are you doing?"

"I don't know."

"Don't be like this. Come back to bed."

"I'm not tired."

"We can talk."

Talk, he sneered beneath his breath. He wanted to get drunk. But he could not let himself, not tonight, not for a long time, maybe never. He exhaled. "I don't feel like talking."

"Then just come back to bed."

He sneered again beneath his breath, wordlessly this time. He returned to bed without removing his shorts, and he lay there with his eyes open in the dark, trying to summon the sensation of that sunny breeze through the open window on East Sixty-seventh Street.

"Do you really love me?" she whispered.

"Of course I do."

"We'll be all right, won't we?"

"Yeah," he said. "Sure we will."

Diane inhaled, a sigh of sorts, and then fell silent. He wondered for a moment at the nature of her silence, then closed his eyes and waited for the breeze to come.

TEN

From where Johnny sat in the café, he could see across Mulberry Street to the nameless club whose windows featured a plaster statue of Christ to the right of the door and a plaster bust of San Gennaro to the left. He had just ordered a second espresso when he saw Willie Gloves emerge from the door across the street and pause to light a cigarette, forming for one brief moment the strangest of trinities.

"Hey," Willie said, taking a seat at Johnny's table. "You been here long?"

"A few minutes."

A waiter came over. Willie pointed at Johnny's cup. "Gimme one of them.

"What's-his-face still own this joint?" Willie asked when the waiter walked away.

Johnny shrugged. The waiter brought Willie's coffee, and Willie drank it down with a snap of the wrist. He put five dollars down, Johnny put ten, and they left.

"How many more stops you got?" Johnny asked as they walked together up Mulberry Street in the late-afternoon sun.

"I don't know. Six, seven. The usual."

They crossed Grand Street, heading north on Mulberry toward Broome. They entered a storefront café. Inside, two pairs of middle-aged men sat at rickety tables playing pinochle for money. An older man in a plaid shirt and an unbuttoned sweater vest sat by himself near the window.

"It's the fuckin' grim reaper," one of the pinochle players, a man in a white V-necked undershirt and jogging pants, announced at the sight of Willie.

"Hey," said another of the pinochle players, recognizing Johnny. "You look good, ya hump. Who you been fuckin'?" This one wore shorts and a fancy silk shirt unbuttoned to the waist.

"Nobody," Johnny answered.

"Yeah, that's the secret."

"Pay or die, you fuckin' stiffs, pay or die," Willie announced.

The old man's face brightened, and the pinochle player in the undershirt reached into his jogging pants and withdrew a thick sheaf of folded bills. He counted out eleven hundred-dollar bills onto the table. Willie picked them up, folded them anew, bound them with a paper clip, then wrote the pinochle player's initials on the outside bill with a black felt-tipped marker.

"How about the numbers, pops," he said to the old man.

From the pocket of his sweater vest, the old man took a folded envelope with a great deal of arithmetic written on it. He handed it to Willie. "The old lady in the Laundromat. Mott Street. She hit. Five bucks," he said.

"I know, pops, I know." Willie looked at the figures on the envelope, counted through the money within, then licked and sealed it. From his left front pocket, he took out a thick bundle of bills held together by a rubber band. He counted out twenty-five hundred-dollar bills and handed them to the old man. "That oughta keep her in girdles and cigarettes for a while," he said, and once again the old man's face brightened.

"All right." Willie sighed, placing the envelope and the pinochle player's money in his jacket pocket. "Anybody want anything? How about you, stiff, you wanna get even or what?"

"What's Philly?"

"Won't get it till later. Call it in."

"Meadowlands. Third race tonight," the opponent of the man in the white undershirt said without looking up from his cards. "Gina's Grace."

"You and these fuckin' name bets. Gimme the OTB letter." Willie withdrew his pen and a piece of folded scrap paper.

"You bet the trotters?" a player from the other table asked in a denigrating tone. He looked sideways at the bettor from under the brim of a cocked hat.

The bettor, who wore a cashmere cardigan sweater and no shirt, did not respond. He merely looked through a newspaper until he found the racing charts.

"D," he said. "It's the D horse. Let me have a hundred to show."

"You know you can't do that. Win or straight across. None of this show shit."

"Fifty straight across."

Willie wrote down the bet. "Anybody else?" The other two pinochle players grimaced and shook their heads without looking up. Willie returned the paper and pen to his pocket.

"Take care, pops," he said to the old man.

Willie and Johnny walked out. Behind them, they could hear the voice of the man in the hat: "Guy bets the fuckin' trotters. I don't believe it."

Several doors up, they came to another café. In the black-curtained window was a sign that said MEMBERS ONLY. Across the street was a tavern. Johnny, ignoring Willie's song and dance, ordered a club soda and let his eyes wander past the familiar photographs above the bar—Tony with Marilyn, Tony with Sinatra, Tony with Reagan—to the television by the window. "*I'm goin' right ahead the way I figured. The spook racket,*" said Tyrone Power, in black-and-white. "*I was made for it.*" The old-timer next to Johnny stirred. "This is a good one. I seen it up Times Square in the theater"—it rhymed with "he ate 'er"—"when I was a kid."

"Look," Willie was saying behind them, amid the shadows in the back room, "I personally don't give a fuck if you pay or you don't pay.

There's a lotta guys like you, Jimmy, they wanna get paid if they win but they don't wanna pay if they lose. I say, more power to 'em. But when they get hurt, I don't give a fuck about that either."

"I get my check on the third," the shadow said.

"What the fuck does that have to do with anything? We're supposed to go by your schedule or something?"

"I get my check on the third," the shadow repeated.

"I think it was the Mayfair," the old-timer said. "I got a knobjob there once, in the loge. Forty-seventh and Seventh. Beautiful the-ate-'er. Beautiful."

"Look"—Willie's voice—"what the fuck do you want me to tell him?"

"I get my check on the third. Tell him I get my check on the third."

"Tyrone Power, he was good. I think he was Irish, though."

"If you make me look bad, Jimmy, I'm gonna make you fuckin' feel bad. I don't believe this shit. Nine kinds of fuckin' grief for a lousy fuckin' twenty-dollar baseball bet. How'd you pay for that fuckin' drink?"

"I'm on a tab. Tony knows I get my check on the third."

"A fag too, they say."

"Fuck you and fuck the third."

"Hell, they're all fuckin' weird out there."

At the corner of Mulberry and Spring, they came to a bar. On the wall over the cash register, there was a trophy shark strung with dead Christmas lights. Johnny knew that shark well.

"Still on the straight and narrow there, kid?" the bartender said to him from inside the half-moon bar. From a cigar box beside the register, he took an envelope and passed it to Willie.

Outside, before turning west on Spring, Willie glanced north up Mulberry.

" 'Quoth the Raven, "Nevermore," ' " he said.

Johnny looked at him, bewildered.

"The Ravenite," he said, gesturing toward the northern stretch of Mulberry that they had bypassed. "That's how that joint got its name. Carlo Gambino's favorite poem. It used to be the Alto, then he renamed it. The day they shut that joint down, the address came out. Two forty-seven. Nobody had it."

"They're open again. Joe the Painter delivered the palms there this Easter."

A penny on the pavement caught Willie's eye, and he stooped to pick it up. As he did so, an envelope fat with money and slips fell from his back pocket. Willie pocketed the penny and, unawares, left the envelope on the ground. As he began to move on, Johnny grabbed him by the elbow and laughed. Willie retrieved the envelope, shaking his head and laughing too. "Story of my fuckin' life. Bend over for a penny and get fucked up the ass." Then, by way of explanation: "I look for the wheatstraws."

They passed a vacant storefront. Johnny glanced at the sign in the window: STORE FOR RENT—CALL MR. YEE, and a telephone number.

"Little Italy keeps shrinking, and Chinatown keeps growing," he said.

"That's exactly what I was thinkin' before. I started out down on Baxter Street today, and that's exactly what I got to thinkin'. It used to be that everything above Canal was Italian, and Little Italy spilled over into Chinatown. Now what's left in Chinatown? That dump Forlini's is still there, that dive Val's, and that's about it. The Limehouse is long gone. There's a fuckin' gook eyeglass joint on that corner it used to be. And look at Mott above Canal, it's all Chink, Korean, Vietnamese, whatever."

"The wops complain, but who the fuck sold out to the Chinks? They did. It's as simple as that." They turned north on Sullivan Street. "Jesus, talk about streets changing," Johnny said. They passed a nondescript fenced-in playground bordered by park benches. "Remember when they had the boccie-ball courts here?"

"And what about the after-hours joint?" Willie said as they passed a Korean dry cleaner's. "Those were some fuckin' times, boy. The old man's dead how long now?"

"Oh Jesus, he passed away when? Eighty-five, I'd say. Spring of '85. They laid him out in Nucciarone, right up the street."

"And that ain't even there no more. Even the funeral parlor's gone."

" 'Quoth the Raven, "Nevermore." ' "

Beyond the dry cleaner's was a black storefront that a New York State charter in the window proclaimed to be the Trapani Knights. The door was open, but there was no one inside. Willie shrugged.

"Out jousting, I guess," Johnny said.

"I get a kick out of this one," Willie said, looking next door into the well-lighted space of the Horodner Romley Gallery. "Remember when old Louie had the store here?"

"Best fucking deli in New York," Johnny said. "We'd come out of the after-hours, seven, eight o'clock, he'd make those fucking sandwiches for us."

They moved on, past Tibetan Handicrafts and Depression Modern, east on Houston to the Genoa Football Club, then back to Sullivan, then north.

"The Venus," Johnny said, gesturing to a shut basement entrance on the east side of the street.

"Push goes to the house. I think those guys are still spendin' my money."

"I was there when Jimmy got shot through the wall."

"They never did figure that one out, did they?"

"Right through the fucking wall."

"Then he had that place on Hudson."

"But that didn't last."

They crossed Bleecker Street and came to a large, shoddy storefront. The remnants of the red lettering on the black windows could barely be read: TRIANGLE CIVIC ASSOCIATION & SOCIAL CLUB. On the door was a circular seal bearing the words ITALIAN-AMERICAN CIVIL RIGHTS LEAGUE, and on the black boarded wall to the left of the door, spray-painted large, the most prominent words of all: NO DOG PISS HERE. The joint was padlocked, and they moved on, toward West Third Street.

"This fucking Village is shot," Johnny said.

"Yeah. I'm surprised at this guy here," Willie said, gesturing across the street to a six-story gray tenement with a black door. "Forget about that Italian-American Civil Rights League bullshit, they oughta tack up a fuckin' Rainbow Coalition sign. They give him this, and look at it.

Right here on Sixth Avenue, two fuckin' blocks from where he lives, it's like fuckin' Nigeria. First that fuckin' basketball court, then that fuckin' *mulagnan'* Sparks, that fuckin' McDonald's, right there on West Third, right in his own fuckin' backyard. I swear to Christ, on a Friday, Saturday night, it's like they were givin' out free watermelon and wine down here. Blackest fuckin' Africa. I don't get it. And these fuckin' faggots. Years ago, back when bein' a fuckin' fruit was illegal, his *cumpare* makes a fuckin' fortune around here with these fag bars. They legalize suckin' cock and what happens? The fags take over the fag-bar racket, and now you got all this fuckin' gay-rights shit. I mean, this fuckin' Vito Genovese—they say his wife was a fuckin' dyke—he starts all this shit, they oughta put up a statue of *him* on fuckin' Christopher Street, and they end up takin' over his own fuckin' neighborhood. Fags and niggers. What a fuckin' perfecta."

"Remember that time, years ago, the kids swept through Washington Square, cleaned out the niggers with baseball bats? Half them fucking kids ended up in Dannemora. All those fucking asshole professors and shit from NYU that live there for free in them fancy fucking townhouses on Washington Square North raised a stink about civil rights and all that shit. Now those same fucking assholes are whining about crime and dope, and the cops ain't doing shit—a sweep every spring, the start of tourist season, that's it."

"You're absolutely right. These fuckin' nigger-lovers, they come here from the fuckin' sticks, and they don't know shit, and they fuck it up. I don't blame the niggers, I blame *them*. They're the ones."

There was one more stop on Sullivan Street, a purple-curtained room near West Third. After leaving the club, Willie dropped quarters into a pay phone.

"Talk to me," he said into the receiver, his pen poised above his scrap paper on the little metal lectern below the phone. He scribbled and mumbled awhile—"Houston-Mets, eight-nine. Philly-Rockies, twelve-fourteen. Yankees-Rangers, even-six. Tigers-Angels, seven-eight"—then hung up and turned to Johnny.

"All I got left is the boys in blue. You wanna walk it or cab it?"

Johnny looked west. The sky over the Hudson River was a deep, rich blue, and the underbellies of rolling white clouds glowed with the melancholy radiance of the falling sun: golden copper and watercolor wisps of rose and red.

They ambled south to a tavern near the Holland Tunnel. Inside, Willie veered to the left, toward a group of men who argued loudly among themselves. Some wore NYPD windbreakers; others, T-shirts or sweatshirts bearing the emblems of football or baseball teams. A few wore neat knit pullovers with Lacoste or Polo trademarks on their breasts. Here and there among them was a Moe Ginsburg suit and patterned necktie. Mustaches and gold jewelry were plentiful.

"Give these guys a drink," one of them called out to the young woman behind the bar, raising his head and gesturing with his hand to Willie and Johnny. They both ordered club soda, then Willie told the woman to wait a minute.

"Forget the club soda," he said. "This flotsky's buying, give us Perrier. No, Evian. You got Evian? Whatever costs more, give us that."

"Nice tits," Johnny observed.

"Ah, she's prob'ly a cop-fucker."

One of the windbreakers sidled up to Willie and gave him an envelope. "Billy's short," he said.

"Whadaya mean? I thought you guys stuck together. I thought you guys were like brothers. I seen it on one of them shows on TV." His shit-eating grin struck exactly the note of ambiguity that Willie wished it to. "I figure, one guy's short, the rest of you guys cover for him." He shrugged. "Maybe the TV lies."

"What's the Knicks?" one of the Ginsburgs asked.

"Two," Willie answered him, then resumed addressing the windbreaker. "So Billy's down what now, five, six hundred? He better start doin' what you guys do best. Besides drink and talk, I mean."

"Fifty times, Knicks," the Ginsburg said.

"You got it," Willie told him.

"How about the Yanks?" asked one of the lizard-tits.

"Even-six."

"Gimme the Yanks twenty times."

"You got it."

"What's the Dodgers?"

"Braves are eight-nine."

"Dodgers, twenty times."

"You got it." He scribbled for a moment, then turned to one of the sweatshirts. "Hey, you, *sfaccim'*," he said. "You got half a fuckin' brain left. Let me ask you somethin'. You know how when you come down Seventh by Bleecker there, the cops got that trap there, ticketin' every tenth car or whatever so they can make some bullshit quota which they claim don't exist? Well, let me ask you. These niggers with these cars that ain't nothin' but boom boxes, these Grand Ams, whatever. There's a law against that fuckin' noise, right? Well, here's what I wanna know. Why don't they start ticketing these fuckin' shines, if they wanna make an easy quota? I mean, it's just as fuckin' easy, ain't it, and they'd prob'ly net more fuckin' tickets."

"That's the Sixth Precinct," the sweatshirt said. "You gotta ask them."

"I can't ask them. The Irish guys got their action. They ain't big shooters in the Sixth like you guys down here in the First. So, you got no answer for me."

The sweatshirt shook his head and ordered another beer.

"That's First Amendment shit, them lawn jockeys with the Toobz," a Ginsburg said.

"First Amendment, your ass," Johnny said. "It's fuckin' unnecessary noise. It's like blowin' your fuckin' horn in a traffic jam. It's illegal."

"The guy's right," one of the lizard tits said.

"That's what I'm sayin'," Willie said. "If it's fuckin' illegal, and it's such an easy fuckin' score, how come they don't do nothin' about it?"

"The EPA handles that. They got stake-out teams with decibel meters. Anything that registers eighty at a distance of fifty feet, they call us. We seize the car for evidence and give the driver a summons."

"Yeah? How many cars you seize? How many summonses you hand out?"

"None."

"Our hands are tied," one of the windbreakers said, and all those around him laughed, shattering the talk into several new and simultaneous discussions, one louder and more drunken than the next.

"Ah, go fight crime, ya fucks." Willie waved them away disgustedly and took a drink of water. "Tell me the truth," he said to Johnny, "don't half of these guys look queer?"

"Shit, man. After show business, the arts, this has got to be the queerest fuckin' bunch in New York. I was with this British bitch once. We were hangin' out, drinkin', and there was a slew of fuckin' cops in the joint. 'Why do they keep glancin' at each other's asses and crotches?' she asks me. 'Are they cock-fanciers?' 'Worse,' I told her. She said they weren't like that in England. I told her, well, here they were."

"Like the guy in the corner here. Look at those eyes."

Johnny looked. The Ginsburg's eyes were bleary and glassy with booze. But in that drunken gaze—the oblique, guarded look did little to conceal it—there was a sense of apprehension, of vague and unclean secrecy, that was unsettled and unsettling both.

"How do you stomach these people?"

"That's a good question. Come on, let's get outa here." Willie placed a five-dollar bill beneath his glass. "Come on, you stiffs," he called out, "it's showtime."

They walked north on Varick Street to Bedford Street, then turned east. They came to a final club, where two gray-haired men in open-collared white shirts sat at a linoleum table drinking wine and smoking. One of them nodded to Willie; the other merely looked away.

On the table before them, Willie lay down all he had collected and written.

"*Brucculin'*," said the man who had nodded, pronouncing the word as if in resigned, familiar, ritual observation.

"*Brucculin'*," said Willie, in resigned, familiar, ritual affirmation.

The man who had looked away looked toward Johnny. "How's your uncle?" he said.

"He's good," Johnny said.

"Good," the man said.

They crossed Sixth Avenue to the south side of Houston Street and hailed a cab. "Make a left on First," Willie told the driver. "We're goin' up to a Hundred-sixteent' Street."

Johnny lighted a cigarette. The driver, who was Liberian, peered into the rearview mirror.

"Allergic," he said.

Johnny looked through the plastic partition at the name on the driver's license. "Fuckin' alphabet soup," he muttered. Then, louder, looking at the driver, "Well, look, it's like this. I'm allergic to that coconut-oil shit you got stinkin' up this cab, and I don't like that shit you got on the radio either. So just let me know, do you want this fare or not?"

The driver sighed and shook his head and drove on.

"I don't tip them when I can't smoke," Willie said.

"I don't ride with them when I can't smoke," Johnny said.

"Oughta fuckin' quit, anyway."

"I know. But it's this kinda shit that makes me not want to quit."

"Yeah, I know, especially guys like us, we always tip the driver five, ten bucks." He elbowed Johnny in his side. "All we want is a little courtesy."

"Of course."

At 116th Street Willie tipped the driver a dollar; "Buy a house in the country," he told him. Inside the joint, they made their way through the shadows of the living and the dead, the ones that seemed forever to tend the gloom of this place, gathering like ghosts in an abandoned temple of some long-forsaken creed, or like dust on the bottles behind the bar. From the doorway of his kitchen sanctum, the old man raised one arm in a slow, slight arc of recognition, which Johnny and Willie returned in kind as they pulled back chairs at their customary table for four.

"The squid, fellas?" the old man asked, as he always did. Johnny and Willie nodded their assent, as they always did. Completing the preliminaries of this long-established liturgy, the white-aproned bartender brought them bread, a bottle of wine, and two glasses. It was the same wine they always drank here, Regaleali, a red Sicilian *vino da tavola* that was cheaper and better than the Ruffino Chianti, the only other wine here that was not rotgut. Johnny had never seen this Regaleali anywhere else. Like the baby squid that was so fresh, its source remained a mystery.

Willie took a drink of wine and breathed with satisfaction. Then, as if the taste of the wine had sombered him, his expression turned pensive.

"You got me thinkin' the other night," he said. " 'Nothin' we do is important,' you said. That got me thinkin'." He took another drink, another breath. "I did some figurin' the other night. Between this, that, the other thing, you know what I made last year? A lousy fuckin' thirty-five grand."

"Well, hell, I didn't do much better."

"Shit. You got that union draw. That's good for what, five, six hundred a week?"

"Four-eighty after taxes. That comes out to shy of twenty-five grand a year. Big fucking deal."

"Yeah. For doin' fuckin' nothin', it is a big fuckin' deal."

"What do you mean, nothin'?" Johnny declared with false umbrage in his voice. "Sanitation management is a fuckin' full-time job."

"Yeah. So's pullin' my prick." Willie drank more wine and lighted a cigarette. "That last fuckin' job, that spic, whatever the fuck he was, we got, what, three grand? Shit. The fuckin' undertaker makes out better than us on this shit. We gotta get a better price outa these guys. We got to."

"Yeah. We'll get signs, we'll picket the fuckin' Knights of *Comu si chiam'* there."

"You gotta talk to your uncle. Maybe they can throw us some better work, somethin' with a price, instead of this tin-duck bargain-basement shit we been gettin'."

"None of this comes through my uncle. You know that. It's Rosario, Jimmy G, those guys."

"Yeah, well, all I know is that them guys ain't got ten years on us, and they're already workin' on their second fortunes."

"A lot can happen in ten years."

"It just seems the breaks ain't comin' my way. I mean, where the fuck am I goin' here? Nowhere. I'm doin' monkey work, that's all. You"—he broke off a piece of bread—"you got that union thing. And you got your uncle. Me, I got you and a couple organ-grinders." He chewed and washed down the bread with wine. "Of course, there ain't no one to blame but me. I thought I was gonna be a big shot. I thought I *was* one. But the shit that was big ten, fifteen years ago ain't big no more. I was a sucker for the rackets. Didn't really have anything else. Didn't have the sense to want anything else. I figured you were different. I remember, we were kids, you wrote that poem, whatever the fuck it was."

"That was just stupid shit. Kid stuff."

"Maybe. But it was somethin'. I used to think you'd go your way and I'd go mine, and between the two of us, we'd have it all covered."

"How you doing with the action? Shit, I saw those envelopes today. You must be doing a pretty penny there."

"I get a lousy fuckin' nickel on a dollar. Once in a while they throw me a bone. I should be gettin' a fuckin' cut, a real cut, but I ain't. *Domani, domani,* for two years, *domani.*" He lowered his voice. "You, me, we shoulda been tightened up by now. Some of these fuckin' punks, they got less blood on their cuffs than us, they already got their fuckin' badges."

Johnny glanced at his forefinger. The carmine line of the cut from Tonio's blade was still sore. It was true: the older you got, the more slowly you healed.

"Fuck the *button'*, give me *u sacc'*," he said.

"Yeah, I know, but you don't get the wallet without the badge."

Only then did Johnny take the first sip of his wine. "I don't know, my friend, you just don't seem to be your happy-go-lucky self tonight. You sound like some middle-level executive planning for the future. You thinkin' about gettin' married and settlin' down, or what? If you are, take my advice. Don't do it."

"Fuck, married. The closest I come to conjugal bliss in the last six months, I picked up some sixteen-year-old whore and pissed in her mouth."

"Doesn't sound like a bad lifestyle." Johnny grinned, and Willie laughed a little from his gut.

"Hey, I don't know about you, but my guy down there's spoiled. Don't straighten out for cunts no more, only mout's."

"When's the last time you were in love?"

"Fuck. I don't know. That fuckin' bitch that ended up rattin' me out a few years ago."

"Donna."

"Yeah. Donna. Fuck her and fuck love. How about you? You still feel like you love Diane?"

"Yeah." Johnny nodded, as if pondering some other, distant thing. "In a strange sort of way."

The bowls of *calamaretti* were set before them, rich and redolent with tomato and basil and garlic and sea, and talk of love, like love itself, was dispelled and forgotten in the heady steam of an old man's magic.

"I think I'm just gettin' old, that's all," Willie said after eating awhile.

"Yeah, well, nobody ever said it was gonna be easy. Most guys our age, if they're lucky enough to be workin', they're doin' nine-to-five, with less of a shot than us at gettin' anywhere."

"Except we're takin' chances, they ain't. Except they got insurance and pensions, we don't."

"What can I tell you? Go legit. Get a fuckin' job."

"Yeah. Doin' what?"

"If I knew, I'd be doin' it. It's not like at this point we have what you'd call career options. You're a carpenter who hasn't picked up a hammer in ten years, and I'm a negotiator. You know what a negotiator does? He says, 'Don't worry about it, they'll be sittin' down and they'll take care of it.' He says, 'That's the way it's gotta be, because that's the way it is.' He says, 'We'll cost it out.' That's what a negotiator does."

"Shit, we got skills. We got the kind of skills they want. It's just a matter of gettin'—what's that line of shit you guys use in that union racket of yours?"

"Honest pay for an honest day's work."

"Yeah, I always got a kick outa that one. You guys shakin' down them fuckin' workin'-stiff suckers, and them suckers walkin' around believin' that line of shit, believin' that you guys are goin' to bat against management for 'em, and all the while you guys are the fuckin' management." Willie snorted. "Yeah, that's what we need all right. Honest pay for an honest day's work."

"No, Willie, the trick is to get the pay without the work."

Willie smiled crookedly. "I guess you're right." He buttered a crust of bread and began use it as a sop in concert with his fork. "I want to ask you somethin'. Tell me to *stare zitt'* if it's none of my business. Just tell me to shut the fuck up, and I will. But I want to ask you: does your uncle ever tell you anything? Does he ever pull aside that curtain and let you see what he sees?"

"You mean, *la bisiniss*?"

"*Sì.*" Willie nodded. "*La bisiniss.*"

Johnny tilted his head somewhat to the right, slightly wincing on that side of his face, as if the answer to this question were a murky one, involving some deliberation. "No," he said, shaking his head, as if the weighing of the matter were done. "No, not really."

"And how do you feel about that?"

"My uncle's an old man, Willie. You know that. Guys like him, guys like Tonio, their day is done. Nobody kneels for those guys anymore." He took a sip of wine. "Hell," he said, "there are guys around today that don't even know who my uncle is."

"Yeah, but the way I figure it, that just goes to show how high up there he is. Guys in the street might not know who guys like him are, but the guys that those guys in the street kneel down to, *they* sure as hell know who they are. It's like with Gotti there. A big man, a hell of a man, a good man. But people only saw as far as him. He was the one in the papers, the one in the fancy suits, the one that fit the role for the government's little production. People knew John Gotti, but they never knew that other Johnny, that Sicilian Johnny, from Cherry Hill. They never knew of guys named Spatola. They never even knew these other guys were there. It's like the old-timers used to say, everybody knows Sinatra, but who does Sinatra know? That's the way I figure it. The guys in the fancy suits may make the news, but they don't move the mountains. The ones you don't see, the ones you don't know—they're the ones."

"You takin' those pills again or what?" Johnny grinned. "I mean, what are you getting at here?"

Then Willie grinned too. "The other day, down the club, one of the guys took me aside. Not one of the usual *citrull*'s—this guy's up there, one of the old *cugin*'s. He puts his arm around me, the usual lovey-dovey shit, smoochy-smoochy, all hush-hush. 'You're a good man,' he tells me. 'A good eye, a good heart.' He gives me one of these"—Willie nodded, winked deeply, turned down one side of his mouth, bent his arm, clenched his fist, and flexed his musculature in a sign of strength —"tells me the world belongs to guys like me. At this point, I figure he's on dope. But he's got work for me, he says. 'You're liked,' he tells me. 'Don't blow it.' And that was that. Short and sweet. The next day, sure enough, this job comes through. Now I'm lookin' at another.

"What I don't get is, I always figured my only prime connection was through you, your uncle. I figured the other day maybe he put in a word, tightened me up. But why would he tighten me up and leave you out? And if it wasn't him, who the fuck was it? It got me wondering."

"Stop wondering and count your blessings."

"But you're okay, right? You're doin' all right?"

"I'm doing all right."

"Because maybe I can get you in on some of this."

"Look, what falls to you, falls to you. What falls to me, falls to me. I always called on you because I needed you. Because you're good and because I trust you. We're friends. This other shit is just work. You deserve what you get."

Willie's features lightened into an expression not unlike happiness. "Yeah," he said. "Honest pay for an honest day's work."

"Damn right." Johnny grinned.

The two men chewed and drank. "I just wanted to let you know," Willie said. "Remember when we first got into this shit? No secrets, that's what we said. Remember? No secrets."

"No secrets," Johnny said, raising his glass and holding it until Willie met it with his own.

ELEVEN

Billy Sing knew that most white men looked on Chinatown as a cesspool, a fistula in the colon of lower Manhattan. They came for the gaudy storefronts, where the gods of millennia, reduced to trinkets of plastic and cheap jade, gathered dust amid brass incense-burners and ashtrays of blue-and-white porcelain. They came for the restaurants, whose red-and-black menus all originated at the same menu-mill on Market Street in the shadow of the Manhattan Bridge, the restaurants that catered to their gross taste for swine-slops of canned vegetables, macerated meat scraps, commercial barbecue sauce, cornstarch, cooking sherry, and sugar. They came for what was false, and they were repulsed by what was real. In the warm months, when they were most plentiful, they did not conceal their repulsion, wrinkling their faces into hideous masks at the stench from the filth in the streets and from the unseen places, the chthonian maze of squalid laundries, sweatshops, and kitchens, the cramped, dank subterranean cloisters that reeked of the excrement of smuggled men and child whores and those reduced by madness, disease, and penury to the world of slithering and scurrying things, the rats and waterbugs and mice and silverfish and roaches whose populations were the true races of this place.

The white man knew nothing but the false face and the scent and effluvia of Chinatown's soul. Less did he know, less could he imagine, of the true filth and stench of urban suppuration. His notions of danger and decay lay in the newsmen's peddled images and fears of Bedford-Stuyvesant and Washington Heights, East Harlem and the South Bronx. His mind could not conceive of the precincts of horror that lay beyond the ken of his innocent nightmares and nervous fears.

Billy Sing thought often of the Walled City, a place older than the white man's dream of America. It had been built as a fortress in the twilight of the Song Dynasty, and so was older than the settlement of Hong Kong, which grew up around it. In the nineteenth century, the fortress had become an official mandarin residence. In the twentieth, during World War II, the walls had been demolished by the Japanese, who used British prisoners of war to build runways from the stones. But in the years that followed, under the din of aircraft roaring to and from Hong Kong International Airport, the Walled City of Kowloon became a fortress of a different sort, whose barriers were greater by far than any walls of stone. Barely two hundred by three hundred yards, with a population of some fifty thousand, it became the most crowded slum on earth, a festering-place of disease and violence, where lawmen did not enter. Its twelve-story tenements were divided into apartments of a few square feet, with communal toilets and cooking-areas. There was little electricity, no sewage system. There were no streets as such, and only two courtyards. In the narrow passages between buildings, garbage rose to heights of thirty feet and more. In the courtyards, amid shifting, windblown heaps of more garbage, were coagulating streams and pools of raw sewage and bloody viscera from the one-room factories where fetid animal flesh was processed into pork balls, fishcakes, and sweet-meats. The putrescent stink was laced with the baneful scent of molten latex and smoldering solder from the sex-toy sweatshops that were the Walled City's other legal industry.

In one of the courtyards, a small forsaken temple was enclosed beneath a canopy of netting to keep trash from its roof. In the alleys and in the warren of tunnels and chambers beneath the Walled City, its young denizens roamed, warriors of a world known only to them. It was a vipers' nest, a breeding ground for many of the Wo triads' most brutal killers. The temple in the courtyard belonged to these youngbloods. There was a temple, too, underground, which they had desecrated with blood sacrifice. It was in that temple, in 1968, that Billy Sing first heard of the thirty-six oaths. He was twelve years old and had not yet killed.

Lung Chung Street, the Walled City's main alleyway, was known as Baat Fan Gai, White Powder Street, for its busy commerce in heroin. In that alley, and in the labyrinths below, little Sing became known as a young tiger. Like the other young tigers of the Walled City, he prowled Kowloon and Hong Kong, stealing from less feral boys and delivering heroin and cash for the youngbloods of the underground temple. Eager to establish face, he killed for the first time at fourteen, when a fat boy called him a little turtle—a faggot—and Sing with an overhand thrust of his three-inch switchblade stabbed through the flab of the fat boy's chest and slashed his throat when he fell, leaving him to die, crying and gasping in his own blood, for all of White Powder Street to see. Twice more within a year he killed, for money.

Not long after, he became an acolyte of Wu Chong, the leader of the Sun Yee On Triad, which ruled much of the Sham Shui district of Kowloon. Wu Chong, who had no son of his own, took a liking to this young tiger so intent on face, and took him into his home. And the young tiger, whose parents were consumptive strangers who barely acknowledged his, or each other's, shared existence in a windowless ten-by-ten cell, was grateful, and for the first time of his own will and heart, he offered prayers of thanks. He served Wu Chong and studied long and hard under teachers of Wu Chong's hiring. By the time Sing was eighteen, he was able, on his own merits, to enter the University of Hong Kong, as Wu Chong wished.

On a warm evening not long before his university education began, Wu Chong took Sing to a house of pleasure near Victoria Harbour. As a child, Sing had known the mouths of the Walled City girls, and in the years since there had been others. But the warm moonlight-drinking mouth of the nightflower with whom he withdrew that evening, and to whom he returned in seasons to come, was wondrous beyond anything he had known.

On the following night, introducing Sing to company of a different sort, Wu Chong received a Taoist priest to dine with them, an elderly man whom Sing had occasionally known to call on Wu Chong in the past. Through dinner, Wu Chong and the priest spoke leisurely of many things. In time the priest turned the conversation toward education, graciously celebrating Sing's achievements and prospects.

"Laozi of the legends said that to rule an empire successfully, one should 'exterminate the sage, vanquish the wise.' Plato, whose vision of an ideal republic perhaps predated the *Laozi*, expressed much the same notion when he said that all knowledge of poetry should be withheld from guardians of the state. These two wise men, while hewing to opposing doctrines, perceived this truth in common: wisdom is the most dangerous weapon, the greatest threat. Your education is important in ways that you cannot now truly comprehend. Remember that. And remember that your master and sponsor, Wu Chong, is a great teacher as well."

Taking pen and paper, the priest drew the classic character *hóng* in expert, fluid strokes:

"In a few years' time," he said, "you will see with new eyes, and you will understand these strokes as few can."

Now Billy Sing lowered a gold-and-lacquer fountain pen to the cream-colored paper of a black leather notepad, drew that same character, and passed it to Johnny Di Pietro, who stared at it a moment, then set it down.

Johnny lighted a cigarette. This restaurant, on Fifty-second Street, had been Sing's idea. In setting up this meeting, Johnny had told him that he needed to pick up a plane ticket at Alitalia and go to the passport office at Rockefeller Center this morning before they met. Sing had suggested the restaurant—he seemed to assume that Johnny knew the place—saying that it was close to both Alitalia and Rockefeller Center and that it was a good place to talk. He had been right. There was a calm quietude to the room and its murals, all autumn and earth colors and rich, warm stillness.

A waiter brought the mineral water that Johnny had ordered and the Château Latour that Sing had selected for himself. Sing dismissed the formalities of the tasting. "I'm sure it's fine" was all he said. The waiter filled his glass, withdrew, and returned with the quail salads they had ordered.

"In the world of lies that the Chinese call history," Sing told Johnny, "the origin of the secret societies remains especially cloaked in legend. I can tell you only what I believe and what I know."

Johnny nodded slightly, pensively, as if to say yes, that was as it should be. He was impressed by Sing's direct, unhalting eloquence. The Oriental hints that shaded his fine English lent the natural sureness of his words an air of subdued, exotic enlightenment.

Sing told a tale that began in the Han Dynasty and ended with the cream-colored piece of paper that lay on the table between them. It was a tale of Buddhist sects and outlaw cults and dynastic upheavals, a tale that wound from the twilight of the last millennium to the fourteenth-century overthrow of Mongol rule by the White Lotus Society, the mightiest of the outlaw cults, whose leader, a former Buddhist monk and murderer, assumed imperial power under the name Hóng Wu and adopted the dynastic name of Ming.

The Ming Dynasty ended in the seventeenth century. China fell once again to foreign rule, this time to the Qing of Manchuria. From the fading White Lotus Society, there rose a new sect dedicated to overthrowing the Manchu Dynasty and restoring the Ming. It took the name of the Hóng Society, Hóng Huì, after the first Ming emperor.

Sing gestured toward the piece of paper that lay near Johnny's left elbow. The character on that paper, Sing explained, was an ambiguous one. Besides representing the family name Hóng, it was, in essence, the character for "flood," "inundation," "vast," "immense." Its main, phonetic element was also that of the verb "to deceive," as well as of the symbol of the rising moon, suggesting the clandestine, the cover of night. Only the diacritical strokes distinguished the meanings of these characters; their sound remained much the same. And when combined with the characters *tu*, "land" or "earth," and *zhong*, connoting China, it yielded *Han*, the name of the Buddhists' earlier golden dynasty and of the ethnic strain that ran strong within the society's founders. In all, there were perhaps sixty different characters in Mandarin that were pronounced *hóng*. In uttering it, one evoked phonetic echoes whose meanings ranged from "rainbow" to "magnificent" to "din of battle," from "the death of a ruler" to "deep" and "mysterious."

He drew the paper toward him, turned it over, and with his fountain pen formed a slightly different character, then enclosed it in an equilateral triangle, as the Taoist priest had done for him four years after that dinner at the home of Wu Chong.

"For their symbol, the Hóng Society took the three strokes that would normally appear to the left of the main element and placed them above the character, thus creating a *hóng* sign of their own, and they put that sign within a triangle, forming the *hóng sanjiao*, the Hóng triangle."

The image of the triangle—the triad, three—evoked another tale, which Sing said was as old as time. In the third millennium B.C., the Sumerians worshipped the holy trinity of heaven, air, and earth. In Babylonia, it was the astral trinity of moon, sun, and Venus. In Egypt, Isis, Osiris, and Horus. In India, the Hindu Tribhuvana, the three worlds of earth, air, and heaven, and Trimurti, the trinity of Brahma, Vishnu, and Shiva. There was the Buddhist Triratna, the triple jewel of Buddha, dharma, and sangha. At the heart of the West, there was the division of spirit, soul, and body, of God, man, nature. The Greeks had the triad of Zeus, Athena, and Apollo; the Romans, Jupiter, Juno, and Minerva; the Christians, Father, Son, and Holy Ghost. In his first epistle, John likened this trinity to the mystical earthly triad of spirit, water, and blood. To the Pythagoreans, three was revered as the first perfect number and the primary geometrical figure was the triangle, three points connected by three lines. The Hebrew character *yod* within a triangle was used by the Jews as a symbol of the ineffable name of Yahweh. According to the Zohar, the triad of wisdom, reason, and perception represented the holy chemistry of all creation. Holy, holy, holy. Thrice-great Hermes. Man, woman, child. Birth, life, death. Shine, shave, shower. Frank, Dean, and Sammy. Manny, Moe, and Jack.

"You get the picture," said Sing, whose next excursus shifted back to China, where script developed from pictographs under the Zhou, at about the same time that the Greek alphabet came to be. The Taoist emperor Qin Shi Huangdi, the so-called First Emperor, ordered, in the third century B.C., the construction of the Great Wall and the destruction of all ancient books. Under his rule, the Chinese script was standardized, and a new official lexicon of thirty-three hundred characters appeared. It was called the *San-chuang*. The first character of the title, *san*, was the trigram of three horizontal strokes that represented the idea of three. The first and most elemental of the so-called primitive radicals of the Chinese script was a simple horizontal stroke sounded as *yi*. It represented the primeval source of all things. The second consisted of three strokes that form a triangle: *ji*, the joining of elements. From *ji* came *ho*, "harmony" or "union," and *huì*, "gathering" or "society."

Three was the mystical number of the *san caí*, the Three Powers, of *tian-dì-rén*, heaven, earth, and man: heaven the father, earth the mother, man the son. Before Kongzi—Confucius—in the ancient *Book of Documents*, there were the three virtues of straightforwardness, firmness, and mildness. There was the Taoist trinity of the three purities, who dwelt in the three celestial palaces. In Zhan Buddhism—Zen, in Japanese—there were the three paths to hell: fire, blood, and swords.

Sing lighted a cigarette and sipped his wine. "As Laozi said, 'The way begets one, one begets two, two begets the triad, and the triad begets all things.' This, the *hóng* within the sacred triangle, became the symbol of the Hóng Society. In time the society was known by other names as well—Tian Dì Huì, the Heaven and Earth Society, and San Hé Huì, the Three-United, or Triad, Society.

"By the time of the American Civil War, the Hóng Society had established a presence in San Francisco under the name of the Chih Kung Dong. From the Chih Kung grew other dongs, or lodges: the Hip

Sing Dong and the On Leong Dong. The Hóng Society reached New York by 1880, when there were about seven hundred Chinese here. In a way, it did succeed in overthrowing the Qing. Charlie Soong, after all, became a Hóng member in the 1890s, and it was he who went on to finance the revolution of Sun Yat-sen, which ended Manchu rule in 1912. But by then the society had for the most part forsaken its crusade and embraced a more realistic course. It had grown into a vast criminal alliance. As its political aspect became little more than a pretense, the society became known as Hóng Bang, the Red Gang—a play on the sound *hóng*, which also represents the character denoting the color red."

In time there was a Green Gang, a Blue Gang, and more. All were known as triad societies, *san hé huì*, after the sacred triangular symbol of heaven-earth-man by which they all swore. In America, their criminal counterparts were the On Leong and Hip Sing dongs, which in New York numbered several hundred members each. White men called the dong men highbinders, and likened them to the Mafia.

Triads had been active in Hong Kong for more than a hundred years. By the 1840s Hong Kong was the triad nerve-center for all of China, but with the Communist takeover of the mainland, when the Green Gang moved from Shanghai to Hong Kong, the colony became more than ever before a city of triads.

"So it was as Laozi said. The way begets one, one begets two, two begets three—Red Gang, Blue Gang, Green Gang—and three begets all."

There was something to Billy Sing's demeanor that gave his erudition a vaguely sinister air, something deeper and darker than those Oriental wisps that colored his voice. To Johnny, the younger man seemed to be a scholar of evil, a professor of infamy. His delicate features, faintly glistening backswept hair, and elegant dress—the open-collared shirt of *leonino* silk, the black cashmere jacket, and the conspicuous lack of jewelry, which seemed to express a disdain for all affectation, a disdain rooted plainly not in humility or in simplicity but in disregard for the eyes and esteem of others—gave him the look that posturing fashion-plates strove for in vain. But the demeanor, rarer than

the exquisite silk, blacker than the hand-tailored cashmere, overwhelmed the appearance. In his companion, Johnny sensed the serenity
of an innate darkness, borne with neither doubt nor pride but a cold,
natural grace.

"You were born when?" Johnny asked him.

"Nineteen fifty-six."

"And you came to America when?"

"Thirteen years ago."

Johnny grinned in a friendly way, in which Billy Sing perceived a
vaguely sinister air. "How do you know all this shit?"

Billy Sing smiled in turn. "Some men devote their days to profes-
sions or affairs of the heart. Some men do crossword puzzles. Some
masturbate like monkeys, feed the pigeons, or watch TV. You might say
that I have squandered my idle time in learning. For many years, it has
been my pastime. Of course, most knowledge is worthless. That includes
all that I have told you. I have met men—your uncle is not one of them,
but men such as he, Italian men of power—who have no knowledge of
their own heritage. They have shared with me the fairy tales in which
they believe, tracing the origin of their so-called honored society to
some imagined response to the French domination of Sicily. It is the
same among the triads, most of whose leaders speak of ridiculous monastic intrigue and a strange red light in the sky. What I have told you,
very few of them know. That does not detract from their power, nor does
it add to yours. But if you remember only the colors, the general picture,
of what I have told you, you shall be less a stranger to their world than
they to yours. I believe in perspective."

The waiter brought their entrées, lamb for Billy Sing, grilled snapper
for Johnny. Sing had smoked two cigarettes in the past fifteen minutes.
His salad still sat untouched before him.

"The Shan Chu, or Head of the Mountain, is the boss of the triad,"
he continued. "Beneath him are many lesser ranks and the army of
soldiers. Every triad title comes with a number, which is always divisi-
ble by three. The Shan Chu, for instance, is 489.

"There are thirty-six strategies which the initiate has to memorize."
Sing withdrew two folded sheets from inside his jacket and handed them

to Johnny, who put down his fork and looked at what had been given him. The first strategy was "To cross the ocean without letting the sky know. To deceive all the people around." The last was "To walk away if there is no better option."

"More important to the triad initiation rites," said Sing, "but not in themselves, are the thirty-six oaths, a series of vows and the punishments by death that one should expect for transgressing. For example, 'I shall not disclose the secrets of the Hóng family even to my natural parents or brothers or my spouse. I shall never disclose secrets for money. Otherwise, I shall be killed by myriads of swords.' "

Billy Sing, Johnny thought, had escaped those swords somehow. After Louie Bones had brought Sing and Johnny together, he had told Johnny that Billy had been a big deal in Hong Kong, the youngest underboss in the triads, but he had turned his back on all except himself and in New York had fallen in with an old Chink named Fang who had long been in league with the boys.

"So these vows, I guess they don't mean shit."

"Like so much talk of honor among your kind."

At Johnny's words, Sing had thought immediately of his benefactor, Wu Chong, whose head had been severed by his own enforcer. Sing had killed and beheaded the traitor, burned a scroll of the thirty-six oaths before the god Guan Di, and left behind him all belief in society and sacred words of any kind.

His tone changed. "They once meant something to me."

He wanted to say more—beneath his glibness there was a hunger to be known and to share the mystery of what escaped him in his life—but he did not, for he did not know how to say it. His voice resumed its forthright timbre.

"In the old days, the rite of initiation could last six or seven hours. Now there is often only a makeshift altar and the ceremony is reduced to its essence, the culmination of the classic ritual. There is a piece of linen paper bearing the thirty-six oaths and the characters *fan qing, fù míng*, 'Overthrow Qing, Restore Ming.' Blood is drawn from the initiate's finger, and the paper is burned."

Johnny recalled the blade of Tonio's bone-handled pocketknife cutting sharply into his skin, the burning Scripture, and the strange ritual sound of the old man's rising and falling phrases.

"Traditionally, the blood and ashes were mixed with wine and drunk. These days, with AIDS, there's not much drinking going on."

Sing paused and lighted another cigarette. There was still pink meat on his plate, and his salad remained untouched.

"What is it with you people and all these fucking vows?"

"Everyone tends to proclaim rather than practice virtue. Look at the churchgoers, moral crusaders, and pontificators of the West. *Konghuà*—empty words. But among the Chinese, it is a deeper matter. The Chinese fear freedom. They are not comfortable with the responsibilities of free will.

"Westerners will never understand the Chinese heart and mind. The Western philosopher Hegel, whom the Marxists never tire of pimping, was a fool. But when he said that conscience and individual morality do not exist in the East, there was an incidental seed of truth in the blind Christian stupidity he preached. I believe that there is ingrained in the Chinese soul a need to have every act and thought decreed from without, with the imprimatur and benediction of some higher power."

"Isn't the same true of the West?"

"No. The West's submission is a pretense. It is not heartfelt, it is not ingrained. Scratch a vow of chastity, find a child-molester. As the fathers, so the flock. The West's obedience to prefabricated morality is all talk, self-serving and hollow—*konghuà*. But in China, throughout time, the entire social and political order has been based on *li*, the all-encompassing idea of correct ritual behavior that governs all human affairs. *Chih*, the will, is nothing. It must be surrendered to the unquestionable forces and authority of *li* and of *dào*, the way. Ethical choice has little place in Confucianism. The *dào* of right and wrong merely is, prescribed and everlasting, in *li*. At the heart of Buddhism is the doctrine of *an-atta*, no-self. In Taoism, the ideal state is one in which men are innocent of knowledge and free of desire. There is no place for conscious decision or judgment issuing from the self. So alien to the Chinese is the idea of free thinking that there was no equivalent of the term 'philosophy' until the phrase *zhexue* was imported from Japan by translators late in the last century. There was simply no conception, even among the men the West refers to as 'classical Chinese philosophers,' of any systematic intellectual inquiry of any kind. The *dào* was there to be pondered and illuminated, not questioned or examined.

"But those old *dào* men, I think, were not without wisdom. In the *Analects*, Kongzi says that he was unschooled in the art of war. But the great Confucian Chu Hsi clarified that statement by placing it in the light of words that the *Analects* overlooked: 'If I fight, I conquer.' Those are wonderful words. But Kongzi, and his disciple Mengzi, believed man to be good. Xunzi's belief is more to be remembered: 'Human nature is evil.' And then there is the phantom Laozi. 'Truthful words are not beautiful,' he said; 'beautiful words are not truthful.' These things made sense long ago, and they make sense now."

Sing ground out his cigarette, ate the last of his meat, and began exploring his salad. He spoke then of the white-powder god.

"Opium was imported from India to China by European traders in the sixteenth century. By 1900, China was not only the world's largest consumer of opium but its largest producer as well, harvesting more than thirty-five thousand tons a year, almost ninety percent of the world's total. But the government continually campaigned against the drug, and in 1907, when Britain withdrew from the trade with a flamboyant display of morality, the imperial government undertook to end poppy cultivation in China. It was then that the triads, long involved in the opium transport routes, took control of the trade.

"In the summer of 1928, Chiang Kai-shek organized the National Opium Suppression Committee, a public relations farce whose governing body included the Green Gang's leader, Big-eared Tu. In its first year, it collected seventeen million dollars in what it called 'opium prohibition revenue' from three Nanking provinces alone. By the fall of 1928, when the Guomindang regime rose to national power, Chiang and the Green Gang ruled the world's greatest opium monopoly, with major heroin refineries in Shanghai and the Beijing port city of Tientsin."

Sing said that to make good heroin was a difficult and dangerous process. First opium must be made into morphine, usually at jungle refineries near the poppy fields, as it takes a hundred kilos of raw opium to make ten kilos of morphine. Then the morphine must be refined in a four-stage process.

The chemist starts with ten kilos of morphine and an equivalent amount of acetic anhydride, which is usually harder to get than the morphine. It is a heavy oil produced all over the world, by Union Carbide and other big chemical companies. Its distribution, however, is closely monitored, so most of the acid the refiners use comes from the industrial assholes of the East, New Delhi and Ghaziabad. From there it is smuggled by truck to Manipur and Nagalind, then across the border to Myanmar, then on to the refineries. The morphine and the acetic anhydride are heated in an enamel basin for six hours at exactly one hundred and eighty-five degrees Fahrenheit. This produces an impure form of diacetylmorphine—heroin. Next the solution is treated with water and chloroform until the impurities are drawn out. Then the solution is poured into a second container and sodium carbonate is added until crude heroin particles begin to solidify and sink to the bottom. The particles are purified in a flask of alcohol and activated charcoal, and this new solution is heated until the alcohol begins to evaporate. This leaves a relatively pure but lumpy and inferior heroin at the bottom of the flask: number-three heroin. Most chemists stop there, with the brownish or grayish stuff—Brown Sugar—that the Chinese commonly use for smoking.

The fourth and final step is where the expertise and danger come in. The number-three heroin is placed in a large flask and dissolved in alcohol. First ether, then hydrochloric acid is added to the solution. Tiny white flakes begin to form. These flakes, filtered out under pressure and dried, result in ten kilos of white powder with a purity of eighty to ninety-nine percent: number-four heroin. It is the volatile gas that is the test of the master chemist. Unless consummately tended for six to nine hours, it ignites and produces a violent explosion, destroying the refinery and killing all involved. In Asia, every one of these master chemists works for the triads. And foremost among the triads is the 14K.

"What's that?" asked Johnny, amazed at the range of Sing's knowledge.

"In the late forties, the Cantonese triad leader Lieutenant General

Kot Siu Wong brought together all the triads of his native region into a new alliance, the Hóng Fat Shan," Sing explained. "The Hóng Fat grew to a vast society of perhaps a million members divided into some forty-four subgroups, all with names incorporating the number 14, after the society's original address. After the fall of the Guomindang, Kot Siu Wong emigrated to Hong Kong with a large number of his followers. The society established itself there and attracted many new members from the disaffected ranks of older Hong Kong triads. The Hóng Fat Shan became known then as the 14K Society.

"As it was the most violent and ruthless of the Hong Kong triads, the 14K was persecuted above all others. But also because it was the most violent and ruthless, it emerged in the 1960s as one of the two great surviving Cantonese triads in Hong Kong. Eventually," Sing concluded, "the 14K became the most powerful triad in Hong Kong and the world. While the Chiu Chao and Wo triads are still central to the drug trade, they have for the most part been incorporated into the structure of the 14K."

The waiter arrived to clear their table. Sing ordered the kumquats, and Johnny went along with him. Both men asked for coffee.

"Where do the New York dongs fit in?" It was the first time he had ever pronounced the word *dong* instead of *tong*. Until today, he had never known how the Chinese themselves said it.

"In essence, the dongs are Americanized triads. Like the triads of Hong Kong, they are all descended from the Hóng Society, the mother triad. The four big dongs who are players today in the Hong Kong triads' world are the Hip Sing, the On Leong, the Tung On, and the Fuk Ching. The Hip Sing, who are predominantly Toisanese-speaking, and the On Leong, the other old Cantonese dong, are the established leaders. The Tung On are a relatively new dong, with ties to the Chiu Chao Triad of the Sun Yee On, now tied to the 14K. The Tung On street gang is only about fifty strong and has the youngest members, but they are also among the hungriest. The nastiest motherfuckers of them all are the Fujianese, the Fuk Ching.

"The Fujianese control almost all illegal-alien-smuggling between China and America—that big bust in '93 only changed the cast—and they've been most violent in their attempts to seize an ever bigger share of the heroin trade as well. Their ways make the bloody dong wars of years ago seem rather civil. In New York, their only peers in brutality are the Vietnamese, the loosely knit gang that police and the media have christened BTK, or Born to Kill, and, in Brooklyn, the Gum Sing."

The kumquats arrived, delicate beggar's purses of sweet minced fruit tied with slender vanilla beans and served with crème anglaise. Johnny, who had never eaten such a thing, found it strangely delicious, and he did not conceal his pleasure. Sing, in contrast, seemed to regard this flamboyant trifle as if it were an everyday sweet to be washed down with coffee, like an assembly-line Danish in a greasy spoon.

"The triads of Hong Kong broker the world's heroin," he repeated. "It is they who tie the highlands of the Golden Triangle to the dongs of New York. The shadow of the 14K is everywhere. There are eight branches, or *dui*, of the 14K in Hong Kong today. Each has its own Shan Chu, but one man stands above them all: Ng Tai-hei, Shun Chu of the all-powerful Ngai faction. Beside him stand Asim Sau, the lord of the Shan Plateau, who controls perhaps three-quarters of the world's opium supply, and Tuan Ching-kuo, the Chiu Chao boss of Thailand and link to the Guomindang of Taiwan. These three men are the triumvirate at the heart of all secret power. Their Uoglobe number-four heroin is the element of that power, and their ways and affairs are truly known only to themselves. Anyone who tells you otherwise, anyone who claims to be an intimate of theirs or to know them well, is a liar or a fool. This is the seal of their power."

Sing withdrew a flimsy folded sheet from his jacket and unfolded it, a red-and-white label about four inches square:

"The prefix *Uo* is a transliteration of the Chinese *wò*, meaning 'grasp.' The name and the symbol say it all. This is the label that appears on every kilo of their heroin, the purest in the world. Already cut and repackaged by the time it reaches foreign shores, it is still potent enough to be cut three or more times again before it reaches the street.

"I understand that you soon may be privileged to be in the presence of one or more of these men. That you have never passed beneath the shadow they cast will be of benefit to you, I think. To many who dwell in that shadow, they are like dark and distant gods, and the idea of meeting them would be unnerving. To you, however, they will be merely men—strangers from a strange world, yes, but beneath that, merely men. And that is how it should be.

"Ingrain in yourself what is ingrained in them. Forget the names of Kongzi, Xunzi, Laozi. But make the black pearls of their wisdom, like the thirty-six strategies, a part of your breath. 'If I fight, I conquer.' 'Human nature is evil.' 'Truthful words are not beautiful; beautiful words are not truthful.' Relinquish all human trust, and remember instead that these men hold to the ancient credo of the warrior-poet Kao Kao: 'I would rather betray the world than allow the world to betray me.'

"Beneath these men, the 14K, like the international triad network itself, is as disorganized as the so-called Mafia, a structured hierarchy that exists only in the bureaucratic minds of government agents and the fables they have spun. Beneath these men there is constant shifting and warring, little of which affects them. The waves of their world are those of the globe itself. Their empire, which runs no deficits and whose currency is sound, is as much a force as any nation. The nuclear-arms trade, international politics, the global economy—their presence is felt, if never seen, in all these things."

During the course of their long lunch, the effects of Sing's words on Johnny were manifold. Once Johnny had grown comfortable with the younger man's presence, Sing's discourse had mesmerized him. Dimly but enticingly, it had rekindled in him an exhilaration in the world that had lain before him in youth, the thirst for knowledge that had been lost in the public school system, its memory since worn away by the attrition of years. It had filled him with a sense of awe for his companion's mind and aroused in him a desire to read once again.

And it had scared the shit out of him. He had grown up thinking he was a tough guy. The trigger fingers of others, the deference of punks in the street, the blood he had drawn in his folly—they had tended this delusion well. But smacking out off-duty cops in the bars of Brooklyn was a far cry from maintaining one's pulse in a world such as Sing's words brought to mind. Who wouldn't have fear? he told himself. Maybe his uncle, maybe old Tonio, men whose cavelike souls seemed to end in hard blind reaches. He wondered about Louie Bones, who seemed to belong more to breathing, wakeful mankind. But fuck it. Fear, he told himself, was a flu he could not afford to come down with.

Sing insisted on paying the check. "Next time," he told Johnny, "next time." Johnny wondered whether there would be a next time, whether Sing thought there would be.

"Those colors, and the perspective, that I spoke of—I hope I've been of some help. I hope that the strange may now somehow seem a shade less strange. Don't be daunted. Don't dwell on how little you know. That's a sign of wisdom, but it's no good. Instead be assured that you now know more than most men concerning the things about which we've spoken."

"Your knowledge astounds me. To tell you the truth, it humbles me," Johnny said, plainly and straightforwardly. "I know you know Louie, and I know you know my uncle. But that doesn't explain your taking this time with me. I mean, it seems to me that what you've done goes far beyond turning a favor. What I'm trying to say is, you seemed to want to teach me as much as you could in the best way that you could. And I appreciate that, and I thank you for it."

"Well, it's like this." Sing smiled. "The more you know, the better off we both are. I don't really know precisely what you are about to undertake. But I do know that if you prosper, I prosper. As far as the time I have spent, it is nothing. I enjoyed it. It gives me an illusion of importance, an illusion that what I've squandered my life on is somehow of more moment than feeding pigeons or masturbating. Not that I haven't squandered my fair share there as well."

The two men laughed. Johnny checked his breast pocket for the thirty-six strategies. Sing had drunk less than half the Château Latour. He returned the cork to the bottle's mouth, placed a fifty-dollar bill in the leather checkfold beside it, patted it, and allowed Johnny to rise first.

"Enjoy the wine," he told the waiter.

TWELVE

Bob Marshall stood before the medicine-chest mirror, his wet hair impeccably parted and combed to the back, his freshly shaved face still glistening with witch hazel. With his chin raised and the starched collar of his white cotton shirt turned up, he shimmied the triangular knot of his maroon patterned Yves Saint-Laurent tie into place. Adjusting his collar, he nodded to himself in the mirror. The suits, shirts, and ties he bought from Barney's and Bancroft were as familiar and consistent in cut as the uniform blues from Frielich he once had worn. He had come to the Drug Enforcement Administration during a time of change. The typewriters had been replaced by computer terminals and the standard-issue sidearms had been supplemented by submachine guns. The street-enforcement and U/C guys had taken to gold chains and pinky rings, blue jeans and T-shirts, fancy pleated britches and open-collared silk. With the passing of time, his conservative SAC suits and neckties gave him a growing and increasingly appealing sense of distinctiveness and nonconformity. Even when working U/C, he did not look like the others. While they relied on their ingenuity to cultivate a convincing image, he ransacked the closet of every apprehended crook who happened to be his size, building for himself an authentic wardrobe that covered the criminal spectrum from street punk to big shot. Other agents went for the cars. By law, seized vehicles became official government property, and confiscated Jaguars and such were understandably often preferred to standard-issue OGVs. Marshall, however, went for the clothes.

Mary was sitting in her nightgown at the kitchen table with a cup of decaffeinated coffee, whole-wheat toast, and fruit spread. Yesterday, unable to button her baggiest slacks, she had spent much of the afternoon, and almost nine hundred dollars, shopping for maternity apparel at Madison Avenue specialty shops with names like Veronique Delachaux and Lady Madonna. The time of stretch pants and tunic blouses, high-waisted panties and four-way-closure bras was upon her.

"Go find an elegantly attired, pregnant, size-ten drug lord and raid her closet for me, will you?" she said.

"I'll run a profile, see what I can do." He poured her decaffeinated coffee from the pot into a saucepan, rinsed the pot and gold filter, added regular coffee from a can of Medaglia d'Oro, and switched on the coffeemaker anew. "Either you get off the decaf or we get a second machine. This is ridiculous."

"No child of mine is going to be born with the caffeine shakes."

"Hell, my mother drank coffee. She drank. She smoked." He shook his head and grinned. "The doctor told her to smoke. She wasn't a smoker. He told her to smoke, told her it was good for her nerves. She smoked Vogues, those pastel-colored things. I don't know if she inhaled, but she did what the doctor said. She smoked. And Rob Roys. That's what she drank. Rob Roys. That was prenatal care in those days. Coffee, a cocktail, a pack of Vogues."

"It shows, dear."

He ignored her little joke. "The doctor tells her to take up smoking, and she ends up dying of cancer."

Mary had heard it all before, and as always, her response was sincere: "That's terrible."

"But it wasn't the smoke," he said. "It wasn't the smoke. The moral is . . ." The loud bubbling and steaming hiss of the coffeemaker distracted him. He filled a bowl with Nutri-Grain almond-raisin cereal, added milk, and fetched a cup. Mary followed him with her eyes as he set down the cup, patted his back pocket, and walked from the kitchen. He returned, suit jacket and Badger shoulder holster draped over his forearm, billfold and credentials wallet in hand, buckling his wristwatch as he walked.

"The moral is . . . ," she said.

He put the jacket and holster over the back of his chair, poured coffee into his cup, then sat and counted the money in his billfold. He slipped the billfold into his back pocket, then flipped open his credentials wallet to check that the hundred-dollar bill he kept tucked away was there. His eyes moved from the leftward-gazing eagle of his badge to the rightward-gazing eagle of his laminated identification card, to the words superimposed on the shaded block letters DEA: THIS IS TO CERTIFY THAT ROBERT J. MARSHALL WHOSE SIGNATURE AND PHOTOGRAPH AP-PEAR BELOW IS DULY APPOINTED AS SPECIAL AGENT IN CHARGE IN THE DRUG ENFORCEMENT ADMINISTRATION, UNITED STATES DEPARTMENT—he turned the card—OF JUSTICE, AND AS SUCH IS CHARGED WITH THE DUTY OF ENFORCING THE CONTROLLED SUBSTANCES ACT AND OTHER DUTIES IMPOSED BY LAW. Beneath the words "Office of the Administrator, Drug Enforcement Administration," there was a western-flying eagle and the legend BY ORDER OF: The Attorney General of the United States. To the left of the eagle was his photograph, stern, unsmiling, staring straight ahead; to the right, vertically, his signature. He shut the wallet and placed it in the inside breast pocket of his jacket. He ate a spoonful of cereal, drank some coffee, and slightly, vaguely smiled. All those fucking eagles.

"The moral is, there is none."

"Thus spake Bob." She stood slowly, kissed his head, and tousled his hair. "The wonderful new world of Helenca superstretch nylon awaits me." She remembered the words on the receipt—"Exclusive Designer Fashions for the Prettiest Time of Your Life"—and something about them made her giggle. "Do you think pregnancy is pretty?"

"I think it's absolutely ravishing." He turned his head and kissed her belly.

"Then how come there's no pregnant pornography?"

"Oh, but there is. It outsells the amputee stuff by a slender but sure margin."

She slapped him playfully on the head. "Go to work."

"Yes, boss."

"And if you go downtown, get bread."

Bob Marshall was one of very few agents who had been fortunate enough to be able to walk to work. From their condominium on West Sixty-fourth Street, it had been only a long stroll to the New York field division headquarters at Eleventh Avenue and Fifty-seventh Street. Then, several years ago, the agency had moved downtown, to Chelsea, and he had become a commuter. Still, by subway or cab, it was a short run. If and when they moved to Spring Lake, he would be traveling back and forth in his OGV—he had his eye out for a Mercedes—like most of the others. That hour and a half each way in traffic loomed steadily more nastily as their dream came closer to being fulfilled. After each house-hunting trip to Spring Lake, especially on rare blue city mornings such as this, he appreciated these easy rides between work and home all the more.

In his office, his assistant, Jennifer Hernandez, had laid out his morning reading neatly upon his desk.

There was a copy of a report from the chairman of the National Drug Law Enforcement Agency of Nigeria to the head of the DEA in Washington, the New York regional commissioner of customs, and the director of the Customs Service's Passenger Enforcement Rover Team at Kennedy Airport. The report updated the Nigerian agency's progress in infiltrating the various heroin-smuggling rings operating out of Lagos, which were becoming increasingly active in moving heroin from Bangkok to America. This report, like its predecessors, had to be viewed in the light of the DEA's strong suspicion that the chairman of this relatively new and high-sounding Nigerian agency was himself a lapdog of the West African drug barons who ran those rings. Affixed to his copy of the report was a Customs Service chart breaking down heroin seizures at Kennedy Airport during the past twelve months according to the arrested passengers' points of departure. The bar graph showed that passengers from Nigeria and other West African countries accounted for more than half of all airport seizures, both in number and in size. Most of these seizures were rubber-glove affairs, as the Nigerians' preferred method of smuggling was to have each courier swallow eighty to a hundred condoms of heroin and wash them down with a thick green okra soup.

Another, interoffice report summed up what little progress had been made in penetrating the new Brooklyn-based heroin-trafficking network that had blossomed among émigrés from the former Soviet Union and used Warsaw as a transfer point between Southeast Asia and New York.

A second interoffice report outlined the route—from the Iran-Pakistan border port of Gwadar, across the Caspian Sea, through the Red Sea and Suez Canal to Bodrum, Turkey, presently being used by Turkish traffickers to ship Afghan and Pakistani morphine base to heroin refineries near Istanbul, the distribution center for seventy percent of the European heroin supply—that Kurdish drug lords had adopted when their traditional overland routes through the Balkans had been disrupted by war. In a single one-month period, DEA and Turkish police agents working this ocean route in concert had intercepted a total of seven and a half tons of morphine base, an amount more than three times greater than the sum of all heroin seizures throughout America in the past year.

There was a memorandum on the resurfacing of street-ready fentanyl, a powerful opiate substitute that was sold as heroin with often lethal results.

A printout from headquarters in Washington summarized the latest evidence of the Colombian *cocaleros'* intention to expand their heroin operations in a big way. The total known land area in Colombia now given over to poppy-growing had expanded exponentially, to some eighty thousand acres in twelve departments.

Another printout dealt with expanding poppy fields in the Bekáa Valley. Once Lebanon's breadbasket, rich with wheat, fruit, and vineyards, the valley, now under the control of Syria, had become the source of riches for a drug trade being run by Syria's highest-ranking military officials.

There was a preview of the new semiannual report of the New York State Office of Alcoholism and Substance Abuse Services. According to the latest figures, emergency-room treatment for adverse effects from heroin had nearly doubled. The preliminary report also noted that while the average purity level of a dime bag of heroin was roughly twelve percent five years ago, street dimes were now being encountered in New York with an average purity of sixty-five percent.

There was an updated interagency directory of the two hundred and fifty officers from the DEA and the New York state and city police who made up the State Drug Enforcement Task Force. There were briefs and queries on cases still pending from the reign of guinea-hunting Andrew J. Maloney, the former U.S. attorney for the Eastern District of New York, and his half-wop executive assistant, Charles Rose, and trial inquiries from assistant U.S. attorney Cathy Palmer. It was little Cathy, known by Oriental drug lords as the Dragon Lady, who had steered the 1988 federal indictment of Asim Sau.

There were memoranda from down the hall—from Group 41, the DEA task force specializing in Asian heroin-smuggling—and from downtown: the FBI; the Bureau of Alcohol, Tobacco and Firearms; the Immigration and Naturalization Service; and the organized-crime and narcotics divisions of the NYPD. There were DEA 202 reports, administrative 12s and 103s, dossiers and file folders, each bearing a two-letter, six-digit identification code, the sum and substance of the office's most important current cases.

It was an average morning load. As the special agent in charge of the New York field division, it was Marshall's job to study, digest, and codify this material. When he switched on his monitor, he would find an even greater mass of data and communications awaiting his attention. Then there would be the regular mail and the usual endless stream of telephone calls and faxes.

He savored these matins. While other agents complained of paperwork and computer migraines, he found in these ordered cerebral exercises a honing sense of satisfaction that appealed to the scholar, the archivist, and the chess player within him. Success on the street, he believed, was built on strategy, experience, and luck, and the only aspect of those three that could be controlled was strategy, built in turn on knowledge, wisdom, and skill. And knowledge is what he found, rare glimmerings of it, here and there amid the data, fragments, and bureaucratic logorrhea that lay each morning on his desk.

Of course, the street, where that knowledge originated and was in turn applied, was what he loved above all. Not as an environment. No. He did not love the city, did not thrive on it as others said they did. He hated the filth and noise and tension and crime more with every passing year. No, not as an environment. But as a place to play. And that is what he did. He went out there in his purloined pants, with the Broad-and-Market stride and the Nicky Newark accent he kept on the back burner; he went out there and he made believe that he was someone and something that he was not; went out there and skinned snakes with their hearts beating and their eyes wide open, beat them at their own lying, thieving, cutthroat racket; brought down the deadliest game with wits and guts and gun. That is what every agent would tell you, Marshall felt, if he was good and he was honest: he was playing. Cowboys and Indians, good guys and bad guys. It was the greatest game of all. Though the pay left a lot to be desired, the job was better than playing baseball for a living, because people did not regard you as a man playing a boy's game. They regarded you as a hero, a tough guy, and there wasn't a man alive who didn't want to be both those things. And it was a dangerous game. There was a thrill in it, a rush that no drug or blowjob or roll of the dice could equal. The odds were long and on your side, but it was always there, the threat of death. Ultimate rejuvenator, reclaimer, it kicked open the adrenaline spigots and filled the soul and lungs with lush life-loving breath. Of course, his street-hustle days were behind him now. As SAC, he only went out to join the agents on big arrests. It was his job to oversee them, and as they said at the agency, you can't judge the problem if you're part of the problem.

But there was still prey. Still an enemy, an adversary. How many men led lives of seething frustration, unfocused anger, and repressed aggression? If destroying an enemy were part of every job description, Bob Marshall felt, America would be a happier place.

At ten o'clock, a dirty black Oldsmobile pulled slowly to a halt beside a beat-up blue van parked on East Broadway, east of Pike Street, near the stone dragons that flanked the entrance to the Fuk Ching Association. The driver of the Oldsmobile, a young, dark-haired, Mediterranean-skinned man in baggy black walking-shorts, white V-neck T-shirt, sunglasses, gold chain, and wristwatch, stepped out from the double-parked vehicle and walked toward the Sun Sing movie theater, in the shadows of the Manhattan Bridge. From the Triple Eight Palace, opposite the theater, three young Asian men, all of whom also wore sunglasses, crossed the street to meet him. One of them had his black hair styled high in *fun-chao* fashion. The white man passed the car keys to him and walked away, toward Chatham Square.

The man with the shark-fin hair entered the Oldsmobile. The other two unlocked and entered the back of the van, which was empty but for a large brown shopping-bag. From the bag, the younger of the two men withdrew a Heckler & Koch MP5K-PDW nine-millimeter submachine gun. He unfolded its shoulder stock, and the gun's length nearly doubled, to two feet. Reaching again into the bag, he removed a curved fifteen-round magazine. His companion, speaking in clipped, hurried Cantonese, gestured for him to disregard the magazine. The younger man, speaking in kind, gestured to the trigger mechanism's pictogram-marked selector switch, which could be adjusted from safety to single-fire or fully automatic firing mode. His companion grunted in comprehension, and the magazine was snapped into place. Then from the bag, the younger man took a wide truncated cylinder that looked not unlike a high-powered camera lens. Affixing the grenade launcher to the muzzle of the gun, he muttered the word *liuxing*, which meant "shooting star," and together the two men sniggered and grinned. He loaded a grenade into the launcher, put another in his back pocket. Making a pistol action with his thumb and forefinger, he asked if the other was ready. The other man raised his shirt to bare, stark against his scrawny pale belly, the brown-and-black stock of the big Italian-made .45-caliber Witness that was stuck down the front of his pants. He stepped first from the van, looked up and down the street, and, removing the handgun from his pants, beckoned to the other, who emerged into broad daylight clutching the machine gun at his side. Only when he raised his weapon to aim deliberately at the second-floor window above the tenement door marked NO VACANCY, directly beside the Fuk Ching Association, did those on the street take notice and flee into grocers' shops, hallways, vegetable stalls. Beyond that window lay the rooms of the heroin-trafficking Fuk Chow.

He fired the grenade through the window. In the single still second between the explosive propulsion of the firing and the disappearance of the grenade within, the sound of the shattering glass was as macabre as wind chimes. Only the first staccato notes of vocal alarm could be heard. The fiery blast that followed shook loose mortar like dusty, stony rain, activated car alarms, and set the building immediately ablaze. By then the other grenade had been loaded, aimed, and fired straight through the door of the Fuk Ching Association. The second blast came before the resounding boom of the first had subsided. Flipping the selector switch to the automatic mode, the gunman fired sweeping rounds on the building's guardian dragons, turning their faces to gruesome spitting eruptions of slivering rock, cement, and smoke. His companion, regarding him obtusely, raised his .45 and fired with unsure bravado into the air.

The three sped off in the Oldsmobile, making their way toward Pitt Street, where they were to cross East Houston, continue up Avenue C, then turn and vanish on East Sixth Street into the Jacob Riis projects. There the *gwailou* men would meet them with two other cars. They would abandon the Oldsmobile, take one of the other cars, and make their way uptown and then across the George Washington Bridge to Fort Lee, where their reward awaited them.

Passing Grand Street, they heard a siren; then they saw it, a wailing, red-flashing blue-and-white gaining on them. The gunmen yelled frantic, opposing instructions to the driver, who yelled in turn for them to shut up. The driver sped through a stop sign, screeching round the front of an oncoming taxi. The taxi skidded to a swerving halt in the path of the squad car, and the Oldsmobile continued up Pitt Street. The yelling gave way to arpeggios of manic laughter, then suddenly resumed as the three argued over whether or not they should turn at Rivington and take Clinton north to Sixth Street or continue straight on Pitt now that other traffic lay between them and their pursuers. They heard other sirens then, coming from the west.

Then the driver heard a strange sound, like a muffled electric alarm, coming from beneath his seat. He bellowed violently at the others to shut up: "*Maihchouh!*" And as they fell suddenly silent, listening as if to ascertain the directions and proximities of the encroaching sirens, they heard it too, a faint but disquieting buzzing from under the driver's seat. They looked at one another, and in that instant, beneath that seat, the little Whittaker digital actuator released the circuit breaker, and the juice from the wire that connected it to one screw of the dry-cell battery beside it passed through it and continued along another wire toward the Mohawk blasting cap that joined it and the wire that was connected to the other battery screw; and the cap detonated the yellowish puttylike one-pound wad of RDX-PETN Semtex, and the blast blew the car to hell, bursting a water main, blowing out cable-TV reception in a nine-block radius, and filling the intersection with a storm of blackened bloody flesh and fiery metal.

Several blocks away from the blasts on East Broadway, a teenage Vietnamese boy sauntered up to the Shing Hau restaurant at 40 Bowery. The glass door was held open by a five-gallon plastic drum of Jadine duck sauce. Inside, chairs were overturned on tables and an elderly Chinese man was mopping the floor with a strong-smelling industrial detergent. Barely discernible from the street was a group of seven men huddled round a table to the rear of the restaurant, near the kitchen. These were senior members of the Flying Dragons and their Hip Sing elders, six of whom sat watching intently as the seventh divided two hundred and forty-odd thousand dollars among them into seven unequal parcels. As he glimpsed them, the Vietnamese boy wondered how much money among them there might be. His older brother, who had been a Flying Dragon in the days before the Vietnamese broke away to form their own gangs, had told him tales of Hip Sing wealth: a hundred and thirty grand a month in five-percent gambling vig from three joints on Pell Street alone; twice that a week from *bach-phien*; a hundred grand here and a hundred grand there from extortion and theft. If only there were a way to get at that table money first, the boy thought. But there was not.

He looked round to see that the car was waiting for him by the newsstand. The white man behind the wheel nodded placidly to him, and the boy turned, stepped toward the open doorway, pulled a thick, cream-colored, eight-inch stick of TNT out from under his shirt, lighted its fuse with a cheap Cricket lighter, and hurled it, fine and hard and far, over the flailing arms and howlings of the old man, clear to the back of the restaurant.

Turning again, the boy moved quickly toward the waiting car. When he was near, the man behind the wheel shot him rapidly, once in the head and twice in the chest, then pressed his foot to the gas pedal just as the billowing blare of the explosion blew asunder the restaurant's front and sprayed the frenzied, fleeing crowd on the street with shards of jagged glass like myriad cutting blades.

In an open garage in the Flatlands section of Brooklyn, a balding, middle-aged man stood at a workbench and pushed aside several wrenches and coffee cans of nails. He set down an empty Chianti Classico bottle. He stuck a metal funnel into the mouth of the bottle, then poured carefully from a can of Quaker State motor oil until the oil filled about a third of the bottle. Then from beneath the workbench he took a red plastic can of gasoline and poured slowly, filling the bottle to the base of its neck. From a box of rags, sponges, steel wool, and sandpaper, he drew a length of stained flannel and crammed one end of it down into the neck of the bottle, leaving a wide two-inch strip hanging out. Holding the bottle over a trashcan, he doused the strip with gasoline. He put the bottle in a gray plastic mop bucket, unlocked his car, got in with the bucket beside him.

"The fucking things I do for love," he muttered to himself. He was, give or take a few grand, seventy thousand dollars in debt. His shitbox house was double-mortgaged, and he was four months behind on the payments. He owed Con Ed, he owed the phone company, he owed MasterCard. He owed the Golden Nugget, he owed Bay Ridge Toyota, he owed Sears, he owed his ex-wife, he owed his ex-wife's boyfriend. He owed the city, the state, the feds. He owed bars, he owed restaurants. He was even into the Church for three hundred, a blackjack debt from the last Lady of Pompeii feast. And he wasn't even Catholic. But most of all, he owed thirty-eight grand to those fucking *lokshen* on the hill. Thirteen grand of it in ever-growing vig alone. He could not even gamble in his own neighborhood anymore. He had to travel to lose. He was like a Third World nation, borrowing just to pay the vig, getting nowhere, replacing one legbreaking creditor with another. If it weren't for GA, he would have killed himself last Christmas. Now, last night, he had been given a hundred-dollar bill, an address, and a stick of dynamite bearing the stamp of the Texas Torpedo Co., Electra, Texas. "Toss this thing and knock ten grand off what you owe." He had driven with that hundred to Howard Beach and looked for a card game. He had found his card game. Twenty minutes later he had been out on the street, selling the dynamite to some acne-faced kid for ten bucks, barely enough for a hand that he could not even afford to see through the first round of raises. Not that it had mattered. It was a losing hand. But what if he had drawn good cards? What would he have done then? He would have borrowed from the house, that's what he would have done. It was ridiculous, simply fucking ridiculous.

He turned off Kings Highway onto Avenue P, then north on East Fourteenth Street. He slowed down, found the address. It was to his right. Above the door were the words HOA-KY NOODLE. In the window there was a sun-faded picture of a smiling Vietnamese broad and a dusty vase of fake flowers. He looked at the clock on his dashboard. It was ten fifty-seven. Three minutes to go. Afterward, he was supposed to return to the club. Then, fuck everybody and everything, he was going to a meeting.

He looked at the bottle. Fuck it, he told himself. What was this, a military operation or some shit? Do it, get it over with. But how, exactly, was he supposed to do it? Lob it left-handed over the roof of the car? Scoot over to the passenger side? Shit. Even if he made an illegal

U-turn, if there was room, it would be awkward using his right arm through the window. He would have to get out and stand there in broad daylight like a fucking Bolshevik—a bald, middle-aged, sour-faced, Toyota-driving, Jewish fucking Bolshevik—and throw it in the open.

He sighed, got out of the car, bottle in hand, and ignited his cheap plastic cigarette lighter against the damp flannel strip. The breeze blew out the flame in an instant. He sighed again, tried again. Little slant-eyed kids were gathering on a nearby stoop, watching him. He heard the jingling song of a Mister Softee truck approaching. Cars passed, honking angrily at his double-parked Toyota. He was trembling. Then, in a moment of stillness, in which his heart sank and his mind went white, the flannel flared and he threw. He had been told that no one would be hurt, and he had chosen to believe that. Now, the instant that the Molotov cocktail left his hand, there were three of them at the door screaming at him. Shit, it was worse than that. They were shooting at him. He could hear fucking bullets passing his ear, hear them punching holes in his Toyota. It lasted less than one terrible second, a nightmarish crescendo of hollering and gunfire and the swelling, sinister song of the Mister Softee truck. Then came the explosion, knocking him down and backwards, hard on his ass, as fire, metal, and glass showered down upon him.

He scrambled back into the car, trembling ever more wildly. He tried to turn the ignition key with a shaking hand, and a pain shot up his elbow toward his shoulder. A heart attack. No, he told himself, he must have hurt his arm in the fall. Then he saw the blood running from his flesh. He was fucking shot. Then the pain spread from his shoulder to his chest. He felt like he was about to puke. He gasped for air, but the constricting pain would not allow it. The key turned in the ignition, and his head rolled back as he gasped once more. He was already dead, of coronary thrombosis, when, seconds later, a late-model Buick sped by and someone shot him twice in the head.

The Bushwick section of Brooklyn, to the north, had changed more in the past twenty years than any other neighborhood in New York. Joe and Mary's, at 205 Knickerbocker Avenue, had once had the best scungilli sauce in Brooklyn. It was there, eating outside on the patio, that old Carmine Galante had been gunned down, betrayed by his *guardia del corpo*, in the summer of 1979. The Italians had ruled Bushwick in those days. Then the Italians had gone soft, there as in many other of the old neighborhoods. And when the Italians grew soft, the streets grew darker. First the niggers, then the spics, the Dominicans, Puerto Ricans, Jamaicans. As old Tonio said, "You couldn't find a wop to spit on in Bushwick these days." Joe and Mary's was now a Chink take-out joint, and those whose fate it was to live there, in that stretch of Knickerbocker between Troutman and Jefferson, that stretch called the Well, right near where Joe and Mary's used to be—those people, their heroin now came not from men like Galante but from the spics.

The young black man behind the wheel of the Toyota drove past Bushwick Park and did exactly as he had been told to do: pulled over to the curb near the corner of Knickerbocker and Jefferson, right by the group of yellow-eyed, dreadlocked men loitering in front of Montego Billiards. He left the car right there, locked it, and walked away, exactly as he had been told to do. His boss at the carting company had given him a fifty-dollar bill to dump the car right here, and looking round, the young black man figured that his boss was right: it seemed a good place to leave a car if you wanted to have that car stolen. The yellow-eyed men called at him in Creole. He paid them no mind. As far as he was concerned, they were a bunch of turd-headed jungle niggers who might as well be sporting bones through their fucking noses. Fuck them. He walked a ways, bought himself a half-pint of Chivas, and continued on toward the M train.

He was halfway back to work, halfway through the Chivas, when the valise full of dynamite in the trunk of the Toyota reduced Montego Billiards and those yellow-eyed men, and whatever and whoever else was near, to mangled oblivion.

Willie Gloves walked out of the bar onto the corner of First Avenue and 116th Street, stood a moment, and belched. Close behind him was a younger, slighter man with unpleasant pockmarked wolverine features. Squinting in the morning sun, Willie took a pair of Ray-Ban sunglasses from the pocket of his rayon Hawaiian shirt and put them on. The pockmarked man unlocked the curbside door of the old gray Cadillac parked directly before them, got in, and unlocked the passenger side for Willie.

The Cadillac moved north on First Avenue to the Willis Avenue Bridge, across the Harlem River to the Bronx, and continued north on Melrose Avenue.

"Slow down," Willie said as they neared P.S. 29. He opened the glove compartment and took out a .40-caliber Smith & Wesson On Duty semiautomatic and a box of Winchester Super-X hollowpoint cartridges. "Pull over here a minute." He loaded the gun with eleven rounds. "Get that other thing out of the trunk."

The pockmarked man left the car and returned with a small Georgette Klinger shopping-bag. He reached into the bag, removed a Mini Uzi submachine gun, smacked a magazine into its housing, and lay the gun at his heels. He dropped the bag, which held three extra magazines, behind his seat.

"What the fuck does that thing spit?" Willie asked him nonchalantly.

"Twenty rounds a second, something like that. They got these little assault pistols now, they convert 'em to semi, shoot the same fuckin' thing."

Willie, gun in lap, lighted a cigarette and told the driver to move on. "Turn here," he said. "It's the second dump on the left."

The two Hispanic boys outside the tenement door did not look more than thirteen years old. One wore a Fuct cap turned sideways and backwards, bright red Global Ghetto shorts that drooped halfway down his shins, Nike Air Jordans, a Homeboy Loud Couture oversized hoodie, and an array of large ugly gold-plated neckwear. The other, whose head was shaved, struck a more somber figure, in passé Vans and Bulldogs. Like most his age who went goldless in these parts, he was a junkie. On the pavement between them was a boom box that thundered forth with gross distortion and endless repetition the series of mixes, the sound-track of his life, that the golden boy had programmed himself: Kool G Rap's "Death Wish" and "Road to Riches"—man, that fucking Tyrone, he *knew*; "Pop That Pussy" and "A Fuck Is a Fuck" by Luke and the Crew; all of the world that was fine and cool and one TDK SA-90 could hold. Right now, the mega-bass of "Suck or Die," by his *main* men, lay hold of him. The golden boy moved his hips, shoulders, and arms to the blare, opening and closing his mouth, jutting his head forward and jerking it back to the arsis and ictus of the lyrics' battering prosody.

> *When I want pussy,*
> *I don't fuck around,*
> *Stick my piece in my belt*
> *And I head downtown,*
> *Find me a bitch*
> *Who done last her way,*
> *Slam her up against the wall,*
> *And I make my play . . .*

Traffic in and out of the door was steady, mostly black and Hispanic, with a few white death's-heads here and there. Directly inside the door, controlling this incoming and outcoming traffic, was another fashion plate, dashing in Giorgio Armani suit jacket, purple-and-pink X-large shorts, a big golden image of Jesus, another of a gun, on chains round his neck, and leopardskin-patterned head rag. A queue of waiting customers stretched down the hallway before him. "Shut the fuck up and stay in line!" he hollered. "No singles, no shorts! Count it out, take it out! Don't fuck with the man!" The line ended at the far wall, by an open apartment door. There sat "the man," a fifteen-year-old spic with a Colt All American nine-millimeter on a chair to his left. At his right stood another kid with another gun.

"You think them monkeys up on the roof have guns?" the pock-marked man asked.

"Fuck 'em," Willie said. "They're just lookouts for the bulls that never come."

> *I use my dick like I use my gun,*
> *Whoever you are, ain't no use to run.*

White motherfucker say the nigger be free,
But ain't no nigger be free from me . . .

"And these two island niggers here?"

"They're just runners, servicin' cars, waitin' for the drop. That ought to be any minute now."

"They ain't servicin' our car."

"Maybe there's a dress code." Willie tossed what was left of his cigarette. "Excuse me, sir," he said, calling out to the two boys by the tenement door. "Where can we get some sharp clothes like that?"

White-powder money is all I crave;
So call your shot, bitch, my dick or yo' grave . . .

"*What* the fuck you want, girl?"

"Why aren't you boys in school?"

"Man, why don't you go fuck yo' mamma or some shit. Go on. Just git before you git hurt."

"Don't threaten me. I have a bad heart."

Ain't but two choices: suck or die . . .

"You're gonna have a bad fuckin' face, you don't git outa here." The cassette in the boom box snapped to a stop, and the golden boy, blareless, stood suddenly still.

"We're waiting for the fellow with the heroin in his trunk."

The two boys spoke to each other in Spanish.

"You some funny-lookin' cops, man."

"We're not cops. We're hit men for the syndicate."

"Oh, man, go hit your fuckin' bozack."

"Fuckin' white spliff-smokin' mothafuckas," the one with the shaved head added. "Go on, git."

"No," Willie said. "We're not really hit men for the syndicate. We're drug addicts. Horse." The pockmarked man beside him was laughing with enjoyment. "We came here for a fix," Willie continued. "We're not going till we get our fix."

"Mothafucka hunkamos be talkin' this black-and-white shit, man," the shaved head said to the gold-laden one.

"We ain't got no fuckin' fix for you, jive-ass. Now fuck off."

Then Willie's voice changed. "Well, that spic in the Lincoln should be here soon. We'll talk to him."

The gold-laden one whispered to the shaved head, "Go get Hector." The shaved head went into the house and came back out a moment later with the boy who stood guard at the side of the seller. As he walked toward the car, he raised his shirt, scratching his belly, to show the handgun tucked beneath his belt.

"What the fuck is your problem, man?"

The pockmarked man, looking in the rearview mirror, spoke quietly: "Here comes your Lincoln."

"Stop right there, kid." Willie aimed the Smith & Wesson at his chest. "This is a bust. Lay down and put your hands behind your back. We'll read you your rights later."

"I ain't done nothin'," Hector said, suddenly sounding like the child that he was.

"Just get down."

Seeing Hector get down on the pavement, the two boys by the door ran into the building.

The Lincoln pulled up behind the Cadillac. Its driver, a middle-aged Hispanic man in conservative brown slacks and a tan linen shirt, did not see the kid on the ground, but he sensed that something was not right. Deciding whether to make a run for the shotgun in the trunk or settle for the pistol in the glove compartment, he reached for the latter. But the wolverine-faced man was too fast, out of the car and upon him with the Uzi before he could fetch it. Willie was out of the Cadillac at the same time.

"Leave that peashooter where it is and get the fuck out the car."

The driver did as he was told.

"What about my rights?" Hector said.

"You want your rights?" Willie said. "Here's your fuckin' rights: you ain't got none." He shot the boy in the spine, then the head. Faces began to appear at windows up and down the street. Willie walked over to the Lincoln, took the keys from the ignition, opened the trunk, took out the shopping bag that was in it.

"Let's talk," the well-dressed man said.

"Lose the knees down," Willie shouted. The pockmarked man sprayed the well-dressed man's kneecaps, shins, and feet with gunfire. The man collapsed to the ground with a bloodcurdling scream, his legs torn apart, his bared bones shattered, his sundered arteries and tissue gushing gore.

"Tell your spic boss he's next," Willie said to the writhing, crippled figure at his feet. From the bag he took a brick of heroin. From his pocket he took a ring of keys. With the rectangular teeth of a safe-deposit box key, he ripped open the brick and the packets within. He kicked the spic hard in the jaw and crammed the brick into his gaping, groaning mouth. He clawed more bricks from the bag, threw them down hard upon the bloody shreds of the man's shattered legs. Then he turned to his companion. "Let's go."

In the rearview mirror, the pockmarked man could see junkies swarming like maggots at the spic's body. The fifteen-year-old man was in the street, making a show of shooting at them; the hall monitor and the shaved head were stealing the Lincoln, swerving off in reverse down the street. In the distance there was a siren, then another.

"Twelve of these fucking things," Willie said, rifling through the remaining bricks in the bag. "Six for me, six for you." He removed his Hawaiian shirt, threw it in the bag, and dropped the bag behind his seat. He plucked at the neck of his T-shirt.

"What do these things go for?" he said.

"Figure ten dimes to a bundle, ninety bucks a bundle. Five bundles to a brick, three-fifty a brick. That's without streetin' it and packagin' it down."

"Twenty-one hundred each." Willie lighted a cigarette. "Make a left, go down Morris Avenue to the bridge. We'll do the other thing, make it back to the bar for lunch." Willie reached back into the Georgette Klinger bag and withdrew the hand grenade, a hexagonal DM 51, that lay among the extra Uzi magazines.

"Those sirens don't scare you?" the pockmarked man said.

"You kiddin'? I hear them in my sleep. I hate them fuckin' things."

"They're gonna make the car, you know that, don't you?"

"They gotta catch us first. I always figure if they were good at what they did, they wouldn't need badges to be crooks."

"Maybe we should dump the guns."

"I suppose you want to dump the dope too?"

"Just the guns."

"Never dump nothin'. It's a sucker's racket, adds to your overhead. This is a five-hundred-dollar piece here." He gestured toward the glove compartment. "I can sell it to some nigger on the street for twelve, fifteen hundred. And that fuckin' matzoh-ball machine gun you got there has got to be worth two, three grand, street. Use your head. Besides, we didn't even kill the prick, we just fucked him up, that's all. Hire the handicapped, all that shit."

"Another fuckin' *brunu* I end up supportin'."

"You pay taxes?"

"I'm thinkin' about it." Then: "Wait a minute. What about the other one, that little cockroach you dusted? I suppose that was a slap on the wrist too?"

"I forgot about him," Willie said in a bemused sort of way.

The pockmarked man looked at him sideways. By the time they turned off Morris Avenue toward the East 145th Street Bridge, the sirens had faded.

"Go straight across to Broadway."

The Cadillac made its way toward the northern reaches of Manhattan. "Make the next left," Willie said as they passed 179th Street, where a sign on a lamppost advertised LA GRAN PARADA DOMINICANA. The driver did as he was told. "Slow down." They neared a storefront with red-and-yellow lettering in the window: SOCIEDAD SAN FRANCISCO DE MARCORIS • CLUB PARTICULAR. From within there was music, fast and loud.

Pues no hablamos inglés,
Ni a la Mitsubishi, ni a la Chevrolet . . .

"There, that's it." Willie held the grenade firmly in his right hand, clutching its curved lever in his grasp. The driver watched him anxiously. "Slower," Willie said. "I never did this before." With his left forefinger hooked into its ring, he abruptly yanked out the firing pin and sidearmed the grenade toward the club's open door. "Go!"

A deafening blast came fast and hard. Watching over his shoulder, Willie could see dark objects—pieces of the building? dead spics?—blown into the street by the squall of the explosion.

Again there were sirens, and again they faded away with distance.

"You got any idea what all this is about?" The driver asked, visibly relaxed for the first time this morning.

"Dope," Willie said.

"I mean beyond that."

Willie looked at him, then looked away, lighted a cigarette. "I used to ask questions like that," he said. "Then I learned. If they want you to know, they'll tell you. And believe me, most of the time they don't even know themselves."

The driver tilted his head, nodded abstractedly. "Somebody's gotta know somethin'."

"As long as they know how to count out our money, that's all you need to worry about." Willie looked with dead eyes at the filthy streets of Harlem. Civilization, he thought, was like an old whore. Despite all its talk and dreams and lies, it just got uglier. Then he stopped looking, stopped thinking. "I'm hungry," he said. "God, I'm fucking hungry."

The fire engines and investigators were still working on East Broadway, the Bowery, and Pitt Street. The traffic in Chinatown was so bad that old Ennio Scarpa had told his driver to drop him off at Broome Street, and from there he had walked south to 187 Mott Street, where a rusted steel door identified a narrow warehouse as the Shing Lau Produce Co. Unlocking the door with keys from his pocket, he slowly ascended the creaking stairs, which were patched here and there with pieces of old tin. To the right of the stairwell was an open freight-elevator shaft boarded across with planks of rough rotten wood. The air here was always musty and had the unclean odor of machinery grease and wet crumbling plaster. From the shaft, there was a strong cold sewery smell. But as old Ennio made his way up the stairs, he became aware of another, unfamiliar odor. He sniffed as he moved closer. It was gasoline, and it was coming from the loft where the *bubbonia* was kept.

"Calò," he called. Then louder: "Calò!" He could never remember the Chinks' names. He only talked to his *paisan*, old Calò. He called him again as he approached the landing.

His *paisan* lay dead, along with several Chinamen, inside, beyond the loft door. Each was covered with gasoline and bled from a hole in his head, and the blood spread among them in tendrils like a lacy wine-red web amid the gasoline that drenched the dirty linoleum floor. In that web lay eleven kilograms of heroin wrapped in blue waxed paper. It was all that had been left behind of a hundred kilograms, worth about sixteen million dollars, that had belonged to old Ennio, and those hundred kilograms were all that he thought of as he opened the door to investigate the silence and fumes within.

The last visitor to this place, however, holding the door slightly ajar, had crooked his arm round it and stood a foot-long block of four-by-four lumber upright, out of sight, and on that four-by-four, crooking his arm carefully round again, he had rested a lighted kerosene lantern.

Before old Ennio's right foot came down upon the puddle of gasoline within, the lantern was toppled and the place burst into booming flame, enveloping him and those who were already dead.

From the club on Hester Street, Uncle Joe could hear sirens, on and off all morning, from afar. He sat alone, enlaced in smoke. Frankie Blue, his driver and *guardia del corpo*, was enjoying the sun. So was the barman.

"Looks like hell's breakin' loose down in Chinatown, Mr. Joe," one of the *cafon*'s ventured, leaving his vinyl-seated post outside to come in for a cup of coffee. "They got it on the TV and everything."

"Ah," the old man said, "you know Chinks."

"Yeah," the younger man enthused, pleased at having been acknowledged by a response.

It was about five to noon when Louie Bones strode in. A moment later, the barman ambled in behind him. Louie sat down at the old man's table and wordlessly gestured to the barman, holding out his thumb and crooked index finger horizontally about an inch apart.

"*E caffè?*" the barman asked.

Louie nodded.

The barman brought a cup of espresso, a shot glass, and a bottle of Thorne's. He filled the glass with Scotch, left the bottle, and asked Uncle Joe if he was all right. Uncle Joe gestured his complacency, and the barman returned to the sunshine. Louie Bones drank his shot and stirred his coffee.

"*Tutto è bene ciò che finisce bene,*" he said, in a tone that was both weary and content.

"End?" the old man said. "Shit, we've barely begun." They were both silent for a while.

"Enio's the only part of the picture I don't get," Louie said.

"Window dressing," the old man explained with a shrug. "We hit the Fuk Ching, the Hip Sing. They figure it's the On Leong, each other, or both. We hit the spics, the Vietnamese, shake them up a little. Before anybody can cry wop, we throw in one of our own. The more they try to figure it, the more confused they'll be, the more they'll start seeing ghosts. And that's what we want. We want confusion and we want fear."

"But why Enio? You worked many a racket with him in your time, didn't you? I thought you two went back to Mulberry Bend together."

"But I never liked him."

"He always thought you did."

"What can I say? A bad judge of character, that's all."

The two men were silent again, and when they next spoke, it was about lunch. Louie was in the mood for soup. Joe told him about the bean-and-spelt soup at Mezzogiorno. Louie finished his coffee and they rose to leave. Joe, cane in hand, moved on first.

"What about that dope we took down?" Louie Bones asked.

"Stash most of it, sell it later," Joe said without turning around. "Cut about ten, twenty kilos with Drāno, put it out on the street, create some more fear."

Louie raised his eyebrows, pursed his lips, grinned, and shook his head.

"Yeah," the old man said, speaking over his shoulder. "Came to me in a dream."

Bob Marshall's morning load still lay on his desk, no longer in neat piles but pushed off to the side in a heap.

At twelve minutes past ten, Mike Wong of the Fifth Precinct had called to tell him that the Fuk Ching had been hit. Twenty minutes later, he had called again to say that the Hip Sing had been hit.

Within half an hour, Group 41 had passed along news of the hit on the Brooklyn headquarters of Du Luong, leader of the Vietnamese Gum Sing.

Soon after that, from the Eighty-third Precinct, had come news of the explosion in the heart of the Well.

Next, in rapid succession, had come reports of the Puerto Ricans being hit in the Bronx, the Dominicans being hit in Washington Heights. The Dominicans, as if eager to uphold the Thirty-fourth's reputation as the most murderous precinct in Manhattan, had quickly retaliated by bombing the police cars and fire engines that had responded. Perhaps they had a point, Marshall thought cynically. The Dominicans of Washington Heights probably paid more to cops in graft than any other group.

Then, from the Fifth Precinct yet again, had come word of the hit on the wops.

The agent had scribbled amid the white space on a sheet of notepaper "Fuk Ching," "Hip Sing," "Gum Sing," "Jamaicans," "P.R.," "Dom.," "Maf." The hit on the Fuk Ching had been perpetrated by three Asians. It was not yet known whether they were Fujianese themselves, or Cantonese, or even Vietnamese, or whether the subsequent conflagration that had caused their death was inadvertent or intentional, the result of an explosive mishap or planned sabotage. The hit on the Hip Sing was by a Vietnamese youth, who in turn was eliminated by either—

eyewitness reports differed—a white man or a Korean. The hit on the Gum Sing was by a middle-aged white man, subsequently eliminated by a person or persons unknown, either by planned assassination or by Vietnamese retaliation. In the Bushwick bombing, there was nothing to go on. The hits on the Puerto Ricans, Dominicans, and Italians had been carried out by parties unknown. To further confuse matters, the Italian hit had included several unidentified Asian victims whose involvement was wholly unknown and whose bodies were charred beyond recognition. Under "Fuk Ching," Marshall wrote "(Hip Sing? On Leong? Viet?)"; under "Hip Sing," "(Fuk Ching? On Leong? Gum Sing? Viet?)"; under "Gum Sing," "Jamaicans," "P.R.," "Dom.," and "Maf.," only question marks. Tentatively, with a pencil, he drew light lines between several clusters. Then, with a heavier, anxious hand, he superimposed a single large question mark over it all.

THIRTEEN

Chan Ling-yueng turned from the open window overlooking Mott Street to the three men he had convened to join him in the second-floor meeting-room of the On Leong Merchants Association. The pale green walls looked gray in the twilight. Chan Ling-yueng walked to the switch by the door and turned on the overhead lamp. The walls, he reflected, had looked better in the twilight. They could use a paint job. The noise from the passing crowd and traffic on Canal Street was great. Chan Ling-yueng shut the window and pulled the cord of the big electric fan that hung above the long table where the three men sat, gathered loosely at one end. He lighted a cigarette and sat among them, at the head of the table.

"I want to thank you for coming," he said. He could sense their tension, their wariness, as they nodded, slowly, politely, but unpleasantly. Chan Ling-yueng paused a moment, as if one of them might speak, but no words came. "I want you tell me truthfully, here, to my face, in the open, any of you, if you suspect me or mine of wrongdoing." He passed his eyes over those of the other men, but saw nothing in them. Even the tension, even the wariness seemed to have been eclipsed by cold reserve.

"Are you saying that you are to be considered the only suspect among us?"

The speaker was Sammy Lau, the youngest of them. Guo Liang Chi, the leader of the Fuk Ching, himself the youngest of the bosses, was imprisoned. Sammy Lau, his acting deputy, still lacked experience in rare meetings such as this. He was dressed casually, not in somber suit and tie like the others, and his words, the others realized, were impetuous. Though he spoke Mandarin to his elders, he did not accord them the venerable form of Mandarin address, did not acknowledge Chan Ling-yueng as Chan Xiansheng, or even as Lao Chan, in respect for his great age. But now that he had asserted himself, the others felt free to speak, as if any sentiments of their own might now be deemed secondary to this opening gesture of Fuk Ching aggression.

"I have lost the most," said Chi-fei Ming, of the Tung On. "There was over twenty million dollars' worth of merchandise in that warehouse up the street," he lied. "In addition to that and several good men, I also lost a good customer."

"You want us to believe, Ah Fei, that this merchandise was not already paid for by your 'good customer'?" asked Benny Eng, of the Hip Sing, with the characteristic smirk to which he seemed to believe his age entitled him. Seeing his smirk, the two others smiled as well.

"If what we say here is not to be believed, I see no purpose in any further talk," said Chi-fei Ming.

"We are not here to discuss who lost what. We are here to air grievances. We are here to lay anger and suspicions on the table so that we might leave them here when we walk through the door. I would be a fool to think that the On Leong were beyond your suspicions. We are the only ones who escaped unharmed, and we are the most powerful."

Benny Eng smirked, Chi-fei Ming smiled, and young Sammy Lau laughed simultaneously. Then the young man made the mistake of isolating himself: "Powerful? You guys are too old and weak to even be pallbearers for one another."

"*Gatzat*," muttered Benny Eng. To accommodate the young Fujianese, who was fluent only in Fuzhou subdialect, the others, who were all of Cantonese descent, had been doing their best to speak English and Mandarin, a dialect understood by him, as by most who had been educated under the Communists, but awkward and unnatural to his elders. Now, when Benny Eng uttered what he did—the word was Cantonese for "cockroach"—Sammy Lau both knew that he had somehow been slighted and realized that he was at their mercy. All these fucking *Guàngdūng giáng* had to do was lapse into Cantonese, and he would be lost.

"Nor are we here to debate our strengths," said Chi-fei Ming, "either real"—he let his final words hang ambiguously in the air—"or imagined."

"To me," said Chan Ling-yueng, "it is obvious that the truth must be known to at least one of you, who attacked the others and left the On Leong untouched, as a scapegoat. To me, this is obvious because I know that the On Leong were not involved."

"This is a farce," said old Benny Eng. "What you say may very well be true, but if it were not, would you say otherwise?"

"Have we ever, the Hip Sing and the On Leong, warred by subterfuge?"

Benny Eng smiled and shrugged. "You're talking now of olden days, my friend. Hatchet-and-revolver days. Those days are gone."

"You call him friend?" Sammy Lau said. "Get a littler closer to him, maybe you can still smell the dynamite on his fingers."

Benny Eng looked at him impatiently. "We go back a bit" was all he said.

"Two of you will remember," said Chan Ling-yueng, "that back in the spring of 1991, Peter Wong, who was then chairman of the On Leong, was murdered, shot through the back of the head, while sitting in the office of his investment firm right here on Canal Street. The On Leong lived with that mysterious tragedy. No rash accusations, no rash, blind reprisals, were made."

The thought passed through the minds of the others in silent concert: that's because the On Leong did it.

"I tell you what I think," Sammy Lau said, looking at no one in particular. "I think that we, the Fujianese, have gotten too powerful too fast for your liking."

"Tell me, Xiao Lau," said Chan Ling-yueng, addressing him as he would a child, "did you get much education under the Communists in Fujian?"

Sammy Lau just looked at him, his eyelids slightly lowered and his brow brooding: his East Broadway look.

"Because you sure haven't learned much in Chinatown."

Benny Eng smiled with surreptitious satisfaction. Chi-fei Ming glanced at his watch.

"Enough of this," said Ming. "I think that we have a new enemy, all of us."

"Odd that you, Ah Fei, with your name in the tablet-house of the 14K Triad, should fret so much over enemies," said Benny Eng.

"The 14K was of no help to me yesterday. Besides, I am not the only one at this table who buys from the 14K. You all do."

"But," said Eng, "you *are* 14K."

"I am Sun Yee On," said Ming.

"Same thing."

"That is neither here nor there."

"This isn't going anywhere," said Lau. "And I've got a date."

"I'm sure you'll impress her with your gun and roguish air," said Chan Ling-yueng. As Chan said the Mandarin word *ta*—"her" or "him," pronouns being without gender in spoken Chinese—Benny Eng casually overrode the ambiguous pronoun with "*gaylou*"—"faggot" in Cantonese. Young Lau did not make the specific connection, construing it as something other than an affront to his manhood, which he would not have allowed himself to countenance.

"If you have something to say to me or about me," he said, "please say it so that I can understand it." He paused. Then, to drive home his meaning, and for his own satisfaction, he appended to his words the mumbled phonemes *suǎn bàbà*, a Fujianese phrase for "ancient cocksucker."

"All right, already," said Chan. "I'm afraid that if we didn't come here as enemies, we'll leave as such. Each of us knows his own truth. Each, the order or disorder of his own house. Each, his own transgressions, if any. Let's hope that what happened today and whatever end, or

ends, it served—known to one or more of us perhaps, unknown to the
rest—are done and die with this day."

"And what if all of us are innocent?" said Ming. "What if, as I said,
we have a new enemy?"

"Time will tell. If so, we fight him. But we know of no such enemy,
and we cannot fight a ghost."

"No enemies?" said Sammy Lau. "What about the Vietnamese?
What about the guineas? What about the spics? I hear those Colombians
are growing opium instead of coca these days. What about the Nigerians, the Russians, the niggers?" To the young Fujianese, New York was
infested with *wū guí* and *sí bān ni giáng*, niggers and spics; and the *bá
jǔng giang*, the fucking wops, were within evolutionary spitting distance
of both of them.

"*Hak gwai?* The niggers?" said Benny Eng. "You must be kidding."
He almost added, in Cantonese: they are even stupider than the Fujianese. But he did not, as it would have been a foolish thing to say. The
young man had taken enough, and besides, as Benny knew, the Fujianese were far from stupid.

"The Vietnamese are too disorganized," said Chan Ling-yueng.
"The Italians are too complacent and subdued these days, and we've
never had any trouble with them anyway. They need us. The *luisung
gwai*, the spics, no. They could never produce enough opium to bother
us. The Nigerians, the Russians—please. These are scum more to be
pitied than considered."

"I don't know," Benny Eng said, turning his palms upward upon the
table. "I just don't know. Does anyone have anything else to say?"

Chi-fei Ming and Sammy Lau were once again as they had been
when Chan Ling-yueng first addressed them. Tense, wary, they shook
their heads, slowly, politely, but unpleasantly.

"I knew nothing when I sat down," said Benny Eng. "I know nothing
now."

"Well," said Chan Ling-yueng, "maybe we have paused to draw a
breath together and to think. Maybe that is worth something."

"Maybe," Benny Eng said. "Maybe."

The four men stood and ambled toward the door. The only words spoken were Benny Eng's. "You really ought to break down for a coat of paint in here."

Six hours later, at twenty minutes past one in the morning, a dozen teenage Fuk Chow stormed down the stone stairs at 76 Mott Street and through the door of the Mayfair Tea Room. Lounging within, smoking their Marlboros and drinking their coffee, were ten teenage Ghost Shadows: one group of three, another of four, in two of the seven red-seated booths along the northern wall; a pair at the smallest of the three tables; another, alone at the counter, turned around, talking to the pair at the table. Like a sudden apparition, the first of the Fuk Chow halted at the door, brandishing a shotgun and hollering *"Dòngjǐe!"*—"Freeze!"—as his eleven cohorts rushed round him, guns drawn, in a furious phalanx. Two white-aproned workers appeared from the kitchen. One of the Fuk Chow ordered them back, and the counterman with them, into the kitchen, where he followed them with pistol raised. Another locked the door behind the boy with the shotgun. The Ghost Shadows did not speak and did not move. There was too much metal in too many chambers. When all had been still and silent for several long seconds, the Fuk Chow who had locked the door stepped to the pay phone, deposited a quarter, dialed, and spoke.

Down the street, turning from Bayard onto Mott, came a band of nine Tung On; from Pell, a group of ten Flying Dragons. The Tung On strode to 66 Mott, to the basement entrance beneath the Western Villa restaurant. One of them knocked on the door of the On Leong gambling-joint. The door opened slightly, and the Tung On, pistols drawn, barged through in force.

At that same moment, across the street, the Flying Dragons invaded the On Leong gambling-joint in the basement of the Hong Fat restaurant. The room was full of Chinese in the throes of their passion: wealthy merchants betting thousands of dollars on the roll of the sik-bo dice; factory and kitchen laborers losing in an hour at the fan-tan table the three or four hundred dollars it took them a seventy-two-hour, six-day week of work to earn; wizened old men whose lives had been reduced to smoke and thirteen-card poker. The sounds of their passion were like a great, jarring symphony, like the noise of weddings and funeral wailings and the slaughtering of beasts at once, rising and falling in discordant waves of hysteria. As awareness of the intruders spread through the room, only the timbre of the hysteria changed, growing softer and less fierce, modulating from passion to dismay. Above the fast-falling hush that followed, from one whose winnings were great, came a single sad sound: "*Diu.*"

The Ghost Shadow at the door lay down as he was told, but there was another, whom the Dragons did not see. From the far wall, near the pai-gow table, he emerged from the crowd, nineteen years old and inspired and wild with desire to make face, to be raised from the gang to the dong. It could be done, he told himself. He was fast, he was blessed, and others in the room would rise behind him. The muzzle of his gun was not far from the nape of the nearest Dragon's neck when the others saw him. He fired and was fired upon at once. There was no more shooting, no more death. The Dragons proceeded to the tables. Three stuck their guns in their belts and removed burlap sacks from their back pockets. The cash was raked from the tables, then the gamblers were told to hand over whatever cash their pockets held, along with whatever jewelry they wore. One gambler pretended that he could not remove his golden wedding ring. A Dragon produced a large switchblade and snapped it open, grabbing the man's hand and cutting into his knuckle joint before he could relinquish his pretense. After the Dragons left, the two dead bodies were dragged out to the pavement and deposited several doors away. Someone unlocked another basement nearby and came out with a hose to wash away the blood as best he could.

The Tung On came away with eighteen thousand dollars; the Flying Dragons, with twenty-seven. At the Shang Chung Tea Parlor on Pell Street, where they met with the Fuk Chow, there was trouble among them. Since they had taken the most and lost a man, the Flying Dragons said, their share should be the greatest.

"*Jian poutungwa,*" said a Fuk Chow, asking all present to speak in the common dialect imposed by the Communists, which all young Chinese understood.

This teahouse was Dragon territory, said the Tung On. There were other Dragons all around, but what was right was right. Without us, said the Fuk Chow, nobody would have taken anything.

"Forty-five thousand, three ways," said one of the Tung On. "Fifteen each."

"Minus five for the dead man's funeral," said the leader of the Flying Dragon group.

"*Sá nú né*," snapped a Fuk Chow: fuck your mother.

"A funeral is eighteen hundred. Ng Fook will let you go for fifteen," said another Tung On.

"Cheung Lung will do it for twelve," said one of the Fuk Chow.

"At Cheung Lung, the rats have you. They ate my uncle's face," said the youngest of the Flying Dragons, a boy of about sixteen.

"Five thousand for the dead man's funeral," said his leader.

"Let the dead care for the dead," said a Fuk Chow.

Flying Dragons around the room began to laugh, in an ominous sort of way.

"*Diu nei loumou*," said a Dragon at the table: fuck your mother.

"Okay," said one of the Tung On, "five grand for the dead man. Now let's just count it out. Forty grand three ways. What does that come to?"

One of the Fuk Chow was ready with the sum. "Thirteen thousand, three hundred and thirty-three."

Several boys began sorting the money into piles of hundreds, fifties, twenties, tens, fives, and ones.

"And thirty-three cents," the Fuk Chow said.

Two Flying Dragons stopped sorting and looked at him.

The money was divided. The jewelry was then spread out on the table.

"We take turns choosing," said a Tung On.

Shining forth amid all that glittered was a five-carat diamond ring. "All right," said a Fuk Chow, beholding this diamond, "we go first."

"Why?" said a Flying Dragon.

"Because we called it."

The Flying Dragon narrowed his eyes, as if weighing this reasoning. "All right," he said equitably. He did not care. He had palmed an even bigger diamond for himself and stashed it in his jockey shorts.

The Fuk Chow chose the big diamond. The boys all thought it was a diamond, anyway. But like the stone in the Dragon's underwear, it was zircon.

A Flying Dragon who stood guard outside the tea parlor saw the pack of Ghost Shadows entering Pell Street, where they should not be. But the sight did not surprise him, for on this night there was no *li*: all boundaries had been forsaken, all territories violated. The guardian ducked inside, called out, "*Gwái yíng!*"—"Ghost Shadows!"

Several Flying Dragons, Tung On, and Fuk Chow dashed to the door with their guns. The Ghost Shadows continued to advance toward them. A Flying Dragon fired a shot in their direction, shooting high and wide. The Ghost Shadows halted, spread out, drew weapons, then retreated. Down the street, there was laughter and talk of *mou min gwái yíng*, Ghost Shadows without face.

The boys returned to the jewelry. Someone produced a bottle of Scotch. Teacups were filled. An argument broke out over whether a pair of ruby cufflinks counted as one item or two. Outside, there was the screech of a car's sudden braking, and a brick came through the tea-room window, and the lighted stick of dynamite taped tightly to it blew the joint to hell, showering the tail end of the fleeing car with glass and gold and plaster and little fiery kite-ribbons of bloody flesh.

Hours later, in the first dim light of dawn, as Giuseppe Di Pietro's green and battered Matilda Sanitation truck rumbled up the Bowery on its daily pickup route, the bombed area on Pell Street was banded with crisscrossed strips of yellow crime scene tape. Nearing Chatham Square, Matilda No. 7 slowed to a stop, and the fourteen-year-old Asian boy who was riding on the truck's hopper jumped off onto the deserted avenue and scampered to Division Street. When he came to the glass door of the Tung On Dong, he looked round, took a can of black Krylon paint from his waistband, and in six fast, sure spraying strokes, marked the door, large and bold, with the character *séi* and three 4s, signifying death. He scampered across the Bowery, up Pell. A few yards from the yellow lattice of crime-scene tape, at the door of the Hip Sing Dong, he sprayed another mark of death. Dashing round to Mott, he defaced the door of the On Leong as well. Then he scurried round to Canal Street, sprinted across, chucked the can of Krylon toward the gutter, and vanished among the narrow streets to the north. On East Broadway, the devastated door of the Fuk Ching, covered with plywood sheeting and yellow crime-scene tape of its own, remained as the sun had set on it.

FOURTEEN

Johnny had known it was coming, but he had not known when. Each day, his anchorage in mundane reality had grown less secure, made shakier by the uncanny, excited marriage of apprehension and expectation within him. The world itself seemed to be growing dimmer, more magical, more vibrant, but more ominous too, a region of unspeakable possibility, sorrow, fear, and doleful shades, as in the haunted black forest of a dream, disturbing and enchanting and fatal, in the blood. Now, with the coming of old Giuseppe's apocalyptic overture, that anchorage, with a sensation of the irretrievable and the irrevocable, had shifted suddenly. As the six-o'clock news last evening had served up the blood feast luridly, with wild speculation, he had felt himself being borne away, with faint shiverings of finality, by that dream-tide in the blood, sundered as if forever from the world of comfortable unknowing that bound men in common delusion. In that moment, it had seemed as if summer, just as suddenly, had arrived. The eerie transmutation of light, the black forest within him, was like a sultry dusk at the day's end of the world as he had known it. Night was falling, and with it his disbelief in demons and the walls that circumscribed his sense of what could and could not be.

In that summery dusk, he saw Diane as a stranger, but a stranger who embodied all that he did not want to leave behind, an embodiment whose image and love and blessing he wished to bear with him, like a cross around the neck, like a gun, like a sacred thought through the night to come.

Now he sat across from her, cultivating her benediction, her surrender, her blindness with a lie. Because in this dusk—so much he knew—there could be no explicit truth between one soul and another. But beyond that, in his lie there was evil, for he knew that he might cherish the blessing and the gun of her love only as long as he needed them, only through the dark night that lay ahead. He could see himself doing that: loosing the chain from his neck, discarding the gun, cashing her in at forty, as the old-timers said, for two twenties.

This luncheon rendezvous had been his idea. Thus far, through the hot-and-sour soup and the dried spicy beef, all had gone well. His lovey-dovey shit, larded with a few personal-growth-through-sobriety lines he had picked up at AA, had her smiling and subdued by the time General So-and-so's chicken and Buddha's whatever arrived. But then he hit her with it.

"What do you mean, you're going away for a while?" She put down her chopsticks and looked at him in that way she had of wielding blades with her eyes.

"It's business," Johnny said.

"What kind of business? You're trying to tell me there's a garbage convention in Paris or something?"

He sighed studiously, attempting to turn the situation around to where he might seem the victim of her sarcasm and lack of understanding. But she did not buy.

"It's for the both of us," he said. "You want us to do well in this world, don't you?"

"It's for the both of us? Then we'll both go. Where the hell are you supposed to be going, anyway?"

His passport and round-trip ticket to Milan were on the dresser in the Manhattan apartment. "I don't have the exact itinerary yet. It'll be a lot of work, that's all I know. But if all goes well, it could be a big break for us."

"What are you talking about, 'itinerary'? Your job hasn't taken you farther than the subway can get you since I've known you."

"Well, it's time to move up. Bigger things, better things. I'm sorry you don't see it that way. I thought you'd be happy for me. For us. I really did."

If she bought that one, he was halfway home. But he could not tell by her tone whether or not she had.

"Tell me what the hell this is all about. Or maybe they haven't told you that, either."

He sighed again, studiously. "Uncle Joe's plant in Jersey. They separate the garbage there, ship most of it down south, to Virginia. Forty-five bucks a ton. Well, there are countries without natural paper resources. They don't have trees, in other words. We're trying to sell our pulp to them." It was all true, except that the deals were already in effect, the pulp was already being shipped overseas. It was these garbage freighters that Joe and Tonio planned to use to transport the heroin. "Forget about Local 958. Forget about Local 813 and Local 23. This is big business. If it works out, I'm in line for a cut of it."

She seemed confused, hesitant. That was good.

"So you're talking about Europe?" Her voice now was more melancholy than hostile.

"Yeah."

"You always said we'd go there together."

"We will. If this works out, we will."

Her fingers touched her chopsticks for the first time since he had broached the matter.

"Believe me," he said, "I'm not really looking forward to this. It'll be work, a lot of work. A lot of pressure."

"What if the pressure gets to you? What if you want to drink?"

"It won't. I won't." He paused. "I'll bring the big book, and I'll have numbers."

"What if some cute young thing wants to talk trash?"

She was almost smiling. That was his cue. He shook his head, grinned, and softly laughed. "You never quit, do you?"

"I love you, that's all."

"And I love you."

Those words, beneath his deceit, were true. But his feelings more and more were becoming occluded, subsumed by an uneasy sense of something vast in the dusk—a stormfront of immense elemental volatility into whose path he had strayed, something that ate souls and drained the vital substance from truth and lies alike. But his feelings were not all that this occlusion obscured. Diane's words were as false as his own.

In the club, Uncle Joe sat bent over, peering through his bifocals and a magnifying glass at the pink pages of *Il Sole 24 Ore*, studying the money-market and stock-exchange figures. Nearby, at another table, a tall, thin man in his early thirties sat drinking a vodka-and-soda and staring straight ahead. Joe looked up as Louie Bones entered, and he told Louie to close the door. Louie turned and said something to those outside, then shut the door behind him. He sat down at Joe's table and looked at the tall, thin man.

"Show him," Joe said to the thin man, his eyes still peering through the magnifying glass.

The thin man nodded, rose, and pulled out a chair for Louie at the table where he sat. He took a brown paper bag from the floor and put it on the table.

"Watch this, Lou," the old man said, still peering, still studying. "The kid's good."

From the bag the thin man removed a cardboard egg tray, then put it to the side. Then he removed a Ping-Pong ball and held it between two fingers for Louie to see. Louie, seeing that the man's hand trembled, looked toward Uncle Joe, then straight into the eyes of the Ping-Pong man. He raised one open hand and grimaced expectantly.

The thin man put the Ping-Pong ball down and from the bag took an identical Ping-Pong ball that had been halved into two small, white, hollow hemispheres. One of these hemispheres had been drilled through its center with a clean little hole about a quarter of an inch in diameter. The thin man held the undrilled hemisphere shakily between two fingers of his left hand and poked his right forefinger inside it. Then he spoke.

"You fill this with a lump of C-4 plastic explosive. Then you add a coating of potassium chlorate, then a coating of gunpowder. Then you put the ball back together and reseal it with a smear of silicon glue." He took a diminutive glass vial, about an inch long and a quarter-inch wide, from the bag. He held this between two fingers of his left hand and tapped its base with his right forefinger. It was then that Louie saw that the man's fingernails had been eaten away to raw, tender flesh and cracked, calcified crescents. He watched the ravaged nail of the forefinger slide slowly, shakily, up the length of the vial as the man spoke. "With an eyedropper, you fill this two-thirds of the way up with concentrated sulfuric acid solution." He took a tiny cork from the bag and stuck it firmly in the mouth of the vial. He then put the vial, cork down, through the hole in the drilled half of the Ping-Pong ball, so that about half of the vial protruded, bottom up, into the air. He ran his finger round where the vial entered the hole. "A little more silicon to close her up here nice and snug," he said.

"The acid takes anywhere from three to six hours to eat through the cork. The time depends on the particular condition and density of the cork. When it eats through and mixes with the gunpowder and potassium chloride, the chemistry causes a slight explosion, which detonates the C-4, which means a bigger explosion. You're not using much C-4, so the explosion won't be that big. The stuff is powerful, though. Its wallop comes from the nature of its explosion—it converts to a gaseous state at very high velocity, sending out shock waves at something like twenty-six thousand feet per second. And in the amounts you're using, each Ping-Pong ball should be the equivalent at least of half a stick of dynamite. Of course, depending on how these things go down, there's bound to be a few duds.

"I tell you, there are companies out there—Microtek, Ronald T. Dodge, outfits like that; don't ask me why, but they're all in Ohio—they got a fancy, big-money name for this sort of thing: microencapsulation."

Louie could not resist: "They use Ping-Pong balls too?"

The thin man took this as a serious although perhaps naive query. "No," he said. "But the principle's the same."

He flipped open the cardboard egg tray. Each of its six concave compartments bore a hole in its center that could comfortably accommodate the diameter of the glass vial. "Of course," he said, "you want to carry your Ping-Pong balls like this, cork up, until you're ready to use them."

Louie stared a moment at the thin man's face and watched him finish what was left of his vodka-and-soda. Then he turned toward Uncle Joe, who was no longer peering through his magnifying glass but was looking straight at Louie and silently chuckling.

"Where the fuck did you dig this guy up?" he said, talking to Joe but facing the thin man with a half-cocked grin.

"Oh, don't you worry, Lou, this kid's all right. A few hard knocks in life, but he come out all right."

The thin man smiled humbly, nervously.

"Now, what I'd like you to do, Lou," the old man continued, "take our buddy here up to see our other buddy."

"Our other buddy," Louie muttered.

"He'll be expecting you. Have our buddy here show him what's what. The two of them are going to take a trip together, get some sun, do a little work. Our buddy here knows what he's got to do, our other buddy knows what he's got to do. Where they're going, there'll be somebody to give them all the Ping-Pong balls they need."

He addressed the thin man. "You listen to Louie, make the best of things with our buddy there. You go where you're going, you do your job, you come back here, you see me."

Then, taking a slip of paper from his shirt pocket, handing it to Louie: "Here's our other buddy."

Louie looked at the paper. "What is this, a fucking *albanes'* curse or some shit?"

"Oh, you'll see. I got all sorts of buddies in this world."

"Never met a man you didn't like, hey, Joe?"

"Something like that."

Louie had Frankie Blue drive him and the thin man to the address

on the slip. It turned out to be a twenty-four-hour peepshow joint near
the northwest corner of Twenty-seventh Street and Sixth Avenue. Louie
grinned and snorted as the car pulled over and came to a halt.

"I think your *cumpare* is losin' his fucking mind, Frankie." It was a
joke, and Frankie took it as such. But in his words, as he spoke them,
Louie tasted a seed of truth, a seed he had been wanting to spit out. As it
grew more real each day, this whole hellish scheme took on the dimensions not of vision hardening into being, but of nightmare becoming
plain reality. Then, yesterday, that look on the old man's face, the way
he said those words, *came to me in a dream*—Louie could still feel the
draft of the spectral breeze that had whistled through his composure.
The thought had occurred to him that old Joe, on his way to the grave,
had no qualm about taking the world with him. Maybe he even relished
the idea. Louie had known men hairless and purple-lipped from fruitless chemotherapy who had brokered deals for nuclear warheads, had
heard of men dying of AIDS who purposely infected others with needle
or cock. But Louie had known Joe all his life, and these thoughts, he
told himself, were hauntings more than suspicions. Still, Louie knew
one absolute truth above all: there was no getting inside another man's
mind.

Bag in hand, the thin man followed Louie through the door into a
long, narrow room. From a large black speaker on the floor by the door,
there issued strange percussive music in a stranger tongue: "*Awa ewe
iwoyi . . .*" The wall to the left was lined with rows of boxed videotapes. To the right was a battery of viewing booths. A skeletal phlegm-
colored man of indeterminate ethnic origin moved slowly through the
room, sluggishly carrying a soggy, Lysol-stinking mop, disappearing into
one peepshow stall after another. As Louie and the thin man walked, the
nature of the videotapes grew more gruesome. Full-color packaging gave
way to white boxes bearing two-color cover sheets in English, German,
and Japanese. *Stump Lovers*, *Pisswütig*, *Up Her Ass and Piss in Her
Mouth*, *Shit for Dinner*.

In the back of the room there was a counter. Behind it stood another
phlegm-colored man. To his right there was a dirty white telephone
mounted on the wall, and beyond it a dirty pink door.

Louie tried to pronounce the name that was written on the slip, but the unwieldy syllables emerged as a cryptic question. "Alhaji Shehu Musa?"

The phlegm-colored man reached around and rapped on the pink door. It opened, and there appeared a rotund black man in an ice-blue silk suit and black-on-black shirt, which, like most of his wardrobe, came from the five-block stretch of sartorial splendor on Eighth Avenue between Penguini Men's Fashions to the south and Farouk Clothing ("Where a Man Can Look His Best for Less") to the north. He smiled broadly and took Louie's hand between both his own, which were sticky and clammy.

"I am honored," he said, in an oddly inflected English. Taking up Louie's hand and bowing, he kissed his knuckles. He then welcomed the thin man in the same way.

Louie raised his eyebrows again. This and *Shit for Dinner* all in one day. The man's lips were as unpleasant as his palms.

"Please," the rotund man said, stepping aside and gesturing toward the open pink door. Louie proceeded but could not fit past his host's stomach. The rotund man giggled and apologized, then preceded Louie through the door. "Yams are my downfall," he declared and giggled some more.

The room they entered was no bigger than a large storage closet. There was not space, nor were there chairs, for the three of them to sit. The walls were the same dreary pink as the door. Hanging in dime-store frames were an autographed photograph of a smiling Chief Commander Ebenezer Obey, a letter from the office of General Ibrahim Babangida acknowledging receipt of a Christmas card, Police Athletic League and American Automobile Association membership stickers, and a Polaroid of Alhaji Shehu Musa himself flanked by two shapely white dog-faced women in swimsuits. There was a bad smell. Louie and the thin man saw its source: an aluminum take-out container of slop that was the same color as the mop-and-counter men outside. An encrusted white plastic fork lay beside it, along with a crumpled, greasy napkin and a container of Yoo-Hoo. Crowding the rest of the room were a sink, a commode, and cardboard cases full of videotapes. A quick glance told Louie that these tapes, unlike *Shit for Dinner*, were not the sort that could be openly displayed. The packages of *Wild Child*, *Winter in Holland*, and others featured young children and adolescents exploring their hairless or pubescent genitals. Other packages bore only titles. *Die Kastration*, *Knife-Fucked Cunts*, *Sacrifice*, *Baby Love*.

"Please," the rotund man said, "help yourself." Then, seeing the look on Louie's face: "To sell to others, of course." The look on Louie's face did not change, and the rotund man smiled apologetically. "Perhaps my urge to accommodate is overreaching," he said. "My quarters, you see, are small, but my happiness in your visit is big."

Louie nodded. "You know why we're here, right?"

The rotund man nodded eagerly. In his mind, he was no ordinary *dudu*. Born just thirty years ago, in the Lafiaji section of Lagos, he had risen mightily to his stature in America. Maintaining his ties to the motherland, he ruled one of the most active of the Nigerian heroin-smuggling rings, the Yaba group. In addition, he personally commanded more than three dozen tribesmen—most of them Yoruba like himself, but also Hausa, Ibo, and Fulani—who peddled counterfeit Rolex wrist-watches and Hermès scarves in the streets of midtown. Through his peepshow emporium, he had come to know men of Italian descent. The *àwon Itálì* had made him feel welcome in their domain, charging him prices, both for merchandise and tribute, that they assured him were reserved for friends and men of mutual respect. It was through these men that he had received his call from Oba Joe, who offered him the opportunity he had long dreamed of. Though it was not true, Alhaji Shehu Musa told men that he was a Yoruba prince and chieftain. It was this pretense of royalty, he believed, and the recommendations of others of Italian descent, that influenced Oba Joe to make an exception to the long-standing rule that forbade men of color from joining the ranks of the powerful. The task that Oba Joe had set for him would entail the betrayal of many of his countrymen, but the reward would justify the deed. Soon men would bow to kiss *his* hand. He would be, as they said in the television shows, a made man.

"All right," Louie said. "Well, I'll leave you gents alone here for a minute to go over this thing in private."

Louie turned and left, strode past the phlegm men, past *Shit for Dinner*, and through the door. He stood and exhaled and shook his head.

In his baggy gray trousers and shabby undershirt, which bore the dark stains of spattered black blood, old Chen Fang sat at the little mahogany table near his bedroom window, bent over mortar and pestle. Side by side on the windowsill were a can of Drāno and a jar of methylfentanyl. He sprinkled some of one, then the other, into the mortar and continued his grinding, mixing the grainy Drāno and powdery fentanyl into a fine white pulverized dust.

Two of the dozen kilograms of heroin that Mr. Joe had given him had been put aside for himself. Some of that heroin now flowed through his veins. It was potent, but he knew it had already been diluted. The guineas, he knew, tended to cut their product with quinine or Mannite Conascenti, a brand of mannitol manufactured in Castelbuono, Sicily, and imported by Pacific Laboratories in Santa Monica. But they used all manner of other agents as well: laundry soap, which rendered the heroin somewhat flaky; vitamin B; even garlic powder. A pinch of fentanyl could increase the potency of weak heroin tenfold; more than that, however, could prove fatal. This heroin, he surmised, judging by its added bit of charge upon injection, had been treated with quinine.

He took one of the kilo packages, tore open its coated blue wrapping paper, and emptied its contents into a large ceramic bowl. He added the mixture from the mortar, then stirred it with a long, small-bowled spoon made from a length of split bamboo stem. Dipping the bamboo spoon into the deadly powder, then leveling its yield with his bony forefinger to a more or less uniform tenth of a gram, he emptied the spoonful into a little glassine bag. Spoonful after spoonful, bag after bag, kilo after kilo, he repeated the process until the pain in his guts overwhelmed him. Then he went to the commode, vomited, wiped the black blood from his face, and lay down. In time he rose, injected more heroin into his veins, and returned to his task.

From a manila envelope, he shook loose an assortment of many small, poorly printed stamps. Some bore phrases: No Mercy, Check Mate, Laundromat, Jungle Fever. Others, symbols: the racing horseman, a dollar bill, two .30-.30 shotguns crossed diagonally to form an X. These were among the trademarks by which heroin was sold in the street, in the hope that satisfied customers in a plentiful marketplace would become the faithful brand-name patrons of one group of dealers over another. Two of the most popular and established brands, stamps that Chen Fang had in plenty, were Body Bag and DOA.

Each glassine bag was sealed with a stamp. As he licked the stamps, the staining streaks of blood and black bile from his tongue grew lighter on each, until in time his saliva became clear, like that of a man who woke in the morning from darkness to light.

"You're keepin' some class company these days, my friend," said Louie Bones. "First this fuckin' weasel with the Ping-Pong balls and the shakes, then this fuckin' orangutang with the dirty movies." Louie told Joe about *Shit for Dinner*.

Joe waved to the barman for more coffee. "*E qualcosa sucari*," he added.

"He wants somethin' to suck," Louie called out. "*Vuole leccare u pacchiu*. Go get that broad from the laundromat. The one with the varicose veins on her *comu si chiam'*."

The barman, grinning, held up a piece of lemon, and the old man nodded. To Louie he said, "I think you been lookin' at too many of the Chief's pictures."

" 'The Chief.' " Louie snorted.

"Oh, yeah, the Chief, he's a big man," said Joe, grinning crookedly.

"Big man, *a culu de tu sorella*." Louie gestured vividly, and could not suppress a grin of his own. With the fingers of his right hand, he rapped the back of his left hand. "He nigger-lipped my fuckin' hand, this ape of yours. Where'd he get this fuckin' *baciaman'* shit?"

"Ah, quit griping. You let Goo Goo's dog lick your fucking hand all the time. And that mutt ain't even fucking Italian. It's a fucking *iresce*, a fucking Irish setter. What's the difference between an Irish dog and a fucking *tizzun'*?"

Louie laughed and shook his head.

"So, Louie, tell me. How do those bones of yours feel?" The old man's voice was different now. Like the look on his face, it was dead serious. "How do you feel about this trip?"

Louie pressed his tongue to the back of an eyetooth and sucked an imaginary morsel through tight lips. He nodded slowly, resolutely. "*Sono preparato*," he said, inflecting the words with assured, straightforward gravity. "*Sono deciso.*" I am ready, he said, and I am determined. Some men were put off by Louie's style of speaking, the way he alternated Italian and Sicilian words and phrases, rather than using just the one or the other, to elaborate his English. But to Joe it sounded as natural and as familiar as the song of a backyard bird.

"*Decisu a tuttu?*" the old man asked. Was he ready for anything?

"*Sì,*" Louie Bones said softly, "*sì.*"

"Chen Fang and Billy Sing, they've told you what you need to know." The tone of the old man's words lay becalmed between a statement and a question.

Louie nodded and inhaled.

"And what about Johnny? How do you feel about him?"

Louie thought for a moment. He had not had to put his feelings about Johnny into words before. "He's nobody's fool, that kid. For a kid his age, he's got a lot on the ball."

"He's not a kid anymore."

"Oh, to me, at my age, anybody whose dick still works is still a kid."

"How scared is he?"

"He doesn't show it."

"What does that mean?"

"You're askin' me? You know what I'm talkin' about. Anybody in this world who says he ain't afraid is either a fuckin' liar or a fuckin' *sciocco*, and I wouldn't trust either one of them."

"So he's told you he's scared?"

"He hasn't told me shit. He's no *fanfaron'*. He doesn't carry himself like one of these fuckin' struttin' cocks with the bouffant fuckin' hairdos and the fuckin' *finocchiu* muscles and the bullshit mouth. He's not like most of these other *citrull'*s his age. He's got something here, and he's got something here." Louie pointed to his sternum, then his temple.

"But does he have the *cughiuni*? Does he have '*a stuffu giustu*?"

"Look, you know what I think? I think because he's the only flesh and blood you got, you're reading into him what's inside you. Maybe you got doubts, you're reading those doubts into him. Maybe you got fear, you're reading that fear into him." Louie hesitated. "Maybe you got second thoughts about your *coglion*'s, you're reading them into him. And I tell you what. If what's inside you, you fucking old *capron*', actually *is* inside him, we're fucking all right." He leaned forward, reached out, and softly smacked the old man's head.

Joe felt good. Talking like this, *dal cuore*, and fucking around with each other—it was like the old days.

"And what about Tonio?" Louie Bones asked. "Has he got our boys ready over there?"

"They're more than ready." The old man lighted a DeNobili and puffed. "These last few years in Sicily—Christ, Louie, you know the story. Things have been bad ever since they brought that fucking rat Buscetta back from Brazil. That was when, back in '84? Shit. He started all this fucking *pentiti* shit over there. He fucking rats everybody out, settles a few old scores, tells those fucking *commissioni* what they want to hear. They set him and his fucking family up over here, nice house, money, the works, as state-supported American fucking citizens under this bullshit Witness fucking Protection Program. To every other fucking cunt-eating rat and his mother, it didn't look like a bad deal. Since then, everybody with his fucking balls caught in the wringer, the same shit, over and over. Now they even got their own witness protection program over there. A world of fucking rats. Contorno, Calderone, Marchese, Mannoia, Drago, Messina, Mutolo. Even Rosario Spatola, the Gambino boys' cousin. You remember him. He used to come by once in a while. Seemed like such a nice boy. Helped out Michele that time."

"*Poviru, brillu, pazzu Michele.*" Louis smiled, recalling how the Sicilian they spoke of had set up Novarca Management Group for them back in the late sixties, how he had explained it to them, even named it for them. Who else made nasty jokes in Latin?

"Even Spatola. *Tutti topi. Tutti canari.* There are hundreds of them now. They don't know shit, these punks. Look at Buscetta's face. That fucking *sfaccim*', he makes our friend the Chief there look like a Botticelli portrait. What *pezzu di novanta* could look into that face and tell it anything worth knowing? Those who know, the *cacocciule di saggezza*, don't talk. But these punks make trouble all the same. Look at what happened to Totò Riina. Twenty-three fucking years, they couldn't find Totò. Then his fucking driver, this little shit-stain Di Maggio, he turns *pentito* and leads the fucking *carrubbi* to his door. But guys like Totò, like Nitto Santapaola, guys like Domenico Libri in Calabria, Carmine Alfieri in Campania—they're from the old school, they're like Greco and Liggio and the *capi bastuni* before them. They may get caught, but they never sing. That much remains true. Never, not once, has a *cacocciula* turned.

"The *commissioni* over there, they have a diagram, a map—I saw it; Tonio had it—something like a hundred and fifty *cosche* in a hundred towns all through Sicily. But guess what town ain't on that map? Piana degli Albanesi. And there he sits. But all around him, these *pentiti*, they've made a mess. This *tangentopoli* shit. Craxi, Chiesa, Andreotti, the Christian Democrats, Contrada and the other *commissioni nella tasca*—it's all changed. But the old man there, he thinks the way we do. He thinks it's time to take back what's been lost. Don't you worry, Louie, they're ready. They're more than ready."

There were feelings in Louie's guts that he wanted to spit out. Words stirred in his mind, seeking syntax and expression.

"Joe," he said, and for a moment that was all he said, and the old man did not press him but bore with his faltering. Then the words came. "Do you think much about death?"

"I used to. I used to think about death a great deal. And I feared death, too. Even as a boy, when there was no reason to fear."

"And now?"

"I just live with it. Slowly our paths, death's and mine, grow closer. It's like, I look aside, I glance through the trees, and I see it. It's there. I sit with it, I sleep with it. It's there. But I don't think about it, I don't fear it. It's different. *U mortu è mortu.* Death is death."

"What do you fear?"

"Pain. Hell." The old man's words came fluently. His answer was not one he had to contemplate.

"So you believe in hell?"

"Not really. I just fear it. Maybe we need to fear something, and I've run out of what I know."

"When you look at what lies before us here, do you see death?"

"No."

Louie waited for more words, but the old man said only that.

"What do you see?"

Again Louie waited. The old man smoked. There were no fluent answers here, it seemed. Then words came through the smoke.

"Nothing. I see nothing."

Louie had wanted resolution, an end to that ghostly breeze that whistled through his composure. He had wanted reassurance. Instead the old man gave him words that rode that breeze like leaves.

"Is that good or bad?"

"It's good," the old man said, strangely, with—it sounded so to Louie, anyway—a sort of blasé indifference, as if reading the result of a coin he had tossed into the air.

Bob Marshall sat in Peter Wang's office. Behind the group supervisor's desk was a bookshelf. There were several books by Jack Morris—*The Criminal Intelligence File, Police Informant Management*, which Wang referred to as "The Care and Feeding of Rats," *Crime Analysis Charting*; *The Standard Telegraphic Code*, the huge lexicon by which the characters of Chinese names can be codified by four-digit numbers for universal identification, reference, and filing; the 1935 Shanghai edition of the four-volume dictionary of classical Chinese known as *Chung Hua Ta Tzu Tien*; R. H. Matthews's *Chinese-English Dictionary*; the U.S. Government's *Report on Asian Crime* and *Organized Crime of Asian Origin*; a framed photograph of Warner Oland as Charlie Chan; an opium pipe; a baseball nestled in the pocket of a well-worn glove.

"So," Wang said, "give me the morning line."

"Here's where we stand. Group 41 met downtown this morning with FBI OCDE and two Chinese detectives from the Fifth. So far, all inquiries among tong and street-gang informants concerning the Fuk Ching and Hip Sing hits have proved fruitless. We know now that the getaway car used in the Fuk Ching hit was rigged. The three Asians have been identified as Cantonese immigrants with no known tong or gang affiliations. Both the car and van involved were stolen and dead-plated. The Vietnamese kid involved in the Hip Sing bombing has also been identified. Again, no known affiliation, though one older brother, now an accountant, once ran with the Dragons. The accountant knows nothing of the kid's activities, and there are no leads on the Korean or Caucasian, or whatever he was, who eliminated the boy.

"According to the Fifth, the tongs and gangs were bristling with confusion all day yesterday. Last night, Chan Ling-yueng of the On Leong called a meeting among himself and the leaders of the Fuk Ching, Hip Sing, and Tung On. God only knows what went down, but a few hours later, between one and one-thirty in the morning, there were attacks on three On Leong locations: the Mayfair and two gambling-joints. Incredibly, the Fuk Chow, Tung On, and Flying Dragons all seem to have been in on this together. Fatalities, two: one Dragon, one Shadow. A little later, at about two o'clock, the Ching Shing was bombed, presumably by Shadows. Among those killed, blinded, and dismembered, besides Dragons, were several Fuk Chow and Tung On. In the morning, the doors of the On Leong, Hip Sing, and Tung On were all found bearing the mark of death."

Peter Wang put out his hand like a crossing-guard. "Wait a minute, wait a minute," he said. "This whole mess is spiraling off into the fucking Hundred Years War and Taiping Rebellion all at once. What was the first act of retaliation? Do we have any idea of that, any idea of where to draw the line between cause and effect, between what we care about and what the Fifth has to mop up?"

"We'll get to that in a minute. Just bear with me. Now, where was I?"

"The mark of death."

"Okay. The identity of the bomber in Brooklyn. One Sidney Drucker, currently under investigation by the IRS for fraud in the bankruptcy of his trucking outfit. Drucker may have had connections with the Vietnamese through his trucking activities at Hunts Point. These possible connections are being pursued. As to the identity of Drucker's killer, we still don't know, though the alleged eyewitness reports describing him as a Caucasian in a passing car may have been fabricated to protect a Gum Sing on the scene who acted in reprisal.

"The job on the Jamaicans remains a mystery. They're having trouble even identifying the make and model of the car.

"The survivor of the machine-gun attack in the Bronx ended up having his legs amputated after seven hours of futile reconstructive surgery at Columbia Presbyterian. He's still under sedation, but so far, in conscious moments, he refuses to speak to police and says only that he wants to die.

"The Thirty-fourth Precinct in Washington Heights is questioning all rival gang members and known informants, but as it stands, the attack on the San Francisco is still a mystery. One theory is that the gang, long established as heroin dealers, had begun to branch out into crack as well, threatening the domain and raising the hackles of neighboring *cocaleros*.

"As to the investigation into the mess at 187 Mott, I'm supervising that one myself. The FBI, the Fifth, they're all in it, fighting one another as usual. Scarpa was under federal grand-jury indictment for murder, extortion, and labor racketeering. Taken in isolation, his murder would seem to have come from within his own crew. But the actual circumstances and context being what they are, the possibilities are . . ." He searched for a word, then merely shook his head. "Calò Onorato, already dead at the scene, was the man who would have gained most by Scarpa's death. The Chinese who were murdered along with Onorato, it seems, were members of the Tung On who, I presume, were Scarpa's heroin suppliers.

"Now, your question. Do we have any idea where to draw the line between cause and effect?

"It's like this. Who would have desired or dared to make those first moves yesterday morning? That's what we need to know. Born to Kill? The Russians? Would the Mob bite the hand that feeds it? Was the first attack, on East Broadway, itself an act of vengeance for some other incident we know nothing about? Could the attack on the Gum Sing have been a knowing retaliation for the Fuk Chow and Hip Sing attacks? If so, where did Sidney Drucker come from? Why the Puerto Ricans and the Dominicans? Going on positive ID and contradictory eyewitness reports, so far we've got three Cantonese, one Vietnamese, one Brooklyn Jew, one unknown Caucasian, and either a Korean or a second, or the same, Caucasian. Who, or what, ties them together? *That's* the question. And the answer could save us, and a lot of others, a whole slew of trouble down the line.

"Right now, nothing makes sense. I doubt that the trouble last night had anything to do with the trouble yesterday morning. Or, I should say, with the cause of yesterday's trouble. *That* cause—the who or what that ties it all together—*that's* what we need to know. Maybe it's just me, but whatever it is, it feels big and it feels bad. It feels like the sort of thunder, the sort of move, that makes me want to say my prayers. I'm paying no mind to anything that happened after sundown. The real storm from that thunder hasn't come yet. According to the Fifth, you can cut the tension in the streets down there with a blade. They're ready for anything. But to me, whatever happens down there—or in Washington Heights, or Brooklyn, or the Bronx—from here on in, it's all smoke. It's got nothing to do with what we need to know. It's just . . ."

"A bunch of crazy Chinamen?" suggested Wang, grinning slyly.

"Yeah," said Marshall, "that's it. A bunch of crazy Chinamen."

FIFTEEN

Ng Tai-hei stood a moment by the parted silk curtains of his office, peering out, trying to gauge the threat of rain in the gray clouds that moved slowly through the Hong Kong sky. To his right, in the open corner between the long mahogany desk and the embroidered silk couch, facing diagonally out toward the center of the room, was a stone chimera of the eastern Han Dynasty. It was more than two thousand years old, six feet long, with a fanged and snarling face that rose well above Ng Tai-hei's hip. So spacious and imposing was the office that this carved beast seemed neither out of place nor oversized. And there was more to the office than met the eye. Down a small hall hung with paintings lay a fully appointed bathroom and windowed bedroom.

This office and the rest of Ng Tai-hei's complex in the Exchange Center occupied much of the thirty-seventh floor of one of the three grand towers of pink Italian granite and mirrored glass that overlooked Victoria Harbour to the north and the Central District to the south. His private office lay beyond a large outer office, where a dozen or so men, each at his own desk and computer monitor, tended to the business of triad money. It was in this room of computers and ringing telephones that the wealth of the 14K Triad was transformed, *mutatis mutandis*, into what appeared to be clean, irreproachable, legitimate income.

This transformation was a Byzantine process involving the buying and selling of currency futures options. The man who had devised this system had assured Ng Tai-hei that he need not know how it worked, that all he needed to know was that it did. But Ng Tai-hei had demanded to know, and the man had explained it to him—through a translator, as the man was a Sicilian, a financier of great renown, an intimate of both Chiang Kai-shek and the pope—in words that Ng Tai-hei could understand.

"As you may know," he had told him, "the Philadelphia Stock Exchange in America now trades futures options on United States dollars, British pounds, German marks, Japanese yen, Swiss francs, and other currencies. Only a fraction, about five percent, of all such options traded are executed on behalf of corporations wishing to hedge the exchange-rate risks of their international trade. The vast majority of trades are purely speculative in nature, carried out by banks on behalf of their clients or themselves. In this international currency flow of perhaps sixty trillion dollars a year, distinguishing transactions carried out simply to realize legal profits from transactions carried out to facilitate our goals is virtually impossible.

"We begin by depositing our dirty money with a friendly face—at the Hongkong and Shanghai, the Chartered, the Bank of China, whoever —in the name of one of our bearer-share ghost companies. Then we buy, say, a one-hundred-million-dollar, six-month call option for yen at two hundred and forty yen per dollar. This option gives us the right, but not the obligation, to buy twenty-four billion yen for one hundred million dollars six months from now. The premium for the option is one million dollars.

"If, during those six months, the yen falls to, say, two hundred and sixty per dollar, we can either sell the option contract or buy the twenty-four billion yen in the spot market for ninety-two million. One way or the other, we make a profit of seven million. That is, eight million less the one-million premium.

"Our counterpart in the deal is officially the bank where we have deposited our money. But in reality, the bank is acting only on behalf of the ghost company in whose name we deposited the money. Our real counterpart is ourself. Therefore, the seven-million-dollar profit we earn is recorded not as the bank's loss but as the loss of our anonymous bearer-share company.

"The deal has turned seven million dollars in dirty money into a clean financial-exchange profit. We haven't even really lost the million-dollar premium, because it's been paid out to the ghost company that is the counterpart in the deal—that is, it is returned indirectly to us. Our final profit from the transaction is reduced only by the commission we must pay the bank for the fiduciary transaction—here, about twenty thousand dollars—and by the income tax we must pay the government. For that is what we have created—clean, taxable income.

"In practice, working prudently and heeding the rapid fluctuations of the market, one who becomes expert at this system might buy and sell the same option many times during the six-month life of the original contract. In this way, hundreds of millions of dollars could be laundered in a relatively brief time. By multiplying the number of contracts, the number of ghost companies, one can launder billions—a mere grain in the constantly shifting sea of sixty trillion—with alacrity and ease."

"But what if the yen rises? What if it goes up to two hundred and twenty per dollar?" Ng Tai-hei had wondered.

"In that case, we allow the option to expire unexercised, and we lose only the million-dollar premium and the twenty-thousand-dollar commission to the bank. But again, that million-dollar premium is not really a loss. It is offset by the million dollars in hidden profits earned by our ghost company as a premium for the option we have granted it. And as we can deduct the million-dollar 'loss' from our other income, not only do we suffer no real losses, but also, through our deduction, we lower the taxes we must pay on the laundered profits of our other deals."

It had seemed too beautiful to be true. But in the years since then—as the system was put to work, first through Philadelphia, then through the Chicago Board of Trade; as it was expanded to bring into play commodity futures options as well—both its beauty and its truth had proven to be unfailing and enduring. And through those years, Ng Tai-hei had never forgotten what the man had answered when asked how such a marvelous system had come to be conceived: "It came to me in a dream."

Now, as he prepared to fly halfway round the world to meet those whose scheme he planned to destroy with his own, the memory of that Sicilian served to remind him not to be brazen in his confidence.

Men in the outer office bowed as he strode past them into the reception area. There, his secretary, Yao Fu-mei, and the outer office secretary and receptionist, May-ling Woo, smiled and subtly lowered their heads. Ng Tai-hei's guard and driver, who sat waiting in his black Baromon suit, stood and took his place behind his master. Beyond the reception area door was a foyer. Concealed in this foyer were Friskem metal detection and Thermedics EGIS vapor-sensitive explosives detection systems, either of which, when triggered, simultaneously locked the bomb-proof reception-area door, set off an alarm, and activated a remote monitor behind the reception desk. Flicking a switch beneath her desk, the receptionist shut off these systems to accommodate the armed driver's exit. A second, outer door, locked and controlled by intercom, bore the Chinese words *Baíshizi Giyè Gongsi* and the English words WHITE LION ENTERPRISES. To the right of the door was a Diebold 1091 access-control system, allowing employee entry by magnetic card and keyboard code.

"*Duhngjihkmaht Gùngyún,*" Ng Tai-hei told the *baobaio* as they stepped from the elevator.

The two men strode southeast across Exchange Square, toward the limousine. They drove south on Peddler Street to Queen's Road, turned left, then right on Garden Road. The driver slowed to a halt near the entrance to the *Duhngjihkmaht Gùngyún*, the Botanical Gardens. Veering from the main walk, Ng Tai-hei followed a winding path that was bright with red-blooming sage and lush with willows. Beyond a grassy lea, there lay an aromatic dazzle of flowering yellow and bronze, pink and red, white and purple. A little wooden bridge traversed a rushing rill that wandered through that dazzle, and across this bridge, on a bench beside a towering pine, a man sat alone, leaning back, his eyes shut to the sky, his elbows raised and his arms draped wide along the bench's top rung. He was about forty years old, neither ugly nor handsome, dressed in a brown suit and cream-colored shirt. Between the thumb and forefinger of one hand, he held a magnolia blossom; between the forefinger and middle finger of the other, a cigarette. Idly, he brought one hand, then the other, to his face: sniffed the magnolia blossom, drew on the cigarette. On the wrist of the hand that held the magnolia, there was a faded tattooed star of blue, the folly of bygone youth. He opened his eyes, tossed away the blossom, smoked the cigarette.

" 'Gay the flower, lush its leaves,' " said Ng Tai-hei with a smirk, reciting from schoolboy memory the opening lines of a poem from the *Shu Ching*, the Book of Songs.

"I have shot my *júngjí*, and my *yàmging* is at rest," said the man on the bench. At the Anglo-Chinese grammar school the man had attended, he and his classmates had devised obscene counterparts for many of the odes in the Book of Songs. The lines he now uttered took the place of the lines—"I have seen my lord, and my heart is at rest"—that followed the opening that Ng Tai-hei had recited.

Ng Tai-hei sat beside him. "And how is your *yàmging* these days?" he asked.

"Prudent, like myself," said the man, whose name was Cho Sin-wo. He grinned oddly, his expression wavering between a sneer and a smile.

"Don't tell me you too have gone condom-crazy."

"Even with my wife." Cho Sin-wo took a final drag of his cigarette and tossed it aside. "Those transfusions and all."

"And how is she, our dear Choi-wah?"

"Terminal. The surgeon could not remove all the cancer from her brain. What remains is inoperable. We have told her otherwise, but her next trip to the hospital will be one-way."

"And you're still making love to her?"

"The cancer in her brain has made her febrile. There are little seizures. They pass through her in waves. Strangely enough, she has become a good fuck."

There was a sudden summery gust, and the willows and the flowers swayed. Ng Tai-hei savored the sound of it: *fan*, the soughing of the breeze through the trees, the rippling of stillness. As Ng Tai-hei believed, it was in characters such as *fan*, which contained in a single simple sound a meaning that other tongues took many words to awkwardly convey, that one found proof of the natural eminence of the Chinese language. In coupling *fan* with *féng*, the movement of the breeze through the trees, the delicate natural psalmody of nature, Ng Tai-hei found his description of paradise: *fan féng*. Early in the morning, late at night, at his home in the hills of Victoria Peak, he would sit out on his terrace. When the sky was clear and filled with the scent of pine, the expanse of Hong Kong, Kowloon, the harbor, and the far hills beyond lay before him like a vision: at dawn, the earth blossoming in the pale new sun; at midnight, a Wang Wei reverie awash in the distant, dreamlike iridescence of neon. He would sit there and let *fan féng* loosen his limbs and breathe away the knots of thought, and he would feel himself replenished. Perception came to him in *fan féng*, and the inspiration for many a death and swindle.

"Talk to me, Ah Wo," he said. "Tell me about the weather in Italy."

"The weather in Italy is fine."

"Weather changes."

"I know. Years ago, you had only to ask Tuan Ching-kuo about the weather in Italy. What few direct dealings we ever had with the Sicilians were through his people, the Thais. Koh Bak Kin, Chiang Wing Keung, Lam Sing Choy, a few others. Even then, their dealings were limited. Santapaola, Partanna, Mondello, Riccobono. Those were the only groups that ever accepted them, and that small acceptance was not warm."

"As I say, weather changes."

"And in our case, for the better. As you know, the Chinese communities in Rome and Milan have begun to grow. *La piccola Chinatown italiana*. Most of the newcomers are from Zhejiang. But nevertheless, I am no longer alone. The innocents in these growing communities call us Hei San Huì, Black Triad Society; the Italians call us Sole Rosso and Tao. Not once outside of our own little group have I heard mention of the 14K.

"As we have grown, our dealings with the Sicilians of Milan have grown as well. And that is why I can tell you that the weather is good.

According to those I know, the word from Sicily is that we, the Chinese and the Sicilians, are about to enter a new alliance of concord and unimagined prosperity."

"These wops you speak to, do you think they know what they're talking about? How close are they to the powers in Sicily?"

"They are close enough to be trusted with the handling of their money, both its laundering and its disbursement. Considering the nature of these men, that leads me to believe that they are close. And you, my friend, know that these are not small sums. You see the kind of shipments I arrange."

"These same men launder money, you say?"

"No. Some launder, some buy."

"And you believe these men?"

"It's as you have often said, Hei Gau: *baak chuen gwai hoi.*"

"Yes, I know. All rivers eventually meet in the sea. *Ging yi yuen ji.* I've often said that, too: respect others but keep them at arm's length. *Lontano*, as your Italian friends would say."

"I tell them nothing."

"And they tell you things?"

"We speak in vaguenesses."

"And from these vaguenesses you've gathered that we, all of us, are about to enter this new alliance of concord and unimagined prosperity, this United Nations, this Benetton advertisement that you talk of?"

"All I'm saying is, the air is sanguine." He smiled. "The weather is good."

"You read the papers. You know men in America. I suppose the air in New York is sanguine as well."

Yat jek gau fai ying, houdoh gau fai seng. That is what he had told Asim Sau: one dog barks at a shadow, and many bark at the sound. Asim Sau, speaking from a jungle outpost near the Laotian border, had known nothing of the bloodshed and violence in Chinatown, and like Ng Tai-hei himself, he had merely laughed at the news. The New York dong leaders had run to the Hong Kong triads for counsel and deliverance. But what befell those who bought and marketed their *baat fan* mattered little to the powerful. For every insect that died, more were born. Beneath their laughter, however, there was concern. The Italians, they saw, had chosen to speak through action, and that was always a cause for concern. It was not what they did that mattered, it was what they showed they could do that mattered. Their insides were strong, their stealth was deep. Moreover, if the dongs' subhuman buyers were thrown further into fear, if the dongs themselves could be rendered insecure in their dealings with the East—if the web of the 14K's power became scorched by a worsening of these things—then damage would be done.

At midnight, June 30, 1997, the British flag over Hong Kong would be lowered for the last time. As that time drew near, the triads had to confront the possible eventuality of their flight from home. It was true that the head of Chinese law enforcement, Minister Tao Siju, had hinted that he foresaw no persecution of the triads. But Ng Tai-hei and others interpreted this, at best, as an offer to share or perish. If the triads shifted their center of power, it would be to New York. They had made millions of dollars in recent years selling forged American passports at twenty thousand a shot to Hong Kong and mainland businessmen wary of Chinese policy changes, and every triad member of any rank had one of these passports for himself. The Sun Yee On Triad had already established itself as a presence in New York's Chinatown. If the 14K should need to prevail in New York, its sovereignty must not be allowed to *diugá*, lose face, among the dongs.

"Tell me," Ng Tai-hei said, "who do you think is responsible for the events in New York?"

"Who knows? It could be your way of saying that prices are going up. Likely it's the Fujianese. I never trust the Fujianese."

"And yet you trust the Zhejiangese. You can spit from Zhejian to Fujian. Those provinces are right next to each other." As Ng Tai-hei spoke, he wondered whether he should have Cho Sin-wo killed here, in Hong Kong, or upon his return to Milan.

"The Zhejiangese are a different people. They're more like the Shanghainese," said Cho Sin-wo. "That is Zhejian's true neighbor, Shanghai, to the north, not Fujian, to the south."

"So you suspect the Fujianese, and yet the Fujianese were the first ones to be hit." Here was better, Ng Tai-hei decided.

"Well, they would want to deflect attention from themselves," said Cho Sin-wo.

"By committing mass suicide."

"I really don't know the details. There was very little about it in the Italian papers." He lighted a cigarette. "So, then, you tell me. Who's responsible?"

Ng Tai-hei shrugged. Cho Sin-wo wondered why Ng did not lay the blame on the Italians. Surely he must know.

"You think it's the wops, don't you?"

"Perhaps," said Ng Tai-hei.

"What do the others think?"

Ng Tai-hei shrugged again. "Do me a favor, Ah Wo. Do yourself a favor. Keep your Sicilian friends at arm's length. I will be in Milan next week. I'll be relying on you to stand at my side while I am there."

"That," said Cho Sin-wo, "will be my honor."

"For now, is there anything else I should know?"

"What little I know, I've told you. May I ask you something that I've been curious to know?"

Ng Tai-hei nodded. Yes, he thought. Better to do it here. He would pack the head in salt and have it sent overnight to Chen Fang in New York. He had heard that wops relished the heads of beasts. Well, here would be something for them and their revenant to feast on.

"Why have you agreed to meet in Italy? Why haven't you had them come to you instead? Have you forgotten the fourth strategy, 'To stay home and let the enemy come to attack you'?"

"I've forgotten nothing. Perhaps I feel as you do, that these men are not really our enemy." He smiled. "Perhaps I have a craving for risotto."

Asim Sau and Tuan Ching-kuo had asked him the same question some time ago. His answer to them, composed in *fan féng*, had been the truth. This business, he told them, would grow more difficult, and more dangerous, as it came to a head. An outsider from the East transported to hold his own among hostile forces in cosmopolitan Milan was certainly at an advantage over one from the West transported to hold his own in the jungles of the Golden Triangle or the urban jungle of Hong

Kong. Better to allow their enemies the first call and reserve the second for themselves. Better to begin in sunny Italy and among their own familiar shadows.

Ng Tai-hei stood and looked down on the younger man. The two were to dine together this evening. Cho Sin-wo expected the driver to come for him at the Mandarin Hotel at half past seven. Ng Tai-hei would send the killer to call at his suite at seven-twenty or so.

"Tell me," said Cho Sin-wo. "How do you feel about what I've said? About the weather, I mean." He stood, and the two men began to walk slowly together toward the little wooden bridge. Ng Tai-hei searched for an answer that, when unwrapped, would turn to vapor.

"I am intrigued," he said. "But you know me, Wo. I am a cynical man."

That tattooed hand. He would send it to Milan. They crossed the bridge to the rippling blanket of flowers. "I will tell you this," he said. "Serve me right, and you won't be forgotten when the next spring harvest comes." He placed his arm round the other man's shoulders. "*Sik neige yidailei fan,*" he said: eat your macaroni. "But don't forget where you come from and the number you bear."

"I never have. I never will."

"And that's as it should be."

Ng Tai-hei had been craving beggars' chicken for some days, and he dined alone that evening in Kowloon at Tien Heung Lau, where they prepared it in true Hangzhou fashion, wrapped in seasoned lotus leaves, packed in mud, and slowly baked over open fire.

The killer had been instructed and given two Federal Express shipping labels. One bore the Baxter Street address of Chen Fang in New York; the other, the address of an importer on Via Bramante in Milan.

"You're early," said Cho Sin-wo, his collar upturned, a necktie in his hand. "I'll be with you in a moment." His visitor was a young man with closely cropped hair and a pleasant smile. Cho Sin-wo did not ask him to come in.

"May I use your telephone?" the smiling man asked.

Cho Sin-wo nodded and led him in. "You brought your dinner?" he said, suspiciously regarding the large gym bag that the man was carrying.

The man set the bag on the floor. "If I lose this," he said, "I lose my job."

Cho Sin-wo gestured to the telephone, then walked to the bureau mirror and began to loop his tie. He kept one eye on the reflection of the man behind him, who, as callers often do while waiting for an answer, glanced at his watch. Tilting his head to the side, he tucked the receiver between his right jaw and shoulder, then, turning casually, with his back to Cho Sin-wo, he began to remove his jacket. He moved the receiver from his right to his left side and withdrew his other arm. His hand emerged from the sleeve and in one fluid movement grasped the pistol, a Hi-Standard Sport-King fitted with an SMG suppressor, that protruded from the jacket's inner breast pocket. The receiver fell suddenly to the floor as he flung aside the cloak of his jacket, jolted his arm straight, and fired pointblank. This mercuric movement was such that Cho Sin-wo's terror and his glimpse of the fiery burst reflected in the mirror—the cognition of danger and the shattering of his vertebrae, the opening of his innards—were simultaneous.

Cho Sin-wo fell face-down. This was good. There were no exit wounds; there would be no blood on the carpet. The killer returned the telephone receiver to its cradle and dragged the body, still breathing and writhing, into the bathroom. He removed Cho Sin-wo's wallet, heaved him into the tub. There was a throaty gurgle of angry horror, an ungodly sound. The killer struck him hard between the nose and mouth with the butt of his gun. He went through the closet, the bedroom and living-room drawers, gathered money, passport, airline ticket. He triple-locked the suite door. This was no time for a chambermaid to come to turn down the sheets and lay mints on the bed. He unzipped the gym bag, took out a heavy, gleaming cleaver, returned to the bathroom. Cho Sin-wo's eyes opened slightly when the killer grabbed him by the hair and jerked back his head, and his eyes were still open when the cleaver came slicing down through the flesh of his neck and opened his aorta. Blood gushed out as from a slaughtered pig.

The killer's work took a while, as cutting through the cartilage and bones involved much hacking and carving. He left the head and hand to drain beside the body while he washed the gore from himself and his cleaver. From the gym bag, he took two plastic bags and a liter bottle of sulfuric acid. Lifting the severed head by the hair, the hand by the middle finger, he shook them, as one might shake a greengrocer's vegetables to free them of excess water. When their bloody drizzle was reduced to a sprinkling, he placed the parts in the plastic pouches, filled the tub with hot water, and poured in the acid. He put the bagged parts, the cleaver, the damp bloody bathroom towel, the gun, the empty liter bottle, the money, wallet, passport, and ticket into the gym bag. He put on his jacket, wiped the telephone and the single lever of the bathroom faucet with his handkerchief, turned the inside lock on the bathroom door, shut it, looked around, unlocked the front door, handkerchief in hand, closed the door behind him, dropped the handkerchief into the gym bag, zippered it, walked to the elevator, and pressed the down button with the knuckle of his forefinger.

He patted his pockets, checking for his cigarettes and looking forward to the day when he ate beggars' chicken while others did such bidding.

SIXTEEN

Big black Alhaji Shehu Musa had managed to sleep during the ten-hour flight, but the thin white man had not. As the Nigeria Airways DC-10 began its descent toward Muritala Mohammed International Airport, he lighted another cigarette, ordered another vodka-and-soda, and gazed out the window at the nearing terrain, which lay beneath an ugly morning haze.

"*Eko Akete, ile ogban*," said Alhaji, grinning broadly, leaning over the thin man to look at the land below. "That is what we Yoruba say: Lagos, bed of sin, house of wisdom."

To the thin man, Lagos, from where he sat, looked like a vast industrial wasteland—like Ponte's place in Jersey City, the thin man thought, grown into a hellish principality of its own and transported to the malarial armpit of ooga-booga land. He scratched the spot on his arm where he had been given his yellow-fever vaccination.

"I will take you to a place only the Yoruba go. Not even a name has this restaurant, but the best yam soup in all the world." Alhaji smacked his lips. "*Gwaten doya*, it is called, and once you taste it, you will crave it all your life. More addictive than *akunnilorun*, great Oba Duji himself," he said, chortling.

The thin man raised his eyebrows and smiled wanly in a halfhearted pretense of enthusiasm.

"And nearby," Alhaji continued, "is a sex house unlike any other. *Agbere* girls from the north. Girls so young they do not bleed." He smacked his lips again. "And often virgins. Yes, yes, in fact, *wúndía*, virgins, not yet disgraced."

The thin man looked at him.

"Well, yes, some are Yoruba."

Lagos looked even worse from the ground. As the battered Peugeot taxi sped west on Apapa Oworonsoki Expressway toward Ikorodu Road, then south toward the Yaba district, the city grew uglier, denser, and fouler-smelling. Alhaji seemed proud of this ugliness, density, and foulness.

"Fastest-growing city in the world," he said. "Yes, in fact. Seven million, maybe more. And the youngest city in the world as well. Half the populace, maybe more, under the age of sixteen." He seemed to love the place. "The yams, the sex houses. Tarkwa Beach. The music— Fela Anikulapo Kuti, Chief Commander Ebenezer Obey, King Sunny Ade."

"Why did you leave?" the thin man asked.

"Median annual income, seventy-five hundred naira. Equivalent to maybe three hundred dollars a year."

The taxi turned onto Muritala Mohammed Way, turned twice more, and stopped at a hotel on Queen Street, a building that seemed to have been erected long ago in ugliness and since decayed.

"Air conditioning." Alhaji beamed. "Television, running water. Ideal proximity for our purposes."

The man from Pantelleria was waiting for them when they arrived: a small, mustached Sicilian in a white suit, white straw hat, and tan-and-white spectators. His English was not good, but words were not important. Alhaji grasped his hand and kissed it, and the man did not mask his distaste.

The sulfuric acid solution, the potassium chlorate, the gunpowder, the eyedropper, the battery-powered drill and quarter-inch bit, the Ping-Pong balls, vials, corks, and tube of silicon glue had all been purchased in Lagos. The odorless, claylike C-4 had been molded into the likeness of a little pony and flown in as carry-on luggage.

"Okay, all we need is the scumbags and the egg box," the thin man said. "And some cotton. We need some cotton."

"I meet you here," the Sicilian said. "When?"

"The cars leave for the airport at nine-thirty tonight," said Alhaji. "We must be there at eight-thirty."

The Sicilan took out pencil and paper. He drew a lopsided circle, passed it back to Alhaji. "Show hands," he said.

Alhaji transformed the circle into a clockface that bore two numbers, the eight and the three. From the center of the circle, he drew a line to the eight, then another, longer line to the three.

The man looked at it, nodded. "*Venti e u quartu.*" He crumpled the paper, put it in an ashtray.

"When we are done, we call Mr. Joe."

"Oba Joe," Alhaji said to the thin man, knowingly, importantly.

The Sicilian stood, raised his hat perfunctorily, and left them.

Alhaji dialed the telephone, spoke with cheerful enthusiasm, part English, part Yoruba, then hung up.

"All is set," he told the thin man. They washed up, and Alhaji led the thin man, like plenty with pale famine in tow, to a tin-roofed shack restaurant. Alhaji ordered for both of them, pepper soup and a seafood-and-yam dish called *ikokore*. The thin man liked the food, but the sweltering heat, humidity, and swarming flies and the stench of shit from the open sewers nearby were overwhelming.

"Many say the sewage and the chemicals from the factories ruin the seafood in the lagoon," said Alhaji. "I don't think so."

After lunch they bought a dozen lubricated blue condoms—"Big party tonight," Alhaji explained, leering, to the man behind the counter —and a box of cotton swabs. To Alhaji's delight, they found a cardboard egg box atop a heap of garbage in the gutter near the corner of Akiwunmi Street. With Alhaji's help, it took the thin man little more than two hours to finish his work. When he was done, he went out and bought a pint of vodka and a bottle of club soda.

The Sicilian was on time, waiting for them outside in a small yellow car. Following Alhaji's directions, they turned left off Muritala Mohammed Way to Oju Elegba Road, went across the railroad tracks, then south on Tejuoso Street, past Yaba Market, to where Tejuoso Street ended. There, in a dirt clearing, dim in the twilight, stood a large corrugated-tin building. Parked outside were several old minivans and a few eight-seater Peugeot 504s.

"Stop here," Alhaji said.

Under Alhaji's watchful eye, the thin man removed the rigged Ping-Pong balls one by one from the egg tray, sheathed them in cotton, and placed them into condoms. Alhaji tied each condom with what he called "the Yaba knot."

"Come back for me at nine-thirty," he said.

Inside the corrugated tin building, men gathered noisily round benches and tables. One man, who wore a seersucker suit, tribal skull-cap, and gold jewelry, hailed Alhaji loudly and embraced him. The place, which was not air-conditioned, was thick and redolent with cigarette and *igi-ogbó* smoke and the smells of sweat, urine, and boiling okra. From a boom box came the thunderous *dundun* song to Shango of Chief Twins Olaniyi Seven Seven. Alhaji let the man in seersucker peer into his paper bag.

"Blue." The man laughed. "Very fancy."

"Special," Alhaji said. "Ninety-eight percent pure. Not to be confused with the rest."

At one table, a group of scrawny young men, most of them shirtless, sat swallowing oversized grapes. Whenever one of them gagged, the older man who watched over them berated him loudly and struck him with a switch. At another table, a group of taller and more exotic-looking men, many of them bearing copper-colored tribal scars on their bare chests, gulped down golf balls. When one of these men gagged, he was merely dismissed. At other tables, swallowers whose training lay behind them—*aláàgbe mì*, they were called—sat opening their mouths, like seals awaiting fish, as overseers fed them one condom after another. At some tables, the condoms were tied into small olive-sized parcels. At others, where the tall men with tribal scars sat, the condoms were packed more grossly: large, fat, and globular. Each condom, no matter its size, was washed down with a swallow of thick green okra soup.

The seersucker man offered to take Alhaji's paper bag and have its contents distributed among the swallowers.

"No." Alhaji grinned. "I shall disperse these myself. Like the old days."

"A lesson from the master."

Alhaji strode to the table of tall, scarred men, and going around with much exuberance, he fed them.

By nine-thirty the swallowers had been given their airline tickets and herded into the waiting vehicles, which departed, one after another, in a motley caravan heading north, toward the airport. Within the next hours, their devious journeys to America would begin. Some, an hour from now, would board Alitalia Flight 845, switching in Rome to TWA Flight 841 to New York. Others, an hour later, would board Lufthansa Flight 567, switching in Frankfurt to TWA Flight 741. Others would fly on Air Afrique to the Côte d'Ivoire capital of Abidjan and continue on to New York from there. Each courier, come tomorrow, when shitting out his cargo for Alhaji's men in New York, would receive between two and five thousand dollars, depending on the size and number of condoms he defecated. Five thousand dollars equaled more than sixteen years' honest wages in Lagos.

Alhaji saw the little yellow car swerve slowly toward him. The thin man got out, walked a few paces, and unzipped his fly.

"Now we eat," said Alhaji, talking to the pissing man's back. His eyes widened like luminous yellow opals in the dark, and he laughed with stentorian lechery. "Then we deflower. *Gwaten doya* and pullet, the feast of kings."

"First we make our call," the thin man said over his shoulder. His free hand thrashed the air. "Fuckin' mosquitoes."

"Yes. We call Oba Joe." Alhaji's exhilaration was great. Soon he would be a man of respect and would walk where no Yoruba had walked before.

"I don't know if we got time for these tar babies of yours. We gotta be at the airport by twelve-thirty. The plane leaves at half past one." He had no great desire to visit the young prostitutes. The way Alhaji described them brought to mind the pictures of skeletal, potbellied Somali kids that those one-for-the-Lord-two-for-me scumbags showed on television in the middle of the night.

"One twenty-five," Alhaji corrected him. There was umbrage in his voice. Tar babies, indeed. "Forty-five minutes to enjoy our meal. Forty-five minutes to ravish. That leaves us more than enough time. Believe me, I have taken Flight 850 many times."

The thin man zipped his fly, turned unsteadily. "I just thought of something," he said. "How do we know none of them swallowers ain't gonna be on the same plane?"

Alhaji laughed. "Nigeria Airways 850 is the only nonstop flight from Lagos to New York. We never use that flight, as it is monitored the most closely at JFK."

The small Sicilian man got out of the car. "*Un momento*," he said, gesturing. They watched him open the trunk. He peered in, waved for them to come over. As they approached, he withdrew an Uzi equipped with a long RFP Encap-U-Wipe silencer, and he sprayed them with fire. For a second the thin man covered his eyes, absurdly, with his arms, wailing "No!" The fat man held his arms at right angles, salmon-colored palms shaking back and forth, imploringly, Jolson-style, his body weaving, his eyes wide, his mouth silently flapping. Then both lay on the ground, groaning. The Sicilian looked down at the thin man, shook his head, and spoke.

"*Scemu figliu di putta.*"

It was the thin man's epitaph—stupid son of a bitch—and its meaningless ring was the last sound he heard.

It was eight in the evening in New York, two in the morning in Lagos, when, somewhere over the mountains of southeastern Algeria, the tall man in seat 32C of Alitalia Flight 845 clutched his stomach and belched blood. In mid-belch, his guts exploded with a deafening blast, violently rocking the aircraft, killing several other passengers, tearing apart seats and overhead console panels, shattering plastic inner windowpanes, rupturing air distribution ducts, and splattering flesh, intestinal matter, and blood throughout the cabin. Horror among the surviving passengers was such that screams of panic still rose among them at the slightest turbulence encountered during the plane's descent to its emergency landing at Touggourt. Panic was greatest among those who were fellow swallowers. Sweating profusely, jabbering wildly in tribal dialects among themselves, they stormed the lavatories two at a time, shoving fingers down their throats and straining on commodes in a manic cacophony of gagging and grunting. At Touggourt, amid the crowd of deplaning passengers, another swallower fell to his knees with an expulsion of blood. The explosion that followed took more lives than the first. In Touggourt's little airport, several distraught swallowers exploded on infirmary gurneys, at pay telephones, and in toilets.

Two Air Afrique shuttle flights to Abidjan went down over Ghana within an hour of each other. The craft were too small, too light, to withstand the force of the blasts. The Lufthansa flight arrived safely in Frankfurt, but the connecting TWA flight was set aflame by explosion over the Atlantic. While the fire was being fought, another swallower exploded in a window seat, blowing a hole through a rear fuselage window panel so the plane was sucked down into the sea in a demonic whirl of blazing black smoke.

International air traffic controllers communicated in anxious dismay over a growing cluster of disasters that passengers, crew, and Germany's antiterrorist unit, GSG-9, alike implausibly attributed to exploding Negroes.

On the sill of a window that was caked with grime and overlooked nothing—an airshaft that stank of rotting garbage—sat a bottle of Olde English "800" malt liquor, an ashtray brimming with Kool Super Long butts and surrounded by smeared ashes, an unlit, half-burnt candle anchored to the sill by a hardened pool of runneled wax, and a scorched, bent spoon. The room was not more than eight feet square. Stained couch cushions were scattered against one wall. Lying on the black, decayed floorboards, his head propped languidly, eyes closed, a thin tendril of saliva running from the corner of his mouth, was a frail-armed black man in his early forties. One of his dirty-sneakered feet moved, not quite in time, to "Land of 1,000 Dances" by Cannibal and the Headhunters, which jived tinnily forth from the cassette in an old portable player on the floor.

The dead refrigerator and oven in the adjoining kitchenette were both doorless, their open racks strewn with seeping, smelling bags and clotted take-out containers. A kente cloth was draped over the refrigerator, the sparse room's only, forgotten trace of decor. Atop it were an open box of Ritz crackers, a near-empty pint of Johnnie Walker Red, and a few unwashed plastic glasses. The drainboard by the sink was yellowed and streaked with gray, encrusted and studded with rock-hard black stalagmites, the remains of what once, long ago, had been the slop and meat scraps from a ravenously devoured souvlaki. Leaning against the sink, smoking a Kool Super Long, was another, lighter-skinned and shirtless black man. He shuffled into the other room, took a swig of malt liquor.

"Fuckin' abscess," he said, cupping his jaw in his hand. His eyelids were drooping, and what showed of his eyes was jaundiced and bloodshot. He sat on a cushion and commenced torpidly scratching his unshaven throat, moving his head in sickly syncopation to the music.

A key turned in the door. A gaunt Hispanic man, younger than his roommates, entered, shaking, sniffling. "*Naa, na na na na, na na na, na na na, na na na,*" he sang along with Cannibal and the Headhunters in a weak, dire monotone, shaking and sniffling in caesura. He sat on the milk crate by the sill, emptied the contents of his shirt pocket: an orange-tip *punto* and three glassine bags bearing the stamp of No Mercy. He sniffled and shook and sang as he did his thing. "*You gotta know how to pony . . .*" He tied his belt above his elbow, began slapping his forearm. "Land of 1,000 Dances" ended; "Cool Jerk" by the Capitols began. He knew this tape by heart. Next would come "You Talk Too Much" by Joe Jones, then "Cloud Nine" by the Temps. He loved that fucking record.

"*I say now, I say now, the moment of truth have finally come, when I'm gonna show you some, some-a that Cool Jerk. Gimme a little bitta drum by himself there . . .*"

He slipped the thin point into his vein.

"*Can you do it, can you do it, can you do it, can you do it . . .*"

He drew blood, plunged. "*Shit!*"

His roommates' eyes opened. They saw the Hispanic man quaking violently, as if jolted by electrocution.

"Caught you a bonecrusher, my man?" the shirtless one said.

The Hispanic man fell from the milk crate, still quaking, groaning.

"That ain't no fuckin' bonecrusher, man," the other said excitedly. "He's goin' out. Shoot 'im wit' saltwater, man."

"Saltwater, shit. Ain't no fuckin' OD. Some kinda seizure, some shit."

The Hispanic man was knotted with pain, palsied, gasping.

"Look at this shit, man." The shirtless one stood over him. Blotches of ink seemed to be spreading beneath the fallen man's skin as the corrosive alkali smoldered through his veins. Tainted blood hemorrhaged through his system, mixing with his body's proteins, forming a second deadly corrosive that turned his tissue to necrotic, gelatinous slush. Clutching his abdomen, he let out a final yelp of agony as the poisons burned through his organs and filled his stomach with bitter, burning blood. Shredded, tripelike tissue rushed from his mouth in a steaming, bloody torrent.

"Damn," the shirtless man said. "*Damn.*"

It was eleven o'clock at night, past old Joe's bedtime. Johnny and Louie Bones were walking west on Kenmare Street, coming from Little Paulie's heading toward the club.

"How the fuck do I know how he does it? He's got this guy with the shakes and a fuckin' Ping-Pong ball cut in half, this big fuckin' *mulagnan'* with the dirty movies. Next thing you know, boomity-boom, bangitty-bang. He never ceases to amaze me, your uncle. Never."

"I still can't believe he did it."

Johnny liked walking down the street with Louie Bones, liked the look and manner of curious deference in those they passed. Even when he walked alone now, Johnny sometimes got that look, those eager, subdued nods of recognition.

"That's him. His warning shots are lethal. Most of the dope flown into this country comes by way of those jungle bunnies. This should fuck it up. I wouldn't be swallowin' any scumbags for a while if I was one of 'em, I know that much. And I also know that airline security is gonna go into red alert.

"One thing, though, Johnny." Louie smiled sardonically. "You say you can't believe he did it. It ain't just him, Johnny, it's us. *We* did it. We're in this together. Share the glory, share the guilt."

Louie's words articulated Johnny's own hesitant thinking. He was not an innocent pilot fish attached to the rising leviathan of his uncle's wreaking. Throughout the destruction of the last few days, Uncle Joe, after all, had pulled no triggers, cut no throats, detonated no bombs. Did the fact that the evil originated in the volition of his mind render him any more culpable than those whose minds and wills embraced and affirmed it? As in his deadly rides with Willie, Johnny preferred to see himself as an accomplice, an occupant of morality's gray zone, an emanation of murder rather than a murderer.

He shook aside his thinking. "Did you see that head that the old Chink got?" he asked.

Louie grimaced with distaste. "Who the fuck wants to see somethin' like that?"

"Just curious," Johnny said. "Just curious what somethin' like that looks like."

"Yeah, well, I wouldn't know, and I wouldn't mind if I never found out. We know whose head it was, that's enough. He was double-crossin' his own kind, workin' for the boys. One way or the other, his time wasn't long." Louie lighted a cigarette. "Curious," he sneered. "Hell, I quit that shit years ago. The only thing I'm curious about is what a nice glass of wine tastes like to an eighty-year-old man. That's the only thing I'm curious to find out. I still don't know why the fuckin' sky is blue."

"Something to do with the reflection of the water."

"Yeah, that's what I used to think. Then I heard that ain't so."

"I think it is," Johnny said. "The earth is three-quarters water."

"Oh, that I know," Louie said with a professorial air. "Just like the human body."

They turned south on Mulberry Street, saying nothing for a while.

"Tell me something, Johnny. How does all this feel to you? In your guts, I mean, does it feel real?"

"The exploding niggers? The head-of-the-month club?"

"No. *Lo schema*. The whole picture. You and me walking down this street here and now. You and me doing what we have to do and coming out clean. You and me walking down this street when it's all over, with enough money to buy this fucking street."

"It's like this. One minute I'm drivin' around with a bad transmission, huntin' spics for chump change with Willie Gloves. Next minute I'm sittin' there listenin' to some story about a horse that went crazy on Cornelia Street when my uncle was plug-high to a fire hydrant, and he's tellin' me there's a few hundred million in it for me. Then Tonio's pullin' a blade across my finger with all this fuckin' mumbo-jumbo, and this Billy Sing is givin' me the secret three-thousand-fuckin'-year history of fuckin' China, and these bombs start goin' off. Well, shit, Louie, to be perfectly fuckin' honest, the answer is no, it doesn't feel real."

Louie said nothing, just nodded pensively. When no words were forthcoming, Johnny spoke again. "How does it feel to you?"

"The same."

"Just what I wanted to hear. The voice of reassurance."

Louie laughed quietly. "I mean, different but the same. I've known these guys—your uncle, Tonio, the old Chink—a long time. Me and your uncle, we've made a lot of money together. A lot of money. It got so nice and quiet. It seemed like it would go on like that forever, us sittin' around nice and quiet, complainin' about how nice and quiet it was. Then this. And your uncle, Tonio, those guys on the other side, they're old men. I mean, don't get me wrong, Johnny, I'm no fuckin' spring chicken, but these guys are livin' on God's sense of humor. I got the feelin' that to them, they're gonna go anyway, why not go out with a fuckin' bang."

"I asked him about that."

"You did?"

"Yeah. He told me it was all in here." Johnny brought his fingers to his chest. "He told me it had something to do with living out the rest of his days in peace."

"I wish he had told me that."

"Does it make you feel better?"

"In a strange enough way, yeah."

"Then you're a sick fuck too." Johnny laughed. But then his face was grave as death. "So," he said, "fuck whether it seems real. It is real. What matters is if that payoff is real."

"Don't jump the gun. What matters is that our heads don't end up in somebody's mailbox."

"And how do *you* feel, in *your* guts, about that?"

"We'll make out," Louie said. It seemed to Johnny as if he were trying to convince himself.

"You really feel that way?"

"Yeah," Louie said, and there was a strange look in his eyes. "We got no choice."

SEVENTEEN

Johnny removed the spreadshot calendar from the wall beside his desk at the Local headquarters on Park Avenue South. He flipped back two of the calendar's leaves, updating it from long-gone April to June, then he hung it again on the wall. He stood for a moment beholding this *dea nova* of the solstice: a vision of suet and bleached blond hair sucking ponderously on her own stretchmarked tit.

"Hey," somebody said to him. "Fancy meetin' you here. I thought you forgot the address." The man, uncombed and unshaven, wore dirty Haband work pants and an International Brotherhood of Teamsters T-shirt, which rode high on his sagging, protruding gut. As he spoke, he slurped spoonfuls from a pint of Häagen-Dazs Cookie Dough Dynamo. Between two fingers of the hand that clutched the container was a lighted cigarette with a long drooping ash.

"No such luck," Johnny said.

"So, tell me about this vacation. Where ya goin'?"

"Away."

"I hear the weather's nice there this time of year."

"So everything's all right? No problems at Lafayette Street? No shit from 23?"

"Nope."

"Good."

"We still got a beef wit' that fuckin' Hindu on the East Side. He don't wanna pay."

"Well, fuck, man, you know the rules. Twenty-one bucks a week, no ifs, ands, or buts. These fuckin' towel-heads wanna sell papers, they gotta pay."

"He says he ain't got no gobbitch."

"Well, tell him to fuckin' make some."

"They told him." The man maneuvered the cigarette to his mouth, sucked on it, dropped it to the floor, and ground it with his shoe. This maneuver left him with a sticky cream-colored crescent across his chin.

"Tell him, garbage or no garbage, it's twenty-one bucks a week. That's that."

"Ah, these guys, they're soft these days. The old days, we just t'row the fuckin' gobbitch can t'rough the window till he figures out what's cheaper, us or the fuckin' glass man."

"Tell him he starts payin' this week or we backcharge him for every week since he's been there."

The man nodded, looking into his ice cream container, scraping round inside it with his plastic spoon. He sucked the spoon, raised the container to his mouth, and made more sucking sounds. There were dark-flecked creamy droplets on his T-shirt and in the exposed tangle of his belly hairs. He wiped his face with his forearm, lighted another cigarette.

"Anyway," Johnny said, "keep on top of things. Don't let me come back to a fuckin' mess here."

The man picked something from the corner of his eye.

"And take a shave while you're at it. You're supposed to be a fuckin' key man here. These bums are supposed to look up to you."

"Ah," the man said, laughing, "who the fuck I'm gonna 'mpress?"

"When's the last time you got laid?"

"Las' night. Why?"

"Just curious."

. . .

It was skivvy weather, but the old man was still wearing flannel.

"Did you see the papers?" Johnny asked him as he pulled out a chair beside him.

"Yeah. Spontaneous combustion, I figure."

"That's what I figure too." Johnny grinned, and he maintained that grin, but the cast of his eyes subtly changed as he went on. "How do you feel about the innocent ones, the people that just happened to be on those planes?"

The old man looked at him unpleasantly, almost indignantly, admonishingly. Then his look too changed.

"Nobody's innocent in this world."

"Is that how you'd feel if it was turned around—if it was you, or me, on one of those planes?"

"When your number's up, your number's up. There's no right time to die." He shifted forward in his chair, peering through his bifocals into his nephew's eyes. "What is it with you and this Sunday school shit today? You wearing lace underwear all of a sudden, or what?"

"It's like this. The more I know how you feel, the better off I feel. You're eighty fuckin' years old. I'm thirty-six. You think we're gonna feel alike and think alike?"

"To a point, yeah." Then his voice grew easier, as he said things that disarmed and unsettled the younger man. "You see, Johnny, I figure it's like this. I figure you feel like I feel. I figure you think like I think. I'm talking about what's in the blood. I'm not saying that you, at your age, could feel and think like I do at mine. I'm not even saying that you should understand how I feel and think. What I'm saying is, the same thoughts and feelings run through both of us. It's just that what's clear to me isn't clear to you. The thoughts and feelings I've grown used to, you're still coming to grips with. So yeah, I think we feel alike and think alike. I think that's why we're sitting here together." Johnny said nothing, and the old man spoke again. "You make your own right and wrong in this life. Don't take the word of man, even if it passes itself off as the word of God, unless you believe in that word. Civilization was built on *'a ouda*, built on killing. There are men who believe that they couldn't live with themselves if they did certain things. Well, I'll tell you something, Johnny, most people can't live with themselves, period. And men who don't see *'a ouda* for what it is, men who don't believe in killing, simply do not understand civilization. They're uncivilized."

It was when Uncle Joe spoke the truth that Johnny found him most fearsome. Listening to his words, Johnny thought of the faded religious print on the kitchen wall uptown.

"You don't remember your grandfather, Johnny. My father, your father's father, I'm talking about. He was something. A cooper. Played the mandolin." The old man snorted a laugh. "Thought he did, anyway. I'll never forget one time, all these guys, these old-timers, were drinking their wine and talking about what's right, what's wrong, the ways of the world, all that shit. And papa just let them all talk. *Bell'arti parrari picca.* That's what they used to say in the old country: to speak little is a beautiful art. And he was like that, your grandfather. So they got their backyard wine, it's Saturday, they're all philosophers. And you know what he told them? '*Sangu lava sangu.*' That's all he said: blood washes away blood. I never forgot that. Church, state, and soul. Those three words said it all."

Johnny listened to the sound of his uncle's breath, which was like a faint, soft bellows keeping the ember of his words aglow in silence. In time, Johnny asked him about the picture on the kitchen wall.

"That's from the little church in the plains," the old man said. He recited from memory the words beneath the picture. " '*San Giorgio, proteggi la nostra casa dall'insidia del male.*' " He spat a speck of bitter tobacco from his lips.

"That white horse he's on, it made me think of you. That horse going crazy on Cornelia Street," Johnny said.

"That was a black horse."

White horses, black horses. The Jockey's back. Many billions of dollars. Exploding niggers. One terrible moment as it gallops toward those flames. Heads in the mail.

"Tomorrow," the old man was saying, "tomorrow we go out to Louie's place, have a little bon voyage. You and me, we'll ride together."

Yeah, Johnny thought, we'll ride.

One of Marshall's group supervisors had spent the morning in Brighton Beach, setting up a group of Russians for a ten-kilo buy-bust operation that had been in the works for several weeks. The numbers had been set, one point five for the ten, but now the Russians had raised their price to one point seven, an increase of twenty thousand per kilo.

"People dying now, everywhere," they had told him. "Everything is poison. Bad *geroeen* everywhere. Everybody is afraid to buy. These ten kilos are good. Guaranteed. With these, you have everybody in the street eating from you. Short count, no matter. These kilos now are like gold."

"Your shit is from Asia just like the rest, just like the poison shit," the agent had told them.

"No, no," they had lied. "No more. From Iran. All pure, confiscated by government."

Less than twelve hours had passed since the first deaths had occurred, and already the notion of Asian dope had become anathema.

"I tell you what," the agent had told them. "You feel free to change the price. Well, so do we. We will pay one million, not a penny more, for the ten."

"*Smeshnoi*! Ridiculous!" the Russians had yelled.

"We'll see about that. I bet there are more people in the market for methadone today than for dope. So we'll see."

He had arrived at the office dressed as he was, in jeans, black T-shirt, and blue silk jacket. He told Marshall and Wang what had happened.

"Three more in Harlem, two more on the East Side," Wang said.

"That brings the total to twenty-four," said Marshall. "All since midnight. I've never seen a plague like this, never."

"Some out-of-town reports have started coming in too. It's starting to spread. Two-bit buyers who came into Mott Haven last night, loaded up on dimes, and took them back to the sticks to sell."

The blue-jeaned group supervisor left to file his report.

"It reminds me of that Tango-and-Cash outbreak back in '91, only worse," said Wang.

"That was just fentanyl, Pete. That was different. That was just one brand. They were trying to bolster the shit, they used too much, and people died, along with a brand name. This isn't just fentanyl. It's sodium hydroxide. Lye. It's intentional murder, intentional mass murder. These suckers're dying ugly, painful deaths. This stuff burns through their veins, turns them black. And it's not just one brand, it's every brand. The streets, the clinics, emergency rooms—it's absolute panic."

"How the hell did they contaminate every brand? That's what baffles me. One cutter, one batch. That makes sense. But not this."

"Well, it's all more or less the same garbage, Pete, you know that. Most of it starts out as Uoglobe. It ends up five bangs later under a dozen different names, as shit in the streets. The baffling part is *when* it was poisoned. It couldn't have been poisoned early on. There are too many dabblers along the way who would have ended up dead. No, this stuff didn't kill until it hit Dimetown, U.S.A. And as you say, there's the rub. One banger, one batch. How did it get into every brand?"

"It had to be somebody who was tied both to the source and to the street, somebody who knew enough stash-to-street characters to slip poison bags into every street source. That would have to be one of your crazy Chinamen. And why would your crazy Chinaman want to put himself out of business? Because that's exactly what he's accomplishing. I'd say the only people shooting up out there today are so far gone that they'd use a spike from a hazardous-waste can outside an AIDS clinic."

"It could be one of your crazy guineas."

"These days, they only supply the black dealers. And even their stuff comes from the Chinese. They couldn't account for something as widespread as this."

"Maybe a crazy guinea and a crazy Chinaman in cahoots."

"Why? They've seen the error of their ways and decided to help us do what we can't do, wipe out heroin through terrorism?"

"The Chinaman's a traitor, the guinea wants to undermine Chinese power."

"Why? Where would he get his dope from then, Greenland?"

"Good question."

"You connect this to the airline bombings?"

"Absolutely. And to the Fuk Ching and Hip Sing hits. The hits in Brooklyn, the Bronx, and Washington Heights too. Everything. It's all one picture."

"That's a pretty big picture."

"Big? It's an apocalypse."

" 'Who is like unto the beast? Who is able to make war with him?' " Wang quoted. The words, which he had learned as a boy at Transfiguration School on Mott Street, were among those he had never forgotten.

Marshall looked at him, impressed. "The Revelation of Saint John," he said, unsure.

Wang nodded, grinning. "The Book of the Apocalypse."

"The beast was a dragon, right?"

"The beast was the creation of the dragon."

"How did the beast end up?"

" 'Heaven opened, and behold a white horse; and he that sat upon him was called Faithful and True.' The rider and his army took the beast. The beast went down."

"What about the dragon?"

" 'And he laid hold on the dragon'—either the rider or his angel, I forget—'and cast him into the bottomless pit, and shut him up, and set a seal upon him, that he should deceive the nations no more.' "

"So it's a piece of cake. All we do is find the rider."

"It's a white horse, remember?"

"White and horse are two things I don't forget on this job."

"A white horse. God, truth, righteousness. Our guy doesn't want to kill the beast or shut up the dragon. He wants to harness them."

"So," Marshall said, grinning, "he's got a flaw."

"Yeah," said Wang, "just like your theory."

"We'll see," Marshall told Wang. It was what the agent had told those Russians in Brighton Beach: "We'll see."

. . .

The first thing that Johnny noticed when he walked into the Brooklyn apartment that night was the new picture on the wall: three men with their shirts off, bent over floorboards with wood planes. His eyes were on the print even as he kissed and embraced his wife. He walked over and took a close look at it. Gustave Caillebotte, *The Floor Scrapers* (1875), Louvre, Paris.

"Do you like it?" she asked.

"Would you like it if I hung up pictures of broads with their tits hangin' out?"

"Sure." She laughed. "Guido Cagnacci, *Dying Cleopatra*, something like that. Why not?"

"Then why didn't you get that one? At least he's Italian. This guy here, what is he, a frog, right? Picture like this, probably a fag too."

"Oh, I'm so sick of all that Italian stuff."

Right. The one he liked, Giotto's *L'invidia*, it was gone.

"But you are Italian."

"So what? Are you serious? You look like you're having a fucking nervous breakdown."

"Where'd you put Giotto?"

"Don't worry." Her voice rose. "It's in the closet. You can have it if you want it."

"I thought you liked that one."

"No, *you* liked it." She screwed her face into an expression of distaste. "That fat, ugly bitch standing in that fire with the snake coming out of her mouth."

He was distraught, angered, but unwilling to state the source of his distress, his ire. She was turning this place into her own, a reflection of independent mind and mood, something other than familiar and comforting uxorial compliance. In those new colors on the wall, he did not see some frog's trifling play of geometry and light, he did not see a woman's passing infatuation with a framed picture or with shopping, or an attempt to allay her confusion and loneliness and depression, to fortify and cheer and assert herself through small indulgence. Rather, he saw all these things, but to him their sum constituted a greater and more disturbing act, a movement away from him, a declaration of desertion from the fragile vessel of their common delusion, an abandonment. These were feelings he would not dare speak, chinks in the armor he would not dare expose. But there was no need to.

"You're the one who left," she said. "All that shit about rediscovering each other, falling in love all over again, taking care of your uncle. What the fuck do you expect me to do, sit here and knit? We don't have a sex life, now we don't even have a life."

What the fuck had brought this on? Who the fuck had she been talking to? A man or a woman? Which was worse, he did not know.

"If we don't have a sex life, it's because you pulled the plug on it."

"No, Johnny, *you* pulled the plug on it. With those pigs of yours and your fucking drunken violent bullshit."

He had never hit her hard enough, that was his fucking problem. Was he addicted to this fucking figment of a fucking marriage, or what? He wasn't even waking up with piss hard-ons anymore. This broad was fucking destroying him. Now here he was, going off to God knew what— it was worse than going off to fucking war—and she pulls this shit.

"Who you been talking to?"

"This is insane. *You're* insane. I hang a picture on the wall and you lose your fucking mind. I don't believe this. You're having a nervous breakdown, you really are."

"Who you been talking to?"

"Who have I been talking to?"

"Yeah. Who you been talking to?"

She snorted a forced, nasty laugh. "I've been talking to *me*, Johnny. I've been talking to me."

"Look. Do you *want* to fight?"

"No," she said irascibly. "I never want to fight. I just want to be able to hang a picture on my fucking wall without feeling like I've desecrated a fucking temple. Shit, Johnny"—her voice rose, it was almost a shout —"you haven't even invited me to that fucking apartment of yours, not once."

"It's not fixed up yet. It's still a mess. Besides, I thought we wanted to spend some time apart, take it easy for a while."

Diane shook her head and sighed. "When are you leaving?"

Whether it was madness or weakness or true need of the heart, he still wanted it: her love, her blessing, to carry with him through the night to come.

"Sunday," he said. "Day after tomorrow."

"Well, good luck."

So that's what it came down to. No candlelight, no blowjob, no legs wrapped around his back and vows of undying love in his ear, no sweet parting sorrow. Just "good luck."

"Yeah," he said. "Thanks."

What the fuck was he doing standing here like a fucking *mammaluccu* with this fucking no-fuck bitch and her fucking *Floor Scrapers* (1875), Louvre, Paris, bullshit?

She kissed him. It felt to him like the kiss of a friend, not a lover. No, fuck that friend shit, worse: the sort of kiss you'd plant on a stiff before they shut the casket lid.

EIGHTEEN

The yellow-flowering tomato plants in Louie Bones's backyard had begun to bear fruit, and the air was sweet with the perfume of rose blossom and basil. In the warm shade of the big Norway maple, a lone sparrow drank from a puddle of cloudy rainwater in the old concrete birdbath. Sitting at the wrought-iron, glass-topped table looking at these things, breathing them in, in the company of men who were older and wiser and calmer than he, Johnny felt good, serene. Diane and all anxiety, and all that lay before him, were distant and faint, like the sound of the Saturday morning traffic that was hushed and far away, all but lost amid the sound of the shimmering maple and the sparrows in its branches.

"Look how big he got," Louie's wife said, standing there in her housedress, looking at Johnny and shaking her head with bemused happiness. "Such a big boy." Her frosted hair was the only thing that did not stir in the pleasant breeze.

"For Chrissake, he's pushin' forty. Will you stop, already?" Johnny saw that Louie spoke to her without looking at her.

"Oh, shut up, you old grouch. Tell him, Tonio, tell him we're going to Niagara Falls. You and me. No grouches allowed."

"Yeah," old Tonio said. He did not seem to be in the mood today for their repartee, and his perpetual scowl did not brighten.

"Did you see my little white eggplants, Joe?"

"Nice," Johnny's uncle said. "Nice."

Johnny watched her with fascination as she counted the four men who sat before her as if there were many, moving her painted lips silently and calculating in the air with her forefinger as her eyes circled the table. She went into the house, returned with a silver tray, and set out four fancy little china saucers and cups of steaming espresso, little silver spoons and linen napkins, sugar and a plate of cookies. "Yell if you need me," she said, then withdrew into the house, pulling shut the sliding glass door behind her.

Tonio's scowl lightened, and he nodded as if he were in a world of his own. Then Johnny saw that Tonio was not alone in that world. His uncle was nodding in much the same abstracted way.

"Tell us, Louie, what you know about *'a Stidda*." Tonio scratched his chest through his white shirt—a shirt that once had been white, in any case. Like his uncle, who also wore a once-white shirt today, Tonio did not like new clothes and wore his old ones till they fell apart. Both men seemed fond of white-on-white shirts that were yellow with age, that possessed a certain *giallo antico* look that could be neither manufactured nor bought.

"*Sì*," Louie said, "*la Stidda*." He put a cigarette in his mouth, turned momentarily to Johnny to explain—"*Stidda* is Sicilian for *stella*, 'star,' something that shoots off from something else"—lighted his cigarette, and inhaled.

"The *stiddari*," he said, "are free guns. If you look at that bullshit maxitrial, that circus of Falcone's, as the beginning of the end for the boys over there, you can also say it was the beginning of the Stidda. Back at the end of '87, around the time that circus ended, that's the first anybody heard of it. From what I know, it came out of Agrigento, that area down there they call *il triangolo della morte*, the triangle of death. Aragona, Raffadali, Sant'Elisabetta. It came out of the wars down there between the Palma di Montechiaro and Porto Empédocle *cosche*. The *stiddari* were guys outside the *cosche*. They moved in when everybody was at everybody's throats. They had their own thing. Whenever the boys got hit by Falcone's monkeys, wherever they left an opening, the *stiddari* would move in, take over. Now it's like the 1850s all over again in Sicily. Nobody heard of this thing called the Mafia, but everyone knew it was there. That's the Stidda today. Nobody knows the word, but everybody knows it's there. It's like in this country. The government goes after *i vecchi uomini d'onore*—a guy like Fat Tony dies in the can in Springfield—while the country falls to a punk pack of wild dogs. There they take old Totò and the *stiddari* take the land." He took another drag from his cigarette. "That's what I know about the Stidda."

"Now tell us what you know about the old man up in the hills, up in Piana degli Albanesi."

"Don Virgilio," Louie said, as if there were nothing more to say. "Greco, Liggio, Totò. He's sat over them all. Don Calò, Genco Russo. Don Virgilio inherited what these men knew, what power they had, and he took it to the hills. And there he is. Greco, Liggio, Totò. Everyone went to them, but they went to him. Don Virgilio. He's the man."

"Okay," Tonio said. "Now put the two together."

"What do you mean?"

"The old man in the hills and the *stiddari*."

"I don't follow you, Tony."

"Well, follow me. The *stiddari* ain't loose guns anymore. They answer to the man, just like everybody else."

"Since when?" In Louie's tone there was a note of disbelief, of suspicion, of being caught out of the know.

"What're you, writin' a book? Since whenever," Tonio answered testily, his scowl contorting into a malefic grin, as if Louie's question were senseless.

Louie sighed. "You sit home all the time, you don't see anybody, you don't say two words to anybody. How do you know these things?"

Tonio said nothing, he merely shrugged, but Johnny's uncle spoke for him. "Little birdies," he said. "The little birdies tell him things."

"Yeah," Tonio said. "The little birdies tell me, then I tell you."

"Then he tells you," Joe echoed, the two of them sitting there,

Johnny thought, in self-decreed oracular majesty in their *giallo antico* shirts.

"So, Johnny," Tonio said, turning his gaze to the younger man. "Who's your man in Milano?"

What the fuck was this, a quiz? They'd been through this over and over. "Vincenzo Raffa."

"And remember, he's with us in this all the way," Tonio said. "It's him and the old man and us. When the deal goes down, we let our kind in. Here, the other side. Everybody. *Tutti i coppule storte.*" He gestured with a wry, ironic glimmer to the cocked brim of Joe's fedora, which Joe seemed to wear only when he journeyed beyond Manhattan. *Coppula storta.* Even Johnny had come to know this arcane phrase by now. It was Sicilian for *coppola a sghimbescio*, which referred to a hat worn at an oblique angle. This was one of the many ways in which Tonio and his uncle alluded to men like themselves. Never once had he heard them use the Sicilian word *mafiusu*, except to describe in sarcastic passing a gold-chain punk in the street or one of the Central Casting *cafon*'s who hung around outside the club. "We give them a better shake than they've ever gotten before, but with a dime tribute, *'a decima*, on every dollar."

Johnny remembered what his uncle had told him about seizing the diseased wild horse of the world for one terrible moment, about riding it and looting all in its path as it galloped toward hell, about jumping off before being thrown and broken. Tonio was not talking about one terrible moment, was not talking about jumping off. Johnny looked at his uncle, and his uncle, with the cast of his eyes, acknowledged that look.

"What Tonio means," Joe said, "is that our deal is our deal. We make our killing and get the fuck out. We pass the reins on to the others, for another killing. After that, we sit back and we continue to receive tribute. Tonio and I and Louie, that is. Johnny understands. We love him, no one more than me, but he hasn't walked through the same blood we have to get where we are."

"Giuseppe here, if he wants to sit back and trust these jackals, that's him. Me, I watch and I count."

"Two, three billion dollars, and you're gonna worry about a dime on a dollar." Joe shook his head and silently laughed.

"That dime," Tonio said, "is a unit of respect."

At times Johnny could not believe these guys.

"So you pay somebody, let them watch over."

"And I'm gonna trust him? *Tu sii pazzu.*"

"Get Johnny here." Joe was enjoying himself. "You trust him. Pay him two cents on every nickel, he'll take care of you."

"No, get somebody else," Johnny said. "I don't plan on lifting three fingers at once after this."

Louie Bones hollered for his wife, and when he heard the sliding door open, without looking at her, he told her to bring more coffee.

"So," Tonio said, as if burying all that had been said in the last moment, "Vincenzo Raffa. You need any muscle, the *stiddari* will be there. You can do no better than them. They're like the boys were in the old days, *'omini di ficati*, tough and hungry and mean."

"But you shouldn't need any muscle," Joe said.

"That's right," Tonio said. "Not yet."

The men ceased talking as Louie's wife approached with the coffee. "Vera just called," she said. "She's going in for the operation next week." She primped her cotton-candy hair. "She's terrified."

"While she's in there, she oughta get the other thing taken care of," Louie said.

"What other thing?"

"You know." He gestured spadelike toward his crotch. "They make the *comu si chiam'* out of the *cacocciul'* and the little man in the boat."

"Oh, shut up," she said, waved him away with her hair-primping hand, suppressed a grin, and waddled off.

When the sliding door closed, Joe spoke. "And you remember what that cocksucker said."

"Which cocksucker?"

"That Asim Sau."

"Right." This too Johnny had committed to memory. In December of 1990 an ABC-TV news program, *20/20*, had broadcast an interview with Asim Sau at his military training-camp in the Burmese jungle. Again and again, mesmerized, Johnny had watched the videotape Louie Bones had given him. "My opium," Asim Sau had said, "is stronger and more potent than your nuclear bomb. It's enough that I just feed you this poison." But Joe was talking about other words. "I have a mission," the warlord had said, "which would cause the people of the world to rejoice. That is to eradicate opium. If you have cash to pay me, I'll give you all the opium produced in the Golden Triangle. You can store it in a warehouse or burn it or throw it in the ocean. You can do what you want with it." Asim Sau had claimed that his deep-discount asking price for six years' opium harvest was two hundred and eighty-eight million U.S. dollars. Each year's crop of about two hundred tons, converted to heroin, was worth some thirty-six billion dollars by the time it reached Dimetown, U.S.A.

"He's full of shit, and that was years ago, but it's still an opening card," Joe said.

"Now, this Chink," Tonio said, "this Ng Tai-hei, he made our Chink in Milano, sent the head to our Chink here. But Raffa, he's got other Chinks who are hooked into that Sole Rosso thing, that Tao. I guess they're one thing, Chinks, that're never in short supply."

"That head," Johnny said. "Do you think that changed anything?"

"It was only a gesture," Joe said. "He didn't trust us before he made our man, and he doesn't trust us now. Nothing's changed. Just one less Chink in the world. Like Tonio said, there are others. Who knows? We probably would've caught this one playing both ends against the middle sooner or later. He was just a *zaffiru*, a two-bit spy."

"And remember," Tonio said, "this Ng Tai-hei, he's no ordinary Chink. You're dealing here with somebody, something. Remember that. But remember that he sits down to shit too, like everybody else."

Johnny recalled what Billy Sing had told him about Ng Tai-hei and the others—that to many who dwelt in the shadow of their world, they were like dark and distant gods, and to meet them would be unnerving, but to Johnny they would be merely men, strangers from a strange world, yes, but beneath that, merely men, and that was as it should be.

"And he knows that Vincenzo and you guys are somebody, some-thing, too," Tonio continued.

"Me?" Johnny said. "Since when did I become somebody, something?"

"The minute he believed it," his uncle said. "Now you had better fucking start believing it too."

"The minute you pricked your finger on that thorn," Tonio said. "The minute you left certain things behind. The minute we asked you to sit with us. That's when you became somebody."

Louie tried to lighten the moment. "Yeah," he said. "It's like the man says. You're nobody till somebody loves ya. And we love ya."

When he was a kid, Johnny had written a poem called "Still/Life." It had seemed to him, not at first but not long after, either, that the title was wrong, that the solidus stank of artifice. Yet he had known of no other way to express that hiss and crackling, that suddenly perceived arrhythmia of being, between nothingness and onwardness. The way he remembered it, the poem had something to do with having his forehead sewn up after someone smashed a bottle across it, an incident that had preceded the poem by some years. Its lines were full of harsh emergency room light and the sickly cool feel of institutional porcelain, and it was about that sensation that time was standing still, a dismal stasis, like a dire ringing in the ears, that he had intended the solidus to represent. The poem had been thrown away long ago, but the feeling had not. All too often, he had remained immobile, static in the eye of the wheel of his life, exerting little or no force to govern its course. He knew this about himself, had told himself that this was the way it was, that he was dependent on the breaks. Well, here was his break. That solidus that separated him from his life would have to be deleted, obliterated. He loved the words that Billy Sing had given him, and they were already a part of him, running through his blood and his breath like poetry about to erupt. He liked that feeling, as he liked the words that China's secret soul had placed in the mouth of Confucius: "When I fight, I conquer."

But beneath it all, beneath the brewing courage and fear and exhilaration and rumblings, time and again there came the troubling thought that in conquering, he would impose another and greater solidus between the breath of being and its fulfillment, that the reverberations of this baptism in evil would be inexorable, that no amount of wealth could bribe Charon to ferry him back from hell.

"And don't forget," his uncle was saying, to him, to Louie, to ghosts in the summer breeze, "bring me back cigars. Toscani Extra-Vecchi. The good ones."

NINETEEN

Black became deepest blue. Johnny gazed out into a cloud-vaulted cathedral of dawn. Stained-glass illuminations of gathering pale light coruscated through dark clouds in a synesthetic symphony, rose and gold, amethyst-violet and sapphire, pink and pearl. Slowly the clouds lightened to baroque billowings of agate gray, then wisps of byssus white. The cathedral evanesced in sighs of accrescent daybreak, and the plane soared low over the Alps. Johnny looked down. It was as if he were seeing from someplace west of heaven, from some colder, less known, and less blessed sphere of disembodiment, but one that shared celestial vantage all the same. Beneath him lay a hushed and haunting vista of snowy blue-shadowed valley slopes, lofty white mountain-brows, glacial crests that commanded the senses like majestic peregrine chords from the organ of creation.

The strange, beautiful world below enraptured and chilled him, breathed into him its immanent power as well as its loneliness. The golden light and pure blue sky of morning seemed somehow sacramental, marrying that power and that loneliness, assuring him that if he could carry the feeling of this moment with him, all would be well; that in moments such as this there was life. A deliverance, not from the fact of the common, foregone end in putrefaction that constituted man's only true brotherhood but from the fear of it, which governed and putrefied men's lives, laying waste to them with an anxious morbidity more devastating than death itself.

The strange cold beauty reminded him too of hell, the frozen region, the nethermost ring of Dante's ninth circle, where Lucifer rose like a mountain in icy crust from the frigid slopes at the heart of damnation, which in Dante's vision was the heart of the world. Dante's Lucifer had three faces, signifying his attempt to supplant the triune God: one face was vermilion; another, yellow; the third, the color of "those who come from where the Nile, descending, flows," that is, Ethiopia—nigger black. Those threes, those fucking threes. A terza rima of endless confluence. Dante had painstakingly set his *Commedia* in the year 1300, had begun it with an encounter with three beasts, had divided it into three parts, had divided his *Purgatorio* and *Paradiso* into thirty-three cantos each. Why had the years of Christ's life been numbered at thirty-three? Three times in the *Inferno*, Dante had invoked the Alps.

"*Le Alpi,*" said Louie Bones, coming awake with a yawn and a bestial stretch of his limbs, leaning across the vacant seat that separated him and Johnny, squinting into the morning. His sudden words, contorted by his waking yawn, were like a startling growl.

Soon Johnny could feel the descent in his ears. The bell tone seemed muffled, distant, as the sign blinked on overhead: FASTEN SEAT BELTS ALLACCIARE LE CINTURE. Then and now, the heart of the world remained the same. The wrathful and the sullen, tyrants and murderers. Sodomites and those violent unto God. Usurers and simonists. Hypocrites, thieves, and falsifiers. And, cursed beyond all, the traitors. ALLACCIARE LE CINTURE. LASCIATE OGNI SPERANZA, VOI CH'ENTRATE. Worse than the damned, however, were those consigned to the brink of hell, deemed unworthy to enter: *i vigliacchi*, the lukewarm, the neutral, the cowardly, those neither good nor evil, who lived with neither disgrace nor dignity. Well, Johnny would not be one of those.

The fifty-kilometer drive from Malpensa airport into Milan was the dearest cab ride that Johnny had ever taken. Louie, who had brought a sheaf of blue ten-thousand and russet fifty-thousand notes with him, peeled off two fifties, then three tens, *una lauta mancia* for which the driver thanked him profusely.

Louie and Johnny carried only one bag of luggage apiece. Both men believed in traveling light. Each had worn a suit and packed only three shirts and three changes of underwear. Better, they believed, to rely on laundry and dry-cleaning services, or to buy anew, than to be burdened. Still, rather than deprive the uniformed *facchini* of *una mancia*, they allowed them to bear the slight bags in from the street to the desk of the Hotel Principe di Savoia. Their two adjoining suites, overlooking the Giardini Pubblici, cost half a million lire each per night.

"There's a little dump on Via Fatebenefratelli, on the other side of the gardens, near Piazza Cavour," Louis said. "Like I say, it's nothing like this. But I'm a walker, and it's closer to things. Here, the Piazza della Repubblica—it's beautiful, don't get me wrong, but there's nothing here. That's where I'd stay if I had my druthers. No shit. The Hotel Cavour. Last time I stayed there, few years back, a fuckin' bomb went off right outside in the piazza. The papers blamed it on the boys, but I'm tellin' ya, there were guys from Sicily stayin' in that same hotel with me, and I know they weren't about to rattle any of their own bedsprings. That's the thing about bombs over here. Half the time, nobody knows who's doin' what. They even got a word for it now, the science of tryin' to figure out what's behind what. *Dietrologia*, they call it."

"Yeah?" Johnny said. "Sounds like they could take a few lessons from my uncle."

Louie snorted in agreement. "Anyway, here we are and here we gotta be. Somethin' like this, it's like fuckin' diplomacy, like a fuckin' summit meeting. We gotta put up a front, come on like we shit gold. That's business. Our Chink friend, he's doin' the same. He's right across the way here, at the Palace. So let's make the best of it. Which shouldn't be hard, since this joint *is* the best of it."

"We'll make the best of the best."

"Yeah, that's us. Best of the best." Louie peered out over the gardens. "Fuck it," he said. "R.P. Corp.'s pickin' up the tab anyway."

Since the day, not long ago, when Johnny had been appointed a general agent of his uncle's interest in R.P., he had wondered whose initials the shadowy corporation held. He had asked Bill Raymond, the lawyer at Novarca who handled what old Joe called paperwork. Raymond had explained that R.P. had been set up by hired lawyers as a bearer-share company in Holland. Protected by Dutch bank secrecy laws, the principals of R.P. were unknown even to those legal hirelings, who acted under unsigned instructions from Lupino, Novarca's phantom fiduciary company in Paraguay, itself a bearer-share company protected by secrecy laws. It was through fake consultancy contracts between Novarca and its untraceable bearer-share shelf companies that Joe and Tonio and Louie transformed dirty money into clean Novarca income. This, like the currency futures options racket that Novarca and its ghosts also employed, they had learned from some mysterious Sicilian before Raymond's time. But as to whose initials R.P. were, Raymond had not a clue, and it had slipped Johnny's mind to ask his uncle. Now he asked Louie, who smiled in a bemused way, as if the question brought to mind something pleasant, even wonderful, a serendipity long forgotten and unsavored.

"Ain't nobody's initials." Louie grinned. "R.P. is—Jesus, gimme a second here. Yeah. R.P. *Rapere pilam*. It's Cicero. 'Seize the ball and go with it.' " Louie spread his fingers as if his hands were grasping a large sphere. "The ball," he said. "The world. Seize the world. This guy we knew, this Sicilian guy, he used to say that."

Johnny thought of the lions of the Uoglobe symbol that Billy Sing had shown him.

The two men went out and walked south on Via Manin, along the western edge of the gardens, then crossed Piazza Cavour to Via Manzoni.

"Fuck New York," Louie said. "This is the greatest city in the world."

They came to an open ivy-covered gate set back from the street: number 12A. Johnny followed Louie through the courtyard that led to Ristorante Don Lisander. They entered an airy room with mint-green walls, arched white stucco ceiling, and fresh flowers. Vincenzo Raffa awaited them, sitting alone at a table for four with a bottle of Surgiva water. He was a handsome man in his middle forties with wavy hair of dirty blond and gray. At the sound of their footsteps on the tile floor, he looked up, and as they approached him he stood, showing himself to be the shortest of the three. He took Louie's hand in his own, smiling and nodding with slow, natural elegance, as if to say, Yes, it is good to see you once again. Louie introduced Johnny to him as "*un amicu nostru, un uomo bravissimu, u niputi a Don Giuseppe.*"

"*Lieto di conoscer La,*" Johnny said.

"*Per favore—dammi il 'tu,'*" said Vincenzo, asking Johnny to address him in the familiar second person rather than the formal third. In Milan, where Sicilian was often sneered at, Vincenzo spoke Italian, though his native tongue's predilection for avoiding *l*'s and turning *o*'s to *u*'s tended to betray his origin. Reflecting on Johnny's halting unease with the language, he said, "The pleasure is mine." His English was as ill-honed as Johnny's Italian, but he was less inhibited by lack of fluency than Johnny was.

Johnny was able to follow most of what the waiter told them. "What's *lanza*?" he asked Louie and Vincenzo.

"Mario's the only fuckin' Lanza I know," said Louie. "I thought maybe he said *manzo*. Beef."

"I was going to ask you," Vincenzo said.

It turned out to be turkey. "Everywhere else in this country, turkey is *tacchino*," said Vincenzo. "Here it is *lanza*. And they look down their snouts at *siciliano*. You figure it."

"What about *busecca*?" Johnny asked.

Both men sphinctered their lips and made sounds of throaty rapture, and Louie leaned toward Johnny and spoke in a low voice, as if he were discussing *la bisiniss'*. "It's this fuckin' soup," he said. "Tripe, eggs, and cheese. *Unh,*" he added, as if striking a fuck-thrusting to the hilt.

They ordered their food, more water, and a bottle of Barbacarlo. They blew on spoonfuls of their *busecca* and brought the thick broth to their lips. Sounds of carnal delight rose from deep within them.

"*Sembra una pipa sotto la tavola,*" laughed the waiter in passing. Even Johnny understood that one: sounds like you guys are getting sucked off under the table.

"*Meglio di una pipa,*" Johnny answered, less uneasy now. "*Meglio.*" The waiter, Louie, and Vincenzo received his words with enthusiasm and laughter.

They did not speak of business until after the soup was eaten. It was Louie who spoke first.

"*Come sta Don Virgilio?*"

"*Bene. Tutto sommato, molto bene.*" Then Vincenzo reminded himself that Johnny was, as they said in Sicily, *u fardu*, an *italo-americano*. Though Louie too had been born in America, Vincenzo did not think of him as *u fardu*, but rather as some errant native seed borne away by the wind. Inside, he thought, Louie was Sicilian. Perhaps this younger stranger, this new *amicu*, would prove the same within. Knowing Louie, knowing Giuseppe and Tonio, he believed that proof would be forthcoming. "Yes," he said, "Don Virgilio is well. I was with him in April. The feast of San Giorgio. And we have been in touch."

The waiter brought small dishes of pasta in veal sauce. Louie and Vincenzo had poured their second glasses of wine, finishing the bottle. Johnny sipped sparingly on the one glass he would allow himself.

"His blessing in this makes me feel good," Louie said.

"Yes. Of course. But a blessing is often only as good as those whose heads it falls upon."

"How do you feel?"

"*Come un toro.*" Vincenzo grinned. "Like a bull. Like a blessèd bull. And you?"

"For a long time, I felt a lot of things," Louie said. "Now I don't feel. It's time to do, not feel."

"And how about you, Johnny?"

"I feel like a season in hell is a small price to pay to get to the other side of this life."

"And what's on the other side?"

"The freedom to find out. Heaven."

"Well, then," Vincenzo said, raising his glass of wine, "here's to heaven." Louie and Johnny touched his glass with theirs, and the three of them drank.

"Now," Louie said, "let's get down to hell."

The waiter set down before Johnny a plate of stuffed anchovies and a dish of grilled vegetables.

"We go head-to-head tomorrow afternoon," Vincenzo said. "*Alle tre.* Three o'clock. He wants to meet on Tao ground. I'll rendezvous with you beforehand. There's a bar on the corner of Via Giusti and Via Braccio da Montone. It's a block away from where we need to be. I'll meet you there at, let us say, a quarter to three."

"*E carcarazz'?*" And guns? Louie said, lapsing stealthfully into *baccàgghiu*.

"*Al bar,*" Vincenzo said, as if lackadaisically stating the obvious.

"Have you ever met this Ng Tai-hei?" Johnny asked.

Vincenzo shook his head. "But to the *cinesi* here, he is some kind of god. The way they speak of his presence here, it is as if Christ came down off the cross to walk among them."

"And how powerful," Johnny said, "is this Sole Rosso, this Tao?"

"Right now, their power is still dependent on our good will. But that is changing. Many still eat from our hands, but trouble has been growing. We look to New York and we see the future. Their strength, our weakness."

"Well, tell us," Louie said. "The ones who eat from your hands, what have they told you about Ng Tai-hei and his friends there, Asim Sau and Tuan Ching-kuo?"

"As I said, they view these men as gods. We had one highly placed rat, this Cho Sin-wo. He knew these men. He went to Hong Kong to see Ng Tai-hei just the other week. He himself never came back, but his tattooed hand arrived here in a package soon after."

"The head came to New York," Johnny said.

"Yes, I know. It reminds me of that *inno nazionale lesbico*, that lesbian national anthem"—he pronounced these English words as "lesspin nascio-nal ahn-tim"—"'I Fall to Pisses.'"

Johnny laughed. Louie had a blank look on his face.

"That Patsy Cline song," Johnny said.

"Oh," Louie said, still blank.

"So, from him, this Cho guy, what did you hear?" Johnny asked.

"You must remember this. Cho Sin-wo was not an intimate of these men. He was not"—Vincenzo's right hand spiraled heavenward—"he was not of their . . . *altezza*. And of course, there must have been bitter blood; otherwise he would not have come with us. But he did know them. He said they moved as one. They are not like three men who argue and fight among themselves, who harbor different notions and live in caution of betrayal by one another. Their heart is one, he said. They are like a beast with three faces. That is their power. He said they are men of great honor, but only among themselves. Nothing they say beyond themselves, either alone or together, can be taken for truth. Nothing they do can be taken at, how do you say, *valore apparente*. Again, these are one man's words. They sound good, but we must learn for ourselves."

"Well, shit," Louie said, "you could be describing us."

"Perhaps. But do we move as one? We have always been our own worst enemies. Our power has been torn apart from within so often that it is like so many broken twigs awaiting an outsider's match. Do we know of a beast with three faces?"

Johnny thought of his uncle, Tonio, and Louie sitting in that backyard less than forty-eight hours ago.

"It's just another fuckin' card game, like everything else in this world," he said. "They're out to fuck us. We're out to fuck them. What else is new?"

"The stakes," Vincenzo said. "The stakes are new."

"It never ceases to amaze me," Louie said. "Two enemies sitting down and lying to each other. That is how we do things. Not just us, I mean. The world. From the Roman Senate to the United Nations, this is how we do it."

"Maybe it's the only way there is. Maybe it works," said Vincenzo.

The waiter cleared their table, brought their salads.

"But we're not out to fuck them," Johnny said. "It's just business. A proposal of partnership."

"I don't know," Louie said. "Blowin' up half of Chinatown. Heads in the mail. Explodin' niggers. Plane crashes. Poison junk. Is that what these *Wall Street Journal* types mean by 'hostile takeover'? I don't know."

"They're meeting us," Johnny said. "That means something."

"Johnny's right," Vincenzo said. "We called, they came."

"Well, let the games begin," said Louie, signaling the waiter to bring coffee. When the espresso came, they toasted again, with their cups.

"To us," Vincenzo said. "*Buona fortuna.*"

"When we fight, we conquer," Johnny said.

"Ah," said Vincenzo, raising his brows. "*Come Confucio*, eh?"

"*Sì.*" Johnny grinned, surprised.

Louie paid the check, waving away Vincenzo's money. He gestured *finito* with his hand over the four fifty-thousand notes he had placed upon the check, indicating to the waiter that he expected no change. The waiter thanked him warmly, rushed off, and returned with three snifters and a bottle of Marc des Hospices de Beune, the stuff that grappa tried to be. But the men declined. "*La prossima volta,*" Louie told him: next time.

On Via Manzoni, in the afternoon sunlight, Vincenzo embraced both men. "*A domani,*" he said.

The meal and the siesta quietude of the city had a soporific effect on Johnny, but he did not want to sleep.

"You got the right idea," Louie said. "Stay awake, get a good night's sleep tonight, wake up fresh on Milano time. That's what I do. I don't believe in this jet-lag shit. It's like that fuckin' PMS with the broads. All in the fuckin' mind. Just another racket."

While Louie strolled among his favorite clothiers—Truzzi, on Corso Matteotti; Castellani, in Piazza Meda; the custom tailor Caraceni, on Via Fatebenefratelli, where he browsed among bolts of new cloth—Johnny set out on his own, directed by Louie in the general direction of Piazza del Duomo. The two had agreed to meet later at the Banca Masini in Piazza dei Mercanti, which Louie said lay close to the northwest corner of Piazza del Duomo.

Johnny emerged from the Galleria Vittorio Emanuele to the sight of the Duomo, rosy white and magnificent amid the tawdry arcades that surrounded the vast piazza like so many transported segments of Manhattan's Times or Union Square. As he made his way toward it, he was overwhelmed by the unimaginable labor manifest in its phantasmagoria of spires and the thousands of saints and scores of grotesque gargoyles that inhabited its façades. It was not so much beautiful as overpowering, as if in this one immense monument, men had tried to cram and crowd all the wonder of their visions and sweat of their brows. Its setting was sublime, a revelation of the soul's aspirations amid its truer actuality.

Inside, the cathedral seemed even more enormous. Stone pillars bigger than any Johnny had ever imagined seemed to stretch before him in endless rows, rising vertiginously toward the place where the lustrous stained-glass filterings of daylight dwindled and gave way to a world of shadows. He turned toward the rays of cool light drifting strongly through the colored windows. His eyes lingered on the stained-glass crest of the Visconti, which had become the symbol of this city: a great twisting serpent devouring a man.

Here and there as he walked, at altars nearby and in the far reaches, somber figures knelt in prayer or sat silently, cowled in the sepulchral twilight beyond where the soft rays and sighing candlelight reached. Johnny made his way slowly along the northern aisle, stuck a dollar bill into a box marked OFFERTE, lifted a taper, and lighted a candle. He knelt nearby, and he blessed himself. *Caro Dio*, he began silently, letting the Italian come slowly, to express as best he could his plain and simple prayer, for wisdom and strength—*dammi sapienza, dammi forza*—and his vow, both vague and strange: *fare buono*. He knew his Italian was not good, but he felt as if some genetic waterlock had been opened by his surroundings, allowing the subconscious memories of his ancestral tongue, the words and phrases and tones of his childhood's immersion, to rise and flow within him.

An old woman approached and stopped before the heavy bronze gate that separated a reliquary apse from the rest of the cathedral. She raised her hand to the sacred symbol on the gate and held it there as her mouth moved without sound. Then she removed her hand from the holy place and pressed it to her lips. Johnny watched her go on to another holy place along the wall of the cult of the dead, where she raised her hand

anew. *Tutti vogliamo qualcosa*, Johnny said to himself: we all want
something.

He made his way toward the main altar, looked awhile at Saint Carlo
Borromeo, who lay, neither man nor ashes, in his casket of glass. He
wanted to go beneath the ground, to the baptistry where Saint Ambrose
had anointed Saint Augustine, but the baptistry was closed for the
siesta. He thought of making his way to the cathedral roof, to the shadow
of La Madonnina atop the dome, where, it was said, on a good day one
could see the Alps. But he had already seen the Alps today.

Johnny found the Banca Masini, which lay amid dark, twisted
streets nearby. Fixing the location in his mind, he wandered further. On
Via Mazzini he paused to study the group of seedy young men that
milled about outside the Bar Mercurio. Junkies, *tossicomani*. Then,
although he had just eaten, the food in the window of Rosticceria Peck,
on Via Cesare Cantù—tender young chickens and game fowl roasted
and stuffed with sprays of rosemary and sage; bright grilled vegetables;
a cornucopia of delicacies, raw, fried, and marinated—filled him with
an ethereal craving, not quite hunger but a velleity. For weeks he had
dwelled on death. Now, in the luxuriance of herbs that blossomed in
earthy celebration from the assholes and gullets of those burnt-gold and
chestnut birds, he saw life, a reason and a desire to live.

He found himself roaming the halls of the Biblioteca Ambrosiana,
browsing among its treasures: Leonardo's *Codice Atlantico* in its crystal
case, Raphael's sketches, Petrarch's copy of Virgil. In Room V, un-
descried amid the treasures, he came upon a small wood-and-glass
chest. This dusty display, assembled by some forgotten curator at some
forgotten time, contained curios that seemed to have been washed forth
by the tide of some unsaid, unsayable truth: shards of human vanity,
remnants of power and glory, broken by mortality and reduced to brittle,
crumbling butterflies by time. There were three objects in the case.
There was a waxen triptych, several hundred years old, that illustrated
the states of blessedness, purgatorial biding, and damnation with a
woman's face that was in turn serenely beautiful, disquieted, and grue-
somely contorted. Beneath this triptych was a tawny ringlet, identified in
Latin as a lock of Lucrezia Borgia's hair, snipped at the hour of her

death, in 1519. To the left of it, simply labeled *"Guanti Portati da Napoleone a Waterloo 18.6.1815,"* was the pair of chamois gloves worn by Napoleon on the day the wind changed for him.

A few strands of brittle hair, a pair of gloves lingering long after the clutching hands that filled them turned to dust—*potere*'s lingering remains—beneath the portrait of that self-blessed, self-damned thing, the shade of every foolish grasping for eternity, every vain craving for power. To Johnny, it was all there, in that case.

Salvia, sage, he read, was recommended for soothing the grief of death. Its slow-wilting leaves were to be scattered on graves, along with that other sweet-perfumed herb of death, *rosmarinum*, used not only to adorn graves and places of mourning, but as a funerary balm with which to scent the dead. He thought of the birds in the *rosticceria* window.

Irony brought home the awareness of the truth that he had suppressed in the breezy blue light of this day, this day that had severed his umbilical moorings in Brooklyn, that had restored some faint sense of the illimitableness of his long-ago boyish musings. It was the eve of his descent. He was not here to feast. He was here to survive.

Johnny made his way through the revolving safety door of the bank. Louie was already there, sitting with the manager, a tall, well-dressed man in his fifties. Louie introduced Johnny to the banker. On his desk, there was a manila folder. He opened it and withdrew several single-page documents bearing the Novarca and R.P. letterheads and corporate seals. Johnny recognized one of them, the power-of-attorney papers that had been signed by him and two of his uncle's shills, chairman Stanley Krauss and president Bill Raymond. Affixed to it was a letter in Italian from the Dutch law firm that acted as the blind administrator of R.P.'s finances and pink and yellow sheets confirming the transfer and receipt of funds from R.P.'s numbered account at the Bank of the Netherlands: one hundred million dollars converted to ECUs at an exchange rate of one point one five U.S. dollars per ECU, with five days' interest calculated at seven percent per annum compounded daily, plus ECU appreciation of three point two percent against the dollar during that same period, converted to lire at an exchange rate of eighteen hundred and nineteen lire per ECU, plus three days' interest at nine point seven percent per annum, less transaction and conversion fees. The account now stood at one hundred and sixty-three billion, five hundred and eighty-four million, two hundred and twenty-six thousand, six hundred and seventy-seven lire, the equivalent of one hundred and one million, nine hundred and sixty-six thousand, one hundred and four dollars and eighteen cents. The hundred million had picked up nearly two million in little more than a week.

"The guy in the paper's right," Louie said. "It really pays to shop around for rates these days."

The banker gave Johnny a form to fill out and sign, then checked the information and signature against his passport. The banker signed the form himself and had Louie witness it. He then had Johnny sign a four-by-six-inch card that bore the number of the R.P. account. When he took Johnny's passport to the Xerox machine, Johnny turned to Louie.

"Did you have to go through all this too?" he asked.

"Sure."

"I figured we'd use fake ID."

"Are you kiddin'? That's a fuckin' federal rap. Here, home, everywhere. This is legitimate fuckin' business. We're legitimate fuckin' principals."

"What about you, with your fuckin' record?"

"Shit, man, I'm recuperated, rehabilitated, whatever the fuck they call it. Ain't you ever heard of fuckin' Fresh Start? Novarca gets a fuckin' tax break for hirin' good, responsible, rehabilitated workin' stiffs like me. Shit, man, I been rehabilitated for years."

The banker returned Johnny's passport with a smile.

"*Mentre ci siamo, possiamo avere dieci milioni*?" said Louie.

"*Dollari*?" The banker was taken aback.

"*No, no, no*," said Louie with a smile. "*Lire*."

"*Ah. Certo*." The banker relaxed, gave Louie a slip to sign, went to the tellers' area, returned with ten million lire in hundred-thousand notes.

Louie stuffed the receipt in his pocket, counted out half the money, and gave it to Johnny. "Between the hotel, eatin', and walkin' around, this oughta cover us."

"Ask him what the current one-month percent average, spot forward, of the lire against the dollar is," Johnny said, knowing that such a question lay well beyond the realm of his own crude Italian. It turned out that the Italian phrase for "spot forward" was beyond Louie as well. But the banker understood his meaning. He went to his computer and in a few seconds gave Louie an answer.

"Down six point seventeen," Louie said, though Johnny had understood what the banker had said.

Johnny's lips moved as he thought and figured. Nine point two less six point seventeen. That was three point three American.

"Ask him about the ECU, same thing, against the dollar."

The banker turned again to his computer, then to Louie.

"Up four point four," Louie said.

But Johnny's lips were already moving again as he thought and figured some more.

"What could we get on ECUs without buying paper or paying commissions at either end?"

The banker said that much to his regret, things were different here from in Holland.

Johnny wanted to know if perhaps the banker could submerge R.P. funds in one of the bank's own short-term buy-sells.

True, the banker said, there were very lucrative Italian *obbligazioni* denominated in American dollars and ECUs—a dollar-valued 1999 Lavoro Overseas at ten and a quarter percent, an ECU 2000 Italia Repubblica at ten and three quarters. The climate, however, the banker told him, again with regrets, was much too warm.

Johnny smiled. He understood.

Outside, Louie lighted a cigarette and grinned. "Fuckin' guy was lookin' at ya like ya knew what you were talkin' about. Where'd you come up with that shit, anyway?"

"I do my homework," Johnny said. He had been dunking doughnuts with union moneymen for years. He knew all sorts of shit through those swindlers, most of it useless. "I'm lookin' to move up in the corporation. I can see it now: Johnny Di Pietro, Boss of the *Baccaus*."

Louie laughed. "You're startin' to remind me of your fuckin' uncle, sittin' there with that magnifying glass and those pink fuckin' newspapers of his."

They walked north on Via Mengoni to Via Santa Margherita and Piazza della Scala, headed back on Via Manzoni toward the hotel. Near Piazza Cavour there was a store that sold nothing but knives: knives for butchering, knives for eating, knives for work and knives for show, knives for sport and knives for killing. Louie and Johnny stood awhile before the glittering array of the store's window display. Louie indicated a *pugnale*, a gleaming dagger with a four-inch blade, curled hilt, and ivory-inlaid handle.

"In Sicily," he said, "they call that a *crucifissu*, the cross of death."

"Stilettos. They're still legal here?"

Louie nodded, staring at the fancy dagger. He looked to Johnny not so much as if he were admiring it or thinking of buying it as contemplating it, revering it, like those who stood before the *crocifissi* in the candlelight of the Duomo.

"I'm gonna take a look inside," Johnny said. He had always wanted a stiletto. At home he could buy guns, bombs, switchblades, name it. But he had always wanted a stiletto, ever since he was a kid, and he had never been able to get one. They were harder to come by than Uzis or bazookas.

"Don't get lost," Louie said, turning away from the store window, lighting another cigarette. "I'll be over here." He gestured toward the tables of a nearby café.

"*Ha Lei gli stiletti?*" Johnny asked the lady behind the counter. She was not pretty, but she had a sort of sultry air. She smiled, uttered a barely audible "*Sì*," opened a wooden drawer, and brought out two long, thin stilettos, one of gray-black mother-of-pearl, the other of brown bone. She held them in her outstretched palm, extending delicately from the soft flesh of her wrist to her slender fingertips. Johnny lifted the mother-of-pearl, feeling the cool of her skin as he did so. He weighed it in his hand. It felt good, not so light as it looked, the heft of the hidden blade substantial and balanced. He eased the little safety switch. Holding the knife firmly in the clench of his closed fist, he pressed the button with his thumb. He felt the propulsion like a swift, sensuous tremor in the pulse of his fist, and the narrow, razory blade of stainless steel shot suddenly forward with intense coil-powered force from the bore of the shaft: four inches of shining, mercuric Judgment Day. He pressed again with his thumb. The blade vanished as abruptly as it has appeared.

"Permesso?" Johnny said, gesturing to a small pile of corrugated cardboard packaging material on the floor behind her. As she gave him what he wanted, it seemed to Johnny that she intuited his purpose. He folded the corrugated packing into a many-layered thickness of perhaps two inches. Holding this wadding, compressed and tight, in his left hand, and with the stiletto in his right, he pressed the end of the knife to it and released the blade with his thumb. The blade shot through the thick wadding as if it were not there.

"È l'uso che intenderar, senza dubbio?" Your intended use, no doubt? the saleslady said, grinning in her sultry way.

"Sì." He grinned in turn. *"S'intende."*

The price was high, a hundred and ten thousand lire. *"Madreperla,"* she reminded him: mother-of-pearl. He paid her and put the knife in his pocket.

At the café, Johnny told Louie to go on to the hotel without him. He wanted to wander again by himself.

"Don't get lost," Louie told him again. "We'll have an early, quiet night tonight. We'll go to Bice. Best seafood risotto in town."

"Sounds good."

As he wandered, there were areas that reminded him of New York. Via Monte Napoleone was like a distillation of Fifth in the upper fifties, Madison in the sixties. Via della Spiga was a downtown, West Broadway variation. But Louie was right, Johnny thought: fuck New York.

Roving through these strange streets, Johnny began to understand what Louie was talking about. Every year, the better parts of New York looked more and more like a nondescript rundown mall. Ghetto-burger, designer-jean, and sneaker franchises had taken the place of small shopkeepers, draining the city of its character, transmuting it into a grease stain, an ugly Plasticville of meaningless noise and sterile pre-fabricated façades and graffiti. Here, Johnny reflected, the ancient and the new struck a balance. The streets were clean and lush with trees, and those who walked them were white and moved more with serene well-being than with anxiety and hostility. This cosmopolitan city, which dated to the third century, appeared to be all that provincial New York had failed to become in the paltry few years of its shining and disintegration. That is, a principality of civilization, a place that possessed a tone and a texture deeper than that of garbage in the streets and the maggoty feeding frenzy of postliterate, Pavlovian consumerism. And the broads here—forget about it.

He walked through the public gardens toward the hotel. He remembered the stiletto in his pocket, the soft, cool touch of that salesgirl's skin, the lilt of her lips. That's what he needed. Blowjob therapy. But in the end, he knew, he wanted it all. That was his trouble, he thought. He still believed, not consciously but in the well of his discontent, in miracles, in gods and goddesses. It was not life's bleak attrition that shrouded him in dysthymia and brooding. It was his sense of deprivation, of his exclusion from these richer dimensions of unarticulated imaginings. Though he had dedicated his life to destroying what meager magic life held, his vague discontent posited the existence of some greater magic, some elusive *magna magica* of the breezes.

For a moment, here and now, this late-afternoon breeze was magic enough. But the breeze turned chill with thought. Why had he come so far to inaugurate the season of his death?

TWENTY

It was rare that Bob and Mary made love in the morning. But he had wakened today with a tumescence that was more than urethral, to the sound of his wife's drowsy purring. In her pregnancy, it somehow seemed more than sex, seemed a communion with something miraculous as well, the sweet mystery of which, theirs and theirs alone, brewed in her belly.

The lingering pleasure of that wakening had left Marshall smiling in the street, late though he was, on his way to work. Now Peter Wang's words turned his subtle smile to a grin.

"I'm serious," Wang was saying, as the two men shared coffee in Marshall's office. Upon Marshall's desk lay this morning's increase in the accruing bureaucratic detritus of fruitless investigations into last week's events and reports of rising death tolls among those still opening their veins in desperation. "Really. If we ever figure out who's at the bottom of this, we ought to recruit them. They've effectively done in one week what we've been trying to do ever since everybody's favorite president created us from dust. They've put a stranglehold on the biggest heroin market in America."

"Listen to you. Wang the Terrible."

"Hell, between you and me, you know I'm right."

"We're not a vigilante group. Contrary to what some of these Hollywood cowboys around here seem to believe."

"No. But we're public servants. This is tax-friendly justice."

"Whoa. Tax-friendly justice. I like that."

"Forget the cost of administration, the cost of investigation, the cost of prosecution. Look what it costs to keep one of these monkeys in prison. Twenty, thirty grand a year."

"More. It's gone up. For Riker's Island now, bottom of the barrel, it's over thirty-five grand a year per inmate."

"That's justice? No. It's subsidy. Show me one decent person in this country, young or old, rich or poor, crippled or blind, that the government ever shelled out thirty-five grand a year to keep in room and board. That's still more than most people in this country make. It's a disgrace. That big riot years ago up in Attica—it was over bad TV reception. They complain about overcrowding. And people listen. It's insane."

"Well, if this conversation were taking place in a public forum, I would remind you that according to a recent study by the Rand Corporation, that thirty-five-grand-a-year felon left out on the street costs society an average of four hundred and thirty thousand dollars in damage for the same year. So, all things considered, it's a bargain."

"This isn't a public forum."

"No, it's not."

"So."

"So I say kill the cocksuckers."

"Looks like that's what they're doing for us."

"Believe me. Mark my words. It won't look that way for long."

"So we'll still have a paycheck." Wang smirked. "Good news all around."

Marshall took a call on line three. The caller was an agent he had assigned to the 187 Mott Street investigation. Caruso or some such shit was playing in the background.

"Guess what I just saw," the caller said.

"A wop."

"Yeah."

"That's good. That's real promotion material. Is that the full extent of your report, or what?"

"Not just any wop. A blast from the past."

"Come on, here. Narrow it down or get back to your *cannolo* there. Wang and I are in the middle of curing the world of its ills."

"Remember Paul Como?"

"Shit. You're kidding. I figured that was one guy we'd never see again. Dead, I figured. Or a thousand miles away. Shit," he repeated. "Are you sure?"

"It's him, all right. A little older, a little grayer. But it's him."

"He's got something to do with Mott Street?"

"No. I mean, I don't think so. I just passed him in the street. And guess who he was with?"

"Another wop."

"Joe Di Pietro. They came out of the club on Hester Street together, got into a chauffeured Mercedes."

"When was this?"

"Just now. A few minutes ago. Eleven-forty, quarter to."

"Shit." Marshall's tone was bemused. He himself had closed the investigation into Paul Como's disappearance several years ago.

"I thought you'd be interested."

"Yeah. I am. Thanks."

Wang had heard only Marshall's side of the conversation. It had intrigued him, and he was pleased, when Marshall put down the receiver, that Marshall chose to share it with him.

"You know about INSLAW, right? Michael Riconosciuto, that whole mess?"

"I was only here for the tail end of it."

"But you know the story."

Wang did not want to appear ignorant, but he had learned from experience, especially when dealing with Marshall, that ignorance was something it was better to admit than to conceal. Besides, there was no shame in his lack of awareness. The case had been winding down when he moved to the agency from the Drug Enforcement Task Force, and his attention, as it should have, lay elsewhere.

"It's something we're not proud of," Marshall said. "If the whole truth ever came out, we'd probably be as popular as the president who made us. There are two versions, the public version, which won in court, and the real version. I guess you'd prefer the real one.

"The whole mess is almost as old as the agency itself. Back in the seventies, the Law Enforcement Assistance Administration funded the development of a software system called PROMIS, the Prosecutor's Management Information System. The developer was a nonprofit corporation known as INSLAW, the Institute for Law and Social Research. By 1980 the system was in use in selected U.S. attorneys' offices across the country. In '81, when Carter shut down the LEAA, INSLAW converted to for-profit status so it could commercially market a new version of the system, called Enhanced PROMIS. Early in '82, the government awarded INSLAW a ten-million-dollar, three-year contract to implement the earlier, public-domain version of PROMIS at ninety or so U.S. attorneys' offices throughout America and its territories. In 1983, under an amendment to the original contract, the government began installing Enhanced PROMIS as well. Once the government had the enhanced system, it began playing dirty. It claimed that since PROMIS had been developed under government funding, INSLAW did not legally have proprietary rights to its enhanced successor. Meanwhile, PROMIS was distributed to the FBI, the CIA, and us. It was a great program. Ran on UNIX, VAX/VMS, all of 'em.

"As INSLAW began the laborious process of taking the government to court for theft of its Enhanced PROMIS system, copies of the software were sent out to Wackenhut-Cabazon, on the Cabazon Indian Reservation, near Palm Springs. They do a lot of national security work out there, a lot of biological and chemical warfare stuff. God knows what else. At Cabazon, Enhanced PROMIS was to be secretly, quote, refitted, unquote. The new, altered system was to be mass-produced and sold illegally to foreign nations. The purpose of this refitting operation was to implant a hidden source code, an intelligence back door, within the program whereby the FBI, CIA, and DEA would be able, by computer, to surreptitiously access and monitor the classified intelligence of government agencies abroad. The man entrusted with this refitting was

Michael Riconosciuto, a shady character whose clandestine involvement with the government seemed to go way back. He was a maverick. A computer master, a scientist. His father supposedly was a business partner of Nixon's. Also involved was another shady government computer whiz by the name of Paul Como.

"PROMIS was sold to Canada, Israel, Singapore, Iraq, Egypt, and Jordan. Interpol in France, the Israeli Mossad. Through this rigged system, we were hooked into them all. Through Eurame Trading, one of our proprietary companies, in Nicosia, the DEA sold PROMIS to drug agencies in Cyprus, Pakistan, Syria, Kuwait, and Turkey. All told, PROMIS ended up as a Trojan horse in something like eighty-eight different countries. It was unreal. They were unwittingly paying us to spy on them.

"In the fall of '89, INSLAW actually won an eight-million-dollar district court judgment against the Department of Justice. But the feds took the case to the U.S. Court of Appeals. In 1990, Riconosciuto, for some reason, decided to tell what he knew to INSLAW, and he provided a sworn statement in early '91. The government saw that statement coming. We called in our man in Nicosia, the same DEA agent who ran Eurame and the PROMIS sales, and reassigned him to intelligence in Washington State, where Riconosciuto lived. His noble mission was to manufacture a narcotics case against Riconosciuto, to destroy his credibility concerning the rigging and covert sale of PROMIS to foreign governments. We went looking for Paul Como, to try to get him to contradict Riconosciuto, or at least ensure he didn't follow in Riconosciuto's footsteps. We never found him.

"Riconosciuto made his sworn statement on March 21, the first day of spring. Eight days later, our agents seized him for possession and distribution. In May, on narrow jurisdictional grounds, the court of appeals reversed the decision against the Department of Justice."

"I remember the Riconosciuto bust," Wang said. "I remember a lot of raised eyebrows and mean faces in the halls. I had my suspicions, but I never knew it was an out-and-out setup. Wasn't there some sort of fishy suicide involved too?"

"Danny Casolaro. The writer. He figured out the big picture. The

PROMIS operation was part of a web. Remember, none of the sales were official. Rumor has it, the money was funneled to a few guys high up in Justice and their friends. Remember Ed Meese's pal Doc Brian, the guy who owns UPI? Friends like that. The funneling was done through BCCI. The Iran-contra affair, that publicity stunt of Reagan's that everybody got so bent out of shape about?"

"Business as usual, I figure."

"Yes and no. See, there was more than arms involved. PROMIS was part of that deal, and the BCCI brokered it. In terms of drug intelligence, Iran is a country that's never leveled with us. In less than twenty years, they go from being the world's primary opium source to executing thousands of drug dealers. They tell us they're drug dealers, anyway. Meanwhile, there's maybe two hundred tons of opium coming out of there every year. Look at Gwadar. Obviously, something like this, a Trojan horse, it's great for us.

"Anyway, you see what I mean about a web. I'm sure the big picture wasn't known to more than two or three of the big guns at Constitution and Tenth. Meese and whoever. But Danny Casolaro, he figured it out somehow. He was writing a book about what he knew. *The Octopus*, he called it. He had also told his friends and family that if something happened to him, they should not believe it was by accident. The book was almost done, and in the summer of '91, three months after the court of appeals reversed the district court's verdict, Casolaro was at a motel in West Virginia, waiting to meet a final source. He was upbeat, his family said, excited by what he was digging up. Who that supposed source was, we'll never know. Danny Casolaro was found in the bathtub with each of his wrists slashed seven times, along with a brief suicide note. The only manuscript of the book, along with his notes, was missing.

"The death was ruled a suicide, and the Judiciary Committee assigned to investigate and issue a congressional report on the INSLAW affair chose not to include it in its formal investigation. The report came out in September of '92, along with congressional requests to have an independent prosecutor assigned to investigate the matter anew. But

Bill Barr, the attorney general, officially shut the book on it for us a month later."

"Where's Riconosciuto now?"

"Still in the can, last I heard."

"And what about Casolaro's book?"

"Vanished. Like Como. Until now. Como, that is."

"What do you think he's doing downtown?"

"Rubbing elbows with Joe Di Pietro. Whatever that means."

"Di Pietro's a dinosaur. A fossil."

"Maybe he's taking a computer course, wants to do some temp work in his golden years. Speaking of which, do me a favor. Dig out whatever we and OC have on him. Get on Joint Intelligence, go through EPIC, see what's there. White Hat, the works. The rest of the unholy three, too. Pull 'em all—him, Tonio Pazienza, Louie Bones. I forget his real name. Check the alias files."

"It seems like we've got better things to do."

"Maybe, maybe not."

"Is this Como that big a deal?"

"He's nothing. A curiosity."

"And Di Pietro. If I find anything that's not yellow and brittle, it'll probably be a blood-pressure reading or a down payment on a plot. That's two nothings. Here we are in the middle of what you call an apocalypse, and you're worried about some computer punk and an out-to-pasture *padron'*."

"Look, number-one son, I'm the boss here, remember?"

"Yeah. For this twelve yards of these three floors, you're the boss."

"No modifiers, please."

"I just want to get inside your mind here. I want to know how bosses think. I have aspirations, you know."

"Okay. Here's how I think. I haven't thought of Di Pietro in years. I haven't thought of Como in years. A guy I assign to investigate one piece of this puzzle calls up out of the blue to tell me he's seen the two of them. It's got nothing to do with what he's supposed to be doing, he tells me. He just thought I might want to know. Well, I didn't want to know.

But now I do. This Como, he was on the edge of a web when he vanished. Maybe he's on the edge of another web now. And I'm sitting here, and this pile of shit keeps growing but it doesn't lead anywhere. That's how I think. It's as simple as that."

"You call that thinking?"

"No. I call it an order. Now git."

Old Giuseppe and young Paul Como sat in a restaurant on Carmine Street. Until forty minutes or so ago, they had never met. Como had been recommended to Joe by a friend who knew a friend who knew a kid who not only had done dirty work for the feds, but had written the spread-making program used by one of the three big sports-book services in Vegas. The kid—kid, shit; he was in his late thirties—was Paul Como, currently free-lancing, under the name Paul Conte, as a covert audit consultant in Texas, where he was bored stiff. He was all right, it was said; he played alone.

It was the feds who had originally fitted him with fake credentials, name of Paul Compton, after he had set up Danny Casolaro for them. With one hand above the table, they had made a pretense of having him sought out by Justice, and with one hand under the table, they had taken care of him. Whoever they were, that is. He still had not figured that part out. He had burned the credentials they had given him—fuck them, whoever they were—took the name Conte instead, after the actor, whom he had always liked. Altering the dummy government recommendations they had given him was easy, a mere matter of pasteup and recopying.

He had preferred the Jews and *paisani* in Vegas to the feds in D.C. and Cabazon. They were a better, cleaner class of people. This Joe here —"Can that Don Di Pietro shit," Joe had told him at the club; "I'm not about to call you mister, so you call me Joe"—he was computer-illiterate, but he was all right. No bullshit like with the feds, and not nearly as scary as he had been led to believe by his friend in Dallas.

"If you're as hungry as you say you are," the old man said, "get the veal chop. Me, I love the food here, but I never eat the meat."

"The meat's no good?"

"I didn't say that. I said I don't eat it."

"Why not?"

"He gets it from these Genoese pricks on Bleecker Street. They sold me a bad pig one year, those Genoese fucks."

The day manager, who had greeted Joe warmly, brought a bottle of Fiuggi and a bottle of Brunello di Montalcino.

"Tell you truth," Joe relented. "I eat the pork here. I love it. All New York, only one guy makes it better. Guy on Bedford Street. And he ain't a restaurant, he's just a guy. The veal chop, too. The veal chop here is delicious. No, I tell you, the meat is good. But that *porcullin'* those fucks sold me, I'll never forget. Smelled like scorched nigger hair, tasted the same. *Guastu.* That was when they were on the corner of Jones, years ago. Should have put a brick through that fucking window."

"Did you tell them about it?"

"No. I hit them where it hurt. The purse. Never spent another penny there. You wanna hurt a fucking Genoese, that's the way to do it. They're worse than fucking kikes." He took a drink of water. "I think they're fucking Genoese, anyway. Then again, any wop in the fucking food racket, they're all like fucking *ammazacrist'*."

The younger man ordered braised fennel with Parmesan and the veal chop. Joe ordered an antipasto of fig and prosciutto, asparagus vinaigrette, and tuna carpaccio, a salad, and fettucine with mushrooms, oil, and garlic.

"I want to fuck up a computer system," the old man said.

"Take an ax to it. Never fails."

"Yeah. Then I wouldn't need you."

"What exactly do you want to do?"

"Fuck it up," the old man repeated. "Fix it so that it screws everything up. Loses its memory. Mixes apples and oranges."

"A logic bomb."

"That sounds about right. Can you do it?"

"Fucking it up, planting a logic bomb, is easy. It's getting into the system, getting past its security, that's hard. What sort of system are you talking about?"

"The DEA."

"That's high-security shit. But I know a little about it."

"Can it be done?"

"The DEA system is part of JICC, the Joint Intelligence Control Council network, which comes out of EPIC, the El Paso Intelligence Center, in Texas. The DEA, customs, the Coast Guard, they're all hooked into Joint Intelligence. And Joint Intelligence, the FBI, everything, they're all networked into EPIC. Even local law enforcement throughout the country, they're hooked into it through the White Hat telecom program."

"I admire your knowledge. But none of what you say means anything to me. I just want to know, can it be done?"

"I imagine they're still using Digital hardware. VMS operating system. That's high-security stuff, much tougher than UNIX, that sort of shit." Como ate some fennel, drank some wine. He still had the Enhanced PROMIS source code. The software for domestic agencies, of course, had never been refitted with back doors, but if he could somehow break in, he could achieve I/O access. That would enable him to modify the system's database, to do anything. Anything. But how could he sneak in, past security and encryption?

The old man saved the fig and prosciutto for last. It was his favorite.

"Do you know what social engineering is?" Como said.

"Sounds like something to do with welfare, giving niggers money, shit like that."

"It's what we're doing now. Talking. Bullshitting. If I want to know something and I con it out of you, that's social engineering. We're all social engineers."

"Something new to put on my résumé."

"Exactly. Anyway, the DEA's not part of a public network. You can't just get on a modem and work your way in through the Net or something like that. You probably need their restricted dial-up number and a high-level password. That's where social engineering comes in." Como paused, took a sip of wine, a sip of water. "You know anything about heroin?" he asked.

"A little."

"Some people, they fall in love with it, they'll do anything to get it."

"That's what I hear."

"There's this kid, used to work for me in Dallas. He went out to work for EPIC. Real low-level shit. He wouldn't have the key to the men's room, let alone privileged code. He was a junkie when he worked for me, and he just got worse and worse. They let him go, but he's still close to one of the system-control managers. A lovely couple. He's about twenty-four, skin and bones, looks like he's going on fifty. The system-control guy is about fifty-eight, wears a corset and a toup'. A marriage made in heaven. Anyway, any password will do. I can get that toup's password for a couple grams of dope. Social engineering. From there it's just a hop, skip, and a jump into the DEA's source code."

"Then you can fuck it up."

"With ease."

"Why go through all this trouble? The junk and the fruits, I mean. I can feed you guys with passwords."

"You can?" Como was incredulous.

"What do you think, this world is on the level? Of course I can. You ever hear of a guy named Eddie Schow? He was a big shot in the DEA intelligence unit, Miami. They kicked his ass out for selling confidential files. Jose Villar, another special agent down there—him and a cop were in cahoots, selling dope and protection. Danny Bunnel, Al Inglerias. You don't know these names, hey? How about Al Mitrone, you ever hear of him? Another big shot, FBI man. Caught him selling something like ninety pounds of cocaine. Tommy O'Brien, another one. DEA staff coordinator, commendations up the ass. Got busted for dealing dope. How about Bobby Peist? Bobby One-Leg. Big-deal cop. Sold police intelligence to the boys for years before they caught him. Look at the Seventy-third Precinct over in Brownsville, the Thirtieth up in Harlem. All running their own fucking dope rings. And look at this big elite unit here, this New York Drug Enforcement Task Force. Supposed to be the *crème de la crème*, the best officers from the DEA, the NYPD, the state police, some bullshit like that. Three of them busted for dealing junk. The fucking supervisor, another donkey named O'Brien, the police commissioner even kicked *his* ass out. Said he didn't know what was going on with these three right under his nose. Guess where they dumped him? The Organized Crime Control Bureau. You believe that? Let me tell you. In my day, I've had more fucking dirty bull mick cocksuckers than stand-up guys come crawling to me for favors. I've wiped my fucking boots on all of them. Believe me, my friend. There's more scum inside the law than outside it. You want passwords, I'll get you fucking passwords."

"The thing is," Como said patiently, plainly, "they're dead passwords. A guy gets caught, they kill his password. They're changed all the time, anyway, passwords. Once every few months, whenever. It's all part of security."

Joe reflected that common sense should have told him as much. He came from a world where things were less mutable. He knew the heart and soul of things, but not the frills, which seemed to change faster and faster as time went on. A few years ago, for Christmas, Johnny had given him a videocassette machine, probably swag. He had never hooked it up. Why should he? He would never use it. He would never use any of this new shit that seemed to do nothing but make the world noisier and busier and emptier.

"Well, get to work on it," he said. "How soon can you be ready? I want to have everything set and ready to go when I give the word. Could be a week from now, could be a month from now."

"A week is tight. It'll take me at least a few days to get the password. I can shoot for it, but I can't promise it."

"Do your best." Joe removed a thick folded wad of hundred-dollar bills from his left pocket. Holding the money close to his belly, he counted out thirty of the bills. "Here," he said, folding the thirty bills in his right palm and passing them across the table, simultaneously returning the remainder to his pocket with his left. "Take this now. That should take care of your trip here. Those grams. A few dollars walking-around money. You do the job, you get paid."

"How much?"

"What do you think is fair? And fuck that social-engineering shit, just give me a price."

"It's a federal rap."

"Not getting caught is part of the job."

"What did you have in mind?"

"Ten grand."

"I get that for five-day system audits."

"Maybe you do, maybe you don't. This doesn't sound like five days' work. Hands on, I mean. Besides, it's tax-free. And you already made a few bucks on that trey."

Como said nothing. The two men ate and drank. "At this point," Joe said, "all I have to do is send somebody from Dallas out to El Paso, look for that loving couple. You yourself said, once you get that password, it's a breeze."

"Only because I've got the fucking source code."

"Look. Let's get this shit over with so we can enjoy the meal. I'll ask you what I asked you before. What do you think is fair?"

"That source code is worth money. I don't expect you to understand that, but it is. I could sell that code for big bucks. After this, it won't be worth a dime. They'll go to a new program."

The waiter brought Joe's pasta and Como's veal chop.

"Jesus," Como said, looking at it.

"I told you it was big." Joe took a drink of wine. "Now give me a fucking price so we can relax and eat this shit."

The younger man was intimidated. "Thirty grand," he said.

"I'll split the difference. Twenty."

"Twenty-five."

"Only because my food is getting cold, you social-engineer bastard."

The two men raised their wineglasses to seal their bargain.

"*Cent' ann'*," the younger man said.

"At my age," said Joe, grinning, "we say *centun'*."

Como was happy, for twenty-five thousand was the price he had had in mind when he said thirty. And Joe was pleased, since he himself would have gone as high as fifty.

Diane Di Pietro spent the afternoon at the laundromat with her girlfriend Jill from up the block.

"Walk away from it," Jill was saying. "Just walk away." She was an attractive woman, in a grisette sort of way: mid-thirties, dark-haired with a single forelock of gray, which, as she said, many men found attractive. Diane believed that this forelock, along with her horn-rimmed glasses, helped to cultivate Jill's "loose-librarian look." She liked what she called intelligent men. To her, intelligent men were those who went to movies and could pronounce all sorts of things on menus. Intelligent men had good jobs, careers, and spoke to her. She never tired of telling about Jewish lawyers she had been with; the only problem was, they all were married.

Just walk away. Divorced people, Diane thought, were always trying to get others divorced.

"He's your husband, and you don't even know where he is," Jill went on. "That's absurd."

"He's working."

"Yeah. They're all working." Jill rose and poured Ultra Snuggle fabric-softener into the rising rinse water of the machine nearest her.

"Look," Diane said. "Let's drop it. I want to enjoy my time. Why don't we go out to eat later, go to a movie or something?"

"Let's go play. We'll find some cute boys, let 'em treat us like the goddesses we are."

"Oh, stop it. Johnny would kill me."

"Jesus, Diane, that's a great way to live. In fear."

"Look. What's right is right."

"Yeah. I'm sure he feels the same way. When's the last time he made you feel good? When's the last time he built up your self-esteem? Come on, already. Live for yourself. If you don't breathe, you die."

If you don't breathe, you die. Really, now. Jill was forever reading these silly little paperbacks with breath and bridges and passages and women who humped wolves or whatever in their titles. And she was so anti-this and anti-that; so anti-pornography, for instance, that Diane wondered what she did in bed. Why is it, she had once asked Jill, that in those cultures throughout history where pornography has been most suppressed, women have been most oppressed? God, Jill had said without answering her question, he's really got you indoctrinated, hasn't he? Actually, the thought had been her own, though she did agree with

Johnny—back before they seemed to disagree on everything sheerly on principle—that the best sex was a marriage of pornography and purity.

"I'm breathing," said Diane.

"Are you?"

"Is that going to be it with you for the rest of your life? Boys, boys, boys? What happens when the rest of your noggin matches that silver strand?"

"I don't plan on being single forever, if that's what you mean."

"So. You liked being married."

"Not to Dwayne."

"Well, look, do you want to do something tonight, or what? I'm a free woman."

"Yeah, you're free, all right. Just relax. It's early. You're not even in the drier yet, you're still on spin."

On her way home from the laundromat, Diane bought a bottle of Beaujolais, something she never would have done when Johnny was around. For several years now, mindful of his drinking problem, she had kept no wine or liquor at home, though she missed her occasional glasses of evening wine. It was one of the small sacrifices she had made that Johnny never seemed to appreciate.

She put away her laundry, took a long bath, showered, and put on her robe. She poured herself a glass of wine. It was a fantasy of hers that her husband kept a secret diary, which she would discover and in which she would find the truth of all that puzzled and tormented her about the distance that lay between them. It was a fantasy that swept away, however briefly, her own sense of responsibility to find the truth within her. This imagined secret diary would tell her to love him or to hate him. But of course there was no diary. As she sipped her wine—a sweet luxury to do so, here, in quiet, in her robe—she browsed along the rows of her husband's books. Most of them were old, from the days when she first knew him. In those days, he had laughed and read and drunk and brooded. The laughter had ceased, then the reading. Then there was only the drinking and the brooding.

But he had kept these books through the years. Maybe there were clues there. His reading had not been rooted strongly in the Christian millennium. True, Dante was there. But beside him were Homer, Hesiod, Horace, and Virgil. She drew down the only book whose title alluded to love, the *Ars amatoria* of Ovid. Leafing through it, she found a passage her husband had noted in ink: "It is expedient that gods should exist, and, as it is expedient, let us deem that gods exist." She looked to the left; the original Latin was printed on the facing page: *Expedit esse deos, et, ut expedit esse putemus.* All that English to say those eight simple words of Latin. She looked further for traces of her husband's hand. There: *Si sapitis, solas impune puellas.* The English: "If you are wise, cheat only women."

Well, fuck you too, Johnny dearest. This was supposed to be poetry? This was the shit Emily Dickinson was up against? Fucking wops. She shoved the book back in its place, poured some more wine, and looked at the floor-scrapers of Caillebotte. The hair above her genitals was soft and still damp. She ran her fingers absently through it, let the breeze from the open window hit it.

The single sheet was a photocopy of a routine report from the Narcotics Bureau CID unit of the Royal Hong Kong Police. If it had not slipped to the floor, Bob Marshall likely would not have noticed it until days from now. His growing preoccupation with the black multifaceted glass of recent events was such that the ritual of his morning had been disrupted and the mundane flow of paperwork increasingly neglected. In fact, he was about to have his assistant go through the mounting mass to cull, collate, and summarize for him.

Returning the report to its place atop the pile, Marshall let his eyes graze its surface. In conjunction with the Royal Hong Kong Marine Police and the Organised and Serious Crimes Group, the Narcotics Bureau had intercepted and confiscated a fleet of heroin-smuggling trawlers operating out of Hainan. . . . In Beijing, Minister of Public Security Tao Siji once again openly acknowledged that the mainland police maintained ties to the Hong Kong triads: "Our public security organs have broad links and ties with different strata in society, including such groups," he said. "As long as these people are patriotic, as long as they are concerned with Hong Kong's prosperity and stability, we should unite with them." In response, T. K. Chan, chief superintendent of the Hong Kong Royal Police, issued a statement that whatever China's view, Hong Kong would continue its war against the triads. . . . More than two high-ranking triad figures were photographed attending a birthday banquet for Thai shadow-boss Tuan Ching-kuo at the Man Wah restaurant. Neither Asim Sau nor Ng Tai-hei, Shan Chu of the 14K Triad, were among them. Ng had been observed leaving Hong Kong for Milan, Italy, the previous evening. . . . Two Narcotics Bureau agents were killed, three wounded, in a gun battle with traffickers at the air-cargo terminal at Kai Tak Airport.

To Marshall, the report was unremarkable, business as usual, and he thought no more of it. He was still trying to trace the source of the poison junk. Fear in the streets was such that the price of spitback methadone had shot from twenty to forty bucks. The area outside the clinic at 125th Street and Park had turned into a twenty-four-hour bazaar. Warm bottles of stolen meth, undiluted by the saliva and wiles of other junkies, were going for fifty dollars and more. Purple thirty-milligram and pink sixty-milligram MS Contin controlled-release morphine-sulfate tablets were selling for five and ten dollars each. Among those whose desperation was greater than their fear, there were still scattered deaths, two and three, sometimes five and more a day. Agents and cops had scoured the streets, trying to trace the trail of each toxic dime from the victim to the streetjack to the runner to the local seller. Most runners were not users, and while there had been several deaths at streetjack and local seller levels, there had been none higher up, in that broad middle marketplace of kilos and ounces that existed between the big dealers and the two-bit pretenders. The local sellers' sources were varied. Someone, somehow, had slipped killer bags into street batches destined for local sellers throughout the city. Now Marshall had rechanneled his search, telling his agents to track down local sellers and brand names whose junk had been unaffected by the plague. Maybe their middle-market sources knew something. Maybe it was one of those sources, or one of the big dealers above them, who lay at the heart of it all.

Peter Wang came to him toward the end of the day, holding a sheaf of perforated printout in his hand. He sat near Marshall's desk, waited for him to get off the telephone.

"Your fossilogical report, as requested, sir."

Marshall smiled. Incredibly, the smile he had left home with this morning had survived the day.

"Giuseppe Di Pietro, FBI number 824437, will be eighty-one in December. Though he continues to consort with known criminals and frequent all the old familiar places, his activities in OC circles for the past ten years have been classified more as social than as active. His name has not appeared in criminal legal proceedings since two federal racketeering trials in 1986. One trial, which sent his old pal Tony Salerno away for a hundred years, ended in acquittal for him. The other ended in acquittal for both him and James Faenza, a.k.a. Jimmy Black, then, as now, president of the Waste Removers of Greater New York. Through his Novarca Corporation, Di Pietro continues to control a sizable share of the city's billion-dollar-a-year private trash hauling industry as well as a recycling concern presently involved in major city contracts and international trade. Though his FBI case file is technically still classified as active, no new sensitive material regarding him has been recorded since 1987, nor has there been any investigation into his affairs since then. Our file on him, inactive for fifteen years, shows his last suspected narcotics trafficking activity to have been in the mid-seventies, although his name in the years since then has shown up sporadically in interoffice and interagency queries and communiqués. Maintains residences both on Sullivan Street and on the Upper East Side.

"Antonio Pazienza, FBI number 753902, age eighty-three, now living on Evergreen Avenue in the Old Town section of Staten Island. No known criminal activities since being released from Otisville in 1982 after serving nine years of a thirty-year sentence for murder and racketeering. He is believed to be suffering from senility—he has the medical papers to prove it, anyway—and is presently under the care of a live-in nurse."

"I bet we can gauge the senility by the looks of the nurse."

"No doubt. As for Luigi D'Argento, a.k.a. Louie Bones, FBI number 899732, age sixty, he too has been a good boy since being released from stir twelve years ago. Like Pazienza, he is a principal with Di Pietro in Novarca. He currently lives with Maria, his wife of many years, on Castleton Avenue in Staten Island. Not this week, though."

"Why not?"

"Late-flash State Department blip on Joint Intelligence. Routine passport activity. The least-fossilized member of your unholy three has journeyed abroad."

"I knew that," Marshall lied with a teasing grin.

"Well, then, where is he? Tell me that."

"Milan."

Wang looked at him. "I suppose you know who he's traveling with, too."

Marshall nodded, still grinning.

Wang put the sheaf of printout on an open corner of Marshall's desk. "Goodbye," he said and turned to leave.

"Wait a minute, Pete." Marshall was no longer grinning. "Tell me. Who?"

"John Di Pietro. The old man's nephew."

"What do we know about him?"

"Not much. He's in his thirties, lives in Brooklyn with his wife, Diane. An up-and-coming force in garbage, you might say. Here and there with the union. Several two-bit arrests over the years. Assault. D and D. Kid stuff."

Marshall thought silently for a moment, then his lingering smile returned. "When age and youth conspire . . . ," he mused. "Seems like there'd be a sagacious clause that should fall right in there."

"Not the way things have been going around here."

"Oh, I don't know about that, partner. Could be our luck is about to change. Call Hong Kong. Get a passport number on Ng Tai-hei. Look here first. Maybe it's on file. Then call our attaché in Rome. Give him the three names and numbers. Have him notify the Italian prefect in Milan. We want to locate these three and try to moniter any contact between Ng and the other two."

"You didn't tell me Ng Tai-hei was there as well."

Marshall told him about the sheet of paper—that if it had not fallen from his desk, he might not have known for days, if at all.

"Do you think it could be coincidence, them being in Milan at the same time?"

"Sure. But I doubt it. Besides, we've chased less promising phantoms. Especially lately."

"Strange things blossom."

"Huh?"

"The missing clause. When youth and age conspire . . ."

"Where's that from?"

"The master."

"Confucius?"

"Warner Oland."

"I must have missed that one."

"Forget about it. No matter how many times they rerun it, you'll never understand our people."

TWENTY-ONE

Johnny's morbid foreboding was exorcised by the light of day. But it was difficult for him to dispel the nervous anxiety with which he awoke. His pulse had seemed to increase with consciousness, his stomach fluttered, and he had no appetite but to smoke. It was not an altogether bad feeling, not a feeling of dread or apprehension, really, but one of restive anticipation, of almost unbearable impatience, of excitement and insecurity dancing wildly inside him. He had not felt like this since he was a kid, maybe fourteen. He had taken Barbara Mason to the movies, and he did not know what to do, did not know how to kiss, did not know how to fuck. It had seemed then, long ago, as if the world had hung in the balance. Now there *was* a world at stake. At least this time around he knew what he had to do.

Though he was not hungry, he joined Louie for a light lunch at the hotel. Afterward, he walked to the gardens, intent on quieting his pulse and calming his nerves. More than two hours remained between now and three o'clock. If it had been in his power, he would have erased those hours from existence. Odd, he thought as he walked, that we are given so few moments here on earth and yet we spend so many of them so impatiently waiting for their passing, looking at clocks and calendars, hurrying the minute or the hour, the day or the week, the month or the year, hurrying our own deaths, wasting our moments and praying for more in one and the same breath.

His pulse softened; his breath grew easier. Smiling, he closed his eyes to the sun. If only he could inject this breeze, like heroin, into his blood and being, infuse the amines and enzymes, the synapses and transmitting cells, with its magic, fuse it, make it one—aura, breeze and breath—with life itself. If only he could feel this way forever. Was it walking brazenly in the shadow of death that had opened his heart to the breeze? Maybe that is why men like his uncle and old Tonio and Louie Bones seemed to move through life with an air of strength and calm, an aura that set them apart and invested them with a power that evoked flinching deference in others, an aura that no loud swagger or gun or three-grand suit could affect. Death's shadow was mere atmosphere, rich with oxygen like any other, an emanation, like dark and light, of every shifting moment. They walked with natural assurance between life and death, seizing and savoring the world of each moment, setting themselves above and apart from those who merely bided. Maybe that was it. Maybe they were the wise ones, who held life as God's patrimony to them, a patrimony that carried no bondage to defer, in matters of life and death, right and wrong, to their bequeather. Maybe their power was a reward for their appreciation, their seizing and savoring, of that patrimony.

He returned to the hotel, shaved, showered, and dressed. Louie knocked on his door at twenty past two. Johnny, who wore a wine-colored three-button knit shirt of Sea Island cotton and a midnight-blue suit of light worsted wool, thought he looked pretty fucking sharp; and he did. Louie, however, was a vision of subdued, sinister elegance. *Azzizzatu*, as the Sicilians say. A coal-gray suit of fine, soft summer wool, a white jacquard shirt with gold-and-onyx links, and a black-and-copper necktie of deep lustrous silk. He had taken a haircut and a manicure. Natural shaved neck on the hair, plain buff on the nails; none of that straight-across or rounded nonsense, none of that clear-polish shit the *cafon*'s went for.

"Ready to roll, partner?" Louie said.

"Let's do it."

They walked west on Bastioni di Porta Nuova and Viale Crispi to Piazzale Balamonti, then west again on Via Sarpi. As they neared Via Bramante, they found themselves moving among more and more Chinese. Italian words on shop windows alternated with Chinese characters. At the southwest corner of Via Sarpi and Via Bramante was a store marked by the primitive character *zhong*, signifying China, and the familiar Italian storefront phrase for "gift items," *articoli da regali*. They turned left. Johnny stopped before the window of an *antiquaria* that bore the words *Talismani Porta Fortuna*. On display, priced at twenty-five thousand lire and up, were various amulets, *"contro il malocchio, per l'amore, la fortuna, ecc."*

"Maybe they got something to ward off Chinks," Johnny said.

"Don't worry, we'll get our *talismani* at the bar."

They turned right on Via Giusti. The city seemed to vanish behind them with a sigh, giving way to a pocket of narrowing, strangely silent paths.

"This must be it," Louie said as they came to the northeast corner of an alleylike passage bearing the name Via Braccio da Montone. A door on the Via Giusti side of the corner was marked CAFFÈ; the door on the Via Braccio da Montone side, BAR. Windows on both sides were curtained to cloak the place from passing eyes.

Vincenzo was sitting at a table. Four other men occupied the room. One, fat and old, with a white apron and white sleeves rolled to his elbows, seemed to be the keeper. He looked at Vincenzo as Louie and Johnny entered, and Johnny nodded to him in return. Vincenzo rose and led the men from New York into a storage area in the back. There, among cases of liquor and *acqua minerale*, he laid out several guns from a Mila Schön shopping bag: a nine-millimeter semiautomatic Desert Eagle; a .45 ACP Colt Lightweight Commander; a pair of .32 Smith & Wesson J-frame Magnums; a Taurus .44-caliber 431 Special; two Smith & Wesson snub-nosed .38 Airweight Bodyguards, and an Airweight Centennial.

"Like my wife said to the milkman," Vincenzo said, smiling, "what feels good?"

Louie and Johnny weighed the various guns in their hands. They both concentrated on the lighter revolvers, as they were not arming for battle but only seeking, as Louie had said, *talismani*. In the end, they took the snub-nosed Bodyguards. Easy to carry, good for close-range killing. Vincenzo brought out a box of Federal hundred-and-fifty-eight-grain semiwadcutter hollowpoints. Each man loaded five bullets into his gun and tucked the gun into his belt.

The fat man paid them no mind as they returned to the bar. Louie put down a ten-thousand-lire note and ordered coffee for the three of them. They drank it down in one shot. It was five to three, time to go.

Louie and Johnny followed Vincenzo north on Via Braccio da Montone, which brought them back to Via Sarpi and the bustle of the city. At the corner, Vincenzo led them to the door of a small Chinese restaurant. He knocked. "*Sono io. Vincenzo*," he called, then knocked again. The door opened. The Chinaman who stood before them, a diminutive man of middle years, had the appearance and bearing of an undertaker. He locked the door behind them, shutting out the afternoon light. Without words, he directed them past the little bar to a room of tables set with pink cloth and flowers.

"Who's he?" Johnny whispered to Vincenzo. Louie's eyes asked the same.

"Tao. Sole Rosso."

Deserted, dimly lighted, and silent, the room possessed an eerie stillness undefined by time or place. From an alcove leading to the kitchen stepped a taller, younger, and brawnier Chinese, Ng Tai-hei's guard and driver, in his black Baromon suit. Standing in the alcove shadows behind him was the unmoving figure of Ng Tai-hei. The little man came forward, stood between Louie, Johnny, and Vincenzo and the guard in the Baromon suit. Again like an undertaker, he clasped his hands before his chest.

"*Penso che non abbiamo bisogno delle pistole qui*," he said: I think we have no need of guns here.

"*Per quanto ne sappiamo noi, questo potrebbe essere un arsenale. Siamo noi, non voi, di essere in terra straniera*," Vincenzo said: As far as we know, this could be an arsenal. It's we, not you, who are on strange ground.

The small man spoke in Mandarin to Ng Tai-hei's guard. From behind the guard there came an undertone.

"*Kui dei ngaam*," the guard said to the small man. "*Zou saanya mou yan gong sunyam.*"

"*Dice che Lei ha ragione. Non c'è posto per la fede, negli affari*," the small man said: He says you're right. There's no place in business for trust. He pulled back two chairs and welcomed Vincenzo and the guard to sit. He invited Louie and Johnny to be seated at the adjoining, corner table. It was a table for six, but only four chairs were in place. Peering into the alcove, the small man cocked his head slightly—an odd gesture, part bow and part directional signal. Louie and Johnny stood as Ng Tai-hei entered.

Johnny recalled Billy Sing's words: "*They will be merely men— strangers from a strange world, yes, but beneath that, merely men.*" Ng Tai-hei struck him as a distinguished man of forthright bearing. In his blue shadowstripe suit and black knit shirt with mother-of-pearl buttons, with his silvering sleek black hair and amber-glinting brown eyes, he moved with that aura, that immanent strength and calm that was both of this moment and forever. But yes, like everyone else in that room, he was merely a man.

"*Piacere*," he said, pronouncing the word eccentrically, holding out his hand first to Louie, then to Johnny. Then, smiling slightly, in English that sounded somewhat less eccentric: "Such is the extent of my Italian."

The small man joined them as they sat. Louie lighted a cigarette. Johnny shifted in his seat, adjusting the gun in his belt with his left thumb.

"So," said Ng Tai-hei, folding his hands on the table. Johnny saw that he too was freshly manicured. "Let me hear this proposal of yours."

"A partnership," Louie said. "Pure and simple. A partnership at the source."

"You understand, of course, that this is something beyond the consideration even of our own people in your country. And they, in this age, are far more important to our commerce than you."

"More important," Louie said, "but not more powerful. We've shown you how much their importance depends on our good will."

"You mean that handful of firecrackers you tossed in New York?" Ng Tai-hei sniffed in dismissal. Chinatown had been transformed into a war zone. The market had collapsed from disorganization and the panic of plague. But in this matter, he would never grant them the satisfaction of his acknowledgment of the truth.

"You're right. A handful of firecrackers. We like to save the best for last."

"What does that mean?"

"Use your imagination. Whatever you imagine, it's worse."

"These psychological parlor games and vulgar attempts at intimidation are perhaps not the best way to court prospective partners."

"Please," Johnny said. "Don't get us wrong. We come in friendship, not enmity. Our little fireworks were only a display. It's always better, don't you think, to manifest power than to lay claim to it in words?"

"Yes," said Ng Tai-hei. "But you must understand, you can not propose partnership merely as an alternative to war. You must understand, we are no quaint little dong. Our power and resources are great. In the jungles of Myanmar, we command an army of more than fifteen thousand armed and able soldiers. And that is only one slight aspect of our strength. What western Sicily was to your forebears, the world now is to us. We do not *need* partners. We do not *need* good will."

"America is your greatest market," said Johnny. "We can ensure monopoly and growth in the years to come."

"These are not insurances we feel we need. We know why you seek such a partnership. It is money. That is as plain and simple as day. You cannot expect tangible wealth in return for intangible offerings. Your proposal involves money and other substantial considerations. That is what I want to hear about. Enough vagueness. You sound like storybook Chinamen. Talk money."

"Several years ago," Johnny said, "Shang Wing-fu stated that he would sell all the opium produced in the Golden Triangle for forty-eight million dollars a year plus subsidies to the Shan for crop substitution and road construction."

Ng Tai-hei was impressed that the young American knew Asim Sau's true name, but his naiveté was surprising. Asim Sau had spoken of selling a total annual crop yielding two hundred metric tons. To begin with, two hundred tons of opium tar, two hundred thousand kilos, were worth only ten million dollars in the Golden Triangle. His offering price thus constituted a profit of four hundred and eighty percent. Furthermore, the annual crop he controlled was closer to two thousand than two hundred tons: two-thirds of the Golden Triangle's total, a full half of the world's. If some well-intentioned sucker nation accepted his offer, allowing him to sell two hundred tons of opium at a four-hundred-and-eighty-percent profit, that would leave him and the 14K with eighteen hundred tons, enough for a hundred and eighty tons of heroin. At a conservative average of ten grand per kilo, that came to one billion, eight hundred million. These wops were dumber than he thought. Bad, he told himself, but dumb.

"You believe what you read in newspapers and hear on television?" He smiled and gently shook his head. "My friend has a great flair for self-promotion, I'm afraid." A flair for salesmanship as well, he did not say. "Do you know what that opium is worth to us once it has been transformed to heroin? It is worth perhaps half a billion dollars. Why should we want partners at the forty-eight-million level when we have all we need at the five-hundred-million level? Of course, what my friend said about the opium would in fact be true of the heroin. We would happily sell it all to a single buyer. Five hundred million from one source is the same as five hundred million from a hundred sources. Actually, it is preferable. And that five hundred million, you must remember, might be worth more than twice that to the buyer, depending on how he handles it. This is what I do not understand. You seek a share of five hundred million instead of a billion or more."

"Our reasoning," Johnny said, "is the same as yours. Things are always easier, much simpler, at the source. We seek the most gain for the least time, energy, and risk."

Louie was pleased with the way Johnny was handling things. When

Louie had first taken him under his wing, Johnny had still been taking his uncle's words at face value: he was to serve as the old man's eyes and ears. But slowly he had taken on duties of mouth and mind as well, as Louie had known he should and would, for it was as neither an observer nor an acolyte that he had been chosen, but as *sangue nuovo*, new blood, mind and muscle ripe for cultivation.

"Of course, you know that there is a great deal involved that is neither easy nor simple. Every spring, mountain fields must be tested for alkalinity, must be burned off, cleared, and hoed. After a summer crop of corn, the soil must be hoed again before the scattering of poppy seeds. The poppy plants must be tended through the fall and winter. The opium resin must be harvested by hand. This resin, wrapped in kilo bundles of banana leaves, must be transported by horseback over long mountain trails to refineries where it can be processed into bricks of morphine base. Then there is the laborious process of transforming the morphine base to heroin. The labor of tribesmen, officials to be bribed, the cost of transport, of running refineries and keeping chemists—there is much involved."

"But the cost to you of ten kilos of opium tar," said Louie, "is only five hundred dollars."

"And the single kilo of morphine base those ten kilos yield, after much time and labor, is still worth only five hundred dollars."

"Yes," Louie said, "but once it leaves the Golden Triangle, once that kilo of morphine base becomes a kilo of heroin—"

"Again, after much time and labor. And danger of many kinds."

"It is worth five thousand. That's your privileged price in Chiang Mai. In Hong Kong, it's twelve thousand. By the time it's consigned to New York, that same kilo carries a price of twenty or twenty-five thousand. Even if your overhead is a thousand dollars a kilo, your profits range from two hundred percent in Bangkok to twenty-five hundred percent in Hong Kong. To us, any process that transforms five hundred dollars' worth of slime into twenty-five grand overnight is quite attractive."

"And multiply that by two hundred thousand," Johnny said slyly.

"That is your true harvest, isn't it? Two thousand metric tons—two million kilos—of opium tar per year? That's two hundred thousand kilos of heroin a year. At twenty-five grand a kilo, that's five billion dollars. Even at ten grand a kilo, it's two billion."

So much for dumb wops, reflected Ng Tai-hei. Not only did they know the truth, but in allowing him to presume and play on their naiveté, they had swiftly established his deceitfulness. The seventh of the thirty-six strategies. They had created something from nothing, confused the enemy with false impressions.

"And two billion divided by three," said Ng Tai-hei, with no breach in his outward composure, "is, in the end, really not that much."

It was the number of the beast, the number of man—six hundred threescore and six—mirrored thrice, a trinity of beasts: six hundred and sixty-six million, six hundred and sixty-six thousand, six hundred and sixty-six.

"It's almost seven hundred million each. And it represents a very conservative figure," said Louie.

"The 14K is a vast organization. There are many mouths to feed, pockets to fill. Asim Sau has his troops, Tuan Ching-kuo his voracious politics."

"It was you who said you didn't like parlor games," Johnny said. Louie was struck by the edge in his voice. But Johnny's next words came forth with placidity and calm. "So let's cut the shit," he said. "The 14K handles all consignments. Every kilo that brings you ten thousand brings those beneath you that and more. And the others, Asim Sau and Tuan Ching-kuo, like yourself, use your heroin as currency. And there you have the greatest exchange rate, the greatest currency unit in the world. Every dollar in jungle money, transformed from tar to powder, becomes two grand's worth of buying power. Goods, arms. *Maaitung, gwoonyuen*. It buys it all."

Louie and Ng Tai-hei alike were surprised to hear Johnny speak these Cantonese words, which Louie did not understand: *maaitung*, bribery, and *gwoonyuen*, the favor of government officials. Even the small, silent figure who sat silently with them raised his undertaker's

eyebrows. To Ng Tai-hei, these utterances of Chinese were like a tres-
pass, an alarming rattle of brush or crackling of branches in the sacro-
sanct woods that lent the comforting illusion of inviolability to the tone,
color, and texture of his thoughts. *Chuengaausi*, missionaries, were the
only white men who spoke Chinese. It was uncanny hearing such sounds
from a man such as this, a man not of *Singling*, the Holy Spirit, but of
cheling, spirits of evil.

"I've heard many numbers from you. But I haven't heard the number
I came to hear. What is your offer?"

"A kilo of morphine, at its source, is worth five hundred dollars,"
Louie said. "We are willing to pay you one thousand dollars per kilo of
morphine, another thousand dollars per kilo of heroin. That is two
thousand dollars per kilo. Four hundred million dollars. In exchange for
that four hundred million, we have the option to buy as much as we
want. From one to fifty thousand kilos, we pay an additional three
thousand dollars per kilo. From fifty to a hundred, five thousand. From a
hundred to two, we pay seven. We also retain a twenty-five percent
participation in all subsequent income on the remaining total output. If,
for example, we choose to buy twenty thousand kilos, we pay you four
hundred and sixty million dollars. If the remaining hundred and eighty
thousand kilos bring in, say, three billion, we get seven hundred and
fifty million. That leaves two and a quarter billion for you, plus the four
hundred and sixty million we'll have already paid you. If we take the full
two hundred, that's a billion and a half. For one single, simple transaction. Something you've never been able to do."

All three men knew that a kilogram of pure number-four heroin
could be sold in New York for a hundred and eighty thousand. At that
rate, two hundred thousand kilos were worth thirty-six billion dollars.

"You speak of things being much simpler at the source, of conserv-
ing time, energy, and risk. So why would you want twenty thousand kilos
of time, energy, and risk?"

"We too are many," Louie said. "We have substantial consignments
planned. Consignments that in turn will mean more growth for you."

Ng Tai-hei's face revealed nothing. "These figures assume a partnership *in esse*. What do you have in mind to effect this arrangement?" He

allowed himself a slight, ambivalent smile. "What's the par value of your much-vaunted good will?"

"Two hundred million," Louie said. "A hundred million upon agreement, a hundred million upon our first settling."

"And the other 'substantial considerations'?"

"We're here to listen," said Louie.

Ng paused for a moment. Then he said, "As you may know, France and America, much to the anger of mainland China, have been selling arms to Taiwan for some years now. F-16s from General Dynamics, Mirage 2000-5 fighters from Dassault, short- and medium-range missiles from Matra. Through Tuan Ching-kuo and his friends in the Guomindang, some of these have made their way to us. Things in Taiwan, however, have been changing fast. The power of the Guomindang has been divided and weakened, threatened increasingly by the Democratic Progressive Party of Hsu Hsin-liang, the New Party of former cabinet members Jaw Shao-kong and Wang Chien-shien. It is doubtful that the Guomindang presidency of Lee Teng-hui will see the new century.

"As you also may know, China, through its North China Industries Corporation, has for some years now been a major exporter of arms. Compared to the American global arms trade of some thirteen billion dollars a year, China's trade, estimated at perhaps a hundred million a year, is slight, but compared to that of other nations, it is considerable. Since the fall of 1988, when the junta of General Ne Maung seized power in Myanmar, and foreign assistance to Myanmar generally came to an end, China has been Myanmar's closest ally and greatest source of arms. In the Golden Triangle, both Asim Sau's Shan forces and the rival Wa have their clandestine supporters within the Burmese regime, and, some Chinese weaponry thus made its way to us, most notably several of the new JL-1/DF-31s and DF-25 ballistic missiles. But when General Ne Maung went mad and was eased from office in 1992, command of the junta passed to General Ye Kyaw, an old man given to astrology and the blood of young girls. As he faded into the mists of his age, active command passed to Major General Saw Win, the head of military intelligence and a supporter of the Wa. At the same time, U.S. sanctions imposed on China for its sale of M-11 missile parts to Pakistan have led to a more restrained and conservative marketplace. Importing technology from America, it seems, is far more important to China than exporting arms to its neighbors.

"In Thailand there have been other problems. Through the military governments of Chatichai Choonhavan and General Suchinda Kraprayoon, Thailand's prosperity and our own were one. Even through the interim government of Anand Panyarachun, we obtained Blowpipes from England, Grails from Russia, Stingers from America. Since 1992, however, starting with the democratic administration of Song Leekpai, the flow of arms has dwindled.

"Through friends in Saudi Arabia, Asim Sau has arranged several purchases from Raytheon in America, but the cost has been exorbitant and precludes any possibility of resale. And our interest in arms has always been more for their illicit market value than for their possible strategic or tactical value to ourselves. So, you see, our interest is in arms. I consider substantial arms to be substantial considerations."

Louie cleared his throat. He looked at Vincenzo, who nodded slowly, firmly. "You want arms," Louie said, "we got arms."

"We want Hughes Amraams for our F-16s, to replace the old AIM-7 Sparrows. Assault helicopters: Apaches, Mi-24s, Mi-25s."

Johnny saw that Vincenzo had taken a pen and paper from his jacket pocket and begun to write.

"Stingers," said Ng Tai-hei. "More Stingers. We can always use Stingers. RPG-7s. Surface-to-air: SAM-7s, SAM-14s, SAM-16s. But what we really want is . . ."

He spoke to the little man in Cantonese, and the little man confirmed his meaning in Mandarin: "*Hé dàntóu yǔ rè hé dàntóu.*" He then turned and spoke in Italian: "*Testate nucleari, testate termonucleari.*" Nuclear and thermonuclear warheads.

Louie looked at Ng Tai-hei. Johnny looked at him too.

"Plutonium," Ng continued. "Deuterium. Tritium. U-235. U-238. Enriched uranium dioxide pellets. Beryllium. Fluorine. We have access to centrifuge technology in Pakistan, so these materials will suffice. But it is finished warheads that we really want. We have tried to obtain warheads from Kazakhstan, but we have had no luck." He allowed himself another smile. "For us, at least, *glasnost* and *perestroika* are not all that we had been led to believe."

"What the fuck do you want with nuclear warheads?" Louie asked him, somewhat grinning, somewhat frowning.

"Hell, we like firecrackers too."

"*Ngodei chongjou kuidei.*" The undertaker snickered. He turned then to Louie and Johnny. "*Li abbiamo inventati,*" he said: We invented them. His sudden happy outburst struck everyone as bizarre, but it left him smiling.

"It is not only a matter of nuclear warheads," said Ng Tai-hei. "We have many political interests. We should like to be rid of Major General Saw Win in Myanmar, see him replaced by a supporter of the Shan rather than the Wa. We should like as well to see the puppet democracy of Thailand overthrown. If you could help us in these matters, we would be most grateful, and I'm sure your proposal of partnership would be warmly embraced."

"These considerations are such," Johnny said, "that before we weigh them, we'll assume that the good-will cash payment of two hundred million is to be waived."

"Two hundred million. Four Amraams. Whatever. Help us, and the keys to the kingdom that you seek shall be yours."

"I'm curious about one thing," Johnny said. "You speak of your power and resources. This general in Burma, this democrat in Thailand —why have you not gotten rid of them yourselves?"

"Because any such action on our part might be perceived for what it is: an attempt to overthrow the government. That would not be abided. Even our friends and allies in these governments would turn against us. Believe me, we have tried to arrange coups through sympathetic forces in the military, but we have been foiled by too many men whose allegiances seem to be divided between us and our enemies. Whether holstered and uniformed or blow-dried and benignly grinning, politicians the world over are the same, it seems to me. Surely our situation is not unlike your own here and in America."

"All right," Louie said. "We'll meet tomorrow."

Ng Tai-hei rose and put out his hand once again, this time extending it first to Johnny and looking him straight in the eye. The six men left the restaurant together, with the little man leaving last and shutting the door behind them. The late-afternoon light was soft and pearly; the *brisa*, a caress, was as delicate as the white rolling clouds overhead. Ng Tai-hei's guard ushered his master into a waiting black Bentley. The little Sole Rosso man walked west; Johnny and the others, south, back to the bar.

"So far, so good," Louie said. He turned to Johnny, put his arm around his shoulders. "When you started talkin' that Chink shit, I thought he was gonna choke on his fuckin' substantial considerations." He turned to Vincenzo. "What about all this Buck Rogers shit?"

"I'll find out."

"I'm curious," Johnny said. "Where does somebody go about stashing an F-16?"

"Hell, we just pick that shit up at the bar here." The three of them laughed, then Louie said, "Tell him. Go on, tell him."

"Muammar al-Qaddafi's ties to the world are through Sicily. His lawyers, for instance, are in Catania. All his Italian financial interests— Tamoil, the thirteen-percent stake in Fiat he holds through the Libyan Arab Bank, and so on—are guarded and manipulated through Sicily. The oil exploration technology he received from SAIPEM, the Western nuclear technology he received from AGIP Nucleare, through SNAM Progetti, it was all channeled through Sicily. His connections to SISMI, the Italian military intelligence agency, are maintained through Sicily. You see, Qaddafi believes that Sicily will someday be restored to Islam, that Palermo will become al-Madinah once again. It is his dream to take over the American missile bases in Sicily." Vincenzo shrugged at the folly of such beliefs and dreams. "Outside of Catania, Qaddafi's hidden strongholds are on the Sicilian islands of Pantelleria and Linosa, which lie in the Mediterranean, northwest of Libya. It is on Linosa, a desolate volcanic speck in the sea, seven hours by boat from the nearest port, that Qaddafi stores his arsenal of Western weaponry. This arsenal has been building since 1978, when Qaddafi paid a quarter of a million dollars to President Carter's brother in return for arranging shipment of a fleet of C-130 military transport planes. And as I say, he is a man with connections. Geidar Ali Aliyev, the former head of the Azerbaijan KGB, is not the least of them. New shipments arrive at Linosa almost every month, through the *contrabbandieri* of Brest, Gdansk, and Prague. We know these things because it is we who guard and maintain the Linosa arsenal. And believe me, yes, it's a good place to stash F-16s."

At the bar, they were alone except for the keeper and a very old man who sat smoking by the curtained window.

Using a SIP card, Vincenzo called Sicily from the pay phone in the bar. Johnny and Louie, sitting nearby with their coffee, heard him ask for Avvocato Signorelli, whom Louie knew to be Don Virgilio's liaison.

"You were cool as a fuckin' cuke in there, kid," Louie told Johnny. "I'm proud of you."

"Hey, I learned it all from you."

"Fuck, man, you learn to mimic, not to be. That was *you*."

They could hear Vincenzo begin to read his list into the telephone. It was plain by his tone and words that there was incredulity at the other end of the line. "*Sì, sì, sì. Testate nucleari. Sì. Lo chiedi a me? Come faccio a sapere? . . . Elicotteri da combattimento. Gli Apache. Mi-ventiquattro, Mi-venticinque . . . Effe-sedici. Sì. Per sparare i missili. Non chiedermelo. Sì, sì . . . Gli Amraam. Sì. A, emme, erre, doppio a, emme . . . Sì, sì, plutonio, bissido di uranio . . .*"

Vincenzo hung up the phone. "*Un Crodino*," he called out to the fat man in his white apron and rolled-up sleeves, "*e un dito di plutonio*."

Johnny and Louie laughed lightly at Vincenzo's request for a Crodino and a shot of plutonium. Their laughter deepened as the fat man shuffled behind the bar as if the order were a familiar one. He placed a tall, narrow glass and a small bottle of medicinal-looking orange liquid on the bar and opened it. "*Plutonio scozzese?*" he asked dryly.

"*Sì, sì. Plutonio Chivas. Liscio.*"

The fat man poured the Scotch generously into a second tall, narrow glass. Vincenzo drank it down in three swallows. He poured the Crodino into the other glass, brought it with him to the table where Johnny and Louie sat.

"I'll know by morning," he said.

"*Dunque*," Louie exhaled. "*Domani. Alla stessa ora, nello stesso luogo.*"

Vincenzo had his car, a peacock-blue Maserati Quattroporte, parked down the street, guarded by a *cafon'* from the bar, and he offered his companions a ride back to their hotel. Johnny and Louie looked at each other. They were tired, but pleasantly so. On their brief way here from Via Sarpi, the soft, pearly light and balmy breeze of the late afternoon had been like a drug to them, and their lingering sense of auspicious exhilaration wanted more of that ethereal drug.

"No, thanks," Louie said. "We're walkers."

The two men moved their guns round to the back of their trousers, so that the breeze fluttering their jackets would not bare them.

That evening, Louie tried to recall the name of an out-of-the-way pizzeria he knew and swore by. He knew vaguely how to get there. It was on a small street beyond Piazzale Oberdan, he said, east of Viale Piave.

"Did you talk to your uncle?" he asked Johnny as they began to walk southeast on Viale Vittorio Veneto.

"Yeah. I got him at the club." He seemed distracted, barely there.

"Well, did he have somethin' to say?"

"Yeah. He said, 'Promise them anything, but give them Arpège.' He said, 'Whatever Vincenzo says tomorrow, do it. It's not him talking. It's me. It's me and the old man in the hills.' And 'Don't forget the cigars.' He said, 'Don't forget the cigars.' That was it."

" 'Don't forget the cigars.' " Louie too now seemed distracted, barely there.

They walked quietly, with the light of the setting sun behind them. The lush green leaves in the boughs overhead turned dark and moved like a glimmering nighttime sea, and their rustling was like the sound of conjuring-gourds, the hissing shimmer of snake vertebrae and bone dust in slow, rhythmic, ghostly invocation.

. . .

At the bar the next afternoon, as Louie and Johnny studied the list that Vincenzo set before them, Johnny remembered his uncle's words. *Whatever Vincenzo says tomorrow, do it. It's not him talking.* He was about to ask if there was anything else that Vincenzo wanted to tell them, but Vincenzo spoke first.

"*Il pontefice* wants us to come and smell the lemons."

"Is that just a polite invitation, or what?" Louie asked, placing the list in his pocket, adjusting the gun in his belt.

"He is not given to invitations, polite or otherwise. You see, he has no need for company, and he believes that any man worth knowing feels much the same."

Louie looked at Johnny. *Whatever Vincenzo says tomorrow, do it.* The two men nodded obliquely to each other, not so much in understanding as in acknowledgment of a foreshadowing that had come to pass, a ghost rising before them in response to the conjuring of shimmering branches and falling light.

In the Chinese restaurant, Louie leaned forward, allowed the smoke from his nostrils to drift toward the face of Ng Tai-hei.

"Two Mi-24s," he said. "Two Amraams. One hundred Stingers. Three kilos of enriched uranium. The death of Major General Saw Win of Myanmar. The death of the Thai democratic leader Song Leekpai."

Ng Tai-hei smiled.

"Effective upon our purchase, according to the terms we discussed yesterday, of two hundred tons of number-four heroin for one billion, five hundred million."

"Next spring's opium crop is not yet planted," said Ng Tai-hei. "What do we see from you in the interim?"

"How much do you now have on hand?" Louie asked.

"I cannot this moment give you an exact figure. I should say somewhere between a hundred and a hundred fifty tons."

"We see no reason to wait," said Johnny. "If the figure is a hundred and fifty, we'll just adjust our terms to compensate for the lack of our twenty-five-percent participation in the profits from the fifty that have already been sold. We'd be satisfied with a discount of two hundred and fifty million on a billion five. One and a quarter billion for the hundred and fifty tons. Ten percent now. Forty percent on shipment. Fifty percent on receipt."

"That cannot be. Eighty percent on shipment. Ten percent on receipt."

"Look," Johnny said. "Let's dispense with the Jewish waltz here. We'll go only as high as sixty percent on shipment. And with that sixty, you pay us, up front, fifty percent of the going price of the goods and services we were willing to give gratis. Two Mi-24s at a hundred million each. Two Amraams at six hundred thousand each. A hundred Stingers at two hundred thousand each. Three kilos of uranium at a hundred thousand each. At fifty percent, that comes to a hundred and ten million, seven hundred and fifty thousand." He turned to Louie.

"A half a million each for the *cappotti di lignu*," he said, as if talking only to Johnny. "They're heads of state."

"*Muk dàyī. Guinchoi*," the little man translated: Wooden coats. Caskets.

"Seventy percent on shipment," said Ng Tai-hei.

"Hey." Louie's voice hardened. "It's like the man said. We're not dancing on this one."

Ng Tai-hei stared at Louie, and as he did, he removed a card from his inside breast pocket, causing Johnny, Louie, Vincenzo to lower their hands rapidly to their belts, and his own guard to reach within his jacket.

"Trust is such a beautiful thing," remarked Ng Tai-hei, passing the card to the little man. "*Da leigo dinwa houma*," he directed. The small man left the room and went to the telephone at the bar. Soon he beckoned Ng Tai-hei, who remained on the line for several minutes.

"We can sell you a hundred and thirty-five tons," he said upon returning. "Ten percent now. Sixty percent, plus goods and services, on shipment. The balance on receipt. The continuance of our arrangement through the harvest season to come will be contingent on our satisfaction with those goods and services."

"A hundred and thirty-five tons," Johnny said. "The strike price is nine hundred and fifteen million. Plus goods and services, as promised. Ten percent down comes to ninety-one and a half million."

Ng Tai-hei put both his palms on the table and smiled. "This calls for a drink," he said. He stood, turned to the little man, and thanked him for tending to the arrangement of these meetings and offering his linguistic assistance during Ng Tai-hei's stay in Milan. In the next breath, he turned to the man in the black Baromon suit, enunciated "*luk*," the Cantonese word for six, and stepped away, toward the bar, as the guard drew his gun and shot the little man pointblank through the base of his skull. The gunfire was loud and reverberating, like an immense metallic crack, and it unsettled the ears and nerves of the white ghosts. But they showed nothing, except for the sudden cringing in Johnny that Louie caught from the corner of his eye.

From the bar, Johnny could see the body of the dark-suited dead man like some obscene larval slough. He suspected that this brazen killing was less a silencing than a display of face, a baring of teeth and clap of command, signature and seal to all that had been said. He remembered the strategies that Billy Sing had armed him with. *To kill a person and scare the rest.* Johnny watched Louie add his own cold sigil to the scene, watched him walk to the corpse, rifle coolly through its pockets, then return to the bar to count out several hundred thousand lire into two parcels on the bar.

"If you're gonna kill it, clean it. That's what I always say. I mean, Jesus, think of them starvin' kids in China." He pushed one parcel toward Ng Tai-hei, shoved half of the other into his pocket, pressed the remaining half into Johnny's hand. Then he went behind the bar. "*Il plutonio*," he muttered, raising a bottle of Chivas Regal from the shelf. He set down five glasses and began to pour.

Johnny regarded the bottle ambivalently, anxiously. He felt good; he wanted to feel better. But the bottle would never enhance the breeze and would make delusion of the moment. For so long that delusion was all that he had known. Everything. Oblivion, the savior. Romance, passion, and sweet, wild madness. Maybe those things were in the breeze as well. He put his hand over his glass: "*Solo acqua per me.*"

Louie neither paused nor questioned him. He knew him. He understood. *"Acqua fresca per il signore,"* he said, barman-like, opening a cooler door and fetching a *mezzo* of Panna Naturale.

The killer seemed pleasantly surprised to be included in the round, but he was not so impertinent as to raise his glass with the others.

"To a new world," said Ng Tai-hei. And to this they drank.

Louie filled the small metal sink behind the bar with hot water and left the emptied glasses there to soak. As an afterthought, he added three more glasses to the sink. He returned the Scotch to the shelf, ran a damp bar-rag over it, then over the handle of the cooler door. He wiped Johnny's mineral-water bottle as well, then tossed it into the trash. He checked the cash register, which was open but empty. Ng Tai-hei's man shut the restaurant door as they left, leaving it unlocked behind them.

It was a long way to the bank in the shadows of the Madonnina, and Vincenzo drove them. They did not stop at the bar; they would return their guns tomorrow. At the bank, Louie and Johnny arranged to have ninety-one million, five hundred thousand dollars transferred, via Lupino in Paraguay and a Bangkok account whose number Ng had given them, to the account of White Lion Enterprises at a bank in Bishopsgate, London.

Afterward, the three men went to a small café on Via dei Mercanti. Louie loosened his necktie and collar, lighted a cigarette, breathed what seemed to be a sigh of relief.

"You got any idea what this Sicily bit is all about?" he said.

"No. But it must be important."

"I don't get it," Johnny said. "The deal is done. Do they want to hear it in person, or what?"

"Not *they,*" Vincenzo said. *"Him.* He moves alone. *Avvocato* Signorelli is his mouth and his ears, who knows no more than he is told. We speak through Signorelli, not to him. It was he who told me of our friend's desire to see us, but he knew nothing of the reason, and I would neither expect nor want him to. As to our friend's wanting merely to hear words from our own mouths, no, I can assure you that this is not so. As I said, he is not a man for company. But he does have something to tell us. Something important. That is the only reason he ever calls anybody to him. To tell them something that must not pass through the *avvocato*. Or to kill them personally."

"Keeps ya guessin', I'll say that much." Louie laughed sardonically.

"What's he like?" Johnny said, turning to Louie as he spoke.

"You're lookin' at the wrong guy. I've never had the pleasure. Or the bullet, as the case may be. Your uncle, Tonio, *they* met him. Long ago. Me, never. Tell you the truth, I'm lookin' forward to it. I been to Palermo a dozen times in my life. I seen the catacombs, but I never seen him."

Johnny turned to Vincenzo and, without speaking, sought an answer to his question.

"I do not know him well," Vincenzo said. His eyes and his voice were grave. There was something odd in Vincenzo's manner as he spoke of Don Virgilio, but Johnny could not assay its nature. "Those who knew him well are long gone, and I wonder, really, how well indeed anyone has ever known him. He rules from behind a veil. Most men, even in Sicily, do not even know of him. To those who do know of him, he is like a god. I am one of his, how do you say, *flamini*. I serve him, but I don't know him any more than a *flamine di Giove* knew *his* god. But to me, yes, he has a face, a voice, a manner. He has, *come si dice, un'aura*."

"*La stessa cosa*," Johnny said. "It's the same: an aura."

"*Sì*. A face, a voice, a way, an aura." His pronunciation of the word wavered between English and Italian: *oh-ra*. "To me, he is all these things. He is real."

"Flamens had to be married, I thought." Johnny smiled, trying to lighten Vincenzo's tone and that of the table. He felt sure that Vincenzo was single. He wore no ring, and he did not seem married. "I thought that was Roman law. *Flamen et flaminica*."

"But I am," Vincenzo said, grinning. "*Sì, la flaminica*. She's home right now, not two miles from here. I would have you meet her, but you're too good-looking, both of you. Not so much this one here"—he gestured to Louie—"but he's a goat, all the same."

"What's she like?" Johnny asked.

"She's a good wife," Vincenzo said, and that was that. "How about you? You bartered your good name for a piece of ass too?"

Johnny nodded. It looked to Vincenzo as if his nod meant nothing.

"And how about her?" Vincenzo asked. "She's a good wife?"

"I don't know what she is," Johnny said.

Louie snorted. Vincenzo smiled. "Then get a new one," he said. Johnny raised his brows in recognition of these wise and simple words.

"Louie here, he's been married how long?" Johnny said. "He's a happy man."

"Happy? Fuck. That's like the two ditch-diggers, two greenhorns. 'Eh, Nicol', you like-a the woman, old-a like you *madre*, she got the big-a fat leg wit' the varicosa vein, she got all-a big ugly mole and a bigga mustache, gotta the big flabby tits like-a water*melòn* hang-a down to the fuckin' *comu si chiam'*?' 'Eh, *Madonn'*, what-a-you talk-a, you crazy, Giusepp'?' 'Then why do you fucka my wife?' "

Louie leaned back, satisfied with their laughter, and he did not speak again until it subsided. "You guys are kids yet. Someday you'll know. You marry one; as long as she's willin' to stand by you, you do the same. It's cheaper in the long run. Now," he said, "let's can this fuckin' modern-romance shit. When do we go? South, I mean."

Vincenzo shrugged. "Tomorrow, the next day. Whenever."

"Not tomorrow," Johnny said. "I wanna get another day in here. I wanna relax."

"Speaking of relaxing," Louie said, "it's about time for my semiannual blowjob." He looked at Vincenzo. "Is that Kent joint still there on Via Filzi?"

"Oh, God." Vincenzo waved his hand in the air. "The *carabinieri* shut that place long ago. You liked that place, eh?"

"They had some good-lookin' head in that fuckin' joint. Nice setup, too. The sauna, all that shit."

Vincenzo mentioned an address nearby, on Via Dante. "Better than the Kent," he said. Then he thought. "But why do you want to go there? I'll have somebody send a couple of girls to the hotel. On me."

"No, no, no, Vincenzo, that's too much."

"Please, please. I insist. What are friends for? You're my guests here."

"Let us pay, at least."

"I'll let you slip them a little something. A hundred, two hundred thousand lire each. That is, if you like them. Nothing more. They'll be taken care of, believe me. Just tell me what you want."

"Gimme a dick-suckin' blonde. Under thirty, nice legs," Louie said, as if placing an order at a butcher's shop.

"What the fuck, 'under thirty,' you old bastard," Johnny said, smirking.

"Hey, shit, anything older than that, I can pin a fifty-dollar bill to my fuckin' vest and go out and get it myself. Anything older than that, it's just piecework to 'em anyway. The slut juices dry up and that motherhood shit takes over. Nice young broad, you can feel the difference. You know that."

"I'll take the same," Johnny said. "But make mine younger and prettier."

"What do you think?" Louie asked Johnny. "Before or after dinner?"

To both of them, the meal was the main event. Some preferred their salad first, some later. Which were they?

"Before," Johnny said. To him, dinner was a ritual of luxuriation and relaxation. Expectations of any impending commitment, even that of tumescence, could diminish and distract from that experience as surely as a bad glass of wine.

"Send 'em by at seven," Louie said.

"I'll drive you back and I'll take care of it right now. I'll handle the tickets to Palermo as well."

Back at the hotel, Johnny and Louie sat in their shorts watching television in Louie's suite. Another prince of industry had taken his own life after being implicated in Italy's ever-widening *scandalo di tangentopoli*. There were scenes of him smiling in happier times, of his wife weeping, gathering her children away.

"What part of a broad do you like to fuck most?" Louie said.

"The leg. The cunt. It's a toss-up. I like both."

"Not the mouth, huh?"

"Oh, of course, the mouth. I thought you meant aside from that. The mouth, yeah. After that, the leg, the cunt?"

"You really fuck the leg, huh?"

"Oh, yeah, get right in there, man. Get 'em in a garter belt, stick it right in under the nylon stockin', right in there, nice and tight, between the stockin' and the thigh. Shit."

"So between the leg and the cunt, you'd really take the leg?"

"I don't know. Depends on if I'm gettin' a lot of pussy or not. Sometimes, you know, I sort of OD on cunt, I go for the legs."

"I never did that," Louie mused. "I fucked 'em between the feet, you know, they make a cunt with the feet, that sort of thing. And I've jerked off on their legs. But I don't think I ever fucked the leg per se. You kiss 'em on the mouth?"

"Yeah."

"See, that's one thing, in the old days, we never did that. Become a cocksucker by proxy, we used to say."

"How about the tits? You ever fuck 'em between the tits?"

"I don't care for it much," Louie said, not distastefully but disinterestedly. "What I like is a little here, a little there, a little this, a little that. You know, take my time figurin' where to ditch my load." He lighted a cigarette. "You eat pussy?"

"Yeah," Johnny said, not quite truculently.

"Okay. You're honest. Now let me ask you this. If you had a choice of either gettin' fucked, gettin' sucked off, or eatin' pussy, what would be third on the list?"

"Eating pussy."

"Do you know that I used to bankroll a bunch of fuckin' kike shylocks from the Bronx who would rather eat pussy than fuck? As God is my witness."

"What can I tell you? It's a strange world."

"I know. But still."

On the television screen, clutching a briefcase, a grim-looking Andreotti scurried down broad steps between columns of state and into a waiting car.

"Sometimes I agree with your uncle: their cunts are too loose, the *culo*'s too tight, and their mouths are too close to their brains."

"What about the *culo*? You go for that?"

"Nah. Once in a blue moon. In the old days, sure. That was Sicilian birth control. But not anymore. You?"

"I don't feel like I've had a broad unless I've plugged every hole. To me, they're still strangers unless I've done that."

"Shit, they're strangers, period." Louie blew smoke. "*U ballu angelicu.* The dance of angels. In a way, I figure I'm lucky. A lot of guys my age, the thing goes down but the desire don't. Me, they're both sort of fadin' away together, nice-like."

The telephone rang. It was ten to seven.

"That must be our sweethearts now." Louie picked up the phone. "*Pronto.*" It was not a call from downstairs. It was Giuseppe Di Pietro.

The corrugated steel door of the elevated loading garage on Broome Street shut out the bright sunlight and sounds of the early afternoon. The artificial glare of an overhead lamp shone down directly on old Joe and the dirty gray metal desk at which he sat. Near the telephone was an old .32-caliber revolver. The stench of burning hair and scorched flesh hung in the close, still air.

Johnny heard Louie greet his uncle, then watched the look on Louie's face slowly change from one of easy pleasance to one of stone. He saw the skin at Louie's temples tighten as he held the receiver to his ear.

Behind Giuseppe, in the softer coronal light of the overhead lamp's conical glare, Tonio Pazienza lay on his back, his wrists bound beneath him. His lips and one eye were swollen. His mouth was caked with black blood. His shirt and trousers were open, revealing a gnarled betel-nut penis and a sparse patch of steel-wool hair. Across his sunken chest and belly were several open burns. The skin around these burns was a bright canary yellow and glistened with blistering blood. One such burn, to the left of his navel, was still bubbling and smoking. His body heaved with stricken breath, and a dire murmuring issued from his mouth. Over him stood a man, casually and stylishly attired in white cotton slacks, blue linen shirt, and beige deerskin loafers, but wearing thick rubber gloves and holding a bottle of piss-colored liquid.

Finally Johnny heard Louie speak. "That fuckin' Chink bastard" was all he said. Now the skin at Johnny's temples was tight as well, and there was a dank draft of dread in his guts.

"No. It's not as you think," Giuseppe said. The man in the deerskin shoes glanced at him as he spoke but made no sense of his words.

"What about Sicily?" Louie said.

"Go there. See our friend. But put an end to your troubles first. Do it now. Get him before he gets you. Now let me talk to my nephew."

Louie passed the receiver to Johnny.

"My buddy," the old man said. His voice was calm, avuncular. It eased the feeling in Johnny's guts just to hear it. "Remember we talked about what hangs between your brains and your ass? Those shirts you might get dirty."

"Yeah." The feeling in his guts intensified again.

"Well, tonight's the night. Just remember, it's you or him. You or the animal at your throat."

When Giuseppe returned the receiver to its cradle, he sat a moment, his hands on the telephone, staring straight ahead. Then he drew breath, stood, and walked, cane in one hand, gun in the other, to stand over old Tonio. He took a DeNobili from his pocket, put it between his teeth, lighted it, and let the thick smoke blossom in the dead air like a censer's slow-furling cloud. He looked at the bottle in the gloved hand, cocked his head toward Tonio. The man drizzled acid onto Tonio's abdomen. Tonio did not cry out. His body jerked and his caked mouth cracked open in a groan, but he did not cry.

"*Mi dicisti tutto. Ma no u picchi*," Giuseppe said: You have told me everything. But you have not told me why.

There was no response, just the heaving and the murmuring.

"*Battezza 'a minchia*," he said loudly to the man with the acid: baptize his cock.

Giuseppe heard a grisly modulation in the old man's groans. He would have knelt to put his ear close to the wound of Tonio's mouth, but he could not. He struck Tonio hard across the face with the end of his cane. "*Avisti vuci sufucienti pi tradirmi. Usala adesso*," he barked: You had voice enough to betray me. Use it now.

"It was not right for you!" Tonio bellowed, as if summoning all the force that remained within him, opening his mouth so strenuously that new blood ran from his lips. "You wanted to sit in the breeze with your wine. For you, it was an end. But not for me. What would you expect? If I were the one who had gone soft, you would have turned from me as I turned from you. '*A bisiniss è 'a bisiniss.*"

"How could one carcass contain such greed?"

"Do you remember, Giuseppe, one night many years ago?" The bellow had dwindled to a dry croaking. "We counted out ten thousand dollars between us. It was all the money in the world. We had never seen so much. You wanted to kill and steal again that very night. 'How can one man have such greed?' I asked. And to that you had no answer."

"It was not you, or your own blood, I talked of stealing from or killing."

"Only because you had not run out of others."

With his gun, Giuseppe gestured angrily to the gloved wrist that held the bottle. Under the guiding pressure of the gun barrel, the contents were emptied onto Tonio's face, evoking from the old man one last, hideous bellow, which overwhelmed the sizzling sound of acid eating through flesh and eyes and nerve endings to scorch the tissue and bone beneath. Giuseppe gazed into the blind smoking sockets, the mouth, open and gurgling, and he fired the revolver twice into the raw monstrous mask.

"Burn in hell," he said, turning the revolver casually to his right and shooting a third bullet pointblank into the stomach of the rubber-gloved man.

When the telephone rang again in Louie's suite, he rushed to answer it. "*Ritorna alle nove,*" he said, then hung up, returned to the open suitcase on his bed, and finished packing. "You ready?" he called out to Johnny through the open door that connected their suites.

"Yeah," Johnny answered. "You get him yet?"

"Still busy."

Vincenzo Raffa was sitting on his couch with his feet up, twirling the black telephone coil with his left hand as he spoke into the receiver.

The telephone rested on a black metal box, eight by eight inches square, three inches high. It was an old, American-made P3 nullifier, a device that protected all calls from being monitored or recorded.

"*Credimi*," he said. "*Prenderanno il denaro da chiunque, purchì le condizioni siano soddisfatte, tratteranno con noi. Quando quella bestia nelle colline è a cavaddu, questo mondo sarà il nostro.*" Believe me, he said. They will take the money from anyone, as long as the conditions are met. When that beast in the hills is out of the way, this world will be ours.

A younger man, tall and trim, in bikini briefs and *biancoazzurro* soccer shirt, playfully tousled Vincenzo's hair while handing him a tumbler of Scotch and mineral water. Vincenzo reached out, stroked the man's thigh and patted his buttock.

"*Sì. Ciao.*"

Less than a minute after he hung up the phone, it rang. The tall, trim man looked at him peevishly as he answered.

Johnny sat and watched Louie as he spoke. "Vincenzo," Louie said, "we've got a problem. No, no. Nothing to do with the girls. We're having them come later. This is serious. It could fuck up everything. Can you be here in ten minutes? We need to take care of something. Out near Morivione. We can't take a cab because we can't be seen near where we're going."

"Give me fifteen minutes," Vincenzo said. The tall, trim man clicked his tongue and let his shoulders droop in a show of petulance.

"We'll be outside. Don't let us down." Louie hung up the phone, turned to Johnny. "Let's go."

In the lobby, they closed their account in cash. When the clerk returned their passports, Louie grabbed Johnny's as well as his own. Taking Johnny aside, he placed both passports in his luggage bag, and from beneath the cardboard backing of his remaining pressed shirt he removed what appeared to be two additional blue passports. He peeked into one and passed it to Johnny. "That's you. This is me."

Johnny opened it, held it sideways. It bore the name of William Morrison, place of birth Illinois, U.S.A. The photograph, stamped with what appeared to be the seal of the State Department, was identical to the one in the passport Louie had just taken from him. He remembered having these photos taken, remembered handing them over, along with his application, to his uncle, who told him he would have one of the *cafon*'s stand in line for him at the passport center. He had gone to fetch the passport himself, the day he had met Billy Sing. What he now held in his hand he had never seen before.

"*Semper paratus*," Louie said. "Don't leave home without it."

They had their bags set aside for later. Each man had his snub-nosed .38 tucked into his belt, his false passport in his jacket. They walked out into the fresh air, lighted cigarettes, and waited. The sky was a deep rich blue, and Johnny could see the first stars of night. Thirty years ago, he had heard his drunken father's voice, smelled his whiskey-sweet breath, as they sat on the stoop together watching the Brooklyn night fall. *Star light, star bright, first star I see tonight, I wish I may, I wish I might, have the wish I wish tonight.* That was another world.

"You don't have to come," he told Louie. "I can handle it."

"I know you can. I'm just along for the ride."

Johnny was not right in his body and mind. He felt no fear, but something worse: a deep, seeping melancholy, as he had felt on that stoop long ago, a sadness that subsumed the world. Just as the long-ago falling night and his father's well-meaning voice had rendered him, or so he had felt himself to be, the loneliest boy in Brooklyn, so this rich blue sky, these breaths on the precipice of— What was it that he felt himself facing? A relinquishing of illusion. A plucking out of that deceiving intercessor, that second party's trigger finger, that familiar moral foil that lay between himself and the truth of himself. An irrevocable parting from the realm of the *vigliacchi*, the lukewarm, the neutral, the safe, those neither good nor evil. It was all this and more. The animal at his throat, it was not Vincenzo Raffa. It was himself. He was doing what his uncle believed was right, what Louie Bones here believed was right. Their morality welcomed him, awaited him. And if their morality was born of old ways and presumed a God whose special understanding and forgiveness was founded in the ancient, sacred grain of those old ways' *moralità*, well, so be it. Who knew if these ways were not of God himself? A time to kill and a time to die. No sacrament had ever changed the way he felt. And yet he assumed that killing would.

"Here we go," Louie said, watching the smooth approach of the Maserati around the piazza.

Vincenzo reached over and opened the left door. Johnny climbed into the back; Louie got in front.

"What has happened?" Vincenzo said.

"There is a thorn that must be plucked. We'll explain later. Go left here."

Vincenzo adjusted his rearview mirror.

"Did you make our reservations?" Louie asked him.

"Not yet. It won't be a problem."

"I think we should get down there as soon as possible. I think we should go tomorrow, if that's all right with you. The earlier, the better."

"Is it the Chinese? Is there a problem with the Chinese?"

"There will be if we don't remove this thorn. Did you have dinner yet?"

"No," Vincenzo said.

"Maybe we can all eat together after this is done."

"Not tonight. Especially if we're to leave tomorrow. I left behind dinner at home."

He turned left on Corso Lodi, passed through the Porta Romana. "Are you sure you know where you're going?" he asked. There was a note of apprehension in his voice. "There is nothing down here but the railroad."

"Just beyond the piazza here. Pull over to the right." In the dark, it could have been a warehouse, a terminal building, a factory.

Johnny raised the snub of the gun to the nape of Vincenzo's neck, and with the finger that no longer bore the scar of old Tonio's blade, he fired. The blast sent the Sicilian's head jolting forward in a spray of blood that showered the windshield like a fine dark mist. Louie reached over and turned off the engine.

The game was over. It was real now. With the resounding report of the shot, Johnny's body had begun to tremble spasmodically. Even the muscles in his face were twitching. He had difficulty getting out of the car, difficulty standing on legs that shook. The noise of the shot still rang in his ear. It was all that he heard: a shrill ringing, a siren in his brain. He felt nothing, only the trembling.

They made their way without speaking to the Porta Romana. Johnny threw the gun down a sewage drain. There was an echoing sound, neither rattle nor splash: a faint, distant, subterranean rumbling.

The sky was still a deep rich blue, darker now, and the world was still the same, more recognizable with every tremulous breath. His limbs loosened, the ringing in his ears subsided. The sound of warm laughter from a café welcomed him back, and the breezes dried away the sweat that had drenched him. Melancholy lay beyond a sea. He smiled. It was a smile of relief, of freedom, of consummation, of deep, visceral florescence. It was as if some lifelong carcinoma of fear had been excised, as if the organs it had cramped and sickened had been allowed at last to draw true breath and thrive. He had foreseen racking guilt, wrenching sunderance from the common soul, anguish beyond satispassion. But what he felt was liberation, strength, an opening of the senses to a wider spectrum of perception, a polishing of the jewel. Murder to those who had never touched it was like passion to a virgin: neither as terrible nor as affecting as the truth of it, but blown all out of proportion. The melancholy, like his father's sad and tender rhyme long ago, had been only a farewell to innocence. He was a new man. Somehow God or old ways would protect him. He felt good.

Outside the café there was a taxi. At Piazza San Babila they changed taxis and fetched their luggage, then took a third taxi to Piazza Cavour. They walked round to Via Fatebenefratelli. At the Hotel Cavour they handed the clerk their counterfeit passports and registered under their false names. Johnny showered while Louie had the concierge make a reservation for them at Gualtiero Marchesi.

While showering, Johnny discovered that his new feelings were more involved, more enigmatic than they had seemed in the cool of night. The artificial light and gleaming tiles were strangely unsettling, and when he shut off the water and stepped out, the ringing seemed to return to his ears. He had a sudden sensation of déjà vu. The harsh light

and tiles—he had been here before, alone and unsettled, his ears ringing, his heart pounding as it was now. It was that poem, that fucking
poem with its solidus and emergency-room ear. With a shock, he realized that he had foretold this moment long ago. He wiped steam from the
mirror and stared at himself. His heart and pulse began to calm. He
smiled, winked, assured himself that all was well.

As he dressed, he found that he was uncomfortable being alone in
the room. It was the new surroundings, he told himself. He missed
Diane. He loved her, needed her. His mother. His father's pathetic
whiskey-sweet rhyme. Anything. He opened a window, let in the sounds
of the night, and felt better. Beyond the lobby's glass doors, in the open
air again, he felt better still. There was a taxi waiting. It took them to Via
Bonvesin della Riva.

Johnny's appetite returned with his first bite of bread, his first sip of
wine. He had a taste for the ocean. He ordered bass with sea-urchin
sauce.

"You still got pussy on the brain here, or what?" Louie said.

Johnny smiled, and Louie saw that it was a good smile, a real smile.
The truth was that, yes, with that first bite of bread, that first sip of wine,
an appetite for more than food had returned. Going back for those
broads Vincenzo had sent would be too dangerous, tantamount to dropping by for coffee at the bar where they had got the guns. Still, it would
have been nice. Within him, a brutal, almost desperate hunger for
disgorging grew with every savorous bite of bread, every savorous sip of
wine.

"You liked him, didn't you?" Louie said. "I mean, until you knew."

"I never would've figured it."

"You bought a lie. You, me, the both of us. We do it all the time. In
this life, we never know who we're dealing with. Never."

"But we trusted my uncle. He said it was right, and we did it. We
trusted him without knowing, took him in faith as blindly as we took
faith in . . ." He hesitated to say the dead man's name, but Louie
understood him.

"It's like this, Johnny. We can never get inside another man's mind.
Fuck psychologists, psychiatrists—they're fulla shit. Even the truth that

a man reveals of himself is often just a lie that he himself believes to be true. We can be convinced, but we can never know. Maybe Vincenzo was our friend and your uncle is our enemy. We're sure that isn't true, but we just don't know. So we go with our instincts. Knowledge, experience, can take us only so far. It's instincts that keep an animal alive. I think that's what wisdom is, a balance between instincts and knowledge."

"Do you trust me?"

"Yeah."

"What if that trust turned out to be misplaced?"

"I would kill you. And if the shoe were on the other foot, I'd expect you to do the same. To me, that's what true trust is based on: a common mind, and common ways. I would *use* a person who would not kill me if I betrayed him, but I would not trust him. Your uncle—I've known him since I was a boy. I've been closer to him than I was to my own father. He's never let me down. And I've never let him down. But if I did, he would kill me. That's what faith is based on. Don't get me wrong. It's not fear. It's not the threat of death. It's the fact of it, as hard and real as the fact of love. The opposite of love isn't hate. It's justice. There's an old Italian word, *faida*. The right of revenge."

For dessert, there were figs in Marsala wine. Louie told the waiter to bring coffee and have the manager call a cab for them. The espresso, and the cigarette that went with it, ended the meal on a note of perfect tranquillity. Johnny was no more a man of violence now than he had been yesterday, sitting in the sun on that garden bench, basking in the sound and movement of the swaying branches and the swifts and swallows that sailed and darted among them in the breeze from the north. He was simply who he was, a man who fucked and ate and loved, laughed and wept, and killed. There was poetry in it all, and no one moment or hue or breeze repealed the others.

As the cab approached Piazza Cavour, Johnny glimpsed dyed blond hair and black nylon: two whores loitering by a newsstand that had closed for the night.

"*Si fermi qui,*" he told the driver. Louie looked at him, then past him to the *puttane*. He laughed wearily and shook his head.

Up in his room, Johnny discharged what remained of the evening's death into the young blonde beneath him. He felt her quake and swoon. It was no whore's simulacrum. It was as if the force of a strange disquiet, a deep black magic, passed from his viscera to hers. He saw it in her open brown eyes: a dark and wild rapture, something profound and disquieting and real, that neither he in his knowing nor she in her unknowing ever would grasp; and he slept that night without dreams.

TWENTY-TWO

With his killing hand, Johnny raised a cup of coffee to his lips. The plane emerged slowly from the soft white underbelly of the high swirling clouds, and he saw the slate-colored rippling sea through a veil of thinner clouds below. In the flashing sun, the shadow of the plane was like a crucifix on the sea. The water turned blue and was laced with whitecaps, then turquoise. Soon Johnny saw the sand and shore of Sicily. The plane came down between mountains and sea, a sort of grand illusion that for a moment obscured the closer reality of the sere, parched scrub all around.

Giuseppe Di Pietro had not killed with his hands and heart together in many years. In the old days, when he had loosed the stench of another's soul, he had gone to church and he had lighted a candle. He did this not for shrift, and certainly not for the spirit of the dead, but, simply and supremely, because it was something he did. The sighing candlelight in colored glass at the foot of the saint was a calmative. The pulling of the trigger or the drawing of the blade across the throat: these and the lighting of the candle were to him the arsis and thesis of one continuous, natural, and ingrained movement of the same hand.

He had not felt the same toward the Church since the abolition of the Latin liturgy. To Giuseppe, the power of the Mass and the power of its ritual were one. It was a mystery rite, rich with the resonance of the centuries. When Pope Paul VI had replaced the sacred language of that rite with the vulgar bland speech of salesmen and newsmen, politicians and children, he had destroyed its power. Still, however, Giuseppe had continued to light his candles. At Saint Anthony's, at old Saint Patrick's, at Our Lady of Pompeii, he had gone in the morning, slipped a sawbuck in the slot, and lifted the taper stick in his hand. Then one day he had walked in, signed himself, and beheld a desecration that turned him forever from the Church of his time. The rows of white wax candles were gone, replaced by gaudy electric candlelike fixtures. Instead of the sand-filled tray of kindling-sticks, each candle now had its own little toggle switch. The sawbuck was halfway in the slot when he saw these things. He withdrew the bill and returned it to his pocket. What next? he mused bitterly. Would the censers of frankincense be replaced with Airwick air fresheners? Giuseppe did not believe that ancient holy ways should be new and improved like the detergents and tampons on supermarket shelves. Then this Polack pope, traipsing around the world in a pair of sneakers, running down the way things were in Sicily. Fuck this Church, he had told himself on the day he saw the toggle switches, fuck this Church where it breathes.

So old Tonio's death was marked by not even a candle.

He thought of these things as he sat across from the man who had the wan soulless features of a faithless priest. They were in the restaurant of a hotel in the east seventies, where the priestlike man was staying. The man was forty-seven years old, a drunkard, a gambler, a doctor of veterinary medicine in New Market, Maryland, and a pathologist at the United States Army Medical Research Institute of Infectious Diseases at Fort Detrick, in Frederick, Maryland. His gambling debts in Baltimore had brought him to this fancy table of prayed-for manumission in New York. He sipped his vodka martini with composure.

"This place you work at," Giuseppe said. "They've got things there, I hear."

Things, indeed, the doctor thought. The windowless, concrete RIID compound was, with the Centers for Disease Control in Atlanta, one of only two places in America that handled Biosafety Level 4 viruses. Hot agents, they called them—lethal viruses for which there was neither vaccine nor cure. The BL-4s were kept alive in blood serum and scraps of meat, frozen at minus seventy centigrade. The HIV virus, from the rainforests of Central Africa, was classified as a Biosafety Level 2 or 3 agent. The far more dangerous BL-4 agents included other African viruses—Lassa, Crimean-Congo, Marburg, Ebola Sudan, Ebola Zaire, Ebola Reston—as well as Junin, Machupo, and Guanarito from South America. Yes, they had things.

"What's the worst thing you've got there?" Giuseppe asked. He buttered a crust of bread, drank some water.

"Ebola Zaire. It's got an eighty-percent mortality rate. When it first erupted, in the fall of 1976, it wiped out fifty-five villages along the Ebola River. The initial symptom is a headache. Slowly, the victim begins to look and move like a zombie. Then fever sets in. Next comes DIC, disseminated intravascular coagulation. The bloodstream throws clots, and the clots lodge throughout the body—the spleen, the liver, the brain. As the organs become jammed, blood starts hemorrhaging from capillaries into surrounding tissues. The intestines fill with blood. Toward the end, blood containing great quantities of virus leaks from the eyes, nose, mouth, anus, and lesions in the skin. Within a week, death occurs from hemorrhage and shock."

"What does it look like? A dose of it?"

"It's a parasite, a filovirus. We keep it frozen in cubes of chuck steak."

"Does the government make weapons with this shit?"

"Not yet. We don't really understand it yet. It's too hot. The only thing that stopped it in Africa was the isolation of that group of villages. If road traffic or travelers had spread it beyond those villages—like HIV, which broke out along the east-west highway connecting Zaire and Kenya—it might have decimated the world's population by now. You wouldn't believe the rigamarole just to get near the stuff. They make you put on a space suit over your surgical scrubs. A helmet. Three layers of gloves. You go through an airlock. Hot showers, Envirochem rinses."

"So say you wanted to wipe out a village somewhere with this beef chuck of yours. What would you do?"

"Introduce it into the local ecosystem."

"Talk English."

"Scatter it around and let it thaw out. The most effective method would be to toss it into the water supply."

"Get me a half a pound of that meat."

"It's not a Burger King. They don't do take-out."

"They do now," Giuseppe said, his voice hard with umbrage.

A bottle of white Bordeaux and bowls of shellfish soup bright with saffron were set before them. Giuseppe did not taste the swallow of wine the waiter poured but simply gestured for the glasses to be filled.

"Let me tell you something," the old man said. "There's this joint down in Texas, they make the plutonium for the bombs. Every year, they do the books, there's a few pounds missing. If they can slip plutonium out of a joint like that, you can get a few scraps of meat out of that fucking jerk-off joint of yours."

There was a time when the doctor would not have envisioned himself being spoken to in such a way. But liquor had relieved him of all but the pretense of dignity, and the blows and threats of the men in Baltimore had since robbed him even of that.

"How much do you owe down there?" Giuseppe asked.

"Seventy thousand." He did not add that he was behind in his alimony payments to two ex-wives. He had gone from brandy and good Scotch to the cheapest vodka the liquor store carried.

"You get me the meat, I'll see what I can do for you."

The doctor took a long drink of wine. "I hope you really understand how dangerous this virus is. Believe me, I'll do anything to get out of debt. I've already told them that. But if you want to . . ." He searched for a word, a phrase. "If you want to do damage, there are far safer means. And if you're looking to sell it, I would think again. Ebola Zaire is far more dangerous than any thermonuclear weapon. This is why the government has not even experimented with it. Unless you can control its spread, you won't just destroy a target population. You could destroy an entire continent, maybe even the entire world. It is infinitely more infectious than something like AIDS, and it kills in a matter of days, not years."

Joe said nothing, just ate his soup.

"Of course, you can't possibly be thinking of fooling with it here, in this country," the doctor said, perturbed by Joe's silence.

"If I am, that's my fucking business. Maybe I want it for security. Maybe I figure, a man's got this shit, nobody's gonna fuck with him. Then again, maybe I'm your worst nightmare. Maybe I don't give a fuck about taking this world down with me. What do you care? You got a reason to fucking live, or something?"

The doctor saw no reason to go on with the hollow show of his eating. He pushed aside the soup, called the waiter, ordered another vodka martini. On second thought, why even bother with the hollow show of the vermouth?

"That's good," Joe said, regarding the double vodka on the rocks the waiter brought. "A man knows what he wants, he doesn't fuck around." He said this as if he meant it, but in truth he looked upon the man as wretched.

The doctor drank. He winced, pressed his hand to the area above his left hip. For years the pains had all been on the liver side. Now they had spread round to his pancreas. The old devil was right. He had no reason. He himself had seen to that.

"A day late and a dollar short," Peter Wang said. "Ng Tai-hei checked out of the Palace yesterday and is already back in Hong Kong. Bones and the young master were registered at the Principe di Savoia. They've checked out too, but as far as we can tell, they haven't returned or shown up anywhere else."

Marshall nodded, as if he had little interest in what Wang told him.

"They found Pazienza in a garage on Broome Street a few hours ago. He was tortured with acid, then shot. The guy who tortured him was shot along with him. They can't ID the second guy. No leads as to the killer."

"How does this fit in with your apocalypse?"

"It fits but it doesn't figure."

"Di Pietro, Pazienza, and Bones. Why Pazienza?"

"You're asking me?"

"You're the man with the answers."

"You draw a check around here too, don't you?"

"Hell, the way I see it, it's like I said the other day. Somebody's doing our job for us. This is just more tax-friendly justice. Pazienza's out of the way. Instead of your unholy three, now you've got only two to worry about."

"No. I still see three."

"How so?"

"Our young master, the prince of garbage."

On Hester Street, the young barman stood in the doorway explaining in his finest formal English that this was a private club. He gestured to the peeled, faded window lettering that stated MEMBERS ONLY.

The two men whose entry he blocked wore dark blue suits, white shirts, and sunglasses. One wore a necktie of blue and black stripes; the other, burgundy and black. Each held a black wallet with a badge that shone like platinum in the afternoon sun.

The *cafon*'s in their tattered vinyl seats looked on, rapt and narrow-eyed.

"I respect that," the barman said, glancing cursorily at the badges, then looking away. "But you are not members. If I want a cup of coffee, do I come to your office? No. It is the same here."

"Look," one of the blue suits said. "We're trying to do him a favor. We could make him come to us. Instead, we're coming to him."

"If I let you in, I must let everyone in."

"*Che c'e? Sono tizzuni?*" Joe's voice from the back of the room carried softly to the street: What is it? Are they niggers?

The *cafon*'s guffawed, and the barman tried to suppress a grin, in the manner of one who is too considerate to laugh impolitely.

Joe's voice drifted forward again: "*Lasciali entrare.*"

The barman stepped aside, let the FBI men pass. Joe gestured for them to sit. Both men entered the cloud of the old man's silvery cigar smoke.

"When's the last time you saw Antonio Pazienza?" As always, one agent spoke and the other remained silent, as backup and witness.

"If he's in some sort of trouble, I'll have to call his lawyer before I tell you anything. It's only right. I know him. I don't know you."

"Maybe you want to call his undertaker instead. They found him dead a few hours ago."

Joe shook his head somberly, almost imperceptibly, as if in resigned disgust at the injustice of fate.

"Where were you yesterday?"

"I was here. I had some lunch. I came back here."

"I suppose he's your witness?" The agent gestured to the barman.

"One of many. As on most days."

"Where'd you have lunch?"

"Little Paulie's."

"Is there someone who can place you there?"

"Who knows better than I?"

"Someone besides yourself."

"Yeah."

"Who?"

"Paulie. Among others."

"Pazienza was a business partner of yours."

Joe nodded, waved to the barman for coffee. He did not include the FBI men in his order. The barman was right. They had their own coffee elsewhere.

"How does his death affect your partnership?"

"One less partner." He looked at the agent as if he were a child who should be able to divide and carry but who could not yet even add or subtract.

"You take over his share of the business, then, or part of it."

"To tell you the truth, I don't know if it's set up that way or not." He had noticed the Semitic cast of the silent agent's face. "We got Jews handle that sort of shit for us."

"Who's us?"

"The business community."

"Could it have been someone in 'the business community' who killed him?"

"Could it have been? Sure. It could have been anybody, from any community. For all I know, it could've been you."

"Who wanted to see him dead?"

"Somebody without much patience, I'd say. Tonio was old and not well. Nature would've taken him soon enough."

"And you've got patience."

Old Joe smiled placidly, as if their underhanded implication were beneath him and all too characteristic of their kind. "Not when it comes to you guys."

He thanked the agents for coming, wished them luck in finding their man. Cane in hand, he accompanied them to the door. As they walked away, he looked after them.

"And whatever you do, don't leave town," he said to their backs.

The *cafon*'s burst into laughter, and when their laughter died, Joe looked at them stoically and said, "Tonio's dead. I want to know who did it."

Asim Sau closed his eyes and drank the cooling quiet of the early twilight. From the wooden porch of the Hmong hut where he sat, in a dirt- and pine-carpeted clearing deep within the forest of Tak province, not far from one of the teak-and-opium-smuggling routes that connected western Thailand to Burma, Asim Sau could hear the sounds of the jungle woods: leaf monkeys and macaques, peafowl and hornbills. From afar there were dholes and jackals and barking deer, crying in the way they did when five or more big cats were sensed within their roaming-ground. Asim Sau had not seen a leopard or a tiger all year. Several of his soldiers, near this season's camp in the north, had seen a black leopard with her cubs. As Asim Sau knew, where leopards moved freely, there were no tigers.

The scream of the wild pig that hung, strung by the tendons of its hind spurs, from the slaughter post across the clearing ripped through the shadowy fabric of the distant forest-sounds. Asim Sau opened his eyes. The pig had been shaved and scalded. The fire of dried and resinous woods, stones and leafy branches glowed in the earth nearby, scenting the air and hurrying the twilight with its glow. A gray metal basin had been placed on the ground beneath the pig's head by a soldier, who, like his master, wore green fatigues and black boots. Clutching the pink screaming head with one hand, the soldier took a dagger from his belt and slashed the creature's throat. He stepped back, watching it jerk and kick and squeal as its blood gushed from it, spraying round and rattling the metal tub loudly with its force. As its spasms subsided, the soldier thrust the dagger with an overhand stab into the area between the pig's asshole and corkscrew cock. He drew down hard, laying the beast open to the gash in its throat. Fat white entrails plopped out in a swaying tangle like coils of sausage.

Asim Sau took a drink from his tumbler of *lâo thèuan*, the clear, strong Thai jungle liquor for which he had slowly acquired a taste during his long years among tigers and tribesmen.

As the Hmong in their loose indigo trousers drifted wearily into the settlement from their long day in the fields, they livened with joy at the sight of the slaughtered pig being dressed. They knew that their honored guest would share the delicious meat with them. Their evening meal of corn, sticky rice, and mouse-shit peppers would become a feast.

While the first soldier finished dressing the pig, another prepared the blood. Like his taste for jungle liquor, Asim Sau's taste for blood had grown with the years. He watched the soldier spoon chalky gypsum into the blood from a tin can, just as one does when making bean curd from slurred soy. The gypsum would coagulate the blood. The coagulated blood would be strained and pressed, then cut into squares and stir-fried with green onions. Asim Sau knew that in Fujian, where this recipe originated, many preferred the blood of fowl and looked down their noses at the blood of swine, but for him, the blood of wild pigs was the tastiest of all. Before frying the blood, the soldier would set aside some of the carmine-black cakes and bring them to Asim Sau, who enjoyed munching on them like snacks of curd.

When the pig was wrapped in broad leaves and buried in the burning pit and the blood cakes were pressed and cut, Asim Sau told one of the soldiers to change into street clothes. He himself entered the chieftain's hut and emerged minutes later wearing light khaki pants and a short-sleeved madras shirt. He walked with the soldier to the Jeep that was parked behind the hut, and together they rode off toward the forest trail that led to the road that would take them to Tak. The setting sun was at their back, and as they sped along, the wooded, flowery hills through which they drove—the cashew-nut trees and waves of beaumontia, the date palms and fan palms and lacy palms and ficus, wild orchids and white-flowering plumeria, red costus and ginger—were like painted temple silk billowing around them, a world of glowing shadows and golden whispering light.

Lo Seng, the driver, was thirty-two years old. He had been a child of the Shan State, born in the Burmese mountains, not far from Asim Sau's own birthplace of Loi Maw. For most of his life, the jungles and the wars were all he had known. He had been a boot-camp charge of Asim Sau's Shan United Army at the age of eight, and had soldiered under Asim Sau's command since the fighting age of sixteen. In those days Asim Sau had maintained a permanent headquarters at the village of Ban Hin Taek, near Mae Salong, to the north. The driver had been there in the summer of 1980, when Thailand's new prime minister, General Prem, had ordered an air attack on the Ban Hin Taek headquarters. Three of the heroin factory's chemical storage units had been destroyed in the bombing, but Asim Sau had stood his ground. The driver had been there eighteen months later as well, when Thai troops staged a full assault on Ban Hin Taek. The fighting had lasted two weeks and left more than a hundred Shan soldiers dead. He had followed Asim Sau then across the border to their native Burma. There they had fought and overcome the allied opposition of Lahu tribesmen and the Communists. By the end of 1983, they had come to rule the Burmese borderlands that contained every major opium caravan route and were operating ten heroin refineries along the east shore of the Thanlwin River.

The only remaining challenge then to Asim Sau's dominion in the Golden Triangle had been General Li, the opium lord of the Guomindang. The driver had been entrusted with delivering and detonating seven thousand sticks of dynamite that left a crater where the general's Chiang Mai mansion had stood. Both the Mong Tai Army and Tai-land

Revolutionary Council had been merged with the Shan United the following year. Asim Sau then had reestablished bases in Thailand as well as in Burma; the headquarters near Mae Salong had been restored. By early 1987, when combined Thai and Burmese forces had attacked the Shan headquarters near Mae Hong Son, Asim Sau's army was strong enough to withstand them. His domain by then stretched across the Mekong to include northwestern Laos as well.

By 1990, when America put a price on his head, Asim Sau controlled more than sixty heroin refineries in the three nations of the Golden Triangle. And still the warring between the Tibetan-blooded Shan United Army and the Mon-Khmer tribesmen of the Wa National Army over the opium-rich Shan territories had not ended. Both Asim Sau and his driver still had gunpowder in their nostrils from last week's conflict with the Wa near Namsang. After that battle, Asim Sau had come south, here, to the Hmong opium farmers of Thailand, whose patron and protector he had long been. Tomorrow he and his soldiers would travel north again, to their Thai headquarters near Mae Salong.

Lo Seng still addressed his master respectfully as Bo Sau, his lord and leader. But they had been through much together, and at times, when they were alone like this, Seng called him U Fu, or Uncle Fu.

"U Fu," he said as they drove through the shadows and whispers, "how do you tell when a wife is unfaithful?" Seng had two wives, one in Burma, the other, his *ma ya nga*, or lesser wife, here in Thailand. By the Shan woman, whom he had married when he was fourteen, he had seven children. By the Thai woman, whom he had married five years ago, he had three. Two of his sons were in the Shan United youth camp.

Asim Sau smiled. "Usually she will change her hair and treat you better." He took a leaf-wrapped blood cake from his shirt pocket and took a bite.

"What if, for as long as you have known her, she just lay there like a dead woman when you fucked her? Then one night, when you came to her after many months in the jungle, she threw her legs wide around you and drummed you with her hips?"

"That, I think, would say more than a haircut."

"What would you do? Would you kill her?"

"Don't be foolish. Who would care for the children then? Besides, the new movements prove nothing, really. The women these days, they tell each other of these things. They propagate them as ways of keeping their men and satisfying themselves. We live in an age when mothers and whores have much in common. Wives believe in their innocence that if they play the slut, we'll have no need of other sluts."

"She didn't learn this from hearing about it. She was practiced. You can tell the difference. The difference between the way a boy loads and fires for the first time and the way he loads and fires after the passing of time. It's the same."

"So she's a fucking whore, that's all. It's through no fault of your own. She won't teach her daughters to be whores. You don't have to worry about that." He turned to Seng and smiled. "They'll have to learn on their own."

"I wanted to kill her. And the dog who fucked her, whoever that may be. But I said nothing, I did nothing."

"Then you're wise. Don't waste vengeance on a woman. When your children are grown and she turns to you for rice and roof in her dotage, then the scales will be balanced. Justice demands patience. Vengeance is a spiritual matter. When it becomes a passion, it consumes you. I've waited for years to destroy certain men, but I wait in tranquillity, not in eagerness. That's because I never allow my peace to depend on another, neither on his prospering nor on his destruction. When you hate, it robs your life, not the life of the one you hate." He lighted a cigarette. "Women are for pleasure, not for pain. I think that when you hurt women, you somehow defile your own strength. Leave them to their own wiles—they'll only end up hurting themselves anyway. We're born from the womb. Only a fool crawls back in to perish." Asim Sau smoked awhile, then smiled again. "You remember your readings in the great books when you came of fighting age? You remember what Kongzi said? 'Women and servants are most difficult to deal with.' "

Seng felt better now. Later, he would enjoy the roasted pig with a happy heart. As he drove on toward Tak, he wondered if he would someday have the wisdom of his uncle, lord, and leader.

From Mahat Thai Bamrung Road, the main street of the little town of

Tak, they made their way to the Sa-nguan Thai Inn, on Taksin Road. Asim Sau stepped from the Jeep, and Seng returned to Mahat Thai Bamrung Road to purchase supplies at the market across from the Mae Ping Hotel. Inside the Sa-nguan Thai, Asim Sau was welcomed as royalty. The proprietor brought him a glass of black tea from the downstairs dining-room and left him alone in the tiny office where the inn's telephone sat like an icon at the center of a small teak desk.

When Ng Tai-hei answered the ring at his home on Victoria Peak, Asim Sau said, "It is I," and lighted a cigarette.

"How is your missionary work coming?" Ng Tai-hei asked.

"Better than we had expected. I think we can look forward to four thousand new converts."

"Congratulations," said Ng, with delight in his voice. Four thousand tons would be their greatest harvest ever.

"And how is your own work coming?"

"My trip went well. Hold the line for a moment, and I'll tell you about it."

Ng returned the receiver to its cradle and went into his study. He lifted the receiver from the telephone on his antique desk and reached over to a switch on a small black box that shared a shelf with other electronic devices. Holding the receiver to his ear, he heard a sound like that of a tuning fork being struck as a high-voltage current passed along the line, burning out any possible transmitters or interceptors in its path. Ng Tai-hei did not believe that his lines were tapped, but he did believe that it was better to be safe than sorry.

"So," said Asim Sau, "tell me about Italy."

"They believe we have only a hundred and thirty-five tons on hand. For that, they will pay us nine hundred million. Plus arms, as you wanted. Two Mi-24s, two Amraams, a hundred Stingers, three kilos of enriched uranium. Plus the heads of Saw Win and Song Leekpai. We already have their payment of ten percent. Ninety-one and a half million. Another sixty percent, plus the arms and the assassinations, will follow upon shipment."

"And that shipment will leave when?"

"*Bayùe*." August's first breath.

"And it will arrive . . . ?"

"Never."

"So it will be as we discussed?"

"Yes. The shipment will be destroyed at sea. That will leave us with six hundred and thirty million. Plus the arms. Plus our situations in Myanmar and Thailand considerably improved. Plus the twenty tons of heroin they don't know we have."

"A hundred and thirty-five tons is a lot to lose."

"Yes. But they are the real losers. Six hundred million dollars, plus perhaps another two or three hundred million in goods and services. That is almost a billion dollars. It is not the sort of money that anyone in this world can afford to lose. It will bankrupt them. It will leave them impotent, and it will leave us far wealthier and with twenty tons to sell in the greatest seller's market we have ever known. We will be happy. Chinatown will be happy. The world will be a better place."

"Our golden sun shines ever more brightly."

To Ng Tai-hei, those words sounded familiar. He had forgotten that they were his own, from this past spring's harvest banquet. It was likely that he had stolen them anyway, from one of the old volumes that filled the other shelves of the room in which he sat.

"Be well, my friend," Asim Sau said.

"My prayers are with you," said his friend.

Asim Sau placed a thousand bahts in bright paper money beneath the corner of the phone. He sat back, ate the rest of his blood cake, and washed it down with tea.

How, he wondered, might a man sitting far off in a jungle know that a price agreed upon in Milan had been reported to him untainted by ulterior greed or common larceny? They had been brothers for more than twenty years. And never in those years had their brotherhood been allowed to degenerate into the *xìnrèn*, the faith and trust, of fools.

TWENTY-THREE

Palermo struck Johnny as a sort of Newark on the sea, a grimy, abrasive arabesque of garbage and dust. Here, as back home, the principle seemed to be *strepo, ergo sum*: I blare, therefore I am. The place wore its two-thousand-year history like a sordid residue, a black crust. Milan had seduced him. Palermo repulsed him.

But that repulsion waned, and seduction came. The black crust of this city hid something, a sort of eternal secret that could never be known but only felt. Palermo, like Sicily itself, had withstood the rape of every race—Phoenician and Greek, Roman and Arab, German, French, and Spanish—by becoming itself a creature of rape. Beneath the endless waves of dominion lay that creature's true and soundless spirit, the ingrained fatal sense. It was that sense, almost palpable in the air, that began to breathe, hushed and Siren-like, in Johnny's ear.

He could see it too in the eyes of Avvocato Signorelli as he sat across from Johnny and Louie in the Bar Il Gattopardo of the Grand Hotel et Des Palmes. He was a tall, stout man in his sixties. What little hair he had was pearly gray and white. He wore brown crocodile shoes, a flimsy beige suit, a pale yellow tie, and a beige straw hat, which he removed when entering the bar. Together they walked round the corner to the trattoria 'a Cuccagna, where, both Louie and the lawyer assured Johnny, *si mangiava sempre bene*, one always ate well. The manager, who obviously knew Signorelli well, led them with pride to view the day's selection of fresh seafood. There were baskets of small silver fish, crabs, urchins, and lobster, and an immense swordfish with eyes so clear there seemed to be life still in it. Johnny, Louie, and the lawyer each chose his flesh, then, from a long table, heaped a plate for himself of roasted peppers and broccoli, cold squid and zucchini. They sat at a large table at the back of the room, where a waiter had already placed Acquabaida water, bread, and wine.

"I hear Signor Raffa will be coming home in a box."

Johnny said nothing. Louie said nothing. Both men found it curious that Signorelli spoke English with the trace of a British accent.

"I am pleased that you gentlemen have arrived safely. Sometimes there seems to be more death than life in this world. Of course, that feeling always vanishes when I sit down to a good meal. This place, 'a Cuccagna, it's been here more than twenty years now. And I've never had a bad meal here in all that time. No pretensions, just food." He turned to Louie. "Don't you agree?" Louie nodded. "Then again," the lawyer continued, "I've never even so much as looked at the menu. Maybe that's the secret, as it so often is."

He did not speak again until he finished his antipasto and his first glass of wine. And when he did, his tone was no longer merely conversational.

"Our friend will see you tomorrow," he said.

The waiter brought their swordfish steaks, which had been grilled and doused with olive oil, lemon, and pepper. There was also a plate of the small silver fish, fried whole in a nestlike mass.

"How long have you known him?" Johnny asked, his voice more casual than inquisitive.

"He is my father."

Johnny and Louie were taken aback by these words, but they showed nothing.

"He was only a boy when he sired me out of wedlock. After me, there were no other sons. He put me through school. Rome, Geneva, London. Set me up in practice. In time, that practice became solely and fully devoted to the handling of his worldly affairs." He smiled, but there was something hard, something sad, in his smile. "He used to say, 'I could never have trusted a lawyer. I had to make my own, from scratch.' Of course, my duties go far beyond those of an attorney. He himself touches nothing. For thirty years, I have been the only man to see even his signature. The irony is, my work to a great extent is cryptic. There is a great element of the abstract. You see, I deal with many unknown factors. I add x to y and come up with z, but only rarely do I have any idea as to the value of x, y, or z. I call them sealed entities. This is the way he wants it, the way he has always wanted it. It is better for me, better for him. If two people know something, he says, it is not a secret. So my practice, you might say, is very private indeed. This is something I do not often speak of. But then again, I'm sure you are exceptional men. He does not often seek to meet people."

"Tell him what Vincenzo said." Louie grinned.

"He said your father summons people either to talk to them or to kill them."

The lawyer snorted and shook his head, as if at some tired old wives' tale. "Well, Signor Raffa needn't be worried on that account any longer."

The men ate and drank. After a while, Louie said, "You must know him better than any man on earth."

The lawyer responded as if to another old wives' tale. "I was twelve before I even knew he was my father. Then for a long time he was like a stranger. But over the years, yes, we've become close. You might say we've shared a great many x's, y's, and z's."

"Do you know why we're here?" Johnny asked.

"No."

"That makes three of us," Louie said.

"You see, when he wishes to speak with someone, it is not my . . ." He searched for a word, but in the end used that which he had sought to avoid. "It is not my place to know why, but only to see to it that the meeting takes place."

The old lawyer's words set Johnny thinking. How much did he himself know about what he had become involved in? He knew the game and the moves and the stakes, all right. But at the same time, he suspected again and again that his bearings were somewhat Ptolemaic, that this game, these moves, and these stakes were not the center of the world that he had entered but merely one spinning force in a vaster cosmology of evil, whose true magnitude and celestial mechanics he neither perceived nor understood.

After lunch, as they walked, heading nowhere, on Via Roma, Johnny asked Louie where they fit in. He asked it as if offhandedly, as if asking where they were.

"What do you mean?" Louie said, the left corner of his mouth curled into a slight smile.

"The big picture."

"The big picture? The meaning of life? You wanna know the meaning of life? Two bucks, same as in town. That's the meaning of life."

Johnny laughed quietly. The streets around them were receding into the sleepy calm and emptiness of afternoon.

"Tell me about this life, this one we're in," Johnny said, pointing with the right angle of forefinger and thumb at the ground of the here and now. "*La malavita*. Whatever you want to call it." He had never heard Louie, or anyone like him, speak of the Mafia. And Johnny did not really care what they called it. But he wanted to know where he was, what he was, and he figured the blood on his shirt in Milan had entitled him to some lowdown, some initiatory explication.

"*Essiri da vita*," Louie said, sighing. "It used to mean something, to be of this life, to be of this thing of ours. Sure, the newspapers, the TV, they still talk about this family and that. But those days are over. The families are dead. All these pinky rings and fancy suits, there's nothing inside them but straw and stuffing. The feds, the papers, the TV. That's what the boys are these days in America. All publicity and no *potere*. The old-timers, they're gone or their bellies are full and they don't give a fuck. Guys like your uncle, they're rare. They still believe in things. They still have values. But they're a forgotten breed. So if you're asking me, do you have some kind of title or position or something, like in the papers and the TV, the answer is no. Maybe the feds'll rank ya. They like that shit. I forget what they call me, but it's somethin' I never heard outa no wop's mouth, I can tell ya that. Give yourself a title. Some guys, it makes 'em feel good. Me, I'm boss of the *baccaus*. That's my throne, the fuckin' turlet. You can be my underboss."

The streets were now empty. Johnny's quiet laughter and their footsteps were all that could be heard. They turned south on Via Albanese, toward the sea.

"What about this whole thing with the Chinks? I mean, I know I'm my uncle's nephew and all that shit. But why me? I'm nobody."

"If you think he threw you a bone or somethin', forget it. He had faith in you. He trusted you. Those *citrull*'s at the club there, they sit around, month in and month out, waitin' for a bone. Believe me, this ain't no bone."

"But how do you feel? You could handle this without me."

"Hey, look, I'm gettin' too old for this shit myself. You, you're a fuckin' comer. You got yout'. You're a natural fuckin' meat-eater. I coasted that whole fuckin' sit-down in Milan. You handled it."

Louie's words made Johnny feel good. He did not know whether he questioned them because he doubted them or because he wanted to hear more of their kind. "I mean, I'm talkin' about hundreds of millions of dollars, billions, and they're listening. To me."

"Why shouldn't they? Whata you got, low self-esteem or some shit?"

"Sometimes, when I think about it, it seems that we're movin' the world with leverage here. It just doesn't seem fucking real."

"Well, it is."

"And when this is done, do we just take our money and walk away?"

"Let me ask *you* somethin' here. When you woke up yesterday in Milano, did you feel clean?"

Yesterday he had woken for the first time as a killer. He had raised his trigger finger to his lip and smelled the scent of the whore from the night before. He had felt somewhat shaken, true. But he had felt sanguine as well, and strong.

"Yeah. Why?"

"Nothin'. It should tell you somethin' about what you can walk away from and what you can't."

"I don't follow."

"A guy who can eat and sleep and laugh and fuck and kill and be alone with himself can walk away from anything."

"But will they let us?"

"What, did you sign a contract or somethin'?"

Johnny could still hear that mumbo-jumbo in his sleep sometimes: ". . . *d'u sangu unu e medesimu . . . un onuri luntanu da chiddu degl'autri 'omini . . .*"

"I've always heard about guys having trouble walking away."

"What kind of trouble?"

"They don't let them."

"Whata you believe in werewolves and silver bullets too? Let me tell you something, Johnny: You can walk away from anything in this life except your promises. The promises you make to your friends, you can't walk away from those. You do, you're wood. Other than that, you're your own man. The thing is, will you want to walk away?"

"Shit, the kind of money we're talkin' about, who wouldn't?"

"You'd be surprised. It's all relative. A young guy, he's never had a hundred bucks in his life, he thinks a thousand is a fortune. He gets the thousand, it don't mean shit. He wants ten. And on and on it goes. A guy might've got the best knobjob he'll ever get in his life ten years ago. That don't stop him thinkin' that the best is yet to come. I used to think once I had a million, I'd become a fuckin' man of leisure, sit around like King Farouk, and fuck it all. It don't mean nothin'. It's all relative. And I'll tell ya somethin' else. It's addictive. Just like anything else. Sex, booze, dope, action. There's a money jones. You'd be surprised."

As they approached the sea, there loomed to their left a massive fortress of pale, weathered stone. In its watchtowers and along its ramparts were machine-gun-toting guards in gray suits and blue berets. At its great iron gate, on a patch of parched grass, was an armored tank with a great long turret-mounted gun and several olive-suited soldiers wearing black berets and red neckerchiefs. There were *poliziotti* in gray-blue pants, dark blue jackets, and berets. Like the guards, they carried machine guns. There were sidearmed *carabinieri* in their gleaming black boots and black suits with red piping and trim.

"There it is," Louie said. "*La casa grande*. Ucciardone. The grand-daddy of 'em all. You ever hear of Don Vito Cascio Ferro?"

Johnny shook his head.

"He was the first great *padron'*. Western Sicily belonged to him. He died here, in Ucciardone, in the twenties. '*Vicaria, malattia e nicissitati, si vidi lu cori di l'amicu.*' He couldn't read or write, Don Vito, but he had somebody put those words on the wall in there: in prison, sickness, and want, one discovers the heart of a friend."

They sat on a bench in the little Piazza Ucciardone, across from the prison's southwest corner. Beyond Via Francesco Crispi lay the wharves and the breakwaters, and beyond them, the Tyrrhenian Sea.

"Our friend up in the hills, he's from that old school, like Don Vito. But Don Vito was supposed to have been an elegant character. The aristocracy, Palermo society, the dukes and duchesses, they loved him. He dressed like one of them. Wore a frock coat, grew a long white beard. They say his barber sold his hair clippings to an amulet-maker. Our friend here, Don Virgilio, from what I know, he's not a fancy man. He keeps to the hills. Piana degli Albanesi, years ago, it was called Piana dei Greci. There was a guy there, Don Ciccio Cuccia, he was Don Virgilio's uncle. One day, 1924, somethin' like that, Mussolini came to town. It was the year the Fascists came to power. Mussolini wanted to see the Albanian dancers. Don Cheech told him that he didn't need his *sbirri* here, his cops. He, Don Cheech, was the law, the only escort he needed. Mussolini knew that Don Cheech was speaking the truth, and that was the beginning of his war on *la Mafia*."

Johnny knew that he had *albanese* blood in him. Once, when he was a kid, he was loitering on a corner with a group of older boys. "Get away from those fuckin' wops," his uncle had called out from across the street. "Get over here with the *albanes'* where you belong." Of course, the old man had been joking. Their bloodline had been Italian since the fifteenth century, when their ancestors escaped Muslim rule. Still, it had stuck with him, and he shared his uncle's distaste for what he called professional wops.

"What do you think happened?" Johnny said. "That call from my uncle, that whole turnaround in Milan?"

"Somethin' in these bones says it has to do with Tonio."

"You think he tried to fuck us?"

"I wouldn't be surprised."

"But he's in on this with us. Him and my uncle. This is their thing."

"Like I said, this shit's a disease. It's a fuckin' jones. You go to bed with a beautiful broad, you wake up with a dick pointed at your brain. Trust is always the fatal flaw. And I don't give a shit what anybody in this fuckin' world says, you can't live without trust. You get on a plane, you're trustin' that pilot. You order a cup of coffee, you're trustin' that monkey who makes it. Trust is everywhere. Another fuckin' disease. Fuck AIDS. They oughta worry about a fuckin' cure for trust. It's killed more people."

Who did Johnny trust? Louie. His uncle. Willie Gloves. What about Diane? No. How could he trust a woman who did not trust him? Then again, why should she trust him? Fuck it. He had not thought of her since his moment of weakness after pulling that trigger. He did not want to start again now. Fuck her and fuck the floor-scrapers.

"It's like we were sayin' the other night," Louie went on. "You've gotta be ready. Ready and able. Ready to kill your own father, your best friend. 'Cause the time can come when they cease to be those things, and a moment's hesitation can be the difference between them and you. He who hesitates is lost. That's what my father used to say."

"Mine too."

"They prob'ly all said it."

"Mine was a loser. How about yours?"

"From day one. You ever see a tailor with the shakes? Believe me. I knew your father. Mine was worse."

"He who hesitates is lost. I guess they hesitated."

They ambled back to the hotel, winding their way through a warren of narrow streets and alleys that returned them to Via Roma. In his room, Johnny threw open the shutters and windows and let the afternoon breeze play on the long sheer curtains. Yesterday, before he had begun to see through the squalid black mascara of Palermo's hardened face, this big high-ceilinged room, and this old hotel itself, had struck him as shabby and sepulchral. Now he found it comfortable, a sort of grand and sheltering preserve of vanished gentility, a sanctuary of older ways whose air, beneath its stole of refinement and worn elegance, somehow reminded him of that in the haunted restaurant on 116th Street. He leaned out the curtained embrasure, looked down on Via Roma, watched the hot summer gust sweep through the fronds of the big palm below.

Johnny had never felt at home in his life. Never, through all the melancholy Octobers that echoed his birth, had he felt that there was for him a retreat of origin, a locus of the heart, a comforting place to which he could return, either in spirit or in fact. He could still hear his grandmother's voice explaining the little plaster figures of a Christmas crèche, the wise men and the donkey and the baby Jesus and the rest. It was the first Christmas he could remember, and with her voice, he could feel the nighttime flannel nuzzling his skin. Where was his mother? His father? He did not know. All he knew was the sadness of those figurines in their illusory manger. A few years later, his grandmother's voice was gone, and along with it the manger and the storybook family. But the sadness remained, and it was a long time before he made sense of its source. In that cheap painted plaster, through the fleeting magic of a grandmother's love, he had found more homely tenderness than in the manger of his own troubled childhood, and it had driven home a sense of loss that would haunt every Christmas, and many a warm night, to come. His star of Bethlehem led nowhere. Star light, star bright. His father had given him a drunken rhyme. His uncle had given him a chemistry set and books with pictures. It all had led somehow to a poem of death, discarded, like the years themselves; had led somehow to that breeze, and to this place as well.

As he withdrew from the window and lay down in silence, a strange feeling came over him. This unknown place, it felt like home.

TWENTY-FOUR

What Bob Marshall planned to do he had done before, in his street-hustle days. He called it his card trick.

As SAC, he was supposed to keep to his desk except for the big, public-exposure takedowns. He was supposed to oversee, not do. You can't judge the problem if you're part of the problem. That's what they said. But he was intent on cracking the seventh seal of this one himself. No one, not even Wang, would know what he was doing until after he had done it.

It was about two in the afternoon when he arrived in Brooklyn, dressed in blue jeans, a dark shirt, and a linen jacket. He did not hesitate but rang the bell directly.

"Who is it?" The subway-quality intercom transformed Diane Di Pietro's voice into a crackling blurt.

"Bob Salerno."

"Am I supposed to know you?"

"Johnny's friend. From the union."

"What do you want?"

"I need to talk to Johnny."

"He's not here."

An old woman entered the foyer with a bag of groceries. She unlocked the second door, made her way slowly toward the stairs. Perfect. By not following her through the unlocked door, he showed himself to be decent, upright, and on the level.

"Then I need to talk to you."

"About what?"

"Look, if you don't trust me, come down."

The buzzer sounded sickly. Marshall pushed open the door and made his way up the stairs. Diane was waiting for him, peering over the length of chain that ran from the door's edge to the jamb.

"May I come in?"

"I don't know you."

"Same here." He smiled. He saw that her eyes were red and puffy, as if she'd been crying. Then he caught a lingering whiff of marijuana and saw that she had a wineglass in her hand. She was wearing a peach-colored silk robe.

"I don't know anything about the union," she said. "Besides, if you're a friend of Johnny's, you should know where he is."

"He's in Italy. But we don't know how to reach him."

So that's where he was. Italy. That was more than she knew. See Naples and die, you sonofabitch.

"Let me put something on," she said desultorily.

She returned a few minutes later in a cotton skirt, white blouse, and espadrilles, with a fresh glass of white wine. Coldly, she let him in.

He sat on the couch. She sat in the easy chair across the room, near the spider plant by the window.

"I guess Johnny told you about the trouble we're having," he said.

"I told you. I don't know anything about the union." He struck her as somehow different from the other characters she had met through her husband. He seemed cleaner, less coarse. "Do you tell your wife about the union?"

"I don't have a wife." He smiled again. There was something sweet, she thought, about the way he said it, not happily but almost regretfully. But wait. Why was he wearing a wedding band?

He saw her looking at his hand. The ring had become such a part of him that he no longer realized he wore it. Why had he told her he wasn't married to begin with? he asked himself. It had just come out that way. Maybe he had been too long off the street.

"I suppose your mother gave you that?" she said.

"It's a long story," he said. "And it's not a happy one, either." The closet must be in the bedroom, he thought. It was just a matter of buying time until she pissed. The way she was drinking that wine, it shouldn't take too long.

"How long have you known Johnny?" she asked.

"A few years." Blowsy or not, she was a pretty woman. How did these fucking sewer rats get these good-looking broads?

"Is he your boss?" She saw him glancing surreptitiously at her legs. It pleased her. She had shaved just this morning. She ran her hand over her knee and shin. They were as smooth and cool as ivory.

"Did he tell you that? Did he say he was my boss?"

"He never even mentioned you. He never mentions anything." She rose, went to the kitchen, poured herself another glass of wine. She offered him a glass as well. He accepted. As she moved, she flaunted her best walk, the subtle river-hipped lilt she had learned as a teenager from watching old Jeanne Moreau movies. She felt as if she were teasing a young neighborhood boy, proving to herself with girlish delight that she still had it, that years of apathetic husbanding and aging cells had not yet robbed her of the power to command. "Do you know he has his own apartment?" She wondered if the men who worked with him had any idea of what he was really like, of what a prick he really was.

Shit, thought Marshall. Right church, wrong pew. "I guess that's your business. I guess that's between you two."

"Yeah. I married a man. Now all I've got is his clothes. That's all he comes here for lately."

Perfect. Right church, right pew.

"And his books. I've still got the books, too. His clothes and his books, they keep me company. Sounds like a bad song."

He looked at the rows of books: the little green-spined volumes of Greek poetry, the red-spined volumes of Latin; Dante and ancient history; *The Bad Popes, The Discourses* of Machiavelli, and *I Married a Lesbian Slut*. He was stunned.

"These are his? He reads all this?"

"He used to. Once upon a time."

"I'm impressed." What the fuck was he dealing with here? Maybe the most dangerous thing of all: a mind.

"Where's his other place?"

"Ask him."

Diane crossed her legs so that her right ankle lay on her left knee. As she sipped her wine, she narrowed her lowered eyes, monitored those of the ivory poacher. Would Johnny even bother to look? Sometimes she felt he did not consider a woman to be a woman unless her legs were sheathed in nylon, like so much meat stuffed into a synthetic sausage-casing of cheap polymer. Then again, did she even care anymore whether Johnny looked or not? Below the belly, she was dead to him. Below the belly, until these last few hot days, she had been dead, period. She thought of the Panabrator she used to have. It had long ago burned out. She finished her wine, went to the kitchen, letting her pelvis sway in that fine fucked walk. She opened another bottle. Marshall had barely drunk from his glass. She lighted a joint, sucked on it, asked her visitor if he wanted some.

"Not right now." Christ. This broad must have a bladder like a camel. He averted his eyes from her. She was getting him excited. He never cheated on Mary. But as much as he loved her, there were things she shied from in bed, especially lately, with the baby on its way. He wondered about this one here. Would she do those things?

Diane had told Jill she would call her by three. They were supposed to go to a movie. Fuck it. This was better than a movie. When was the last time she had been alone here with a man? Except for a few repairmen, never. But enough was enough. She had had her fun. She wished she still had her Panabrator.

"Well, what did you need to tell me?"

"If I tell you something, can you call Johnny and give him the message?"

"What makes you think I can reach him?"

"Doesn't he call?"

"Not even a postcard."

"Well, then, it doesn't make sense to go through you. I'll just wait till he comes back. If you don't mind, I'll just finish my wine and leave a little note for him."

The sealed note was in his pocket. *Did you get a good fortune cookie in Milan?* it said. But he had already made up his mind to trace Johnny's other address and send it there. For now, the card trick, if he could pull it off, was all that mattered.

"Please yourself." She wheezed, drawing on the joint. She did not know why she smoked this shit. It always ended up making her dwell on things, such as her childlessness, such as all the times that Johnny had hurt her. How often in their years of marriage had he been alone with a woman? Had he ever been a gentleman like his friend here? Shit, Johnny didn't even have to be alone with them. He dragged them into public toilets in bars. He was probably fucking some bitch right now, for all she knew.

Marshall sipped his wine, looked at the print on the wall. "Nice picture."

She craned her neck, then stood, took a few steps back, and stared at it.

"Johnny doesn't think so."

"Why not?"

"It makes him jealous."

"I don't get it."

"You don't get Johnny. And like you said, it's our business." She'd had enough of this. She was getting morose. She wanted to be alone.

"Would it make him jealous to know that I was here?"

"No." Fuck it. She turned around, faced him, took another step toward him, felt something like a wolf rush up inside her. "But this would." She took his hand and put it under her skirt to rest on her thigh.

This was ridiculous, he thought. But his erectile tissue stirred like a boy's. He stood, bringing his hand up and around to clutch her as he rose. Her neck loosened, and she opened her mouth to his, feeling that stirring in his britches strong against her abdomen. She stroked it, grabbed it, slaked her tongue within his mouth. He slipped his hand beneath her cotton panties, moved his fingers from the soft flesh of her ass to the warmth of her crotch. When he discovered that she was sopping wet, a groan escaped him, soft and low, a falling, abandoning sound.

"Do you want to fuck?" she whispered into his ear. He felt more than heard her: sounds not so much of voice as of breath. She could feel his heart pounding against her bosom.

He couldn't fuck her. He couldn't do this to Mary. No, that was bullshit. He could do this to Mary, all right. But he couldn't risk getting caught. God only knew what this slut might dose him with. No. Fuck that. One way or the other, it would weave an indelible lie into the fabric of their marriage. Could he live with that lie? Maybe a blowjob. Could you get AIDS from a blowjob? A handjob. Maybe a handjob. Mary was good for neither.

"I'll be right back," she said.

He waited till she closed the bathroom door, then took off his shoes and crept into the bedroom. From his jacket pocket, he took out a small stack of DEA calling cards and began slipping them into the pockets of Johnny's suits, jackets, and coats. He returned to the living room, stood near the bathroom door.

"Give me your panties," he said boyishly.

"Why? Do you want to sniff them? Does that turn you on?" She was sitting on the toilet, brushing her teeth, grinning, with a look in her eyes like that of a cat playing with a mouse.

"Yeah."

The door creaked open slightly. He took the cotton panties from her hand.

"Don't jerk off in them. Wait for me."

They were scented and stained with her juices. He wrapped them around a calling card, returned to the bedroom closet, and tucked them neatly into the inside breast pocket of a black kid-mohair suit. That should unhinge this fucker but good.

Johnny, he figured, was the youngest, the most vulnerable, the least hardened—the weakest link in this chain. Unhinged, that link might very well break. Marshall's belief in psychological warfare had paid off in the past. He had fucked up the brains of bigger game than this Brooklyn prince of garbage. Were it not for those books in the other room, he would have little doubt as to the efficacy of his scheme. What if the garbage prince, like Marshall, knew that chapter of *The Discourses* that proclaimed "that it is a Glorious Thing to use Fraud in the Conduct of a War"? What if he possessed the composure to see this deceit for what it was, an incendiary excitant that could be defused simply by being ignored? But who could possess such composure?

He was still in the bedroom when the bathroom door suddenly opened. Hurriedly, he pulled off his jacket and threw it on the bed, then began unbuttoning his shirt.

"What did you do with my panties?" she asked, standing there in her peach-colored silk robe.

"It's a secret."

"Tell me. I want to know." Her voice fell to a whisper. "Did you kiss them?" She unbuckled his belt, unzipped his fly with two hands. "Tell me."

She took him by the hand, lay down on the bed, drew him down beside her. She couldn't fuck him. She didn't even want to fuck him. She wanted to jerk off while he fucked her mouth. But drunk or not, she wasn't about to let a strange cock between her lips. Now that she thought about it, what the fuck was this all about?

He had done what he had come here to do. He should just get up, piss off his hard-on, and git.

"Does he ever hit you?" he asked.

"Don't even think about it," she snapped.

"No. I was only curious." What if this cocksucker beat the shit out of her when he found those cards? Maybe the bit with the panties had been too much. Fuck it. This guy wants to play with fire, fuck him. But what about her? What if she caught a beating over this?

He heard a small wet clicking sound. She was playing with herself. Her breathing grew heavier, strained and wild at once.

"Come on my tits," she said, panting. She repeated it again and again, like a chant. What would Johnny do if he knew? Would he kill him? Would he kill her? She imagined Johnny standing over them, watching, masturbating in a rage, like a caged and cornered beast.

Marshall knelt over her, fondled her breasts, watched her face contort. She opened her eyes, watched him caress his cock. Her hand moved more furiously.

"Now." Then she began to moan, low and long, and as he watched her writhe beneath him, he shuddered and shook the hot, pasty sap from his cock onto her breasts and across her shoulder and neck. She called out for God, then wilted and lay there gasping. Even through the general anesthesia of the wine, she hated herself. She had never before laid bare her nature for a stranger like this. What had gotten into her? She had felt miserable before. She felt wretched now.

Marshall skulked with his clothes into the other room. He felt like shit. He had come here as an agent and was leaving as a fool. We're all fucking animals, all of us, he told himself. When he was dressed, he went to the bedroom and looked down on her.

"I guess we'll keep this afternoon our little secret," he said.

She said nothing. It did not seem that there was anything to say.

Back in his office, Marshall sat at his computer and began merging data on Giuseppe and Johnny Di Pietro, the late Antonio Pazienza, Louie Bones, and Ng Tai-hei and the 14K Triad into the directory he had named Apocalypse. He was still there at eight o'clock, when Mary called. By then he had washed his hands three times. Before he went home, he washed them once again.

TWENTY-FIVE

Standing on the northwest corner of Piazza Ruggero Settimo, Johnny had looked around. To his left and to his back, there were mountains. To his right, the sea. He decided to walk straight ahead, along the shaded, moneyed boulevard of Viale della Libertà. That is how he had happened upon the Giardino Inglese.

Beyond Piazza Crispi, the English Garden lay before him like a smack in the face to his early dismissal of Palermo as a Newark by the sea. He had spent the last hour of sunlight there, wandering along its winding paths amid the towering palms and cacti, the flowery knolls and lush-boughed trees. There were old men gathered here and there around *tarocchi* and poker decks. And everywhere—around the fountain, on benches amid blossoming bushes, under trees, and on the open grass— were lovers. From the venery of youth to the venality of age, this vast green place was a morsel of paradise for all. Johnny found a bench just beyond the shade of the most remarkable tree he had ever seen, a gigantic, ancient plane whose roots had risen from the earth with the passing of the centuries, lifting the great trunk toward heaven on a sinuous chaos of massive veins that ascended like a nest of Laocoön-killing serpents.

From somewhere nearby, Johnny heard a soft, light, girlish giggle, so sweet that it merged with the songs of the birds all around. It was the sound of love, and it made Johnny smile. He leaned back, closed his eyes, and raised his face to the setting sun.

Here, as at the public gardens in Milan, it was easy for him to open himself to the breeze and beauty of the moment. He imagined himself trying to do the same amid the boom boxes and nigger dope-hawkers of Prospect Park or Washington Square. The thought made him grin, not so much at the absurdity of it as at his fortune to be here rather than there. Here, where he felt strangely at home.

A squirrel scurried by. A group of sparrows in its path took flight, vanished into the foliage of the big plane.

In moments and places such as this, the blood in Johnny's brain ran calm. He had not been drunk for more than a year, and as he sat in the tranquillity and voluptuous waning sunlight of the English Garden, the accruing pressure of those long months of restraint evaporated in the breeze.

Alcohol had very nearly destroyed him. He had not even been aware of entering Lenox Hill Hospital at the end of his last go-round. When his trembling consciousness had returned to him, he had found himself bearded and kneeling in a back-tied gown on the cold hospital floor, an intravenous catheter in his wrist connecting him to a feeding-sack tree, immersed in studying, as if it were the lost key to the hermetica of the ages, the manufacturer's plate at the foot of his bed: MODEL NO. 68 ALL ELECTRIC BED. HILL-ROM COMPANY INC., BATESVILLE, INDIANA. He had risen then to stalk the corridors, toting his IV tree as he moved, searching out the nurse with the red band around her waist. She was the one. He had known that much. He could not remember how he got here, or what season it was, but he remembered that: on every shift, the nurse with the key to the Schedule 4 cabinet made herself known to the doctors by means of that red waistband. The Schedule 4 cabinet was where the narcotics and barbiturates were locked away. With that key, he could knock himself out, go back to where he liked it best: oblivion. How would he get the key? He would sweet-talk her, bash her with his tree; he did not know.

By the time he found her, he knew what season it was. He had been taken off the IV and put on Librium and folic acid. The doctors had wanted to know about his drinking. He had leveled with them. He either drank or he did not drink; he was not one of the lukewarm. He might go months without so much as a glass of wine. Then, for two or three months, he would drink. Every waking moment he would drink, eating barely enough to stay alive, until his body no longer accepted even this subsistence, and then he would merely drink, for days or weeks without eating, until he could drink no more; and then, with all the will and strength that remained within, he would taper off with cold beer, then suffer and await renewal. How much did he consume in a day? they wanted to know. A dozen or so beers or Bloody Marys to quell his guts and steady his nerves. At least a fifth of Scotch, usually more. A bottle of wine if he was eating. Five or six brandies. God knew what else. They told him that he was lucky to be alive, that drinking far less had shut down younger bodies than his. He knew this. Everyone he had ever known who had drunk as much as he did was dead. He had watched them go, one after another. In the bars where he was most comfortable, "Guess who died?" was a familiar greeting.

His liver, they had told him, was bad. He had both gastritis and gastroenteritis. He was suffering from malnutrition, neurological degeneration, and alcoholic myopathy. But he was alive. It must be that Albanian goat blood, Johnny had thought.

The doctors had persuaded him to go to AA when they released him. And he had gone. But after a while, he had begun to see it as a racket. Most of those who attended, by his standards of reckoning, had never really drunk all that much to begin with. They came to meetings, he suspected, as others went to bars or did church work: to socialize. For some, AA seemed to be a substitute for life, a microcosm with its own mythology, hierarchy, and language, a refuge where those who failed to find elsewhere the attention, love, and sense of importance they craved could preen and thrive. For others, it seemed to be a counteraddiction that built not strength but weakness. Elevating themselves from drunkards to alcoholics, from fuck-ups to suffering souls, the not-so-anonymous followers of AA seemed to enjoy the self-importance and self-sympathy of pretending to be in the throes of a disease. They were snobs that way, skid-row elitists who bestowed delusory dignity on drunkenness by calling it alcoholism. Johnny had watched his mother rot away slowly and painfully from cancer. To him, that was a disease. What kind of disease could be controlled by volition? he asked. But then again, AA had not much use for free will. Its credo of powerlessness and blind submission to a lackluster deity of drunkards insured the stunting of souls, the snuffing of willpower, the dousing of what ancient wisdom called the heroic spark. Surely more people put down the bottle in the centuries before AA than in the decades of its existence. With its dictatorial insistence on endless meetings, indoctrination, and conversion, it denied that there are men, and women, whose powers are diminished, not enhanced, by the strictures and influences of conformity, who find no comfort in gathering, who are lessened, not greatened, by remanding their destinies to others. Like every religion and cult, its ultimate message was: there is no other way. And that message, as always, was anathema to Johnny. It was bad enough coming from the Church, whose sword of authority had been drawing blood for nearly two millennia, but coming from a cult whose history went back only sixty years to some schmuck named Bill, it was preposterous. So it was not long before Johnny had discounted what the doctors had recommended. But for a time, he had kept his little forty-eight-page *New York Area Meeting Book*. For him, it had served as sort of a modern-day, New York *Tenderloin 400 Blue Book*, a twenty-four-hour-a-day, five-borough "where the girls are."

To the doctors, and to the gadabouts of AA, Johnny's drinking had made no sense. Other men who were drunkards were beset by impotence. But Johnny was never so hindered. Reduced by myopathy and malnutrition, lurching at death's doorway, he could raise a fucking hard-on for a puke-drenched barroom sow. Other drunks told of their inability to have only one drink. Johnny had never, not once in his life, set out to have one drink. His goal was drunkenness, pure and simple, and he knew beforehand that drunkenness would ultimately seize him and not let go until long after the pleasures of oblivion had ceded to pain. And yet his urge to be drunk was not such that he would ever choose to become instantly loaded. If given the opportunity to take a pill that would make him drunk, he would never take it, whereas he believed that most drunks would. To him, the slow descent into oblivion, with its endless expectations and possibilities—a winning bet, a broad, a fight, a frisson of joy in song or laughter, a memory come to life—was the main event. Sometimes it took days and nights without sleep to get there, but he loved every moment of it. In time, however, those expectations and possibilities had dwindled, and he just drank, without delusion or false happiness; he just drank. And when he realized that the expectations and possibilities were gone forever, he wondered what it was that lured him still. Then he knew that it had never really been the broads, or anything else. It had been oblivion all along. That was his true love: oblivion.

In Milan he had killed with purpose. But through the years he had been killing himself, and had not known why. He made more sense as a killer than as the protagonist of his own life.

He wondered whether Diane missed him, or if that bitch Jill and the floor-scrapers of modern womanhood had got her. He knew that deep down she was good; that deep down she would never betray him. What love remained for her within him was not all weakness and muted cry. Besides, she was his wife, now and until the moment he renounced her. If she turned her back on him, if she lay with another man, then Johnny would turn to Leviticus, and to the wisdom of that Albanian shylock named Lou with whom he had once run. Or would he? If the events in Milan had taught him anything, it was that no man could foresee his response to an unknown occurrence.

This was the lesson not just of the murder, but of the parley itself. As smoothly as it had gone, he had thought that he would come away with a greater sense of confidence and relief, even elation. But such had not been the case. The more he had reflected on the relative ease of those negotiations, the more dubious and discomfited he had become. As he had sat in the English Garden, what Billy Sing had taught him had seemed to drift, blood-red and violet, through the western sky, illuminated by the sun's last golden rays. *To cross the ocean without letting the sky know. To deceive all.* As the rays had softened and fallen, he had been able to look straight into those colors with open eyes. *To pretend to hit the east and actually attack the west.* Perhaps he had dwelled too long on one stratagem: *to transform oneself into a wholly new man during crisis.* Perhaps in his dwelling and pride, he had blinded himself to the rest. *Human nature is evil.* To forget that for one moment, as Vincenzo Raffa had forgotten, could prove fatal.

Johnny and Louie made their way that night to Via Castriota. Johnny followed Louie down a flight of stairs to the dining-room of La Briciola, which Louie recalled as the best restaurant in Palermo. It was a small room, with tiled floors and lower walls of white and upper walls of beige, separated by a chair rail of dark wood. The beige walls were hung with paintings and prints, and bottles of old wine rested on corner shelves. The lighting was soft; the tablecloths, tangerine. The owner, who remembered Louie, led them through an arched passage to their left, to another, smaller room of four tables, where they were the only diners. A waiter brought them a plate of wild-boar prosciutto and bottles of water and wine, then wheeled in a cart of fresh fish and raw meats and told them what pastas were being prepared.

After they ordered, Johnny broached the subject of his vague doubt and discomfiture concerning the meeting in Milan. Louie listened to him intently, nodded slowly, and thought for a moment.

"So," he said, "it ain't just me."

Johnny had hoped that Louie, with the perspective of his years and experience, would be able to explain away his apprehension. The older man's words were not what he had wanted to hear. *Truthful words are not beautiful.*

"You know, that trouble with Raffa there, it came so fast that for a while, in my mind, it was all connected. But that was different trouble. That was Italian trouble. It had nothing to do with the meeting itself."

They still did not know that Tonio had betrayed them and was dead. And they did not know that Raffa was part of that betrayal. Giuseppe would not speak of such things over the telephone. All they knew was what he had told them, what he had had to tell them that night, in urgency: that Raffa, not the Chink, was the thorn to be removed.

"In my mind," Louie said, "it was all mixed up. I felt like, hey, this wasn't such an easy deal. But the trouble and the parley were two different animals. The meeting *was* easy. Maybe a little too easy."

Johnny played devil's advocate to himself: "But then again, we did lay a hell of an offer on the table."

"That we did. And he didn't jump on it, either. There was a hell of a lotta back-and-forth with the numbers there."

"And all that World War Three shit."

"Yeah. He couldn't hide his fuckin' hunger there."

"And he made that call to check on those final figures."

"Now that I think of it, it wasn't that fuckin' easy, was it?"

"Maybe it seemed easy because we got what we set out to get. Maybe that was it." Johnny laughed.

The waiter brought them the fennel salads they had ordered.

"I used to believe," Louie said, "that everything a man suspects is true. I'm talkin' a man with eyes to see. Not everything he fears, but everything he suspects. There's a big difference. I still believe it in a way. But now I know that sometimes it's almost impossible to tell the difference between suspicion and fear."

"How *do* you tell?"

"By never fearing."

"And how do you do that?"

"When you find out, let me know."

TWENTY-SIX

The Albanian Plain lay only fifteen miles south of Palermo, but those miles twisted along winding mountain roads that made the journey seem much longer. The roadside was a garland of gold and white and purple blossoms, dense with cactus and pine, lemon and orange, silvery olive trees, clusters of dewy lavender grapes.

There was not much to the town itself, which seemed to cling to the age as well as the hilly rock of its fifteenth-century founding. Signorelli parked the car in an alley off Via Kastriotta, near the center of town. Goat hides and cloven-hooved carcasses hung in the morning sun outside a shop advertising *carnezzeria* and *testa di castrato*. Outside a café, a group of men on the dusty pavement raised their hats solemnly as Signorelli passed. Johnny and Louie followed him from sunlight to shadows as they made their way up Via Barbato, a steep path that led to a little church, identified in both Italian and Albanian—Chiesa di San Giorgio, Klisha Shën Giergji—as the Church of Saint George.

"Wait here," the lawyer said, then disappeared down another, nameless path.

Louie stood there, smoking on the old stone steps. Johnny opened the creaking door and entered the dim, silent church. In the cupola over the altar, a blue-robed Christ held a book that bore the marks of alpha and omega, the beginning and the end. Johnny was drawn to the left, to Nicolò Bagnasco's wooden sculpture of Saint George and the dragon. He put several two-hundred-lire coins into an offering-box and lighted a candle.

Less than a minute after he rejoined Louie on the shadowy steps outside, they saw Signorelli returning, and with him Don Virgilio.

He was an old man all right, older than Johnny's uncle, but he moved with more strength and vitality than Joe had summoned in years. He was shorter than his son, and dressed in clothes that might have been tailored eighty years ago, or yesterday: nondescript shoes of thick black leather, beltless black straight-cut trousers held up by black galluses worn over a white V-necked T-shirt, a cocked cap of brown herringbone tweed on his head of white hair, and an open notched-lapel jacket of brown calf suede. As he approached, his eyes remained set on Louie, Johnny, and the church. When he came to the base of the steps, he stopped and stood. His face was like an image from a Roman aureus: cold and grave and august.

"*Manciamu,*" he said. His voice was deep and gentle.

Johnny rolled the word over in his mind. *Mangiamo,* perhaps. Yes, that is what it must mean: let's eat. He knew then that it was not going to be easy to follow Don Virgilio's words. But when the old man saw that Johnny's comprehension was halting, he spoke again, saying this time, "*Mangiamo.*" And that is the way it was to be: the old man would weave his words of Italian and Sicilian, and sometimes even of the strange, isolated *albanese-siciliano* dialect of this little town, and Johnny, looking to Louie whenever he was lost, would try to follow what was being said.

Don Virgilio's invitation to lunch was fulfilled slowly and with the arcane air of ritual. First they entered a baker's on Via Kastriotta, where they were given, directly from the oven, at no charge and with much fuss by the baker over size, freshness, and warmth, a loaf of rich-smelling *grana.* From there—as they passed the café again, hats were not only raised, heads were bowed as well—they proceeded to a shop that had no door, merely a curtain of beads. There they got a bottle of water and a bottle of red wine that bore no label or seal. The proprietor screwed open the wine, pushed the cork back in. Again there was no charge. From there they made their way to Piazza San Nicolò, where several old benches were arranged around a well. On one side of the tiny, sun-bleached piazza, there was another shop, a *salumeria*, where Signorelli, who had been carrying everything, handed over the bread to the woman behind the counter, who proceeded to slice it and prepare thick sand-wiches, four of local salami and four of prosciutto and tomato. She accepted no money and pressed upon them, too, four of the blood oranges known as *sucasangu* and a hunk of goat cheese studded with peppercorns. They adjourned to the benches by the well, and there they ate, in the sun and the air, looking out at the mountain that the locals simply called Pizzuta, the Peak.

Johnny could remember no better lunch, no meal in which the rare simple flavors of food and wine, the pleasures of air and sun and mo-ment, were so perfectly joined and balanced, savored and imbibed together in wordless tranquillity.

Don Virgilio did not mix eating and talking. When they were nearly done, alternating their last pieces of cheese and sweet orange with swallows of water and wine, he looked at Signorelli and nodded. To Johnny, they did not seem like father and son. That bond seemed to have been tempered to a more enigmatic one, a sword of covenant, perhaps, which both men held in common, the elder hand clasped on the younger.

The four men washed their hands and rinsed their mouths with well water, shaking their hands dry and spitting on the ground. The lawyer gathered up the rinds and bottles and told Louie and Johnny that he would await them in the café.

Don Virgilio placed a short, gnarled cigar between his teeth and lighted it. There had been no introductions. Signorelli had not intro-duced them, and the old man had not introduced himself. Yet he spoke to them as if they had been here at this well forever, drinking from it together and sharing the same sunlight.

"Dimenticate tutto che sapete di quest' affare. Tutto che credete è una menzogna," he said: Forget all that you know about this affair. Everything you believe is a lie.

Louie and Johnny looked at each other, then at him.

"Tuttu muht," he said, not so much to them, but as if to reaffirm to himself, in the tone of his own strange dialect, what he had said. Oddly enough, Johnny recognized the sound of the word *muht*, which was Albanian for *shit*.

Though the sun was still shining bright, it seemed to Johnny and Louie that the sky had darkened, such was the startling pall that came over their minds. Johnny tried as best he could to follow what Don Virgilio said.

There was, the old man said, no true intention of forming a partnership with the Asians. There never had been.

"Un'inculata per i cinesi," he spat: fuck the Chinks up the ass.

The Pakistani-Afghan borderlands were poised to resume their dominance over the Golden Triangle as the opium heartland of the world. Men close to Don Virgilio, *uomini d'onore della cupola palermitana*, were already preparing the hill farmers for greater production and overseeing the construction of new refineries in the region and throughout the Middle East, from Karachi to Istanbul. All that needed to be done was to deplete the Asians of their current stock, through the initial transaction of the false partnership that Johnny and Louie had arranged. The arms from Linosa would never be delivered. Instead, support would be given to those rulers who sought to destroy the power of their common enemies.

"Il generale Saw Win in Birmania," Louie said. *"Il primo ministro Song Leekpai in Tailandia."* He did not even have to look at his notes; he remembered those names, which Ng Tai-hei had pronounced with venom.

"Bravissimo," Don Virgilio said, and for the first time, he smiled.

In this manner, he said, rightful sovereignty would be restored. Of course, Don Giuseppe could never have burdened them with this knowledge beforehand. Men who knew they were lying were never as effective as those who believed they were telling the truth.

He asked who had killed Raffa. He used a strange expression for "murder"—*abbucari u brodu,* to overturn the broth—which Johnny did not understand. But the inquisitive tone of his voice and the name of Raffa made his meaning clear. Johnny looked at Louie but said nothing.

Don Virgilio, observing the men's faces, settled his gaze on Johnny and thanked him. Then he asked both of them if Tonio Pazienza was a good man.

They assured him that he was.

"*Avrei detto lo stesso di Raffa,*" he said, slowly and deliberately: I would have said the same of Raffa.

He saw that the two Americans were stunned.

"*Non si sa mai,*" he said: you never know.

What followed was what men such as Don Virgilio called *stagghiacubbu,* a profound silence. Johnny recalled Tonio's telling them that the *stiddari,* the island's free guns, had been brought to answer to Don Virgilio. He asked about this.

So I had thought, the old man said. Raffa was Stidda. That Chink whose hand was sent to Milan was Stidda. Though at the time we did not know it, whoever sundered him did us a great favor. That was Tonio's dream, perhaps, and Raffa's: to create a new regime from the Stidda.

No, he said, *un'inculata per la Stidda.* From now on, the *stiddari* would be fed to the commissioners like mice to snakes. Some men, he reflected, were more suited to extermination than to slavery.

Don Virgilio repeated what he had said before: "*Non si sa mai.*" This time, it was little more than a whisper. Then he stood. Looking away, he nodded abstrusely, as if his true business were with the sun, the air, the sky.

The three men walked to the café. As they entered and those at the bar and at the tables raised their hats and lowered their heads, as those outside had done, Johnny noticed that the eyes of the townsmen never met those of Don Virgilio. It was as if, while respectfully acknowledging him, they purposely, absurdly made a show of not seeing him or those who accompanied him.

Signorelli sat alone at a table in the back. Don Virgilio asked Louie to write down the names of the Burmese general and the Thai prime minister. These names were given to Signorelli.

What Italian government official in that part of the world is *obbligato a noi*? he asked.

The lawyer raised his brows and turned down his mouth. He mentioned the name of a chancellor at the Italian consulate in Shanghai. Through his appointment to China, Signorelli said, the chancellor had escaped implication in a political-corruption case in Turin, and that appointment had been arranged through friends in Rome. Perhaps this friendly and indebted chancellor could arrange introductions through diplomatic channels in Bangkok and Yangon.

You must arrange meetings for our friends here, Don Virgilio said. Meetings with this general and this prime minister.

And what should the purpose of these meetings be said to be?

Political and military support. Our friends here represent a consortium of Western business interests who wish to make a very generous commitment to what they deem to be great humanitarian causes that will further both democracy and trade.

Johnny looked at Louie, and the old man looked at both of them.

"Wear a suit," he said.

That afternoon, as they sat together over coffee in the Caffè Opera in Piazza Verdi, Johnny realized that for the first time he felt himself to be on an even footing with Louie. This was because Louie, it was clear, was as uncomfortable as he himself was with the prospect of their mission as legates to Burma and Thailand, as put before them by Don Virgilio.

"That sorta shit ain't my *métier*," Louie said, pronouncing the final word with a crooked grin, trying to make light of his uneasiness.

"Christ, Louie, you got class like people got dandruff."

"Nah, pal, you're the one. They look at me like an old warhorse. You're the one they wonder about. You're the young lion."

"Well, now that we've jerked each other off . . ."

"Yeah." Louie laughed. As Johnny had noticed before, laughter was medicine for Louie. It came rarely, but when it did, it rejuvenated him, lighted his hazel eyes like a matinee idol's. Hell, it was everybody's medicine.

Louie said he was going to visit an old friend, a guy who ran the rackets in the Capo zone, not far from where they were now. He invited Johnny to come along. Johnny passed, told Louie he wanted to see the sights.

"You already did," Louie said. "We had lunch with the sights, both of us."

Louie had told him about the catacombs, and he wanted to see for himself. He walked Louie to Piazza della Stigmate, then went off on his own. He took the number 27 bus to the northern outskirts of town. He got off near Via Pindemonte and walked east to Piazza Cappuccini. To the left of the Convento dei Cappuccini, there was an entranceway. Stepping from sunlight to shadow, Johnny encountered a brown-robed monk, wizened and hunchbacked, who gestured silently at a small tray of woven palm, on which were several crumpled thousand-lire notes. Johnny placed two bills on the tray and began his descent of the stone stairs that led to the catacombs. The way grew darker, the air drier, cooler, and more rarefied. There were wisps of an unknown scent, an ageless mulch of holy water and dead souls.

Neither in his dreams nor in his nightmares had he envisioned such a place as this ghetto of the dead. Crowded everywhere throughout this underground maze of passages and galleries, lying in niches and hanging from spikes, escaping from disintegrating caskets and peering sightlessly through cloudy panes, were the remains of some eight thousand *palermitani* from centuries past. From the oldest among them, Frate Silvestro da Gubbio, *inumato 16 ottobre 1599*, all skull and white leathern hands in his sack of monkish brown, to the child Rosalia Lombardo, *morto 6 dicembre 1920*, perfectly asleep with her chestnut hair and yellow bow, theirs was a population as varied as any that breathed. There were cardinals in their copes and miters, suspended like grisly dolls, some full-skinned and hairy, others with grasping skeletal hands bursting forth from splayed gloves of brittle flesh. There were gentlemen in frock coats, their faces screaming, a rotten eye still peering here and there, strands of long white hair and parched strips of husklike hide dangling from yellow skulls. There were children, like little monsters, in their nursery bonnets; infant carcasses, crushed, flattened, and froglike. Here a woman's raised hand bizarrely beckoned; there a prelate's face froze in a wide, silent, endless groan. Straw matting protruded from robes where bodies had sunken and turned to dust. There were footsteps other than his own on the majolica tiles; here and there, the form of another intruder could be seen, or sensed. In time, the footsteps and forms vanished. Johnny turned up his collar, shoved his hands in his jacket pockets against the chill.

He approached the chamber of virgins, where ghastly maidens in white were arranged upright on either side of a large crucifix. He studied the faces of purity, rotten and bereft and bony. One of them, its head fallen, grotesque and demure, transfixed him.

Then suddenly death was upon him, with a hissing voice so close that he could feel its warmth on his ear and neck, a sensation so terrible that the shuddering that overtook him in a wave seemed to disembowel him. The arm was around his neck, the forearm pressed to his throat before he knew it. All he could see was purity's rotten face, and he felt himself enveloped and overwhelmed by the drumming of his own wild heart.

"Ti farò manciari 'a sua ficu, fottutu strunzu!" The words came in a hushed, violent rush: I'll make you eat her cunt, you fucking piece of shit.

Johnny could feel something pressed to the small of his back. A gun? A knife? The breath in his ear seemed almost sexual. He clenched his hands in fear.

The forearm pressed tighter against his throat. He wheezed, straining to fill his lungs with breath, swallowing what he could of the scent of holy water and death.

The drumming in his ears slowed. Everything slowed. His throat grew numb to the crushing pain. His field of vision darkened and contracted. How strange to die in such a place.

Had a second passed, an hour, since that last drawn breath? He tried to speak, but he could not. He could not die like this, not like a woman clinched tight to the heat of a raptor's breast. And yet he could not move.

His hands wilted open. He had crushed a pack of cigarettes in his left hand. In the clutch of his loosening right fist, he felt something cool. A pen. No. He eased the safety switch on the mother-of-pearl stiletto.

"*Questo è per Vincenzo*," hissed the voice in his ear.

With his thumb, Johnny pressed the release button of the stiletto and at the same time drove it backward in his pocket with the sum of all the power that remained within him.

Now it was the voice in his ear that turned womanly, with the *oh*! of a girl taking a deep thrust to the cervix. Hard metal dropped to the ground: a dagger. Johnny wrenched the stiletto blade from his attacker's liver and from his pocket in one fierce movement. Spinning round, he saw the young Sicilian gripping his side with two hands, blood streaming through his fingers and cascading to the floor. He was one of those woodpile Sicilians, one of those long-distance swimmers from Africa, with hair like a fucking *tizzun'*. Johnny kicked him hard in the groin, watched him fall to his knees in the puddle of his own blood. He grabbed him by his nigger hair and lowered his mouth to his ear. It was his turn to whisper sweet nothings.

"*Sei stiddaru?*"

The bleeding man said nothing, only panted.

Johnny brought down the bloody blade before his eyes and put it to his neck. The man begged for life.

"*Sei stiddaru?*" Johnny asked again, angrily, impatiently, jerking back the man's head.

"*Sì*," he said sadly, imploringly.

Johnny drew the blade like a cello bow across the man's throat, which opened like a mouth to cover him with an apron of blood.

When he stood, both his hands—one held the stiletto, the other his victim's wallet—were drenched and slimy with gore. He shut the knife and returned it with the wallet to his jacket pocket.

Somewhere in the catacombs, he heard other steps. He wiped his hands on his jacket, then removed the jacket, turned it inside out, rolled it up, and placed it under his arm. He was still trembling when he made his way to sunlight.

He wound through the crooked streets east of Via Mosca. He was certain that he could hear a faint scream from the catacombs. He knew he heard sirens and blaring horns. By the time he reached the Archbishop's Palace, he had rid himself of the jacket, knife, and wallet and put the dead man's identification and money in his back pocket. Near the Biblioteca Nazionale, he caught a cab to Via Roma, then walked to the hotel. He removed his clothes, examined them for blood. His shirt was spattered with stains he had not seen. One shoe, one sock, and one trouser cuff were smeared with blood as well. He emptied his pockets and shoved everything into a plastic laundry bag. His fingernails were dark with a red-and-black bloody crust. His thighs and shorts, he realized, were dank with the piss of animal fear.

The trauma of the attack reverberated deeply. In the shower, he was overcome with panic, hearing creaks of entry in his own breath, shadows of approach in his every move. His hands shook so badly that he could not shave. It was not the throat-cutting that unsettled him; it was the arm from nowhere around his throat, the sudden fatal hissing in his ear.

He lay naked in the breeze, waiting for his breath to ease and his nerves to calm. When they did, he trimmed and cleaned and filed his nails, brushed his teeth and shaved, and put on fresh shorts. He counted the money he had taken from the man: only eighty thousand lire. Then, with odd entrancement, he studied the dead man's photo ID—odd because this man seemed as nondescript as any other who had ever breathed, odd because to Johnny this plain-faced nobody and the face of abject fear had been one, odd because he passed such men in the street every day, men whose documents of identification lent their existence more credence than their lives would seem to merit, men who, like this one, might at any moment dart forth from the milling blur with fangs bared and venom bubbling.

As a boy, Johnny had always wanted a stiletto. He had wanted a stiletto for the same fool reason that he had taken to smoking. He thought it was cool. Many years later, in Milan, on a whim, the man had indulged the boyish desire. He remembered the feel of the mother-of-pearl and the saleslady's soft skin. If the fool boy had not wanted to be cool, if the man had not still sheltered the ghost of that boy, if that store had not been there and that whim had not overtaken him, he would now be dead. Should one thank the child or the man, or the God that blessed them both? The wisdom that lurked in folly, or the kaleidoscopic chain of moments, the spiraling triplets of flux, that were fate's genetic code?

Who had been behind the attack? Had his assailant taken it upon himself to avenge Raffa's death? If so, why had Johnny been chosen and not Louie? Maybe they got Louie too. Maybe Louie was wood. Maybe Louie was behind it. A bigger payday for himself, a sacrifice to appease the *stiddari*. What about Don Virgilio? He seemed the sort who would always be eager to cut a budget. Had his own uncle come to doubt him? His paranoia ran like a ballock-cinched bull, trampling all reason and lucidity. But was it paranoia, even in the vulgar sense? In a world turned upside-down, a world where illusion and actuality rattled like dice in the hand of a furious god, was he not better off unburdened of all good sense and reason? But no, sense and reason were not his enemies. Even in this upside-down world of shifting shapes and shifting truths, there was reason, there was sense, however hidden. No, the enemy was fear, which had overcome him in the catacombs, which even now had him gazing nervously at the double-locked door. In its victim's mind, fear could make a horde of a single fallen adversary. He had taken care of the one who had attacked him, but what of the invisible many that lurked and silently advanced?

It was as much to exorcize his fear as to dump his telltale sack that he braced himself to venture back out into the light of day. When he opened his door and saw someone close upon him, his breath was taken and he flushed.

"You okay?" Louie said.

Johnny laughed weakly and held out his tremulous hand in answer. He led Louie into the room and told him what had happened.

"Look," Louie told him, "it's natural. Don't worry about it. You get happy, you laugh. You get sick, you cough. You get shook up, you shake. It's natural."

"You ever shake?"

"Yeah. Whenever I think of fuckin' my wife." Louie grinned, then his face went grave again. "I used to, Johnny. I used to. Like everything else, it passes." He lighted a cigarette. "I'll tell you one thing. You're really earnin' your fuckin' wings this go-round."

"Who do you think was behind it?"

"Your guess is as good as mine. I'd say it was a friend of Raffa's. Somebody who was in with Raffa. Somebody he told about us meeting him in Milan."

Johnny showed him the photo ID. Louie shrugged.

"He said he was Stidda."

"He prob'ly was. Then again, you put the word in his mouth. A guy with a knife to his throat, he'll say anything."

"When we were in the café, he must have been watching us. We split up, he followed me. Why me, not you?"

" 'Cause I'm the one who set ya up."

Johnny stared at him, watched him reach into his jacket and pull out a compact .45.

"Jesus, you *are* fuckin' shook up. Here." Louie put the gun in Johnny's hand. "Hold this, you'll feel better."

Johnny looked down at the gun in his hand. It was a lightweight Para-Ordnance P12-45.

"My friend in the Capo, he's got a slew of 'em."

"Thanks."

"Why'n't you go get a good rubdown, a nice blowjob?"

"The way I feel, I'd come out with more knots than I went in with. I'd be afraid she'd strangle me, bite it off."

"Well, look, you go dump that shit. Take some air. We'll go have a nice dinner."

"Let me ask you something. The last hour or two here, I been seein' ghosts. I suspected everybody and their mother. How do you deal with that?"

Louie shrugged. "Deal with what? The less you trust, the less likely you are to get fucked. You know that."

Johnny thought of the story of Zampante of Lucca, the fifteenth-century henchman of Duke Alfonso I of Ferrara. Believing that his enemies were plentiful, Zampante ate only pigeons bred in his own house and would not cross the street without a band of armed guards. But as the fate of Zampante illustrated, it did not pay to live on pigeons and in fear. For all his precautions, he was murdered one day in his sleep.

Leaving the gun behind in a drawer and discarding the bag in a trash cart on Via Principe di Belmonte, Johnny made his way once again, in Louie's shoes, to the English Garden, where dusk cured him. It was better to be without the gun, alone like this with his lingering fear. Besides, he already disliked the burden and discomfort of a gun. At first, walking around with a pistol shoved down his pants had pleased him in a way, had made him feel tough. But that feeling had quickly waned, and only the physical discomfort had remained.

In time he stopped seeing an enemy's malevolence in the face of every passerby, and the lovers and the children by the fountain left him smiling in the breeze. He stopped for coffee at the Gran Caffè Nobel on Viale della Libertà. The barman looked at him the same as he looked at every other man: as neither a throat-cutter nor a priest, or, more accurately, as one who could be either. That was the great democratic look of Palermitan barmen. When it came to coffee, all men, saints and sinners, were equal and one. While Johnny drank, he looked at the bottle of Brunello di Montalcino Riserva 1945 that was on display, bearing a price tag of three million, six hundred thousand lire. A two-and-a-half-grand bottle of guinea red. He wondered what it might taste like, fancied coming back someday and finding out. Would Diane like it here? Would Diane like it anywhere?

Diane. She was getting old, he told himself. If he was ever going to have a son, it wasn't going to be with her. What was it that still held them together, without passion or pleasure? The word *love* was too easy. It was used too often to explain too little, a sludge trap, a catchall. What kind of love could exist without passion or pleasure between man and wife? Only the wrong kind, the sad and melancholy kind, the kind that hurt and wasted lives.

What had kept him this long from getting something going on the side? The world was full of dumb young girls who wanted to fuck their fathers. Something nice and soft and sweet and creamy, all panting youth and *auroque puellae*. Why had he sat around like a fucking gelding after she had withdrawn from him? Had he felt somehow that she was right? Yes, maybe he had. But guilt and penance had their end, and one neither should nor could live any longer in atonement than in fear.

There was something about Diane that he never would find in another, something in her soul that complemented his. He knew that. But this Virgin Mary shit, the psychological sideshow of suffering and deprivation, had to end. True, his view of marriage had always embraced the prospect of a mistress in his wife's golden years, but Diane was still in her prime.

In a way, they were strangers now. He would never tell her he had killed. He would never tell anyone, except another killer. He was two different men: the one he knew and the one she, or any woman, could know. But what of the one he knew? The one who felt strangely at home in this place he did not know? The one who stood in borrowed shoes staring at a two-and-a-half-grand bottle of wine? The one, caressed by breezes and stained by blood, who could not see where his journey would end? What about him?

There was a shoe store on the corner where Viale della Libertà opened to the piazza. He bought a pair of deerskin loafers. On Via Ruggero Settimo, he bought trousers and a shirt. That night, after dinner, he and Louie walked together among the lovers and the stalkers and the beggars. The mendicants of Palermo were a wretched crew, not so plentiful as, but far more pitiful than, the vagrants of New York. Here in Palermo, begging was not a racket, and those reduced to it were neither pampered nor elevated to a euphemistic social class—"the homeless" —by a suckered populace. Some wandered with their litanies of woe; others moved silently with hands outstretched. A few, cripples and old men clinging to pride, gathered round Santa Lucia and other old churches, offered little picture cards of Gesù Crocifisso in exchange for alms. It was into the baskets of the humble Gesù beggars that Johnny unloaded his coins.

Back in his hotel room, he turned on the television and found himself watching something called *Colpo Grosso Story* on Italia 7. One after another, housewives came on stage, stripped off their clothes, bared their breasts, and danced around in panties and garterbelts. There was something about other men's wives that Johnny liked; something, anyway, that the lizard in his pants liked. He began to stroke himself, then looked through the pages of that day's *Giornale di Sicilia*. There, in the back, among the *linea rossa* ads, he found what he was looking for.

"*Sia sicuro che abbia belle gambe*," he told the guy who took his call: make sure she has nice legs.

This was like asking for a medium-rare hamburger at McDonald's. The girl who showed up was cute but scrawny. The hour-long *Colpo Grosso* show was still on, and Johnny sat in a chair watching while the scrawny girl sucked his cock. He turned down the sound by remote control, all the better to hear her slurp. Once again, as on that night in Milan, he felt the force of the day's deathly disquiet pass from his viscera to the stranger's.

In his dreams that night, the girl's mouth and the slit throat in the catacombs were one. *Don't do that*, he told her, recoiling in his love-making. But the more he rebuked her, the more she laughed, and the more she laughed, the more horrendously the blood flowed from the mortal gash of her laughing, lipless mouth. It was the rollicking, meta-static Coney Island grin of George C. Tilyou's Steeplechase grotesque— as a boy, that hideous smiling countenance had been for him the face of fear—transformed into a fount of blood. There was blood everywhere, all over the wound-mouthed whore, all over him; it filled the room and flowed into the hall. Soon the door shook with the banging and pounding of unseen persecutors. When he awoke, he was sweating and breathing hard.

Signorelli met them for breakfast at the hotel. He brought with him a legal-size manila folder containing several sheets, which he ruffled through as he spoke.

"I've spoken to our man in Shanghai," he said. "The Italians have no consulate in either Thailand or Burma. There are Italian embassies, however, in both those countries, and our man will arrange for your meetings through *cancellieri* of those embassies. I will let you know the dates of these meetings as soon as they are scheduled. In addition, to facilitate your movement into and within both Thailand and Burma, I will be providing you with *lettere di presentazione*, from both our embassies and the native authorities. These documents will be in Italian, English, and the languages of the appropriate countries. I understand you also will have business in Hong Kong. I'll take care of all your travel arrangements. Just give me an address and fax and telephone numbers where I can reach you in New York."

Louie gave him a Novarca business card.

"I will try to get you diplomatic passports through the Knights of Malta," Signorelli said, "but I don't know if there will be time. As to your visas, when the time comes, you'll have to take care of those yourselves, through the Thai and Burmese consulates in New York."

"Diplomatic passports? Is that possible?" Johnny asked.

" '*In Sicilia tutto è possibile. Questa è la terra dove un cactus fa i fichi d'India.*' " In Sicily all is possible. This is the land where cactus bears figs.

He passed them a letter. "This is a letter identifying you and your organization." The letterhead bore the name of the Società Padre Carmelo, a Rome address, and the motto "*per un mondo migliore*": for a better world.

"*A chiunque riguardi*," it began: to whomever it may concern. The letter went on to state that its bearers were respected and trusted representatives of the Padre Carmelo Society, a nonprofit organization dedicated to world peace and prosperity. Through the society, many of the most important businessmen and humanitarians of Europe and America anonymously and generously sought to better the world that had been so kind to them. The letter was signed, with a majestic paraph, by the society's *presidente*, the honorable Dottor Avvocato Camillo Signorelli.

"Founded 1968. Three orphanages in the western provinces," he said matter-of-factly and with a hint of modest pride. "Now. The Linosa list. Do you still have it? Good. I'm to tell you to memorize it. Keep it here." He pointed to his white crown. "Not on any paper that you bring through customs. Offer the bulk of the arms to the general in Burma. Speak of a crop substitution program as our condition, but give no funds toward that end, for he will surely use the money elsewhere. To the Thai prime minister, offer to underwrite the implementation and enforcement of a full crop-substitution plan and to supply a small complement of arms to help overcome those responsible for the opium plague. I am also to tell you that the enriched uranium is to be held out as a reward upon the achievement of your common goal. In other words, promise them anything—"

"But give them Arpège," Johnny said.

The pleasure of yesterday's alfresco lunch in the hills led Louie and Johnny to the great open-air market known as the Vucciria. There, in the Piazza Caracciolo, an immense man stood behind a plank counter with a drum of boiling water to his left and a mass of slimy, gray-purpling octopi to his right. Set out on the plank were four plates and a sea sponge. The creatures emerged from the drum, one after another, transformed, with bulbous pink heads and pink-white tentacles. With his cleaver, the fat man split their heads in two, scooped the glop from them with his fingers, and chopped their bodies into mouthfuls. Whenever someone stood before one of the four plates, he served up a heaping handful of head and tentacle segments and, if one wanted it, a piece of lemon. Behind the counter was a thigh-sized length of tentacle; occasionally a customer would ask for a slice of it.

One ate with one's fingers, and the sponge was for the use of all. When someone finished wiping black muck from his hands, the proprietor squeezed the sponge in a ceramic bowl of inky water and wiped the plate clean for the next man. Though he himself ate constantly as he cut and served, the *maestro del polpo*, whose hamlike hands were permanently dyed, did not use the sponge on himself but merely licked and sucked. The price was two thousand lire a plate.

From the Vucciria they walked to the sea, to the shabby, carnival-like strip of Villa a Mare, which reminded Johnny of Coney Island, and of that face. All along the Foro Italico, young black men solicited money to guard rather than rob the parked cars of carnival-goers. Johnny and Louie made their way to a quiet bench on a grassy knoll near the seawall.

"How long do you figure it would take to really get to know this place?"

"You know, Johnny, a long time ago, a bunch of us, we were at a villa here. In Torretta. West of town, up in the hills, out near Isola delle Femmine."

"Island of Women. Shit. Let's go there."

"Eh. It's nice, but it ain't what you think. The name, I mean. Utopia Parkway. Garden State. Same principle. Anyway, a bunch of us, a few guys from New York, a few guys from here. And we got to talking. I remember, I kept my mouth shut, and I learned something. Before this island was Sicilia, it was Trinacria. That's what the Greeks called it, that's what the Romans called it. It came from the Greek word for 'trident.' See, the island's shaped like a triangle—it's got three points. And the Greeks and Romans, they called this town Panormus. The Arabs, who took over in the 800s, pronounced it *Balarmu*, and that's where Palermo came from. Greek, Arab, Provençal, German—they all left their mark. But still, Sicilian stayed closer to Latin than regular Italian. All these words that end in *u*'s instead of *o*'s, that's from the Latin *-us*. When these people say *u* instead of *il* for *the*, that's from Latin, too: *illum*.

"You know Latin?"

"Yeah. *Amo, amas, amat. Veni, vidi, vici. Semper paratus.* Someday I'll teach ya. Anyway, in Old Sicilian, they said *lu*. But Sicilians don't like *l*'s, so it became *u*. They're like Chinks when it comes to *l*'s and *r*'s. With these people, *palma* becomes *parma*. In fact, I've heard it said that Parmesan cheese wasn't really named for Parma. That's a myth that everybody believes. It really came from down here, from Palma." Louie paused. "I still don't know if I believe that one or not. Tell you the truth, I don't even know if they make cheese in Palma.

"Of course, it's all changed now. I don't think kids down here these days talk Sicilian. Just yesterday I heard some kid in the street use the word *cazzu*. In the old days, no Sicilian, no matter how young, would call his prick *cazzu*. To a real Sicilian, the cock is *'a minchia*. And don't ask me where the fuck that one comes from. It don't mean 'mink,' if that's what you're thinkin'. *'A minchia e u pacchiu*. It's funny. They give a feminine name to the cock and a masculine name to the cunt.

"Anyway, these guys were talkin'. And somebody—one of the New York guys—he asked that same question you asked me. And I never forgot what somebody told him. If you're born here, the guy said, and you live a long life, and you die here, then you've got a shot at beginnin' to understand it."

"That's what I figured," Johnny said. "What I don't figure is why I feel so at home here."

"After what happened to you yesterday, you feel at home here? Whadaya got, one of them fuckin' death wishes or somethin'?"

Johnny grinned, and Louie laughed.

"It's hard to explain," Johnny said.

"You tryin' to tell me you'd rather live here than in Milan?"

"No. Milan is beautiful. I'm not talkin' about livin' here, I'm talkin' about feelin' at home."

"What's the fuckin' difference?"

"When you're at home somewhere, it's like you belong there, even if you don't like it. Y'know what I mean?"

"You mean like a kid. He's at home but it sucks."

"Not really." Johnny groped for the right words, but the nuances of his meaning were too murky even to himself, and he quit. "Hell," he said, "I don't know what the fuck I mean."

"Then maybe you do belong here." Louie laughed and smacked him on the shoulder.

Passing through the Giardino Garibaldi, they came to the Museo delle Marionette.

"Before there was cock and pussy, there was Punch and Judy," Louie said. "When I was a boy, that was a big deal at the feast. *Il teatrino di Pulcinella*. I used to love it. Man, I didn't know how true it was."

Johnny saw where this was leading.

"This one's on me," Louie said.

"You bet it is."

They made their way through the dimly lighted rooms of ghostly puppets, remnants of a bygone age that were as eerie in their way as those that occupied the catacombs. They came to a grand tableau identified as the set of Il Giardino di Alcina, from the Teatro di Don Liberto Canino, Palermo, circa 1920.

"What does *alcina* mean?" Johnny asked.

"I don't know. But it looks like a good one."

There was the devil, a serpent, a winged dragon, a skeleton, sirens, a centaur, and more: a panoply of pagan spirits reduced to haunted wood and paint.

Farther along they came to an older tableau, where a long-haired knight in ármor raised his sword to the *drago a tre teste*, the dragon with three heads.

That night, not far from the hotel, near forsaken little Piazza Florio, green neon script captured their gaze. The neon spelled out the words *Hong Kong*. It was Johnny's idea to eat there. He did not believe in luck. Like his uncle, and like Louie, he believed that luck was the religion of failure. But he wanted to eat there. The place looked like it had been there forever, waiting for them; it was the sort of place that seemed to Johnny as if it might vanish if he turned his back.

They both ordered the same meal: *ravioli al vapore* and *maiale in salsa di ostrica*, steamed dumplings and pork in oyster sauce. One of the waiter's eyes was opalescent, like a blind man's. He looked at Johnny as if he knew why he had come—not for the food, but to inhale the sense of something he did not fully comprehend: the indomitability and adaptability of a people who not only survived but prevailed wherever fate or will took them. To the Americans, they sold their *shiu mai* as steamed dumplings; to the Italians, as *ravioli al vapori*. It made no difference. Wherever they were, they could appropriate the language and make themselves understood to their *gwailou* hosts. But they allowed themselves to be understood only so far as was necessary to make money. There was China, *zhong*; the rest was merely a barbarian babble of Chinatowns.

Dumplings. Heroin. *To reveal oneself barely enough to bring forth a hidden enemy. To occupy a country while passing through it.*

" '*A chi vuole, non mancano modi.*' Where there's a will, there's a way. Wha'd you get?"

Johnny cracked open the almond-scented cookie and removed the little strip of white paper. He stared at it for a moment, translating it. Then he almost laughed, but he did not.

" '*Ignori tutte le profezie anteriori,*' " he read: disregard all previous fortunes.

TWENTY-SEVEN

The floral arrangement that stood near the head of Antonio Pazienza's open casket at the Companello Funeral Home was dressed with a scarlet ribbon of tender words. *Che tu possa riposare, caro amico, nella serenità dei giusti e rivivere nella luce di Dio.* May you rest, beloved friend, in the serenity of the just and live again in the light of God.

Many men praised Giuseppe Di Pietro for the beauty of his flowers and the loveliness of his sentiment.

Several blocks to the south, in a basement chamber in Chinatown, a blue-gowned embalmer labored to lend the lie of peaceful death to the wretched remains of old Chen Fang. *"Diu nei loumou,"* he cursed, as a long ash dropped from the cigarette in his mouth to an open pocket in the Y-shaped incision that the coroner had made in Chen Fang's thorax. It was not that the ash impeded his work or would affect it in any way. It was simply that he was a professional.

Chen had died with a needle sunk in his arm, and when he was found, his naked scarecrow body was stuck fast to the floor in a coagulated pool of gravelly black blood. His insides were abscessed and rotten with cancer, a spongy mass of perforated tissue, carcinoma, melanemia, and pus; and his face in death had been frozen into the hideous green *èmó* mask of a screaming demon.

As the embalmer worked, he kept the tip of his shoe on the foot lever that controlled the lid of the white steel BIOHAZARD waste can into which he tossed shreds of Chen Fang's fetid viscera. Close to the can, beneath the metal drain-table, was one of several large rattraps distributed throughout the room. The embalmer pried open Chen's mouth and looked for gold fillings.

"*Diu nei loumou.*" There were none.

Giuseppe, of course, would not attend Chen Fang's wake. But Billy Sing would, and that was why it was important for Giuseppe to send flowers: to show Billy Sing that he accorded old Chen, in death as in life, the respect due him. The ribbon on his flowers read *May you rest, beloved friend, in the serenity of the just and live again in the light of God.* The wake would be attended mostly by old men, who remembered times and events that the younger dong men did not know. Many of them would remark upon the beauty of these flowers and the loveliness of this sentiment received in anonymity. It was an anonymity that insured that Billy Sing would have no doubt as to whose identity it cloaked.

Before long, the seventh moon and the feast of All Souls' Day, the season of the dead, would arrive. In death as in life, Chen Feng, with no descendants to perpetuate his memory, would be an orphaned spirit.

"And what if it's a girl?"

"Mary."

"You know I hate my name."

"But I love it."

"It's too generic."

"Too generic, she says. What do you want? One of those air-freshener names? Heather?"

"No, I hate that precious shit."

"How about Louise?"

"Louise? You're kidding."

"Louise is a sexy name."

"It's a washwoman's name. Besides, you want your daughter to have a sexy name?"

"Look, babe, we've got a lot of time."

"I know. But it's fun."

"Mary?"

"Yes?"

"You know I love you, don't you?"

"You say it so sad. What's wrong?"

"Nothing. I was just thinking. Thinking how lucky we are."

"You don't sound like you feel lucky."

"Do you know the DEA has the highest divorce rate of any profession?"

"Why do you think that is?"

"The mandatory overtime. The sixty-hour work weeks."

"Maybe we're together just enough. Maybe that's it."

"Maybe."

"Is something bothering you?"

For one dreadful instant, she was afraid he had found out. But no, that could not be. He would never react like this, would never be so subdued and melancholy and oddly passive. Besides, she had put an end to her foolishness months ago, when she first discovered she was pregnant. There was just no way he could find out now. But why had he mentioned the overtime, the sixty-hour work weeks?

"I got some new listings yesterday from the realtor."

"Anything good?"

"A little high. One's three, the other's three and a quarter. Still, it'd be a good excuse to get away for a day or two. You seem like you could use a break."

He muttered something about summer rates. Why had he done what he had done? Why had he stained something that was pure? Every time he looked at Mary, he hated himself and he hated that fucking mafiosa slut in Brooklyn. He was weak. He had proved that much. It was not really the deed that bothered him. It was the weakness. He had degraded Di Pietro's wife, but there was no sense of strength or conquest in that, for she had degraded him as well. He had moved against her husband in strength but had emerged in weakness. Was she anything more than her husband's bitch? In weakening him, had she not let her husband weaken him as well? There was no sorting out these vague notions within him, and there needed to be none. All that mattered was the fact of his sense of weakness, the fact of his feeling that Johnny had the edge. For now, anyway, Marshall told himself; only for now. As soon as Johnny put on a jacket or suit from that closet, he would come apart; and when men came apart, they were as easy to discover and destroy as rabid dogs.

When that moment came, he would be ready. In his Apocalypse directory, the crude elements of his theory now occupied a file of their own. The more he thought about it, the more convinced he became that his early instincts were right. Everything—the hits on the Fuk Ching, the Hip Sing, the Gum Sing, the Jamaicans, the Puerto Ricans, the Dominicans, and the Scarpa–Tung On alliance; the plague and the terrorism—was an aspect of a single concerted drive to disrupt the market and unnerve its players. He was sure that the two Di Pietros, Pazienza, and Louie Bones had been central to that drive. Perhaps they were in league with the On Leong. Either their show of power had been a move to press the 14K Triad's hand toward agreeing to a new market arrangement with the Italians and perhaps the On Leong, or the 14K had been a party to this violence as a prelude to their anticipated shift of power from Hong Kong to New York. Either way, an arrangement had been made or was in the works. Something central to this arrangement had transpired in Milan. The Pazienza hit, he suspected, had been an act of retaliation from Scarpa's people. Though it had shaken up the OC desks, he classified it only as a repercussion, like the outbreaks of gang violence that had erupted in Chinatown in the wake of the first wave of violence.

He knew in his guts that something vast and almost unthinkable was under way. But he knew also that the crude elements of his theory would yield the bricks of his case. He had kept these elements too long to himself. It was not the DEA's way, but it was his way. Soon Johnny Di

Pietro would be back, and before long he would panic, as surely as those junkies in the street had panicked. Then Marshall would share his files and his theory with them all: not only Wang and the other agents, but the field officers in Chiang Mai, the Narcotics Bureau and Triad Bureau in Hong Kong, the Servizio Centrale Antidroga in Italy, maybe even the FBI, if he was in a good mood. Together they would cast their prey into the bottomless pit. It would be the bust of the century, and there would be glory enough for all.

Four years ago, overcome by the feeling that the man she had married was turning to stone, Diane Di Pietro had undergone several months of psychotherapy. Johnny had always told her that psychiatry could be reduced to a fundamental formula: "You wanna fuck your mother. Gimme a hundred bucks." He said that Julius Caesar, as a quaestor, dreamed one night of fucking his mother, and when he told the sooth-sayer of his dream, the soothsayer told him it was a good dream, it meant that he would conquer the world. To Johnny, psychiatry had never much improved on soothsaying, except in its refinements as a racket. But Diane had disagreed. There were doctors for the mind, she said, as for the flesh. Besides, if Johnny's mental health represented the argument for disbelief, she was all the more eager to believe.

After a while she had found herself observing the therapist as much as he observed her. It became sort of a game, comparing Johnny to the doctor, the disease to the cure. Much to her consternation, she came to the conclusion that Johnny had it all over the doctor. Sure, the doctor was all those things that Johnny was not: understanding, patient, sympa-thetic, supportive. But she was paying him to be so, just as a john paid a whore. Who knew how this guy treated his wife? That is, if he even had one. Maybe one grain of real emotion, no matter how unsatisfactory or unpleasant, was worth more than the fullest fifty minutes of the prorated compassion that money could buy. By the time she quit seeing the therapist, she felt that psychiatry was at best a sort of medieval pseudo-science veiled in fancy sheepskins and high-sounding cant, a grand placebo whose active ingredients were desperation, weakness, and gullibility. At worst, it was pandering, a legal but insidious form of big-money addiction, plied by charlatans whose real stock in trade was dependence and illusion.

Maybe it was the wrong therapist, she told herself. Maybe that was it. But then she looked around at those, like her friend Jill, who were satisfied customers of long standing. They weren't happier. They weren't wiser. They were just more fatuous. Where did that leave her? She didn't want the misery of her worsening marriage, and she didn't want the pabulum of "finding herself" either. She knew where she was, and it sucked. Sitting around with some high-priced Jew making a slow-motion fuss about figuring out how she got there seemed to her about as sensible as sitting in a plane that was going down and trying to figure out the cause of the engine failure rather than bailing out. But how could she bail out? She hadn't worked in years. She was dependent on Johnny. Even the luxury of her abortive psychotherapy had been subsidized by Johnny's union coverage.

If only she could break that stone, wrench out the soul that she once had known and loved, the soul of the man who had danced to "You Belong to Me" and held her and bathed her eyes in the light of his and made her feel, no matter how briefly, no matter how rarely, as if mornings were magical, nights serene. Sometimes she wondered where that soul had gone, whether it had been washed away by drunkenness or— she hated even to think it—subdued and starved by austere sobriety. Lately she had begun to feel that it was merely being borne away by darkness. It was more than a feeling, really. It was almost a vision. She could almost see it: an elusive, captivating leaf blown finally away and out of sight and grasp, swallowed by the somber wind of that realm where men like his uncle lived their lives.

On Stanley Street, not far from the offices of White Lion Enterprises, Ng Tai-hei and Tuan Ching-kuo sat in the Luk Yu Tea House at the table that was kept reserved at all hours for Ng and his associates.

"So," said Tuan, "tell me about our Italian friends." With his elbows on the table and his hands raised, he held his cup of warm black-dragon tea with two hands, inhaling it; and when he spoke, his shifty grin curled over the horizon of the cup's rim like a creeping mean mist.

Ng waved dismissively with the back of his hand.

"You're sure you're not underestimating them?"

"Their greed makes them blind."

"And your own greed—it sharpens your sight?"

Ng smiled. As usual, the chef had placed several honorific delicacies among the *dím sàm* they had ordered: clear fresh fish eyes, chicken feet, frilly morsels of bright orange intestine. Ng ate an eye, then a stuffed duck's web, and washed them down with chrysanthemum tea.

"The older one looked the part," he said. "He was *haksau dong*, old-school Mafia, all the way. The younger one was more baffling. He seemed to know more, and he seemed to hate us less. That was my impression, anyway. But what struck me most was their weakness. What was it that Chi-fu called them? Do you recall? That day at the Tin Hau temple?"

"Evil dregs of a dead society."

"Yes. And what struck me was that these men were envoys of other men who were too old and too feeble to tend to their own affairs. The fountainheads of their power are dry and disintegrating. Theirs *is* a dead society. Even their allies are recruited from graveyards. Who else would have given face to the ilk of Chen Fang? Believe me. When we cripple them, I don't think they will ever stand again. They will be an extinct breed. I believe that. And I believe the day will come when whatever feral dogs they leave behind will heel to us."

"And what about the young one?"

"He has no face. He is nobody, *ját* to one of the old and dying ones in New York."

"Then he has the face of blooded mandate."

"The mandate of what? Believe me, he is insignificant. His mandate, as you call it, is insignificant."

"What if he is legion? What if there are hundreds, thousands like him? You should know better than any: if the army is there, one leader is all it takes."

"He is not a leader."

"You said that when you had that Sole Rosso shot, he looked at you and seemed to see through the strategy of your little show."

"Well, wisdom alone doesn't make leaders."

"No. But it makes formidable enemies."

"Look." Ng lowered his voice, even though no man was near. "When we have their money and the sea has their heroin—appraise their wisdom then."

"So. You take their offer at face value?"

"It is no longer an offer. It is a deal. We have already received their good-faith payment of ninety-one and a half million dollars."

Tuan Ching-kuo sneered happily: "Good faith."

"*Bing bù yàn zhà*," said Ng, smiling: there can never be too much deception in war.

"That's why I ask if you take their stated intention at face value. What of *their* deception?"

"Oh, I'm sure they have deception enough planned. I should be surprised if this were not just a first step for them toward usurping our power in our own house. Then again, it is they who are desperate, they who are dying, they who need us. I think there is more veracity of need than deception in their hearts. Besides, what could they do until they received their dreamed-of heroin? That heroin represents billions to them. It represents their resurrection. Until then, we hold the cards, not they."

"And you foresee no retribution?"

"I foresee the wrath of the impotent. Maybe they'll blow up half of Chinatown again, or detonate a few *hak gwai* in mid-air. Maybe they will attack us like wounded dogs. What do you care, Ah Kuo? You always manage to see that no battle dust ever sullies your lapels."

"I'm not a violent man," he said. "I'm an entrepreneur."

"And your mother was a virgin."

"In my eyes, yes."

Ng Tai-hei found Tuan's sentiment of chaste devotion to the memory of his mother rather whimsical, as the Guomindang in Taipei never tired of telling the tale of how young Tuan Ching-kuo had raped his own mother in a drunken rage after failing a civil-service examination many years ago in Bangkok. As far as Ng knew, it was only a tale. He had never asked Tuan about it, as he did not see it as the sort of question to which one would expect an honest answer.

Tuan ate a shrimp and bamboo-root dumpling and signaled to the waiter for more tea.

"When does their ship arrive?"

"I will give them clearance soon. First there are some details that need to be worked out."

"Details that need to be worked out with them?"

"Some. Bills of lading. Dockage. Entry papers. The usual. Most of what needs to be worked out are what you might call details against them."

"And what will they supposedly be exporting?"

"Rubber dicks."

"And what is the lading code for rubber dicks?"

"It's their idea. They have outlets for such things."

"Is this where the Silk Road ends? All the riches of the Orient to choose from, and they take rubber dicks."

"What can I tell you?"

"I don't suppose they'll get their dicks either," said Tuan with a note of sarcastic pity.

"Oh, I don't know. One or two might bob to the surface and float ashore."

"Will our friends be accompanying this cargo back to America themselves?"

"That is their choice. In making it, they'll also choose unknowingly between life and death. I certainly shall urge them to oversee shipment personally. It only seems prudent, after all, for such a valuable cargo to be closely guarded from port to port."

"Of course."

"Do you want that last eye?"

"Be my guest, old friend, be my guest."

TWENTY-EIGHT

The *cafon*'s outside the club were resplendent in their new standard-issue summerwear of silk and cotton workout suits, Bally loafers and Nikes, Ray-Ban shades, Rolexes, and diamond and onyx rings. Since each of them operated at least one restaurant or after-hours gambling-joint on the Upper East Side, and since this was a busy season for them, talk had turned from matters tonsorial to matters entrepreneurial.

"You crack that new barmaid's ass yet?"

"*Ah, fa'n'cul', eh?*"

"She don't want him. She wants his fuckin' *cummar'.*"

"They're all fuckin' lezzies these days, these kids."

"I had this one up on Eighty-sixth one time. All she did, this broad, she'd eat cunt and she'd take it up the ass."

"What about that thing, used to come in your fuckin' joint?"

"What thing? I get a lot of 'em."

"That thing. Was a guy. Decided he wanted to be a broad. Went to fuckin' Denver, took the operation. Came out. Turned into a fuckin' lezzie. I mean, you needed a fuckin' pen and paper to figure this one out. What the fuck was that thing's name?"

"Samantha."

"Yeah. Samantha."

"Face could stop a fuckin' clock, this thing. I swear. A mug like fuckin' Goo Goo's dog."

"And that kid fucked it, remember? Before it went lezzie. That bartender from the Village, used to come in after work. He thought it was a real broad."

"Yeah. Ladies' man. Man of the fuckin' world."

"Well, shit, Fonduzz' took a fuckin' blowjob off it."

"That's Fonduzz'. We were kids, he had a shine box and a fuckin' mutt. Friday nights, the guys outside the joint, they'd take a shine, throw 'im an extra pound to jerk off the mutt."

"Whatever happened to him? I don't see 'im no more."

"He's in the fuckin' joint."

"Again?"

"I think he likes it. Makes 'im feel like a man."

"Some guys are like that."

"He was good in the kitchen, though. I'll say that much."

"You still got that spic cookin' for ya?"

"Oh, shit, he's good, man. You gotta come up."

"Is there a fuckin' 'talian rest'rant left in this fuckin' town with a fuckin' 'talian cook?"

"I doubt it. All spics. A few old-timers here and there, but the cooks in the money joints, all spics."

"That one fuckin' *mammalùcc'* you had that time, that fuckin' Ramón. He's out his fuckin' skull wit' that fuckin' wine o' his, stagg'rin' round the kitchen, 'I no git, I no git. You say *burro* is fuckin' butter. He says *burro* is a leetle donkey. I no git, I no git.' "

"Boy, and he could gamble. Ended up into my joint for six, seven grand. We tol' 'im it was the river and you talked us into the hospital 'cause you loved 'im so much. We had 'im fuckin' shakin'."

"Did he ever pay?"

"Oh, he paid."

"Yeah. I wanted to fuckin' fire 'im. This guy here, 'Oh, you can't do that. He owes us.' Two fuckin' mont's I gotta carry this fuckin' guy, just so's he can pay."

"What can I say? You're a nice guy."

"Too nice."

When Johnny passed among them, they hailed him respectfully. Just this past spring, they had barely been able to place him. Now they knew. He was up there, all right. He was above them, they figured: *punciutu*, pricked. Someday, perhaps, he would need them. More likely, they would need him.

Johnny put down the carton of Toscani Extra-Vecchi five-packs on the table.

"Thanks, buddy," the old man said. He withdrew one of the packs and held it in his hand. " *'Nuoce gravemente alla salute,'* " he read aloud: gravely endangers health. "Sort of like your trip, huh?"

Johnny smiled, and his uncle told him he looked good, told him he'd gotten some color. The barman brought coffee, addressed Johnny warmly as Signor Giovanni.

Giuseppe listened intently as Johnny gave him the details of the deal that had been struck in Milan.

"Sixty percent on shipment," the old man repeated. He began silently to reckon, but Johnny provided him with the figure.

"Five hundred and forty-nine million."

"Five hundred and forty-nine million," his uncle repeated.

"And what about the arms, and the money for that prime minister?"

"Don Virgilio will take care of that."

Joe opened the pack of cigars, removed one of the six-inch cheroots, and beheld it. It looked like a piece of twisted black branch. He tore off its tricolor band. "These are the real thing," he said, lighting it and drawing smoke. "These other fucking things, the ones they sell here, they're from some goddamn factory in Pennsylvania." He sat quietly for a moment, enjoying the real thing. "A hundred and thirty-five tons," he said. "A hundred and thirty-five thousand kilos. We sell it pure. Eighty grand a kilo to our friends. That's less than they've ever paid. They'll be grateful to us, and they'll flourish. But we'll flourish above them all. Everyone else, the price is a hundred. Other Italians, I mean. No spics, no niggers, no Chinks. Those who buy from us will sell to them. They'll make their own prices. Only one Chink will get the price our friends get: Billy Sing. That's because he's been a friend to us.

"If we were to sell it all for eighty a rap, that would still turn a pretty penny." The old man reckoned. "Ten billion, eight hundred million. Don Virgilio and our friends in Sicily are in for a third. That's what? Say three point six billion. That leaves us with seven point two billion. Of course, once the old route is working again and the Triangle is wood, we'll be operating fifty-fifty together. Me, I'm gonna move aside, make people even more grateful. You, Louie—you do what you want."

"Seven billion," Johnny said. Distractedly, he took one of the cheroots and lighted it before he fully realized it.

"So, you see," his uncle said, "your cut is just crumbs from the cake. With Tonio pushing up daisies, I'm giving you more than you would have got. I was figuring ten percent of my take. But with the cigars and all, I'll make it an even five hundred." The old man sensed that his nephew wanted to hear the word he had left out, so he spoke again. "Five hundred million."

Johnny's mind could fathom that sum no better now than when his uncle first had spoken to him of "a few hundred million." The storm of murder and near-death that had shaken him seemed inconsequential in light of the reward that now awaited him. That such wealth and the breeze should both be his filled him with a sense of wonder that he had never imagined to exist.

"I want you to go downtown today," Joe said. "Go to the office, see Bill. You tell him to get working on that five hundred and forty-nine million. You tell him you're gonna need to have it at your disposal in Hong Kong. It's a lot of money. He may have to cash in the Bank of Pakistan bearer bonds. Tell him that if he bitches. State Bank of Pakistan. But one way or the other, we're gonna have to have that five hundred and forty-nine million free and ready in Hong Kong. Don't take any shit from him. You're his boss. He gives you any lip, smack him."

The idea of smacking a lawyer, any lawyer, was not without a certain pleasant appeal to ethos and equity.

"Then, later on, come by the apartment. Seven, say. We'll go out, put on the feedbag."

Johnny stood, bent to embrace his uncle, and turned to leave.

"Hey, buddy."

Johnny turned round.

"You did good. You're all right."

Absolution. Dispensation. Benediction. His uncle's voice seemed to deliver all those things. It seemed to appose the imprimatur of blooded authority to that cleansing Johnny had already performed on himself.

At the Novarca office on Wall Street, Bill Raymond gave him no lip. He merely sat and shook his head forlornly.

"Do you have any idea what Novarca is worth, John?" Unlike his uncle, Johnny had never discouraged the lawyer from addressing him familiarly.

"Book value or market?" Johnny grinned. He had no idea.

"Plain old net current assets."

"Could we speed this up?"

"Sure. With current and projected assets and liabilities, including those of Lupino, R.P., and its other undeclared subsidiaries, the Novarca Management Group, after our little R-and-D jaunt in Milan, is worth approximately six hundred million dollars."

"Does that include the Bank of Pakistan bearer bonds?"

"That includes the Bank of Pakistan bearer bonds. Of course, you understand, six hundred million dollars is nothing to sneeze at. There are publicly traded corporations worth far, far less. But at the same time, an outlay of five hundred and forty-nine million would leave us without funds to meet our operating costs. Novarca does not have five hundred and forty-nine million dollars to lay out.

"As you know, I am not a privileged officer of Novarca. I do not know, nor do I wish to know, the exact nature of the sanitation industry's inner workings. And I am not going to ask you what it is that you seek to do with this five hundred and forty-nine million dollars. I am just telling you the facts. We don't have that kind of money."

"Then we'll have to borrow it."

"You want me to walk into 23 Wall Street and borrow fifty or a hundred million dollars?"

"It's right down the street."

"And what do we offer as collateral?"

"Novarca."

"That means if we don't pay, we're finished. And I'll tell you something else. If we don't pay, it also means we go into Chapter 7, and if we go into Chapter 7, there'll be a lot more questions asked as to what goes on around here than I've ever asked."

"We'll pay."

"When do we expect to see our money back? What sort of payment schedule are we talking about?"

"Payment in full within thirty days of our investment."

"The first thing they'll ask is what it's for."

"Well, it's like this." Johnny lighted a cigarette. Raymond hated smoke. Johnny would give him a choice: fetch an ashtray or have his office used as one. "We've got those fancy new recycling machines out in Jersey, and those minimum-wage monkeys who sort through the garbage for us. Paper from paper, not from trees. Work today for a cleaner tomorrow. That's our motto. Like with this sludge-removal thing, we're in the vanguard of waste management. We've gone from green packers and green lift-offs to green thinking. Our true business today is the environment."

Bill brought an ashtray, and Johnny flicked his ash. "You gonna remember this shit, or you want to write it down or what? This is good stuff. They'll eat it up."

"I'll remember it." It *was* good, Bill Raymond admitted to himself.

"Ecology. *International* ecology. We've begun to sell American pulp to paper companies overseas, where their own natural resources have been depleted and their own recycling industry is inadequate. At present we use outside shippers. But the field is burgeoning, and we need to build our fleet. We want to buy a ship. At the same time we've begun to explore import and export possibilities, which would enable us to generate profits both coming and going. In fact, we've begun arrangements for our first return consignment, a container shipment from Hong Kong that has already been presold to an import group here in New York."

"And what is it that you're importing?"

"Rubber dicks."

The lawyer looked at him in disbelief. No, it was not disbelief. It was total incomprehension. Johnny slowly raised his left hand, made a circle with his thumb and forefinger, moved the forefinger of his other hand languidly in and out of the circle.

"Rubber dicks," the lawyer said. "They'll like that. I mean, it's not as if they're not big on sanitation to begin with."

"They're very fancy, these dicks. Works of art. Lifelike latex. Battery packs. They're like sculptures: a beaver at the foot of a totem pole. You turn on the juice, the pole rotates and the beaver's tongue goes crazy. Two speeds. I'm tellin' ya, Billy, these are fifty-dollar dicks. You got a sweetheart?"

"Look. Bring me broker papers for the ship you want to buy."

Johnny was sure he could get dummy papers from the triad people.

"Bring me the papers, and I'll take them to the bank. Of course, they'll check."

White Lion Enterprises. They were in the book.

"I just hope you know what you're doing."

"Me too." Johnny grinned. "Me too."

He wondered how his uncle would take the news that Novarca would be wiped out and in hock until they brought in the dope. When he arrived at the old man's apartment that evening, he wasted no time in telling him.

"Well," Johnny said, "you're broke." He could smell something good.

"Not unless my mattress catches fire."

"He looked like he was gonna cry when I told him what we needed."

"Yeah. Cry for his fucking job."

"He's really not that bad once you get to know him."

"No? What's there to know? What're you, running for fucking alderman or something? Don't mix with the fucking hired help."

Joe expressed surprise that Johnny thought he could move the rubber dicks. "That whole racket these days, every one of them dirty movie joints, it's all Israelis. I figured they did to that racket what the Hindus did to the newsstands."

"The Israelis got the stores," Johnny said. "But the Italians still got the distribution."

"It was never just the Italians. That's what went wrong. It was Italians and Jews. And the Jews let these fuckin' Israelis in. Ten, twenty years ago, that was a nice little business for a young guy: the peepshows, the girlie books, the fag shit. Now, forget it. All Israelis. Everything they touch, those Israelis, they make it dirty. They're dirty people. No class at all."

"Whatever. The rubber dicks ain't the main event."

It was stuffed peppers baking in the kitchen that he smelled. He loved his uncle's peppers. No one made stuffed peppers like his: bread-crumbs from the baker's brick oven, fresh parsley, anchovies, walnuts, garlic, chicken stock, and Parmesan. The fact that Joe was cooking meant that he was feeling good.

"I figured we'd have a little antipast' here before we went out. They should be done by now. Why don't you run them under the broiler for a minute? It's hard for me to bend that low."

"*Shit*!" Like a fool, Johnny had opened the oven and taken hold of the roasting pan with his bare hand.

His uncle stood watching him hold his blistered fingers under cold running water. "What the fuck, did you leave your brains in Sicily, or what? Fucking pot holder right there in front of you."

"Every time I come here, somethin' happens to my fingers." Johnny went to the refrigerator, took a tray of ice from the freezer. As he did so, he saw a strange package sticking out behind a box of Bird's-Eye green peas. It was a metal box banded with yellow tape that was imprinted with what seemed to be some sort of code—USAMRIID BL-4—and the words DANGER and BIOHAZARD.

"What the fuck is this?"

"What?"

"Behind the peas here."

"Oh, that. Stay away from that."

"What is it?"

"Bad meat."

"Bad meat?"

"*Bad*, bad meat. A gift for our friends in the Golden Triangle." Joe told him about the alky veterinarian, about the virus that was frozen in the meat. "Makes this AIDS bullshit look like a fucking head cold."

Johnny let the ice cube drop into the sink, thought about those green peas.

"What're you gonna do with it?"

"I told you. It's for those jungle Chinks. You know what an ecosystem is?"

Of course he did. The environment was his business.

TWENTY-NINE

Johnny smiled as he sat in the café on Mulberry Street and saw Willie Gloves appear, dressed in one of those fancy, unsweated athletic suits, between the plaster statues of Christ and San Gennaro that framed the doorway of the storefront across the street. He crept up behind him as he neared the corner of Grand Street. He stuck his forefinger in the small of his back.

"Hand it over." He knew Willie's moves, and he sprang back as Willie vaulted around.

"Fuck," Willie said, and his face broadened into a beaming grin.

"What's shakin', stranger?" Johnny grinned back.

"Where the fuck you been?"

"Hey, garbage is a full-time job. Let's eat."

"I got my rounds."

"So, we'll do your rounds and then we'll fuckin' eat."

Johnny began to cross Grand Street.

"Where you goin'? Over here." Willie walked toward a gleaming new silver Buick parked in a tow-away zone near where two men sat on folding chairs. "My walkin' days are over," Willie said.

"Prosperity suits you."

"Better me than the next guy. How about you? I hear you're goin' places, pal."

"Who says?"

"The guys on Hester Street." Willie lighted a cigarette, double-parked on Broome. "Then again, where the fuck they goin', right?"

Later, over squid at the old restaurant uptown, Johnny told Willie that things were looking up in the garbage racket.

"Yeah, well, me and the undertakers are in the midst of a bull market too, ya might say."

The garlicky, wine-rich sauce brought Sicily back to mind. For the first time, Johnny realized that it was far more than a recipe for a meal that the ghostly keeper of this place had mastered. It was the recipe for a memory, an evocation, of place and spirit and breeze.

"So," Willie said, "how's married life treatin' ya?"

"Fuck married life."

Johnny had been back a week, and he still had not made his return known to Diane.

"What the fuck did you ever get married for in the first place? I mean, it wasn't as if you had fuckin' monogamy in your fuckin' blood or some shit."

"Love," Johnny sneered.

"Love." Willie's voice rose, took on the timbre of operatic declamation: "Un' schiavo d'amore." He buttered a crust of bread, dipped it in the sauce. "You fuckin' people kill me. You don't bother wit' a license for a fuckin' gun, but you stand in line like a fuckin' citrull' for a fuckin' license to fuck. I don't fuckin' get it."

"I wanted to have a kid. You know that."

"So ya knock her up, then ya get the fuckin' license. Ya save all this fuckin' trouble. I mean, do you even have a life wit' this broad anymore?"

"We don't talk. We don't fuck."

"Hey, the stuff of the troubadours. Love in the first degree."

"Don't worry about my fuckin' life. Worry about your own." Johnny grinned when he spoke, but there was umbrage in his voice that his grin did not wholly conceal.

"Whadayou kiddin'? I live for love these days. High on love, that's me. I even went on a fuckin' date last month."

"*You* went on a fuckin' date."

"Damn fuckin' right. Flowers, a show, dinner, the works. Set me back three hundred bucks. As Christ is my fuckin' witness. Three hundred bucks and not even a fuckin' stroke."

"Modern romance, man, modern romance."

"Take your modern romance and stick it up your ass. It costs more to come up empty than it does to fuck in this goddamn town."

"It costs money to meet a nice girl."

"What nice girl? A broad, she's into this date racket, she's a bigger fuckin' whore than a broad who bends for fifties. She's a fuckin' no-fuck whore. It's fuckin' sick."

"Where'd you meet this fuckin' broad, a fuckin' gin mill?"

"Church. I met her in church."

"You go to church now too?"

"Why not? What the fuck, you think the statues are gonna walk out or somethin'?"

"It just doesn't seem your style."

"Hell," Willie said, smirking, "ya gotta hedge your fuckin' action in this world. Plus, I tell ya, Johnny, they got some nice fuckin' leg there. No shit. I'd say, pound for pound, tit for tit, church draws a much better class of head than the gin mills. Besides, I been startin' to help this guy Bareback run the Friday night games in the basement."

"What kind of split you work with the church?"

"What split? The church is the house."

"You're doin' charity work? I don't believe it."

"Yeah. Charity work. Sort of, anyway. See, they got a ten o'clock curfew at the church. After that, we take ev'rybody down the club and take their fuckin' socks."

"Goodman Willie. Before you know it, you'll be sellin' fuckin' indulgences."

Willie smiled demurely and drank his wine.

. . .

When Johnny finally did go to the Brooklyn apartment, Diane was not there. He sat awhile, looking at the Frenchman's floor-scrapers.

The idea of life without Diane saddened him, and the prospect of foundering for love depressed him. He did not think he had it in him to spill his guts and tell his life story—no matter how censored and edited a version—all over again. He did not even know if he had it in him to seek without the succor of booze. And yet booze was no longer any good. In the old days, every binge would bring him new flesh, new beauty, new thrills. Then the binges got longer and the broads got uglier. Then he was like the rest of them: a pathetic drunken no-fuck drowning in his own desperation, waiting like a fool for a train that had stopped running years ago. The blowjobs he took standing up in restrooms did not build strength. They were as sickly and as joyless as pissing and retching.

Without liquor, without Diane, all that lay before him seemed seeped in melancholy. He had discovered that murder in deed was not the spiritual dilemma it promised to be in thought. Compared to that precarious kindling of souls called love, compared to openly entering and receiving the heart of another, compared to piercing a soul, taking a soul was nothing. There was the mystery, the arras world of subtle, woven shades. And when love died, or was murdered, there was a devastation that blades and bullets could not bring.

And this love was dead. He himself had killed it, and that murder troubled him far more than the carnage he had wrought across the sea. He knew it was dead, but he could not accept that death, and he was like one who clung to a corpse in bereavement and denial both. He knew that he had fallen from the paradise of a friend and lover's grace to the hell of cold possession, and in that fruitless possession they would waste away, shackled enemies in a cell to which he held the key. Yes, that is what he needed to think, here and now, in Brooklyn, where there was no breeze and the moment was one of dead breath; he needed to think, to know, that it was he, not they and certainly not she, who held the key.

He stood. For a moment he thought of leaving her a note, but when he pictured it, try as he might, it remained blank.

A few days later, when he was at the union, he received word from Novarca that Signorelli had concluded all necessary arrangements. He called Louie, who told him that he would contact White Lion through Novarca to see that all was in order.

That evening Johnny returned to Brooklyn. He told Diane that he had just returned from Europe and he wanted to pick up some things, that he had one more trip to make. In truth, it was the shackles that had drawn him.

She had a look in her eye that disturbed him. It was the look of neither a stranger nor an enemy, but of an orphan in a storm, a look that seemed to recognize him only as a figure from a recurrent and troubling dream. He knew then that they would never make love again, and the thought seized him that he should rape her. Surely their shackles should be sundered with as much brutal passion as they had been soldered. But instead of raping her, he merely stood there and surrendered himself to the strange final flickers of what once had been love.

"How do you feel?" she said.

"All right," he said, unsure.

"About us, I mean."

To that there was no response, real or feigned, within him, other than to embrace. He did, and she began immediately to weep. And before he knew it, what would never again happen between them was happening. Her mouth seemed to want to drink in whatever cure there might be for the aching, draining loss of her tears, and her body filled with the greatest passion of all, a passion not of pleasure or love or heat or hate but of blind rage and sorrow. And that is what it was, not a fucking but a sorrowing, a sad, slow, carnal dance of loss. They lapped at each other like two beasts licking their mutual wounds in soundless instinctive ceremony. Her cunt was hot and wet and clenching, and his cock struck within her like a misericord.

They lay together silently until the slow beating of dark night became too much to bear.

He was about to leave. Maybe he would not see her again until he returned from the East. If he returned from the East. It was she who reminded him: "Didn't you want to pick up some things?" She reached up and turned on the wall light over the bed, then rolled over into her own darkness.

He started pulling some clothes from the closet: the jacket of soft olive silk he had bought on sale at Burberry's, his black kid-mohair custom-tailored suit, a pair of blue wool summer slacks, a few light shirts. At first he thought the bulge in the breast pocket of the black kid-mohair jacket was a necktie. When he pulled out the balled-up pair of stained panties, Bob Marshall's DEA calling card fluttered to the floor. He stood there awhile, pondering his wife's oddly misplaced panties, then he stooped to retrieve the small white rectangle that had fallen to his feet.

The notion of raping her had been mere velleity. The urge to kill her, to crush her throat, was overwhelming. It was an urge that banged with ramming violence at the door of his sanity, turning pulse and heartbeat and breath and mind to a blast of sudden shock. If there had been a quart of Scotch nearby, he would have broken it at the neck and cocked it, jagged, to his mouth.

His mouth was dry with anger. The words barely came. He stood over her. "What the fuck is this all about?"

She turned to him, barely saw what he held in his hand, recoiled at the demonic anger in his eyes and quivering lip. He grabbed her chin and jaw and jerked her toward him, then rubbed the panties hard in her face, hurting her nose. She began to scream, and he stoppered her mouth with the wadded panties and the force of his hand. He could feel her breath, hot and frantic and gasping, through the cloth. Her eyes widened in panic. The cloth covered her nostrils too. She was sure that he was smothering her, killing her. With a trembling hand, he held the card close to her eyes.

It made no sense to her. Only when Johnny uncovered her mouth, allowing oxygen to temper her panic, did she remember those panties; only then did she piece it together.

"Look," she said finally, summoning the voice in her jagged breath, "I don't know what's going on here any more than you do."

He raised his hand to smack her. She flinched and yelped. But he did not strike.

"I tell you what's goin' on, you fuckin' bitch. You rat me out to this fuckin' cunt-eatin', cocksuckin', motherfuckin' fed fuckin' bastard, then you fuckin' let him fuck you."

He raised his open hand again.

"Stop it! You're insane!" she screamed.

The last thing he wanted to hear was any of her stock fucking phrases. A moment after the blow flushed her face, tears welled in her eyes and a drop of blood appeared at the corner of her mouth.

"Who do you think you're fuckin' with here?" he spat.

"Listen to me," she whimpered. "You know what I think of cops."

It was true. She had always been a stand-up broad that way. She had nothing but disrespect for them. And how could she have ratted him out if she knew nothing?

"They must've broken in here for something. They took those panties from the hamper. Maybe you know what they were doing here. I don't."

He almost believed her. He wanted to. He could not accept that his possession had been defiled. The thought that she could have done what he had accused her of doing was unbearable. If anything was as low as a nigger-lover, it was a cop-fucker. Then again, when one sought to harm another, one's own morality was often abandoned toward that end.

But none of this mattered now. Whoever left this card, this Special Scumbag Robert J. Marshall, was onto him.

Johnny raised himself from his wife. Half an hour later, he was at his uncle's apartment on Sullivan Street. He laid the DEA card on the kitchen table. He told how he had found it.

"It's a bluff," the old man said. "A guy, he's got something hard to go on, he doesn't pull this shit. He wants to throw a scare into you, get you to fuck up."

"What if they followed me here?"

"So you're visiting your uncle. What's wrong with that?" The old man paused. "See, this is what he wants. You're all off-kilter. You're not thinking."

"Look. He knew enough to come for me."

"That's why he has to go. But let me ask you this. And I want you to remember that anything but an honest answer can finish us all. Does your wife know anything about our business? Anything at all?"

"No."

"Well, then we're okay."

"You think he fucked her?"

"You're asking me? She's your fucking wife. I barely know the girl. What do you think?"

Grains of composure had begun to separate fear from suspicion. "I think she fucked him."

"You're like me. You figure if they fuck you, they'll fuck anybody."

For Uncle Joe, the world of sex and jealousy was a dim and distant memory, like the mingled imagined scents of lemon blossom and the sea. In a way, he envied Johnny the mad heat of his passion.

"Let me do this guy," Johnny said. He knew what he would do, too. Diane owed him. Yes. *To use women as bait.*

"Are you crazy? Did that taste of blood turn you into an animal? This is not a fucking personal matter. I'll take care of this." Joe placed the card in his shirt pocket. Then his tone softened and was more compassionate. "Do you want him treated as if he gave you the horns?"

Johnny thought awhile, then said, "Yeah. I'd like that."

"One other thing. If your wife is telling the truth, your line may be bugged. Shit, even if she's lying, it may be bugged."

"I haven't used that phone in fuckin' ages."

"Good. It doesn't matter then."

"You really think we're okay?"

"These things happen. Like I said, I'll take care of it."

Johnny lighted a cigarette, sat back, and drew smoke.

"Did you hurt her?"

"I smacked her."

"But beyond that?"

Johnny shook his head.

"Good. Let her be for now. Don't let this thing drive you crazy. Remember, it's like the man says. Cunt is cunt."

"Yeah. Like the man says."

The heavyset, middle-aged man whom Joe summoned to the club the next morning listened intently as the old man spoke. As he listened, he held the little white card between two fingers of his right hand.

"And remember," Joe told him. "Make it look like cocaine and spics all the way."

The man nodded slowly. He flicked the card with the forefinger of his left hand. "This is not ordinary *quaglia* here."

"You know me, Berto. Just do your work and do it well. The envelope will not disappoint you."

Joe had intended to call Paul Como, the computer kid, when the shipment was in transit. Instead, he called him now.

Three mornings later—it was Friday—Bob Marshall's assistant, Jennifer Hernandez, switched on her terminal and called up a letter file that she had been working on. The system did not respond to her command. Instead, on her monitor, the prompt line flashed AQUI SE HABLA ESPANOL. At first she smiled. Someone was playing a trick on her. Probably Valdez, on the floor below. She tried to call other files. Every time the same message flashed. She tried the directory command. What she saw stunned her. The list of her files had all been transformed into ASCII gibberish. Had she herself done this somehow? She moved quickly down the hall. It was early. Few were in yet besides herself. She knocked on Peter Wang's door.

"I think something's wrong with the system," she told him.

He was calm and smiling when he turned on his machine, but after a few minutes he was pale and distraught. Not only had all files classified as sensitive, confidential, or restricted been erased, but their directories had been wiped clean by Norton. Unclassified files had been encrypted, and all but the most basic commands had been transformed to logic-bomb signals, programmed to wreak even deeper and more wide-ranging havoc throughout the system and its networks upon execution. Sporadically, as the logic bomb spread, the system flashed FUCK YOU and VAYA CON DIOS, CONCHA DE TU MADRE and VIVA LA BLANCA.

Washington ordered the New York system shut down. The viral tendrils of the logic bomb, however, had already crept far beyond New York. The uproar at the office was such that it was half past ten before

Jennifer Hernandez realized that her boss had not yet shown up for work.

In a deserted weighing-station terminal in South Kearny, Marshall lay bound and gagged with duct tape on the dirty concrete floor. The left side of his face was red and swollen, and a gash at his temple oozed dark, clotting blood. His nostrils flared and his shoulders heaved with the labor of his breath. His eyes were wide with fear. Cowboys and Indians, good guys and bad guys. It was the greatest game of all. Now, for him, the game was over.

The heavyset, middle-aged man leaned against a post. A younger man stood over Marshall and spat in his face.

"Where's that phone?" the heavyset man said.

The younger man gestured to a milk crate near the wall. The heavyset man sauntered to it, fetched the cellular telephone that the younger man had placed upon it, along with the roll of duct tape and a Coast Guard knife.

Taking a slip of paper from his pocket, he recited Marshall's home number as he dialed another.

"You have the wife?" He looked straight at Marshall as he spoke. "Good. Here's my number." He glanced at the phone in his hand, then gave him the area code and number. "Call me back when you got your cock in her."

He laid down the phone, lighted a cigarette. In two or three minutes —it seemed like thirty days and thirty nights to Marshall—the phone rang.

"Put the phone near her cunt." The heavyset man held the cellular phone to Marshall's ear. "Listen," he said.

At the other end of the line, a receiver lay on a kitchen counter. Near the mouthpiece, two right-hand fingers beat a soft slurring rhythm against a left palm.

Marshall's eyes closed, as if he were overcome by something beyond fear. The sound of the rape of his wife and his world wrenched him from sanity and delivered him to hell.

"Now kill the bitch," the heavyset man said, and once again he lowered the telephone to Marshall's ear.

At the other end of the line, a right hand fired a gun through an open kitchen door into a suburban backyard.

Marshall's eyes opened slightly and filled with tears. Then they closed, and not only his shoulders but his whole body heaved. Only when his trousers were torn open by the younger man did his eyes open again.

The younger man drove the big Coast Guard knife hard into the inguinal region. Marshall's body screamed in horrible silence, then went into convulsions as the blade sawed around his fear-shriveled testicles and penis, pierced his left femoral artery, and dug into his pelvic cavity, severing his urethra and vas deferens. When blood squirted hard from the femoral artery into the face of the cutter, he cursed, as if at some personal affront on the part of his victim. Finally, he gouged out the pound of bloody flesh and venous roots in a single, sodden mass. By then Marshall's body was still.

"Should I finish him?" he asked the heavyset man. Blood splattered onto the floor from the organs in his left hand, dripped from the blade of the knife in his right. He looked with repulsion at the gore in his left hand. "Fuckin' disgusting," he muttered, as if he had nothing to do with it, as if he had happened upon it and only now realized what it was.

"He's already finished." The heavyset man reached down, pulled the tape from Marshall's mouth, which fell open but made no sound. He was still breathing, but his life was gathering in the drenching pool of blood from his femoral artery.

"Go 'head," the heavyset man said, "make it pretty."

The younger man crammed the handful of gore into the open mouth.

"There's a spigot out back," the heavyset man told him. "Go wash up." From his pocket, he removed a small spiral notepad. The pad was old and worn and missing many of its blue-lined leaves, all of which were blank. The first leaf, however, bore the impression, invisible to the casual eye, of a notation that had been made on a previous leaf. The impression was that of a Colombian nickname, Cabezon, and a number, 24. The pad had also been lightly dusted with cocaine. He tossed the pad onto the floor behind the milk crate.

It would be more than a week before Marshall's gruesome remains were found. In the ensuing investigation, Peter Wang would help the FBI tie it all together: the Spanish-spouting logic bomb, Marshall's murder, the case that Marshall had called Apocalypse. While pursuing his theory about the Mafia and the 14K Triad, Marshall must have stumbled on the truth. For several years now, there had been intimations that the Colombian cocaine cartels were about to get into the heroin business big-time. It had been the Colombians who had set New York aflame with violence and plague. Marshall had gotten too close to the truth. Convinced of this, the FBI and DEA stepped up full-scale investigations into those Colombian groups who were known to have expanded from cocaine to heroin. Wang would see to it that his friend had not died in vain.

THIRTY

They arrived in Bangkok during Buddhist Lent. The sun was so strong and so hot that the streets shimmered in simmering mirage, like streams issuing from the Chao Phraya, the River of Kings, which wound like a serpent through the city's heart. From the veranda of his suite in the Oriental Hotel, Johnny could see the teak-hulled barges of rice that flowed endlessly by.

From the hotel, in the heart of the old business district, it was but a modest walk to the Italian Embassy, on Nang Linchi Road. At the office of the chancellor, they were introduced to the clerk who would serve as their escort and translator. The three men rode together in a chauffeured limousine north along the Phadung canal to Government House.

The limousine was air-conditioned. In their black suits and ties, Johnny and Louie rode in comfort, insulated from the terrible heat of the morning and the maddening din of the traffic. They were comfortable, but they were not at ease. Louie read the anxiety in Johnny's face.

"Look at it like this," he said. "Who turns down money?"

Johnny nodded in estimation of those words. But nothing more was said. The clerk had no idea of what they were up to, and they wanted to keep it that way.

Guided by the clerk, they made their way through the halls of
Government House, coming finally to a large, burgundy-carpeted room
on the third floor. On the wall were portraits of the king and the prime
minister. Louie studied the latter.

"Looks just like the rest of them." He shrugged, but he could not
conceal his nervousness from Johnny.

A door opened, and a man in a drab brown suit led them into
another, smaller room. The drab man vanished beyond yet another door.
A woman at a desk said something to the clerk, who turned to Johnny
and Louie and asked if they cared for tea. They did not. Their appointment had been for ten o'clock. It was now twelve minutes past. Johnny
did not like to be kept waiting. Louie was even worse. Usually, if
someone was fashionably late in meeting him or let other business tarry
him, he simply left. Nervous or not, prime minister or no prime minister,
they grew resentful at this impropriety. Louie asked the clerk to remind
the woman that their appointment had been for ten. The clerk did not
have to translate her reply, as her bemused expression implied clearly
enough that here the only time that mattered belonged to the prime
minister.

Eventually, the drab man reappeared. The prime minister, he said,
apologized for keeping them waiting. There was, he said, trouble today
in the north. Then he smiled, a shit-eating grin that seemed to say that
this was of course merely an absurd and threadbare formality, that the
prime minister could not have cared less about keeping them waiting,
that there was no trouble in the north, that this was merely the excuse
offered everyone, day in and day out.

From the prime minister's office one could see the lush green
grounds of Wat Benjamabophit and, to the east, Chitrlada Palace, the
royal residence.

The prime minister stood and greeted his visitors as if they were old
friends. Grasping their hands, he welcomed them to the City of Angels.
Smiling boyishly, he gestured toward Wat Benjamabophit and said
something to the clerk.

"Prime Minister Song should like you to know," said the clerk, "that
this lovely Buddhist temple is builded of Italian marble."

The prime minister nodded enthusiastically as the clerk relayed his observation.

"Please tell him," Johnny said, "that it is a most fitting metaphor for the nature of our business, a quest for a true universality of strength and peace."

As Johnny spoke English, Louie helped the clerk follow his words by offering brief Italian explications here and there. Johnny opened his leather attaché case and presented the prime minister with several documents concerning the Società Padre Carmelo.

"In you, Khun Song," Johnny began, "we feel that for the first time in modern Thai history, we have an ally who shares our hopes for a better and more democratic world. We are neither a political nor a governmental organization. And while our society bears the name of an Italian holy man, our precepts are no more sectarian, or nationalistic, in nature than the marble in that temple that you show us. We seek no considerations, no recognition, in return for the good that we try to do. We are seed-planters, if you will. Our only rewards are the fruit of our efforts, which we believe belong to the world and to its children."

Seed-planters, Louie thought. Way to fucking go, kid.

"We should like to make it both feasible and profitable for you to eradicate opium production and drug trafficking throughout your country. Opium, as you well know, is a source of some of the world's greatest woes. Furthermore—and this you know better than anyone—it has greatly stigmatized your country's international standing. We are willing to subsidize an extensive crop-substitution program in the north. Furthermore, we are willing to donate matériel that will help to ensure the continued strength and security of your democratic leadership."

Their meeting developed into a luncheon. The drab man was summoned, and soon waiters appeared bearing trays of catfish curry and roast duck, prawn-and-lemon-grass soup and stir-fried vegetables, rose apples and the red, hairy-skinned fruit called rambutan, chilled bottles of Kloster beer and iced Thai tea.

His honored visitors did not know, said the prime minister, how many times his own attempts to initiate a full-scale crop-substitution program had been vetoed or aborted on economic grounds. He would have a declaration of intention drawn up and presented to them. The program would be inaugurated as soon as his benefactors' funds were received at the Bank of Thailand.

"Please tell Khun Song that no declaration of intention is necessary. We are far from naive, but we believe that when men of honor and good will can no longer trust one another, the Società Padre Carmelo will have lost its battle."

From his attaché case, Johnny removed the blank check, drawn against the Rome account of the Società Padre Carmelo, that had been signed and supplied by Avvocato Signorelli. He filled in the amount: one hundred and fifty billion lire.

The prime minister was so visibly impressed that when he got a mouthful of green-and-red mouse-shit pepper and his eyes teared, he appeared to Louie as if emotion had overtaken him.

"Can we presume that the program will commence with this coming season?" Johnny asked.

He assured them that it would. The necessary plans were already laid out, and had been awaiting an opportunity, a godsend, such as this.

"Of course, the prime minister himself will have to arrange for the shipment of our gift of arms. Our associate, Avvocato Signorelli, will be in touch with him."

Of course.

The prime minister seemed indeed an upright sort. Johnny and Louie both wondered how much, or how little, of the money he would steal for himself.

When their long, amiable, and fruitful meeting was concluded, the clerk from the embassy seemed to regard them anew, as saints among men.

"I was gonna ask him about the whores, but he was lookin' at us like we had halos," Louie said.

And Johnny and Louie regarded themselves anew as well: as men who could slither among the mighty and the exalted as sinuously and as effectively and as finely as among the scum of the earth.

Wandering the streets that afternoon, they came upon a homely placard posted outside a bar.

NO ENTRANCE FEE
PAY ONLY FOR DRINK
FIRE STICK IN PUSSY SHOW
PUSSY WRITING SHOW
PUSSY CHOP BANANA SHOW
RAZOR THRILLING SHOW
BOTTLE CRACKING SHOW
CHOPSTICKS IN PUSSY SHOW
PUSSY IRRIGATION SHOW
FUCKING SHOW

No entrance fee, Johnny thought; pay only for drink. Razor thrilling show. Fucking show. It sounded like a syllabus for life itself. Soon, he reckoned, he would be able to write his own syllabus:

MONEY SHOW
HAPPINESS SHOW
PARADISE IN BREEZE SHOW
ETERNAL BLOWJOB SHOW
BANKBOOK IN PUSSY SHOW
TOP-OF-THE-WORLD SHOW
NO WORRY SHOW

He felt now, in his heart, that it was all within reach, that it was only a matter of days. So intimidating at first, this place of temples and whoredom, this gold-and-emerald sideshow of Bangkok now, after their success at Government House, seemed less surreal and less dangerously seductive. It seemed just another carny midway in a world, Manhattan to Milan, Brooklyn to Bangkok, that felt more and more their own.

"Get a load of this joint," Louie said, drawing Johnny's attention to a sign that read

CABBAGES & CONDOMS
Thai Cuisine Restaurant
Open Daily 11 A.M.–10 P.M.

"Appetizing," Johnny said. "Very appetizing."

"I knew that AIDS was big here, but this is fuckin' ridiculous."

Eventually, they found out about the whores, who were everywhere. They ranged in price from five hundred to fifteen hundred bahts, more if you were an Arab, as the many Saudis who came to Bangkok for sex were considered *saca poch*, dirty. Here, as among the Italians, to fuck an Arab was to risk social stigma. *S'è fatta scopare da un arabo*, as they dismissed certain women in Italy: she let herself be fucked by an Arab. A certain caste of Thai whores fucked only Arabs. But most whores also fucked them, in secrecy, as Arabs were willing to pay a premium for women who had been with white *farang*. There were places in Bangkok that offered nothing but *kathoy*, lady-boys, men who had undergone sex-change operations. There were places that specialized in "smoking girls," or cocksuckers; places for men who liked to watch; even a place where unscarred girls from the hills allowed themselves to be cut. Bangkok, where a woman could labor all day for a hundred bahts or sell pussy for five hundred bahts a crack, was indeed a city for whores. But as Johnny and Louie were warned, one was wise to assume, even if presented with a barely pubescent girl selling herself as virgin meat, that every one of them carried death in her body.

Neither Johnny nor Louie believed that AIDS could be sexually transmitted from a broad to a straight. As they saw it, there were only two ways for a man to get it: through a spike in the vein or a dick up the ass. All this bullshit about heterosexual AIDS was just a fag plot to deflect discrimination and scare the general population into funding and affinity. But this knowledge did not prevent them from using scumbags, any more than rationalism prevented them from knocking on wood or rubbing a negrillo's head for luck.

The whores in Chinatown were cheapest of all. Their pimps were their fathers, brothers, husbands, and boyfriends, who lived in broken-down buses parked across the street from where the girls congregated. One chose whom one wanted, went across to the buses, pointed her out, and a relative or beau fetched her. Louie picked out a little girl that reminded him of a Danbury Mint porcelain doll his wife had bought through an ad in the *TV Guide*. The doll was called Lotus Blossom, and it had cost Louie five monthly payments of thirty-three bucks plus shipping and handling. The whoreling cost three hundred bahts. Much to Louie's amusement, Johnny took three girls at once: a mother in her early thirties and two teenage daughters, all of whom had scrawny but stockinged legs. "Go git 'em, Farouk," Louie said as they parted at the doors of their suites.

Two days later they boarded a Thai Airways International flight to Yangon. Riding in from Mingaladon Airport in a government taxi, they beheld a landscape so ravaged and lifeless that the vultures flapping languidly overhead seemed to be scavengers more of the dead soul of this militarized land than of the carrion that littered it. In the city itself, the lingering decayed traces of a grace that must have been Rangoon's still escaped here and there—a glimmer of golden pagoda through a breach in ancient foliage, a dragon-prowed bark drifting downriver— like errant trills of birdsong from a soulless cage.

The clerk from the Italian Embassy drove in from Golden Valley to meet them at the Strand Hotel. On their way to the junta headquarters of the State Law and Order Restoration Council, the clerk translated the red-and-white signboards that were everywhere: DOWN WITH MINION OF COLONIALISM. CRUSH ALL DESTRUCTIVE ELEMENTS. IN DISCIPLINE LIES SAFETY. No need of cursèd condoms, no chopsticks in pussy shows here.

Major General Saw Win showed them no Buddhist temples made of Carrara marble. He merely listened, neither acknowledging nor denying that his country's opium fields were the ultimate source of most of the world's heroin.

"We share a common enemy, Bo Saw," Johnny said.

The general asked him whom that might be.

"Shang Wing-fu. The one they call Asim Sau."

This was true, the general said. Shang was an enemy of the people, responsible for much of Myanmar's fraternal conflict. As such, yes, he was the general's enemy as well.

Was it true that Shang's army was as powerful as the Tatmadaw, the government army, itself?

Nonsense.

Then why was Shang, alone of the state's enemies, allowed not only to live but to prosper?

He was no longer in Myanmar. He was in Thailand.

He was there. He was here. He was everywhere.

To this, the general had no answer to make.

Johnny said they were here to help annihilate Shang Wing-fu and raze the opium fields of the Shan.

Tapping the Società Padre Carmelo documents that lay on his desk, the general said that he did not understand. In one breath, he said, they spoke of benevolence, and in the next of bloodshed.

The righteous road was not always a bloodless one. Surely the general knew that.

What sort of assistance was being offered?

Mi-24s. Amraams. M60s.

Expressionlessly, silently, the general wondered if these men could know of the Shan and not of the Wa. As if reading his mind, Johnny let him know that men of good will were not necessarily men of innocence.

"We know that you have a certain sympathy for the cause of the Wa in their struggles against the Shan."

Like them, said the general, he merely took the righteous path.

Be that as it may. The Società Padre Carmelo only hoped that he would not allow the Wa to supplant the Shan as poisoners of the world.

These cross-worshipping fools knew nothing, after all. That men such as these had weapons such as those of which they spoke was, to the general's thinking, truly dangerous.

"In any case," Johnny said, "we hope that the Wa don't forget who their friends are."

No, he told himself, it was he who had been the fool. He knew now who these men were, knew the true name of their society. The embassy clerk, meanwhile, was convinced that they were intelligence operatives —SISDE, SISMI, CIA, or some combination thereof—involved in some unknowable cabal.

The general wanted to know, what did they ask in return for this support?

Nothing.

Nothing?

"As we said. Only to be remembered as friends."

Louie saw what Johnny had expertly done: struck the perfect tone of desired ambiguity. The Wa warlords, of course, would never prevail. They and the Hong Kong triads would have no time to develop the sort of international organization that was needed. The restored Middle Eastern network would foredoom them, and General Saw, to the role of secondary players before Asim Sau's body was cold in its grave.

They would be remembered, the general said. Of that much, he assured them.

Johnny and Louie found themselves that evening at a Shan restaurant, the 999, on Thirty-fourth Street. It was just north of the Sule Pagoda, a two-thousand-year-old monument said to contain a hair of the Buddha. By gesturing at what looked edible on the tables of nearby diners, they ended up with steaming bowls of rice noodles, peppery cured eel, and spicy raw vegetables smeared with fermented shrimp paste.

"Those wops Virgilio's sending to Hong Kong," Johnny said. "How are we supposed to recognize them?"

"We're not," Louie told him. Holding a chopstick up to the light and muttering something, he rubbed away at it with his napkin. "If we did, that could give them away. They'll be there. Let's just worry about us, not them." Looking more closely at the napkin, he muttered again and gave up entirely. When the waiter came, Louie grabbed fresh chopsticks from him and gave him a dirty look.

The cold Mandalay beer tasted good, and it made them realize how hungry they were. The food came, and they dug into it like wolves. They looked at each other, then at the contented patrons around them. The eel tasted like sewer eel. The fermented shrimp paste inspired Louie to new poetic diction: "This shit tastes like cancer-ward cunt slime."

It was the time of year when the monsoon passed through Yangon on its way from the Indian Ocean to the up-country jungles. The sweltering twilight, a thick yellowish haze of biting insects and humidity, gave way to a black moonless night of hard steamy rain. From the window of Johnny's room, the river and the torrential sky seemed to be one, and the world itself a place without light, or breeze, or time. Or truth. That he had beguiled and deceived men—a prime minister, a general—who were princes of power, lords of nations, did not fill him now with any great assurance, satisfaction, or pride. It filled him instead with the eerie and dire suspicion that he had succeeded only in discovering that lies and truth were but different cheap copper castings of the same debased but universal currency. Had any government ever run on truth, beyond demanding it of the enemy and propagating its value to the common man? Was the idea of truth between men in itself anything but a lie that men chose not to face?

He thought of the mother and daughters he had taken to his room in Bangkok the other night: the lamprey-mouth of the mother fixed to the breast of the daughter whose emaciated skull lay between his legs like a tribal war trophy on a stake, the other daughter licking weakly, hungrily at his chest, stroking the skull and stake with dry, bony fingers. The uroboros they formed, writhing round him like casket snakes, seemed a strange funerary rite of the senses. Maybe they themselves were dying, withering from this world in slow marasmus. Maybe there was something in him that they could sense—a heartbeat, a pulse in cock or wrist—something pullulating deep inside him, where the secret of the souls he had stolen with gun and knife resided.

He thought of Diane—thought of her sucking that fed's rotten cock. A death rite of her own. A death rite for that motherfucking fed, that much was for sure.

Had she? One copper coin or another. He would never know. And here, in the hot black downpour where a world once had been, it seemed not to matter. Here pride seemed even less of worth than wealth.

In his dreams that night, he lay down with serpents. And when he awoke in the streaming sunlight, the sensation of their presence was so vivid in his memory that the sweat that drenched his body struck him unpleasantly as the secretions of their visitation. He showered and shaved without seeing it: coiled round the cool plumbing under the sink, glistening black and utterly still.

THIRTY-ONE

Coming into Hong Kong by night, they emerged from stormclouds and turbulence to a phantasmagoria of neon colors, myriad magic lanterns of rainbow light, that shone like a cove of jewels through the sable summer sky. Johnny and Louie had never seen anything quite like it. To Johnny, it was as if the black hole of the Yangon night had spewed him forth into another world: Babylon, a land of dreams, shimmering and sleepless, with open mouth and gleaming blade.

After settling in at the Mandarin Hotel, Johnny called his uncle in New York, where it was the afternoon of the previous day.

"You forgot the meat," the old man said as soon as he heard his nephew's voice.

"What're you talking about?"

"The meat. The bad meat."

Johnny inhaled, exhaled audibly. He was too much, his uncle, he really was. Here Johnny was, halfway around the world, he had just skinned a prime minister and a dictator, he was on the verge of closing the biggest fucking deal the flat-earth society had ever swung, and all his uncle, whom he was about to render a billionaire, could think of was that scrap of poison meat in his freezer. Not even a how-are-ya or a good-to-hear-your-voice. Nothing. Maybe he was losing his fucking mind.

"What is it with you and this bad meat? What was I supposed to do with that shit, anyway?"

"Introduce it into the ecosystem," his uncle said, as if stating the obvious.

"Whose ecosystem?" Fuck. Now he was talking like him too. Maybe they were both losing their fucking minds.

"The jungle Chinks. That Asim Sau and that fucking army of his. You were there, weren't you?"

"No. Not really. He's way north of Bangkok, way south of Yangon."

"How far could it be? From here to Philly? Here to Baltimore? You could've put it right in his fucking lap, right in his goddamn water supply."

"Just like that. How the fuck was I supposed to find him?"

"Hell, you got business with the man. That Chink in Hong Kong could've got you to him."

"Look. Why don't you take that fuckin' meat and feed it to the fuckin' feds or some shit? Feed it to Goo Goo's dog."

"You don't understand. This could've wiped them all out. This could've done what those fucking aldermen over there may not be able to do. This was all Virgilio's idea, you know, this diplomatic shit. I wanted to go with the meat all the way." Then, as if it were an afterthought: "How did that go, anyway?"

"What?"

"What 'what'? Your business with those fucking monkeys over there."

Johnny resented his uncle's demeaning tone. The old man showed no appreciation of what Johnny and Louie had done. He made it sound as if they had merely tossed a handful of sugared nuts to monkeys in a zoo, as if they were on a vacation that he was paying for.

"Oh, that," Johnny said. "Piece o' cake."

"Good." The old man's tone was different now, was warmer and more benevolent. It was as if Johnny, in demeaning the work himself, had shown Joe what he wanted to see: the aspect of one who was bigger than anything set before him, who did not pause to honor himself but instead washed away the sweat and got on with it.

"I'll see you," Johnny said.

"Sleep with one eye open till you do. Get home in one piece."

May-ling Woo, the receptionist at White Lion Enterprises, was a beautiful woman. At her desk, beneath a seventeenth-century landscape by Dong Qichang, she was, like the painting, an image of exquisite delicacy and composure. Standing there looking at her and around her, Johnny thought of old Rose and her ashtray of lipstick-stained butts beneath the assembly-line painting of the skyline at sunset in Novarca's outer room.

Ng Tai-hei had the necessary papers in order: bills of sale, invoices, tax forms, tariff schedule, and country-of-origin statement. Signed copies would be delivered, along with the carrier's bill of lading, to Novarca's licensed customs broker in New York, who would transmit all documentation to the appropriate authorities via Automated Broker Interface.

The paperwork detailed the sale and transport of twelve thousand marital-aid items at a bankruptcy clearance price of nineteen and a half cents per unit, the price which Johnny had asked to be put on them, though in Japan and Europe these same deluxe dicks sold for as much as thirty dollars a shot. Per Johnny's request, the transaction had been documented as two separate sales of six thousand units each. There was some confusion as to whether, according to the *Harmonized Tariff Schedule of the United States of America*, these battery-powered rubber dicks should be classified as 9503806020, Toy Models Incorporating a Motor, or 9021300000, Other Artificial Parts of the Body. In the end, they went with the less macabre toy category.

"I really thought you'd double the price," said Ng. "Launder a few grand that way, kill two birds with one stone."

"There's a method to my madness," Johnny said, smiling. "You see, I don't want to press my luck."

"And the money?" said Ng.

"It's right here in Hong Kong," said Louie, "waiting to be transferred. The ship arrives from Singapore in two days. Once we have our cargo, once we've examined it and it's loaded on that ship, you can witness that transfer."

"Very well, then. Tuan Ching-kuo, who will be honored to meet you, will be flying in from Taipei early tomorrow. He has planned a little banquet of celebration for us in the evening."

"And Asim Sau?" Johnny asked.

"He is already here. He will join us as well."

From White Lion, Johnny and Louie walked to the Macau Ferry Terminal. *Made in Macau.* Every pack of firecrackers Johnny had bought or sold as a boy had borne that legend. *Do not hold in hand. Lay on ground. Light fuse. Get away. Made in Macau.* Nowadays, firecrackers came not from Macau but from the Communist mainland, the Special Economic Zone of Guangdong Province, north of Hong Kong. But to Johnny, the Sino-Portuguese territory Macau still beckoned as a symbol of all that was faraway and exotic and romantic. In adolescence, he had pictured Macau as an island of lost souls, of rickety firecracker sweatshops and one-eyed, pigtailed coolies laboring under the whips of gunpowder-mad Fu Manchus. Now, aboard the jetfoil, he still thought of it as an island and was surprised to discover that it was a peninsula, connected, like Hong Kong, to mainland China. It was a belated realization of the sort that served to keep Johnny aware of how ignorant he was. Insignificant in themselves as they were, he was grateful for these little humiliations that came his way, for he was a great believer in stupidity. An awareness of one's own stupidity, he felt, was the better part of wisdom. When one realized how little one knew, one not only opened himself to knowledge but also was able to place that knowledge—and the relative incompleteness of all knowledge—in proper perspective. *Ex stupiditate, sapientia.* In stupidity, wisdom. *Lay on ground. Light fuse. Get away.*

At the Casino de Lisboa, Johnny played blackjack, Louie played craps. Johnny well knew that system gamblers were gamblers who made a science of losing. But he himself had a system of sorts. It had nothing to do with counting cards or splitting or doubling up. He called it the hit-and-run system. He never played two consecutive hands at the same table. Starting out with three hundred-dollar chips, he was up eleven hundred Hong Kong dollars within an hour. He cashed in and walked over to the craps table. Louie was rolling the dice, cursing in Italian, much to the amusement of the Chinese gamblers gathered round. By the sound of things, he was losing his shirt. Then Johnny saw the five-hundred-dollar chips that were stacked on the green felt before Louie in three staggered piles, one of which lay in the pass line. Two of Louie's chips lay in the hardway layout, surrounded by the lesser chips of other gamblers.

"Porco Maria!" he exclaimed as he shook and threw the dice hard across the table: that pig of a Virgin Mary!

"Pawlco Maleea!" echoed the Chinamen in exuberant chorus, right and wrong bettors alike.

Johnny watched Louie throw the dice four times, exclaiming at every roll. When two fours came up, Louie stood back and nodded obliquely at the resting dice, as if they had done well. The croupier placed a second stack of five-hundred-dollar chips next to the stack that Louie had placed on the pass line. In the hardway layout, he added eighteen chips to Louie's two. Louie threw one of the chips to the croupier. Five-hundred-dollar tips were very rare, and so also was the savoir faire with which Louie had tossed it visibly across the table, setting an example for other gamblers to aspire to and emulate. The croupier twirled the chip sharply between his fingers and dropped it into his pocket. *"Pawlco Maleea!"* he sang.

Louie took his piles of chips to the cashier, who counted out thirty-one crisp thousand-dollar bills.

"Is that how you got that name?" Johnny said. "Is that why they call you Bones?" Johnny had always assumed the nickname had a more sinister origin, something to do with making one's bones, or with burying them.

"Always a sucker for the bones," Louie said, without really answering the question. "That's me, all right."

"That ain't no sucker's purse you got there, pal."

"This? It just looks like a lot. A lousy four grand American. Shit.

You look at the big picture, I'm down. Over the years, I'd say, I'm into the bones maybe a hundred grand. It's a sucker's racket. And I'm a sucker."

"Well, you're a richer sucker now than you were when you woke up."

"What're you, buildin' up to a pinch for dinner?"

"Yeah."

"Like I said," Louie said, grinning, "I'm a sucker."

They walked along Avenida do Amizade, which followed the coastal curve of the Baia da Praia Grande, then ambled up Rua do Comendador Kou Ho Neng to Penha Hill. According to the croupier at the casino, the Bela Vista on Penha Hill had the finest restaurant in Macau. There, on the terrace overlooking the bay, they ordered a chilled bottle of Martin Codax Albariño, roasted pigeon, and a paella of fresh crab.

"Do you think they'll try to fuck us?" Johnny asked.

"Fuck us how?"

"Any way they can."

"It's like this. If it were a one-shot deal—I mean, if they thought, if they knew it was a one-shot deal—yeah, definitely, they'd do everything they could. They know we're gonna spot-check, and they know we got the little *comu si chiam*'s, the little testers, like the feds. But still they'd try to burn us, a few dummy tons here and there, that sort of thing. Like it is, though, I'd say no, they'd be fools. There'd be no more deals. More than that, if we cut into one of their dummies, or a streeted batch, or whatever, they wouldn't get their fuckin' money. Even if we missed it, we'd catch it later, and they'd never see the final payment. Not that they're gonna see it anyway, I mean, but they think they are."

"I wish there was a way to load that shit and fuck 'em *before* the money changed hands."

"Well, there ain't. Believe me, if we tried that, even if that ship did get outa port, we'd lose everything. They'd have every fuckin' fed in New York waitin' for these rubber dicks."

"What's to stop 'em from doin' that anyway? That way, they win, we lose."

"But they wouldn't win. We'd have the feds on that transferred money quicker than a Chink can blink. They know that."

"After those wops dust off this Ng, you don't think they're gonna wanna get back at us?" Johnny was thinking of what Billy Sing had told him about men who learned the ethic of vengeance from the cradle.

"Are you kiddin'? With that money sittin' there, there'll be more of his own kind glad to have him out of the way than sorry to see him go."

Johnny sucked crabmeat from a claw. "Beats hell outa that joint in Burma."

Louie snorted. "Tell me somethin'," he said. "We got four forty-foot containers. We're declarin' a few thousand rubber dicks in each one. What about the real weight? What about those hundred and thirty-five tons?"

"Half of the dicks are registered as LCL shipments of Novarca import cargo, half as R.P. cargo."

"What's LCL?"

"Less than container load. Ocean shipments are classified either as FCL, full container load, or LCL. The containers are owned by us. But it's all untraceable, through one of the shelf companies. We lease them to ourselves through the Inter-Continental Equipment Group in Basel. We're sharing each container with LCL shipments registered by Lupino in the name of the Lighthouse Society. Again, untraceable to us. The Lupino cargo, also handled by our customs broker in New York, is faked as a charitable shipment of Braille textbooks, printed in Hong Kong by the Lighthouse Society for free institutional distribution by the American Foundation for the Blind, the Jewish Braille Institute of America, and Lighthouse, Inc. Thirty-three tons in each container. All of it loaded behind our rubber dicks. Technically, Novarca has no knowledge of who owns the containers or who or what it's sharing the containers with. Since we couldn't fill a container of our own, the broker squeezed us in on the four book containers. When the containers are trucked out of port in New York, the paperwork will indicate destinations for separate warehouses, one for Novarca, one for Lupino. Those dicks are our legal reason for opening and partially unloading those containers upon delivery in Jersey. The rest of the shit, which we unload by mistake, we know nothing about."

"Rubber dicks and Braille textbooks," Louie mused. Then his expression changed. It grew more serious. "You know," he said, "you're doin' a hell of a job. For all I'm worth to you on this trip, I coulda stayed home."

"Ah, you said the same thing in Milan. It was bullshit then, it's bullshit now."

"No. It was bullshit then, all right. Now it's the truth. You got what it takes, Johnny. You got more than what it takes. You can go places in this world. Places me and your uncle, guys like us, places we only dreamed about."

"I tell you, Lou, we pull this off, I already been as far as I wanna go." Johnny shook off the subject. "You know the captain of this ship, don't you?"

Louie nodded. Though it sailed under a Liberian flag, the steamship *Golden Stella* was an American-owned container vessel with an Italian crew and American officers. Operated through a bearer-share company in the grasp of men like Johnny's uncle, it was the ship that hauled Novarca's paper pulp to foreign lands. Its business, until now, had been completely legitimate. And even now, only its owners, whom Giuseppe would smile upon when selling time came, knew the secret of its hidden cargo. The ship's captain, a man named Petrillo, had been told only that Louie and Johnny were important friends of the *Stella*'s owners.

"Yeah," Louie said. "I mean, I know about him." He thought of the videotapes in the back room of that orangutang's store on Sixth Avenue. "He's got a thing for little boys."

Johnny shook his head. "Those guys are the fuckin' lowest. Them and rapists. They oughta cut their dicks off, all of 'em."

"I agree. You know what gets me? These clay-eaters, these fuckin' Jesus creeps down South, they run around gunnin' down abortionists. What the fuck is that all about? I mean, you wanna do good in this world, go kill some fuckin' rapists. Make 'em eat their own fuckin' dicks."

"What gets me about these right-to-life assholes is, they're a bunch of rednecks, they hate niggers, right? But who's havin' these babies? Niggers, that's who. They hate 'em, but they want more of 'em. I don't get it."

"They should penalize these welfare cows for havin' babies, not reward 'em."

"Then again, that would reduce our market."

"Yeah." Louie grinned. "It's like, years back, this guy asked Colonel Sanders what he thought of niggers. Colonel says, 'They eat chicken, don't they?' "

Their feast of celebration was held the next evening at Man Wah, in the penthouse of the Mandarin. Introductions were made, and the chef, Fok Kam Tong, presented himself at their table to describe the menu he had prepared for them, a medley of nouvelle delicacies and celebrated dishes from China's imperial past. The sommelier brought out a bottle of Château Mouton-Rothschild 1864 and made his way around the table, letting each man behold its tawny vellum label. The wine was opened with slow, gentle ritual and set down to breathe. As the sommelier raised the cork daintily to his nostrils and placed it upon a linen square in a small silver tray to the right of Tuan's plate, Ng joked about the new vending machines operated by the yakuza in Tokyo. For three thousand yen, the machines coughed out used panties guaranteed to have been worn by a Japanese schoolgirl.

While the wine was being poured, Johnny turned his gaze from the incandescent Hong Kong nightscape to ponder the faces of Tuan Ching-kuo and Asim Sau. Tuan possessed the most readable countenance of the three. His was the banal, fatal look of perfect falsity, a look familiar to Johnny from the flickering and graven images of uncounted Western politicians. His molly-mouthed smile was disarmingly sincere, in that it so faithfully conveyed the insensate emptiness within, an emptiness that was as dangerous as it was odious. He struck Johnny not so much as a man but as a beastly parasite, bloated and content and holding fast to the host of the world. His eyes were those of a coward and a killer, a falsifier not only in word and deed but in spirit and soul as well.

The emerald eyes of Asim Sau, in contrast, were like those of the hooded serpent-demons and temple snakes that his people called nagas. Mesmerizing, cold, and reptilian, they were like shards of stained glass that turned the hellfire of a deadly soul into icy, untelling light. When his handsome lips parted with the slightest of movements, one almost expected to hear a venomous hiss.

Billy Sing's words came to Johnny as if from another life. *I understand*, Sing had told him, *that you soon may be privileged to be in the presence of one or more of these men. That you have never passed beneath the shadow that they cast will be of benefit to you, I think. To many who dwell in that shadow, they are like dark and distant gods, and the idea of meeting them would be unnerving. To you, however, they will be merely men—strangers from a strange world, yes, but beneath that, merely men. And that is how it should be.* Snake-eyed Asim Sau, however, did not seem to be merely a man. He seemed to be an Abbadona, one fixed eternally in evil, who could do not but evil, think not but evil.

Asim Sau was the first to taste the wine. He closed his eyes dreamily, savoring it, as if it nourished and renewed him. Then, smiling, he spoke.

"So. Who will win the World Series?"

"Still a long way to go," Louie said.

Tuan Ching-kuo grinned, as if this exchange represented a great cross-cultural triumph between East and West.

"I hope someday to visit America," said Asim Sau, who detested America and these vermin from its shores who shared his wine.

"We'll take you to a ball game," Louie told him, "do it up right." You dead cocksucker.

"Peanuts and Cracker Jacks," said Tuan, who always felt a need to lower the intelligence of his conversation in the company of Americans.

"I propose a toast," said Ng. He raised his glass. "To a new age." An age without *haksau dong*.

"And a new prosperity," said Louie. You rat bastard.

"Bravo," said Tuan. *Diu nei loumou*: fuck your mothers.

The five men drank. Waiters set before them aromatic servings of braised bird's nest, diced shrimp, crab coral, and night blossom.

"Will you be flying home as soon as the ship leaves?" asked Ng.

"We haven't decided." Louie shrugged.

"Maybe we'll take the boat back," Johnny said.

"But it's such a long trip," said Tuan. But not as long as you think.

"And it's a merchant ship," said Ng. "Surely you'd rather fly." It was the height of the typhoon season as well, but Ng said nothing of that.

What was this all about? Johnny and Louie both wondered. Why should these fucking Chinks care one way or the other whether they flew or sailed? Why would they want to keep them off that boat? Did they have something up their sleeves? Were they going to hijack the ship once they had their money?

Louie and Johnny had discussed sailing home as PACs—persons in addition to crew—aboard the *Stella*. Johnny had told Louie that he had reasons of his own for wanting to do so but that Louie should not feel obligated to accompany him. What he had to handle, he said, he could handle alone. Now, listening to these Chinks, Louie made up his mind. They would both ship out on the *Stella*. They would do whatever these shifty-eyed scumbags seemed to want them not to do.

"We'll see," Louie said. "We'll probably end up flying. But then again, the idea of a slow boat *from* China has its appeal."

Ng nodded. They had bought it. Reverse psychology. Simple as dealing with laboratory rats.

"How are things in Myanmar?" Johnny asked Asim Sau.

Asim Sau looked at him. It was a momentary glance that carried the piercing effect of a long, inscrutable stare.

"Maybe I should ask you the same thing."

His words chilled Johnny to the bone, blinded him, dumbfounded him. *He knew.* Somehow he knew.

"Surely you don't expect an outsider's ignorant perceptions to compare to a native son's?" He spoke as easily as he could, without hesitation or circumvention, as if answering one casual statement with another.

Though they knew what Asim Sau knew, Ng and Tuan remained aloof, commenting quietly to each other, in English, to avoid any suspicion of secrecy, on the taste of the night blossom, the rarity of the wine.

Louie, who did not skip a mouthful, chewed without taste, feeling for a moment that it was the end of the road.

"What were you doing in Yangon?"

Louie knew that it was Johnny's roll of the dice. To come to his aid would be too suspicious. He did not have the presence within him to pray or to hope. He merely listened to the roll of Johnny's words against the backboard of the warlord's ominous composure.

"Didn't Ng Seng—"

"Please. Ah Hei," Ng corrected him, asking him to use the more familiar form of address. Ng returned to his food as if the rest of the conversation were of no import, as if his only concern were that there be no more formalities among them, imagining meanwhile what the face, first of Johnny, then of Louie, would look like in death. This was his penchant. Mothers tried to discern the face of the man-to-be in the child that was. He looked for the mask of death in the face of the unknowing damned.

Good Chink, bad Chink, thought Louie.

"Didn't our friend here tell you the details of our bargain? There is more than money involved. We promised wooden hats for Major General Saw Win and Song Leekpai. We went to give them a fitting, you might say."

Louie was so delighted by Johnny's ingenuity that he laughed with relief, and his laughter seemed nothing more than an untroubled, natural response to Johnny's turn of phrase.

"We were going to try to visit you," Louie said, "but we didn't know where to look."

"Who told you we were there?" Johnny asked offhandedly.

Asim Sau looked at Ng and smiled.

"They have a saying around Chiang Mai," said Ng. "East of the Bay of Bengal, west of the Mekong, even the eagles ask Ah Fu."

"Then you know we've lost no time in preparing to honor our part of the bargain."

The warlord said nothing. It did not matter. Soon these fools would be dead, and with the next harvest, all would be restored.

The waiters brought a dish of fowl and seafood called "the rousing of the rooster by the deer," and another of many kinds of mushrooms and many kinds of onions.

As they ate, Asim Sau surreptitiously studied the Americans with an almost clinical fascination. The older of them struck him as a product of pure evil, a creature neither of cause nor of reason, led by base and brutal appetite alone. The Italians as a bloodstock had always seemed to Asim Sau peculiarly diabolical, a race that had in turn crucified and forced upon the world the god of their choosing. Murder and devotion. It was their way.

In the younger man, he saw the traits of that bloodstock and more. If the other was the product of pure evil, this one represented something far more dangerous: a man of thought, not merely a product of evil but one who understood evil as well; one who had broken the seventh seal and beheld the greatest of dark secrets, the mother of murder and devotion, of all holiness and horror, the mind and heart of man.

Civilization, however, had made them weak, like pampered emperors or sated demons. Like Tuan here. Or even Ng, with his manicures, his courtesans, his sybaritic whilings. He, Asim Sau, was the strong one here. It was he who moved with the leopard, the flying snake, and the wind. Ng and Tuan knew this. But these *gwailou* did not. He should like to kill them himself, on their knees, before him.

"We must do this more often," he said.

"Yes," Johnny said. "We should make it an annual affair." By the time the *Golden Stella* reached New York, he told himself, these three would be history, and when he and Louie sat down again to celebrate, they would be the powers to whom men raised their glasses.

"Do you know much of the Shan, or of our struggle for independence?" the warlord asked.

This guy was too much, Johnny thought, crusading for the freedom of a godforsaken tribe of jungle mongrels while enslaving the world to junk.

"Will there be an end to that struggle? Or will it go on forever, like the Arabs and the Jews, the Irish and the English?"

Kid sounds like he fucking cares, Louie thought.

"If we did not see an end, we would not fight. No, perhaps that is not true. Sometimes we must fight even without hope. Don't you agree?"

No, actually. Johnny agreed with the last of the thirty-six strategies: to walk away if there is no better option.

"If we fight without hope, we may not live to fight with hope."

"He that runs away lives to fight another day," said Louie, bringing a smile to Tuan's face. *Diu nei*, he thought: fuck you.

All this talk of living from men who were about to die, thought Asim Sau.

Louie remembered a day of spring shadows and an old man's words: *Avimu a fari comu San Giorgio. Avimu a fari muriri u dragu.* We must be like Saint George. We must kill the dragon.

The alpha and the omega, Johnny thought. The church in the hills. The picture on his uncle's kitchen wall.

Strange, thought Ng. Many years ago, with a robbery and a killing, he had embraced the sign of the *hóng sanjiao*. Now, risen to the top of the world, he faced robbery and murder again. A ten-thousand-dollar last supper, perhaps, many millions instead of a merchant's purse, but robbery and killing all the same.

The waiters brought coffee, snifters of Quinta do Noval 1931, and Hoyo de Monterrey Double Coronas. Ng raised his port and once again proposed a toast.

"To harmony, strength, and longevity."

And your mother's cunt.

May no ancestor know your name.

And one through your brain and two up your ass.

May the living eat the dead.

Die painfully and be fucked by God.

"This port," said Tuan, smiling, "like the company, is superb."

The five of them lighted their cigars, sending up slow silvery-white plumes of rich smoke laced faintly with scents that hinted at nutmeg, chocolate, cinnamon, and palm.

At the foot of Louie's bed that night, beside the laundered clothes that the chambermaid had returned to his room, was a gift-wrapped package bearing a square white envelope. Inside the envelope was a card imprinted with the words *Buon Viaggio!* Louie removed the wrapping and opened the shoebox within. Enclosed in wadded tissue were two Beretta 96 .40-caliber pistols, eleven-round cartridges, and a prayer card from the Chiesa di San Giorgio in Piana degli Albanesi.

· · ·

As dawn spread its fingers of pink light across the eastern sky, the stern lines of the six-hundred-foot *Golden Stella* were swung out around the bollards of Harbour City Pier, Kowloon. Like dead prey, from her deck and her hatches, twenty- and forty-foot cargo containers, stainless-steel IMCO tanks, loose crates, and industrial-equipment flats rose in the tenebrous talons of the booming hundred-ton dock cranes. Other containers, freed from truck cabs and railcars, were hoisted aboard in their place. And there, as the sun rose unkindly upon her, the old *Stella* waited, black-hulled and sea-scarred and leprous with rust.

One hundred and thirty-five tons of Uoglobe number-four heroin had been tightly packed in five thousand rectangular plastic bundles of twenty-seven kilos each. Each bundle was sealed in a box imprinted with the characters *shu bùláiyè mángwén*, the words BRAILLE BOOKS, and the symbol of a lighthouse and its rays. Affixed to each box was a counterfeit green-and-white tax exemption stamp.

No one—not Ng Tai-hei, not Asim Sau or Tuan Ching-kuo, not the silent, wiry, dark-skinned Chiu Chao who drove the forklifts and hoisted the boxes—had ever seen so much heroin in one place at one time. The government of the United States had intercepted big shipments in its day: two point seven tons of morphine base in the anchor-chain bins of the *Lucky S* in 1993, eight hundred pounds that old Peter Woo had brought ashore in rubber tires in 1989. But the government did not even think in terms this big. Discounted to the *capi bastuni* of New York, it was worth ten billion, eight hundred million dollars. Beyond that, as it passed down to the streets, God only knew.

In an abandoned military warehouse on Stonecutters Island, Johnny and Louie stalked to and fro among the five thousand boxes, opening them at random, cutting into the heavy, dense bundles within, spooning pinches of white powder into the vials of their testing kits, adding droplets of acid reagent, and watching the milky mixture turn a lovely pale purple. Moving behind them, the Chiu Chao resealed each bundle and box they opened. As they moved, they sprayed the boxes with a fine mist from plastic canisters of dark amber liquid. The chance of any shipment being caught by customs was one in ten. According to their own estimate, that is what they seized: ten percent. Their dope-sniffing dogs were effective, but there was a substance that scared off those dogs, made them shy away and sniff elsewhere: wild-dog piss. The Chiu Chao kept pens of these dogs and gathered their piss for sale to smugglers and to use in their own operations. Whenever they handled anything, they christened it with wild-dog piss.

Johnny and Louie were satisfied: every sampling of bitter white death turned the color of violets.

The trucks were loaded, walled in with crates of rubber dicks, and driven to a private ferry on the northeastern shore of the island. At the pier, Asim Sau boarded a waiting launch. Before parting, the warlord paused to look long and hard into the eyes of the two Americans. In the light of the sun, the reptilian emerald of his gaze was not so unnerving. He seemed less a naga than a monster of more earthly origin. Slowly, his mouth broadened into a smile.

"Life is short," he said. "You are right to live it big."

He said these words so like an epitaph that neither Johnny nor Louie was sure that he had not said *were* instead of *are*.

The ferry made its way to Kowloon. Johnny and Louie did not take their eyes off the containers until they were unhitched, cleared, and hoisted aboard the *Golden Stella*. Louie remained by the ship. At the dockmaster's office, Ng stood by as Johnny telephoned the Bank of East Asia, Limited, at 10 Des Voeux Road. Three minutes later, Ng telephoned the Hongkong and Shanghai Banking Corporation at 1 Queen's Road and received confirmation of the transfer of five hundred and forty-nine million dollars.

"The arms," said Ng, "and the wooden hats."

"Assassins are in place in Bangkok and Yangon," Johnny told him. "Within forty-eight hours, there will be letters edged in black. The arms are now in transit. The ship carrying them has cleared the Suez Canal and is approaching the Strait of Malacca. Men from Italy will be in touch with you later today concerning the necessary arrangements."

"What if, God forbid, you are intercepted?"

"That will not affect our deal, except for the final payment. You have lived up to your end of the bargain. Besides, you will have your black letters and your arms long before we are in any danger."

"You are honorable men."

"It takes one to know one."

On Stonecutters Island, even the Chiu Chao who handled the cargo had not noticed that one of the four containers yielded less free space after loading than the others. Inside the front end of that container, a lead-lined space about a foot deep had been fashioned behind a false partition. Sealed into that space was enough RDX-TNT to blow a battleship to hell. A thirty-day timer had been set to detonate two weeks hence.

It was startling, it really was, Ng Tai-hei had told the others, how many ships vanished on the high seas every year.

Johnny and Louie stood on the bridge deck, looking out over the piers. Their bags from the hotel had already been delivered and stowed. The *Golden Stella* was fueled, stocked, and set to sail.

"You're sure you wanna do this?" Louie said.

"Yeah. I'm sure."

"Twenty-eight days."

"I don't trust them."

"I don't trust 'em either. But eleven thousand miles. Twenty-eight days. That's a long fuckin' haul."

"I know. But if somethin' went wrong now, after all this . . ." Johnny did not finish, as if there were no words to convey what he meant.

"If they did hijack us, what could we hope to do, us and our two peashooters?"

"I don't know. They'd have to get close to us to hijack us. Maybe that peashooter at the right guy's head—this chicken-hawk captain, the engineer, whoever it is that steers this fuckin' thing—could prevent them from answerin' any goddamn distress calls. I don't know. I really don't know. I don't even believe they're out to fuck us anymore. Not now. I think maybe we were just bein' paranoid when they gave us that shit about flyin'. Besides, that fuckin' Ng'll be wood by the time we're a hundred miles out."

"Yeah, but that second ship'd be on our tail by then anyway."

"Then I'll make sure we stay clear of them."

"But you think it's a long shot?"

"Real long."

"Then what the fuck is it you're worried about?"

"I don't know. I just keep feelin' that somethin' ain't right."

Louie said nothing for a while. He lighted a cigarette, turned his back to the piers, looked out toward the sea.

"Did it ever occur to you, Johnny, that this whole thing ain't right? I mean, look back on the last couple of months. What we did, where we been. And now. Shit. We just bought, what, two-thirds of the world's supply of heroin? It ain't like we went to the corner for a pack of smokes. At this point, how the fuck could we know what *right* feels like? What we're doin' has never been done. It's unreal." He laughed and shook his head. "Now that I think about it, how we made it this far, I don't fuckin' know."

Johnny laughed then too. "Look," he said. "Why don't you get the fuck outa here? Jump on a plane, go back and relax. There's no need for both of us to ride this beast home."

"And what about you?"

"I have to make sure everything goes all right. There are last-minute details I have to take care of. I have to do this. If I flew back, every one of those twenty-eight days would be like doin' time. Besides, I got some thinkin' to do. A nice long cruise might be just what the doctor ordered."

"What kinda thinkin'?"

Johnny told him about Diane and the fed.

"Yeah, well, do yourself a favor, pal. What's done is done. It's been taken care of. Don't think yourself into the joint. 'Cause if you do, you might drag us down with ya."

"What would you do?"

"What would I do? Well, first of all—no offense—I wouldn't've married a bitch like that. Don't get me wrong. It's not your fault. A guy, he wants to settle down, he wants more than just a good wife. He wants a broad he can talk to, a broad with somethin' upstairs. And this is what he gets. You can't have everything in one broad. You can't have a mother and a whore, a wife and a *cummari*, a thinker and a follower, an equal and a squaw in one broad. When you get sucked into thinkin' you can, this is what happens. You didn't have these problems in the old days. You took her to the altar, smacked her once across the face, and brought her home. That was that. Not that they weren't a pain in the ass then too. But it was differ'nt. You gotta remember, fear is the better part of respect."

"Then why even bother with a wife? A guy like you, I mean. Or my uncle. No kids. Why not just go it alone?"

"Because whatever they are, we're worse. We're weak. We're shit. They may be broads, but if we need them, what does that make us? Lower than broads. I tell ya, it's a sucker's racket. No matter how you look at, it's a loser's game."

"What would you do?"

"What would I do? I'd treat her real sweet, that's what I'd do. I'd forgive and forget. Then I'd kill her."

"Now you're tellin' me to kill her? First you tell me don't think myself into the joint, then you tell me to kill her?"

"No. You asked me what I would do. I'm tellin' you what I would do. You're too smart to do what I would do. You'll do what's right."

"And what's right?"

"Hey. She never snored in my face. That's up to you to figure out."

"Yeah, well, like I said, I got some thinkin' to do."

"I guess you do. And I'd be a hell of a friend if I left you alone to do it."

"No, Louie. Go home."

"Fuck you." He looked toward the sun. "I'm gonna work on my tan. A little rest and relaxation. I deserve it."

The steam horns blew. Their stentorian blast reverberated through the membrane of the morning: a salute to the sun, a summoning, a blowing asunder of all indecision. Johnny thought of the old Frankie

Ford song "Sea Cruise," and he grinned. He looked at Louie, standing there smoking in his shades and his black silk shirt and his Tanino Crisci shoes and his Beretta stuck down his mohair trousers—an Odysseus of the age—and he grinned all the more. Soon the engines and the slow-swelling breath of the South China Sea bore them away under the brazen sky.

THIRTY-TWO

In the dwindling heat of twilight, in the sweet pine breeze that carried the faint notes of unseen birds, Ng Tai-hei and his driver stood for a moment at the entrance to Ng's home in the hills of Victoria Peak, at the edge of the woods, where no one came. Something, like the echo of a human sound, a heartbeat, a presence, seemed to hang in the warm air. The low-cutting rays of the falling sun whispered through the wild lush darkness of the trees, breathing soft light across the trembling shadows of the cool mossy ground.

It was nothing.

Through the lithium-powered scope of the Oakshore Electronic Ultra-Dot 30 sight that was mounted on the fat, heavy, silenced barrel of the Casull .454, a tiny glowing red point lighted like a ladybug on the temple of Ng Tai-hei.

The loud snap and rush of hushed velocity flushed the unseen birds from the trees. The ladybug became a neat round hole, and like a clump of sod blown from the earth, the other side of Ng's face burst away in a bloody mass of scalp, skull, and brains. The driver, jolting to a crouch and drawing his gun, took the second shot full in the face, which, through the lighted sight, seemed to the painterly eye of the killer to blow open like an Arcimboldo pomegranate.

Aboard the sea-worn *Stella*, Johnny and Louie knew nothing of the end of Ng Tai-hei. They merely assumed that it had come to pass. That night, as the police swarmed on Victoria Peak, they sat in the navigation cabin playing cards with the captain, the pilot, the chief engineer, the deck-and-engine mechanic. It was dealer's choice. The deck passed to Johnny, and he tossed out two rounds of down cards, one round of up cards.

"Is this your first time out?" said the captain, peeling up the corners of his down cards.

"Yeah," Louie said. "How about you?"

The other players laughed, and the captain smiled. He did not look like a man given to children, Johnny thought. He did not even look queer. Then again, it had been so long since he had seen a man without a mask that he wondered whether he could even recognize someone who appeared to be what he was.

The demech, who had a pair of sevens showing, threw up a buck. "I understand you know the powers that be," he said.

"You might say that," Louie said.

No one asked anything further of them, though they all yearned to know why men in their right minds would want to spend a month on this crate without drawing pay and overtime for it.

After midnight, Johnny and Louie checked the locks on their containers. Two were on the upper deck, two were on Hatch 4, Bay 1, about halfway between the bridge and the bow. The abbreviation STC—said to contain—was everywhere in the cargo manifests. Their containers were designated as "STC 33½ tons Braille books, STC 3,000 marital aids." Near the entrance to Bay 1 was a yellowed U.S. Customs notice listing the items that could not be brought into the United States under any circumstances:

Counterfeit articles
Obscene, immoral, or seditious material

Products of convicts or forced labor
Endangered species of birds and animals, including their skin,
    tusks, feathers, and fur, and products made from them
Lottery tickets
White or yellow phosphorous matches
Switchblade knives

"Don't say a damn thing about heroin," Louie said.

Later, when Louie said goodnight and retired to his cabin, Johnny ambled alone around the deserted decks, savoring the Pacific breeze. They were lucky, the pilot had said. This was typhoon season through a hundred and fifty degrees east longitude, and yet the way was clear.

As Johnny lingered on the port bridge, the constellations seemed to enfold the world, each shining star a mystery, a witness to eternity, a guider of breezes and of lives, an ancient god unto itself, hallowed with the prayers and wonderings of the ages. Astraea, the Starry Maid. In the Golden Age, she lived among men. Then, repelled by their wickedness, she withdrew to the evening sky.

Could men ever draw the gods down to earth again? With their hollow words and their snares of theology and morality, could they ever bring back the vain imaginings of their dream of eternal life? What in his self-seeking came first to man, the harnessing of fire or the precept of good and evil? Surely the harnessing of fire, for in doing so, he learned from nature. In inventing good and evil, he interpreted nature, took a further and more imaginative bound. Here, on the open sea, beneath the midnight stars, it was easy to imagine men gazing into this same dark and dazzling sky in the time before good and evil, the time before right and wrong, the time before gods. Man had devised these things for ulterior motives: to shield himself behind the illusory skirts of a threat greater than his own. And yet morality, conjured to protect him, ended up tormenting him. Fear, guilt, and trepidation. These were the disfigurements that the soul bore like the battle-scarred flesh of a warrior in the days before right and wrong. Was it man's wickedness that drove Astraea from him, or was it the wretchedness, the cowardliness of his flagellant soul that repulsed her? Did she recoil at his weakness, his failure to live and die according to his nature, without the threat of damnation or the promise of eternal life?

He thought of the containers, of the death and pestilence and waves of crime and ruin they held, like the myriad demons waiting to be loosed from the brass vessels of Solomon. A gunshot in Milan, a thrust of the knife in Palermo—these were grains of sand compared to the desert storm in those containers. How many innocents would die and suffer so that the wretched might slake their sickness in these poison riches? The answer, like the sum of money involved, was imponderable in its enormity.

The world will follow the streets to hell, old Joe had said, and no one man, no army of men, will turn the tide. Johnny remembered that spring day in the club. *The question I'm asking you is this. Does your morality —call it whatever you want: your code, your principles, your sense of right and wrong, that scrap of something in your heart or your soul that separates you from the beasts—does it allow you to make money from the business of hell?*

And what was his morality? What part of the self-inflicted wound of humanity had he inherited and cultivated? He looked at the stars as if the answer were there. But he saw only Astraea returning his silent glance.

It was not eternal damnation that he feared, and he did not believe in eternal life, except perhaps through metensomatosis. Why then did he do good in this world? Why had he sought love, and why had he felt bereft without it? Why had he never cheated or dishonored those in whom he saw the light of probity? Why did the sight of a dying or crippled child reduce him to sorrow? Why had he hungered to be seduced by the wordless poetry of the breezes? Did these things have anything to do with goodness, or were they merely in his nature, traits and ways that would have defined him even if he had drawn his breath beneath these stars in the time before the gods? Could it be that these things were not good, that they merely *were*? And what then of the capacity to kill, the lust for vengeance? Could the same be said for them?

And what of a man who would destroy the world for his own gain? Well, if the world sought, or accepted, its own destruction, so be it. If the scum of humanity craved heroin, so be it. If the laws of man, and man himself, did nothing to save him from that scum, so be it. Let the self-oppressors go down together, down to the wasteland of gutted souls and assembly-line minds. "The devil is apparently making a comeback," he remembered the Chinese newslady saying on *ABC Eyewitness News.* "Why him? Why now?" she had asked. She was from their world, the world of whiter whites and prefabricated thought, and she did not understand who the hero of *Paradise Lost* really was. Why not him? Why not now?

Those containers carried the sustenance, the transubstantiated host, body and soul of man's chosen savior. It was not a matter of delivering evil to a good world. The old man was right. The world was a black horse running wild to hell and filled with disease. All they were doing was riding that horse for one terrible moment. Just one moment. This one terrible moment.

Fuck this world, and fuck those who would impose their frail conceits of good and evil on it. Fuck the black man and the white, the junkie and the crusader, the philosopher and the fool. Fuck those who swagger and those who cower, those who pretend to truth and those who flee from it. Fuck the poet and the book-burner, the leader and the led. Fuck God and justice and every other lie that ever held men back. Only when one set it all aflame and forsook it could one return, if only for a breath, to that time of purity, that time when fire was the only philosophy.

In that garden in Milan, a secret breeze had opened to him, revealing every moment as a world of radiance unto itself. That breeze had caressed him again and again, diaphanous and miraculous and true. And that breeze was with him now, like Astraea above him and the devil within.

As the ship made its way easterly across the Pacific, veering toward ten degrees north latitude, Johnny came to love his nights alone on deck beneath the stars. The days were hot and brutal beneath the blinding equatorial sun, but the nights, like that first night, were wondrous. The second mate told him of the days before SatNav, the satellite navigation system that now guided ships across the seas. He took him to the chartroom and showed him the tools of celestial navigation: calculator, dividers, and sextant. He took him to the port bridge and showed him Sirius, the brightest star, and Spica, the jewel of virgin Astraea; explained how Saturn during their voyage turned from a morning star to an evening star. In the slow, easy cadence of sunlight and stars, it was easy to lose track of time, and of a world beyond their oceanic coursing.

"How long have we been on this ship?" he asked Louie one morning as the two of them lay on deck, smoking in their boxer shorts, coated with vegetable oil in the waxing sun.

"Damned if I know. A week, maybe more."

The timer in the hidden compartment of their container showed that nine days had passed since the trucks were loaded, that five days stood between this day and the day of detonation.

"We're turnin' into fuckin' bronze gods."

"This is the life, all right."

"I tell you, Lou, if it wasn't for the fuckin' food, I wouldn't care if this thing ever got to shore."

"I'm with you on the food. That fuckin' guinea cook's got some moxie. *Risotto ai frutti di mare* he called that shit he made last night. Tubful of Uncle Ben's, a can of tomato juice, and a handful of fuckin' brine shrimp. Jesus."

"That and something to read. I should've brought a book."

"Hell, they must have fuckin' books on this boat."

There were many back issues of the *Mariners Weather Log*, a beat-up paperback of *The Bridges of Madison County*, a Reader's Digest Condensed Bible, and an Australian "Men's Special" called *Bawdy Ballads for Barroom Blokes*.

"No," Johnny said. "Not really."

"Write your own. You got enough time. Shit. They had this old British broad in the paper, her obit or something, they said she wrote a book every two weeks. She woulda got two outa this fuckin' trip."

Johnny smiled, his eyes shut to the sun.

"Hell," Louie was saying. "Write about how we spent our summer. Write the story of these containers."

Yeah, Johnny thought: *In the beginning was the Shit* . . .

"I don't know how it ends yet," he said.

" 'They lived happily ever after.' "

"That's what I figure." Johnny smiled blindly into the sun. "That's what I figure."

The digital timer in the hidden compartment showed high noon: precisely one hundred and twenty hours to detonation.

Major General Saw Win's arms had been shipped from Linosa to the Israeli port of Haifa, and from there had been flown to Yangon. As the *Stella* passed into the Western Hemisphere, news spread around the world that what General Saw called the regrettable fraternal conflicts of Myanmar had escalated to an unprecedented scale on the Shan Plateau, where Wa warlords had somehow gotten hold of advanced Western military technology. Casualties to Asim Sau's Shan United Army were considerable and mounting, and the Shan warlord himself, while believed to have escaped injury, was said to have fled across the border to Thailand.

There, in Thailand, he would find that Prime Minister Song Leekpai's crop-substitution program was fully under way in the northern hills. As the sowing season neared, the Hmong had been assured of greater prices for grain than for opium tar, and that assurance had been accompanied by a subsidy for seeds and new agricultural implements. As this came to pass, the Democratic Party of Prime Minister Song drew support away from the six right-wing parties that constituted his opposition.

The Padre Carmello Society had done well in making the world a more humane and democratic place.

Incommunicado aboard the *Stella*, Johnny and Louie knew nothing of these things, and they knew nothing of certain events in America.

Special Agent Peter Wang had done what he had hoped to do. He had tied everything together: Bob Marshall's death, the past spring's plague and violence, the logic bomb, and the Colombian cartels' move to overtake the American heroin trade. Together, the FBI and the DEA virtually crippled the Colombian network throughout New York and New Jersey. And yet Wang, who had meant to see to it that his friend had not died in vain, could not escape the sense of that vanity. Not only, he felt, had his friend died in vain; all that he stood for was also in vain.

Then, by accident, Wang found it: the glyph that led him to believe that he had tied together nothing at all. It had been left behind in Wang's office, not in Marshall's, but the handwriting was unmistakably that of Wang's dead friend. It was a matchbook from a Chinese restaurant in Brooklyn, and inside its cover Marshall had scrawled a telephone number and the words *J. has own apt.* Wang had called the number and reached an answering machine. "This is Diane. I can't come to the phone right now, but if you leave a message, I'll try to get back to you as soon as possible." Diane. J. Brooklyn. It came to him that night, at home, and the next day he checked it out. He was right. It was all there in the report that he had compiled for Marshall. John Di Pietro. Lives in Brooklyn with his wife, Diane. Maybe Marshall had been right all along. Maybe he had ripped through the veils of subterfuge to the truth. Maybe the circumstances of his death had been only more veils.

And the FBI in its own way, and for different reasons, had been drawn back to old Giuseppe as well. His second visit from the blue-suited agents was not so laconic as the first.

"I don't think Antonio Pazienza was the friend you made him out to be," the speaking agent said.

"Why's that?" Joe asked, showing neither patience nor impatience, neither curiosity nor disinterest.

"Because friends don't kill friends."

"Are you accusing me of something?" he asked, with a slight, truculent grin.

"Do you know the riddle of the Sphinx?"

"You sure you guys don't have something better to do?"

"The riddle of the Sphinx. You're supposed to be a smart guy. You know the story of Oedipus?"

"I seen the picture. Guy fucked his mother, ended up in the dark. Now I'll tell you something. I'm not in the mood for this shit. You want to fuck around, go do it somewhere else. I'm always nice to you guys. Be nice back. Get outa here."

"The riddle of the Sphinx. 'What is that walks on all fours in the morning, on two at noon, on three in the evening?' In that garage on Broome Street where your old pal got it, all we had to go on was footprints in the dust. By the time we got there, the cops had done a pretty good job of covering those with their own. But there was a partial imprint of a heel, nice and clear, at the edge of the blood. You can't tell much by a partial heel mark. You can't even tell what size shoe it was. As a matter of fact, unless you find the shoe and match the blood, you're nowhere."

"You want to go through my closet now, is that it? Well, I'll tell you something. You put on fucking rubber gloves and aprons, you clean my fucking oven, scrub my floors, do the toilet, the windows. That's the only way you get near my closet. That or a fucking warrant."

Those shoes, like everything else he had worn that day, had long since been reintroduced by Novarca into the ecosystem.

"We don't care about your shoes, Joe. See, there was this other print in the blood, too. Sort of a bull's-eye, a polka dot, a little circle about the size of a quarter. And here and there in the dust, you could see it too. Couldn't figure out what the hell it was. Then somehow I thought of the riddle of the Sphinx. What walks on three legs in the evening of life?" He reached over and gently patted the crook of the hardwood cane that leaned against the chair between him and Joe. "Man," he said. "That's who walks on three. Man."

Old Giuseppe did not flinch. When the agents looked into his eyes, they saw nothing.

"You guys are pulling your pricks, you know that? And you're doing it on my time. You think I'm the only guy who walks with a cane in this world, or what?"

"And I got to thinking," the agent said, as if Joe had not spoken. "These rubber cane-tips, they're porous, and they show the particular wear of the individual who uses the cane. Under magnification, I wouldn't be surprised if they were just as good as fingerprints, with or without traces of blood."

The cane on the chair next to Joe was not the cane he had used that day.

"And this cane isn't going anywhere either."

"Well, Joe, you're wrong about that. And you're wrong about your closet too. About ten minutes ago, a few guys with a warrant entered your apartment by means of an Omni-Guard jamb spreader. Wonderful tool. Wonderful. And much neater than those old twelve-gauge Shoklock shells. Don't worry, they'll fix the door when they're through. And don't worry, I won't leave you without a cane-tip, either."

The agent placed a brown rubber Futuro cane-tip on the table. "That's two bucks and change, but we'll call it a fair trade." The un-speaking agent was already prying off the old cane-tip. He put it in his pocket, replaced it with the new one.

"Now come with us, Joe," said the agent with the voice. "It's time to do some paperwork."

As the *Stella* made its way toward the Panama Canal, as the timer in the hidden compartment counted ineluctably down, as the golden days and starry nights rolled on like the waves beneath him, Johnny thought little of his uncle, or the feds, or the world beyond this seaborne cradling. He thought of the new life, of the riches that awaited him, beyond customs, in the cascade of breezy moments that would wash the darkness away.

And he thought of Diane, who had sinned against him, and who now must suffer.

As for Diane, she had no idea where her husband was, and neither did his office. She had even gone so far as to gather her courage and call his uncle. "He's all right" was all the old man had told her. Wherever he was, it was better this way. It would give him time to cool off. The thought made her laugh in a sad sort of way. Cool off for what? So that they could get divorced in peace? For that was the only solution she saw. They were married not to each other but to misery. It was the only way.

To Johnny, hate was love's weak sister. To hate was to be consumed and obsessed by one whom the hater invested with power over his or her own peace and happiness. It was to be reduced to a weakness beyond that of love. One was a passion that strengthened the soul, the other a passion that tore it apart. And he had hated Diane, with a fever that screamed its weakness to the heavens. But he was calm enough now to see that only when his hatred subsided and weakness left him would he know how, or be able with justice, to deal with her.

But there was time. A new world and the first lustrum of new life lay before him, like a land of dreams. The *Stella*, under a darkening sky, passed a hundred degrees west longitude. The timer in the container showed twenty-one hours to go.

THIRTY-THREE

By the following morning the sky was as gray as slate, the sun a blur of hazy glare. The ashen pall through which the *Stella* passed laid a silence on her crew. They had been two weeks without the sight of land or fellow vessel. Now it was as if the heavens had faded from sight as well, leaving them adrift, alone and ghostly, in a world of bleak eclipse. The ship slowed on the turgid sea. Men moved more languidly. But the hidden timer did not slacken. In less than six hours, its unseen face would show zero days, zero hours, zero minutes, and there would be a small click and a slight whirring sound as the combined masses of trinitrotoluene and cyclotrimethylene trinitramine were detonated, sending forth, at a speed of several thousand feet per second, an obliterating, volcanic blast of shock waves that would fill the gray sky with destruction.

The lookout, far up in the bow, was the first to see it: a speck, a blot, to the northeast, on the murky line of the dim horizon. Johnny was with the captain, waiting. As it came into sight, they hurried to the bridge. The captain overrode the autopilot, conferred with the helmsman. The *Stella* slowed and soon was motionless upon the calm and open sea.

Louie came to the bridge and asked what was going on. Johnny led him away from the others. They leaned against the port rail, watching the nearing ship.

"Here comes our side bet," Johnny told him.

"What do you mean?"

"The *Cobán*, out of Guatemala. We're breaking up the shipment. Two containers stay on the *Stella* for Port Newark. Two on the *Cobán* to Long Beach, then by rail to New York."

"Why?"

"We needed four containers."

"Right."

"We needed to get a dummy order in each of those containers, to give us access to them without tying us directly to the dope."

"Right."

"The lowest value I could put on those rubber dicks was nineteen and a half cents each. That's way below cost as it is."

"Right."

"I had the dicks doped into two separate shipments of six thousand units each, valued at eleven hundred ninety dollars per shipment."

"Right."

"But if they arrive on the same ship, we've got a total of two thousand three hundred and eighty dollars in import cargo."

"So what the fuck's the differ'nce?"

"Anything over twelve hundred and forty-nine dollars and ninety-nine cents, we're fucked."

"How so?"

"That's the dividing line between informal entry and formal entry. Anything valued under that amount is eligible for informal entry. Anything valued over that amount requires formal entry. With informal entry, chances are we get whisked right through customs. The broker shows our paperwork, the inspector stamps it 'Cleared U.S. Customs,' and that's it. We're home free. Formal entry, we're looking at a lot of shit —bonding, an audit—and odds are maybe ten to one that we'll be searched. And if those containers are opened, those inspectors are just an arm's length away from those Braille textbooks. Informal entry, Lou —that's the name of the game. Besides, this way we come into the country from two coasts. Instead of a ten-to-one risk of losing everything in one shot, we go off at twenty to one. Me, I think our odds are even better than that. These ships aren't gook-owned. And the gooks are the only ones who've been bringing in dope by sea for a long, long time."

"Well, what about those Braille books? How do they get around formal entry?"

"They're charitable goods. Not-for-profit. Tax-exempt."

"You're somethin', kid. You're somethin'."

"So where do you want to go, Long Beach or Port Newark? Long Beach, you cut the trip by almost a week. You can fly back from L.A. You pick it."

"What about you?"

"I don't know. I just figure one of us oughta stay on this thing, one of us oughta go with this other thing." He gestured toward the looming *Cobán*.

Louie blew smoke and thought. He knew people in Los Angeles, people he hadn't seen in a while. They even had a decent Italian restaurant there these days. That Conda Veneta, whatever the fuck it was, on West Third there.

"I'll go to Long Beach," he said.

The bow of the *Cobán* was rigged with an engine-powered deck crane, and as the ship tied alongside the *Stella*, two of her crewmen began maneuvering the controls of its drums and its wire rope tackle. A seaman from the *Cobán* boarded the *Stella*. Johnny led him to the two containers secured to the open deck. The seaman, with hollers and waves of his arms, directed the crewmen who manned the crane. Slowly, like a bony black forearm, the boom of the crane reached out in a sidelong arc over the deck of the *Stella*. Most of the crew of both ships had never seen a mid-sea ship-to-ship transfer before, and all hands were on deck, watching and wondering. Soon the word spread around: illegal animals—big cats or jungle birds—making for a back-door port in Mexico. First one container, then the other was hoisted aloft and brought across to a place among other containers on the deck of the *Cobán*. As the crane worked, its wire ropes creaked monstrously, and the Plimsoll mark of the *Cobán* dipped beneath the sea with the weight of the swaying tons. The captain of the *Cobán*, a red-faced man with a Southern accent, confirmed to Johnny that Novarca's customs broker in New York had made all necessary arrangements for unloading in Long Beach.

Louie stood beside Johnny, a cigarette in his right hand, his travel bag in the left. He placed the cigarette between his lips and held out his hand to Johnny.

"See ya in New York," he said.

"Yeah," Johnny said. "See ya in New York." He felt as if he and Louie had been through hell together these last months. He hated to see him go.

Louie was aboard the *Cobán*. Crew members of each ship freed their vessel. Engines began to sound.

Johnny watched as Louie stood waving. The older man looked suddenly like the figure of an orphaned child, forlorn and solitary. Johnny waved back, and to Louie, he looked the same way. The ships began to part.

"Right twenty," bellowed the pilot of the *Stella*.

"Left twenty," bellowed the pilot of the *Cobán*.

"Right twenty," answered the helmsman of the *Stella*.

"Left twenty," answered the helmsman of the *Cobán*.

"Midships," shouted the pilots.

"Midships," shouted the helmsman.

"Dead slow ahead."

Louie's travel bag landed wide of Johnny. Louie scrambled from one ship to the other just as the space between the two widened beneath him to a good three feet. Johnny had him and pulled him aboard.

"I just thought of somethin'," Louie said, winding his legs over the rail. "You can't smoke there no more. I ain't goin' to no fuckin' town where you can't smoke in the rest'rants."

Johnny laughed, and Louie looked at him. "Well, hell, would *you*?"

The *Stella* continued east on its way, following Trade Route 12 toward the Bay of Panama. The *Cobán* wound north, toward the Baja coast. In time, each ship once again became but a speck on the horizon of the other.

Then suddenly the northern horizon burst with fiery light, a blast that filled the slate-gray sky and shook the *Stella* with the thunderous, sea-roiling force of its might.

Johnny turned pale in the breath of the blast. Then he thought of the containers on Hatch 4, Bay 1, and he flushed, sure that a second blast would end his world before the next beat of his heart. The decks swarmed with officers and crew. Louie held fast to the rail, his knuckles whitening.

In that moment, in that heartbeat that came, like a miracle, like a work of the God that he had cursed, Johnny grasped the meaning of those sums—billions, hundreds of millions—that from the very outset had been beyond the ken of his understanding. They were worth less than a heartbeat. He knew that now. For in his horror, it was not the money his being had screamed for. It was the next breath, the promise of which enriched every pauper to wealth beyond his.

Only when panic ebbed and breath returned did he mourn his loss. A third of the world's heroin. Five billion dollars. Up in a sea-swept storm of white powder that hung in the sky like fine ashen fallout.

"It ain't the end of the world," Louie said.

"It almost was," Johnny said.

"We still got half. That's more than we need."

Need? Johnny thought. Maybe Louie was right. Maybe for them, maybe for everyone, greed was need, need was greed.

Louie stared straight ahead, at the northern horizon.

"You all right?" Johnny asked him. It wasn't the sort of question you'd ask a tough guy, Johnny thought. But then again, they weren't tough guys anymore. They were friends.

"I'm here," Louie said. Then, still staring straight ahead, as if to convince himself, he said it again: "I'm here."

They emerged from the fifty miles of the Panama Canal to the open blue water of the Caribbean Sea. Within days, the sky cleared and the slow, easy cadence of sunlight and starlight resumed. Time and the world, however, no longer seemed a realm apart. Instead of Astraea, Johnny saw only those pale and scattered stars—*star light, star bright*—to which his drunken father had drawn his eyes in the long-ago Brooklyn night. Twenty-five degrees north latitude, sailing north. They were in the Atlantic now, the Brooklyn sea, the sea of dirty dreamland, and of *l'America*. They were home.

It was not yet dawn when they pulled into Port Newark. Johnny and Louie were already awake and on deck.

"Judgment day," Louie said, and Johnny merely nodded. His heart pounded as they drew nearer.

It was midmorning by the time the ship was unloaded and customs had arrived. Johnny, who had chain-smoked and drunk coffee incessantly since waking, felt like a mass of raw ganglia.

"You better cool out or let me do the talkin'," Louie told him. "You look like a fuckin' advance man for guilt. Go get some pills off somebody. Do somethin'. You're makin' me fuckin' nervous."

Johnny got some Valium from a seaman, and he went to his cabin, lay down, and shut his eyes. It was a moment like all others, he told himself, just one passing moment. But it was for him a moment of fear. He breathed deeply, thought of the breeze and calm of the Giardino Inglese. Whatever was meant to be, he told himself, would be. Fear could never save him, it could only destroy him. The commotion on the dock and throughout the ship was intense, but he had almost drifted to sleep when Louie rapped on the cabin door.

"Show time," he said.

Johnny rose, and together the two men strode down the gangway toward customs. Johnny looked for their broker but did not see him.

The inspector held their paperwork in a clipboard.

"You're Novarca?"

"We're Novarca," Louie said.

"You're coming from the *Stella*?"

"Yeah."

"What the hell were you doing on that ship?"

"Cutting costs."

"How so?"

"Our boss, his idea of entertainment expenses is a six-pack and Chinese take-out. Travel expenses, same thing."

"So you're PAC. Let me see your passports."

They showed him their passports. He returned them, looked down at the clipboard.

"Toy Models Incorporating a Motor," he read. "What kind of models?"

Johnny reached into his luggage bag, took out a black cardboard box seven inches long by three inches wide by two and a half inches thick. It had a pink label with Chinese and Japanese writing. He gave it to the inspector. Inside, the inspector found a black six-inch molded latex effigy of a phallus-shaped totem pole with a long-tongued beaver at its base. A thin two-foot red, white, and blue wire connected it to a purple plastic battery pack with two control switches for speed and rotation.

"Keep it," Johnny told him, breaking his silence, feeling both the Valium and the pounding of his heart, fearing that the dream of his artificial composure might burst at any moment, leaving him a panicked, prison-bound mass of jagged nerves and sweat.

"Nineteen and a half cents. That's pretty cheap." There was a note of skepticism in the customs officer's voice.

"These are old hat over there. They can't sell them anymore. They've got all sorts of new models. They took a loss. Over here, we figure, they're still novelties, they're still something new."

"Since when does Novarca import? I thought Novarca only exported. I thought Novarca shipped pulp."

"That's right," Johnny said. "But we're thinking of getting our own ship. If we did that, we'd go import-export. We're starting to feel things out."

"Here's your broker now." The officer gestured beyond them. "Get those passports stamped, you can get out of here."

With the broker was an elderly blind man wearing dark glasses and a yarmulke and feeling his way with a tensile cane. The broker barely acknowledged Johnny and Louie.

"Mr. Rothstein here is from the Jewish Braille Institute in Manhattan. He's very worried about his books."

"What books?"

"Containers YCEU 410167-3 and 250009-1. He just wants to know that they've arrived safely."

The inspector looked at his clipboard.

"Hey, pal," Johnny said. "We were here first. You're working for us too, right? Let's do one thing at a time."

"You should be glad that I got your two-bit shipment in with these books," the broker said.

"What do you mean, two-bit shipment," Louie said, taking the cue. "These books, I suppose they're worth somethin'." He sneered.

"Yes," said the frail old man in the skullcap. "To children who hunger for knowledge but have no eyes to read, they are worth something, indeed. They are worth a great deal."

The inspector looked at Johnny and Louie. "There's more to this world than a bunch of nineteen-cent tchotchkes, you know. And if you're going to get into import, you're going to need some patience, too. We warehouse goods here for certain audits, you know." There was the barest hint of threat in his voice. "Sometimes an audit can take a year. Say a guy brings in goods he values at nineteen cents. Say I think he's dodging duty, that he's undervaluing his goods. That's grounds for an audit. He gives me a hard time, I give him a hard time. Patience. It goes a long way. Besides, I told you, you don't need to be here." He turned to the broker. "Sign here for the books," he said. Then he looked at the blind man. "Everything is in order, sir. As soon as your drivers are here, your containers are ready to roll."

By the time the trucks arrived at the Novarca plant in Jersey City, the blind man had regained his sight and was bitching about the money he was to be paid.

"Come on, guys," he said. "My ass was really on the line there. I mean, what's right is right. I said a grand, I wasn't thinking."

"That fuckin' beanie really suits you, Max, you know that?" the broker said, and everybody but Max took to laughing.

Louie put his arm around Max, drew him slightly away from the others as they walked from the trucks to the work office. "I tell you what, Max. I didn't know you were in on this. I'll throw in an extra grand. You just keep your fuckin' mouth shut about this, you hear? You don't, I'll fuckin' rip your eyes out for real." He made a clawlike gesture with his right hand, patted Max on the back with his left.

The containers were parked and unhitched. Johnny's mind and body sang. He had never felt such exhilaration, such elation, in his life. This hellish compound through which he strode seemed to be paradise itself. The minimum-wage spics scrambling through the garbage at the huge funnel-mouthed maw of the sorting bins seemed to be angels of triumph and bliss. The stench of decay, ambrosia. The rumbling of packers and lift-offs, a symphony, a song.

They had done it. The world was his. He could do anything now: drink, dance, open a joint, buy a 1481 *Commedia*, a 1495 Hesiod, murder his wife, buy a stone villa, pin hundred-dollar bills to his vest and fuck teenage girls. He had lived the first half of his life as a fool. He would live the latter as a prince.

It was the foreman in the office who took the grin from his face, and from Louie's as well.

"They got him for murder," the foreman said. "He's out on bail."

He was there on Hester Street, sitting with his coffee, enlaced in smoke, as if this day were like any other. He smiled as Louie and his nephew approached.

"Is it true what they say about Chinese broads?" he asked, cutting the air horizontally with his hand.

"What happened?" Johnny said.

"What? This shit with the feds? I think they're on fucking dope, these pricks. They say they can place me at Tonio's murder by my cane print. Did you ever hear such shit?"

"A cane print? Is that possible?"

"My lawyer said he'll let me know."

"They'll never get a fuckin' conviction on a goddamn cane-print. It's fuckin' ridiculous," Louie said.

"That's what he says."

"You'll never do time on this."

"Shit, I won't even do court time. I'll blow my fucking brains out

first. Jump fucking bail. Whatever. Take my money and vamoose. I ain't
got time for this shit. It's like the guy says in the commercial: these are
my fucking golden years. So," he said, as if discussion of his fate were
so much small talk to be dismissed, "where's the shit?"

"Jersey," Louie said. He looked at Johnny.

"We lost half of it," Johnny said.

The old man's expression remained one of stone. "How do you lose
sixty-eight tons of dope?"

They told him about the explosion at sea, about how they almost
lost it all and their lives along with it. Giuseppe nodded philosoph-
ically, as if to say that such was life. He called in Frankie Blue from the
street.

"It's time to make those rounds," he told him. "Go see all five. Tell
them supper's on the table."

He turned to his nephew. "Have Bill downtown put in invoices for
two hundred grand in consultancy fees to Lupino in your name. You'll
have to pay taxes on that, but it'll wash some of your cut, show a legit
source for it, cover any conspicuous-consumption bullshit you'll probably fall for no matter what I say. The rest, you'll get cash. So get yourself
a safe-deposit box. A big one." Then, to Louie: "You, get yourself a
fucking wheelbarrow. You're gonna need it."

Johnny walked all the way uptown to the apartment on East Sixty-
seventh Street, stopping off on Park Avenue South to pick up the six
weeks' pay that was waiting for him. As he walked, even the oppressive
heat and glare of summer's final days was a celebration of the senses;
the white glistering sun, a golden shield that radiated glory and promise.
He felt as if God had saved and affirmed and smiled down upon him as
never before. He did not even want to kill Diane. It was as if the
purifying, empowering wave that had delivered him to new life had
washed away the petty poisons and burrowing jealousies of his soul's
grubby chrysalis. Diane knew nothing. As far as she knew, he was still a
scuffling union stiff. If he was going to dump her, now was the time,
before the new cut of his cloth aroused her suspicion and greed. Based
on his union income, alimony would not be so bad at all.

So it was, later that afternoon, when he dialed the Brooklyn number and heard her voice, he found himself saying words he never imagined he would utter: "I think we should talk."

He met her that night at Lespinasse, where some big shot from Jersey had once taken him on union business. It was the most elegant joint he knew.

He had been awake since before dawn, had started the day as a mojo sack of raw nerves, caffeine, nicotine, cold sweat, and Valium. Drained by ordeal and elation both, he had walked miles in the heat on this, his first day on land in a month. But he had taken a hot bath and a cold shower, shaved, and dressed, and he felt all right. That is, until he looked at the black kid-mohair suit hanging in the closet. Had she fucked that rat cocksucker, or what? He would never know. But it did not matter now, he told himself. They were history; their marriage was wood.

She looked beautiful when she arrived, and Johnny saw in her the woman who had enraptured him years ago. Would that this were his first glimpse of her; would that they were coming together tonight as strangers, playing in the light of each other's eyes for the first and fatal time.

"It's good to see you," she said softly. It was amazing, he thought, how violence and upheaval worked as a catharsis on the soul, how they drained enmity and left placidity, even timidity, in their place.

As they ate, their conversation was so trifling that it devastated them, she in her way, he in his.

"You gave me these," she said, touching the string of pearls on the flesh of her neck and the black of her dress. And when she touched them, she began to weep. And as she wept, she said she was sorry.

Johnny could not bear to see her cry. Seeing her so vulnerable made him doubly so. He did not understand what she was sorry for. Her public tears? Her sins? The end of them? His fate, or fate itself?

"We'll be all right," he told her. "We'll be all right." The words sounded strangely familiar, almost ghostly to him. It was what he had told her on that cool spring night when Tonio drew the blade across his skin.

"I love you," she said, weeping. "I'll always love you."

He could not do this. He could not do this and yet he must. To take a life was not so dreadful as this. To have destroyed love and to bury what one had destroyed: it turned the thews and sinews to sap. Those moments in the catacombs of Palermo did not seem so terrifying as the soft-lighted opulence of these.

"You're more than my love," he told her, feeling his own blood curdle at the deceit of his words. "You're more than my love," he told her. "You're my friend."

The restraint of her sobbing seemed then about to burst, and she rose, shaking her head, and rushed to the ladies' room. Johnny sat alone, staring blankly and sucking on his tooth as if to extract a morsel of bitterest fruit.

When Diane returned, her tears were stanched, her face abraded, reddened, and hard.

"I want a divorce," she said.

Thank God. She had rescued him, ruddered her own destiny. He listened to her, and as she reviled him without rancor and in the name of love, he found himself savoring her anguish, feeling that in renouncing him, she would find his vengeance.

He walked her to Fifth Avenue and embraced her in the night. He watched awhile as the cab he had hailed took her away, south toward Brooklyn. The moon in the starless sky was waning. Johnny walked north, along Central Park, inhaling the leafy perfume of maple and oak. There was a melancholy, a languor, in the heavy swaying of trees in the last long days before their season of sleep. Tonight, it ennobled the melancholy that echoed within him, and instead of sadness or anger, he felt a great poignant strength. His past was in the swaying of those trees. He could sense it calling after him, like an old friend who returns from death in a dream.

Within three days, Joe had sold all but twelve of the sixty-seven tons. His own crew had come in for a baker's dozen. President Street had taken ten; Mount Carmel, another ten. Sullivan Street, seven. Newark and Cherry Hill, five each. Philly, three. Billy Sing, a deuce. At eighty grand a kilo, that came to four billion, four hundred million. A billion and a third to the Albanian Plain left just under three billion. After what had been laid out and interest due on the bank loan, that left a net profit of roughly two billion, three hundred and eighty million and change. The unsold twelve tons were worth another nine hundred and sixty million—six hundred and forty million after Virgilio's cut.

Three billion and change. It was not what Giuseppe had envisioned, but it was not bad. And it was only the beginning. Once the Middle Eastern caravans began to move next spring, duty would be paid to Giuseppe and his chosen on every shipment imported to the States.

When Johnny arrived at the club to collect his cash, Louie was there but the old man was not.

"Where is he?" Johnny said.

"That's what I was gonna ask you."

They sat and they waited. They smoked and they stared at the door. They called his apartment. They called Frankie Blue's. After an hour and more had passed, Louie took a deep breath and spoke.

"He told us the other day. He told us right to our fuckin' faces. He told us he'd jump fuckin' bail, take his money, and vamoose. What he didn't tell us was that he'd fuck us in the process."

"I can't believe it," Johnny said.

"No? Well, let's hear your fuckin' theory. For all I know, maybe he paid you and fucked me."

"Go fuck yourself."

"Where do you bury your dead, punk? You talk to me like that, you better have more in your hand than fuckin' sweat."

This was a side of Louie that Johnny had never seen: rabid, unthinking, hateful. The shirt he was wearing, it was an eight-hundred-dollar piece of silk. Johnny knew because he had been with him when he bought it, at de Lisi. He drew thick phlegm from his lungs to his throat and drew a bead. That is when Frankie Blue walked in.

"He had a stroke. It don't look good."

Thirty minutes later, they were at his bedside in a private room at Lenox Hill. Cerebral infarction had stolen his power of speech, and the right side of his body was partly paralyzed. They could tell by his eyes that he knew them, that his mind was still there.

"Where's the money?" Louie asked him.

The old man tried to speak, but the sounds that came out of his mouth were garbled.

By the telephone were a pad and pencil. Louie placed the pencil in Joe's left hand and held the pad for him to write upon. Straining in his illness to write with a hand he had never written with, he was capable only of an indecipherable scrawl.

Johnny's anger toward Louie had not subsided; it had merely been shunted aside. When Louie and Frankie Blue left, he remained by his uncle's side, watching over him as he slept, wondering at how a man with the vigor of a bull could be reduced to a slobbering child in the drawing of a breath.

When Joe woke, his left hand reached out, groping for the drawer of the nightstand by his bed. Johnny opened the drawer for him, and the old man dangled his hand within it. Johnny examined its contents: a bunch of hospital admissions papers and his uncle's wallet. Johnny took out the wallet, and the old man nodded. Tentatively, Johnny began looking through the wallet. But there was nothing there that seemed to indicate the location of the money. The old man uttered a harsh guttural sound. Johnny removed each item from the wallet. As he held one card and scrap after another to his uncle's eyes, the old man shook his head. At the sight of his Social Security card, he nodded. Johnny stared at the card. He read out every word that was on that card, and every number as well. The old man lay motionless, his eyes fixed on Johnny. In those eyes, Johnny could see the light of thought screaming for a voice. When he came to the number seven, Joe nodded forcefully.

"Seven," Johnny repeated.

Again the old man nodded.

"Is that it?"

Yes.

"There's nothing more."

Yes.

"There is more."

Yes.

Johnny continued through the contents of the wallet. Again and again, old Joe shook his head. There was nothing left but a ragged

Columbus Civic Club membership card and a tattered little photograph of Johnny's aunt. To the picture of his dead wife, the old man nodded.

"Aunt Matilda."

Yes.

"Aunt Matilda and seven."

Yes.

"That's where the money is."

Yes.

Johnny looked blankly, hopelessly into his uncle's eyes. Aunt Matilda and the number seven. He wandered to what used to be the smoking-lounge and sat awhile with the patients in their gowns, recalling the days when he had been one of them, in this very same room. Aunt Matilda. The number seven. Four billion, four hundred million dollars reduced to an imprisoned thought, lost to a tiny bursting bubble in the blood as surely as their fortune's other half had been lost to cataclysmic explosion at sea. He shook his head and closed his eyes. Through the window, from Seventy-seventh Street below, came the bang and crash and groaning churning of garbage trucks.

Suddenly his eyes opened wide. He returned hurriedly to his uncle's bedside.

"Matilda No. 7," he said. "The money's in Matilda No. 7."

The old man nodded, and though his face could form no expression, there was a fire in his eyes, a fire bigger than death or crippling fate.

Johnny went to the closet and reached into the pocket of the trousers that hung there. He jangled a ring of keys.

Yes, his uncle nodded, yes.

"The lunchbox?" Johnny asked, referring to the locked compartment beneath the driver's-side chassis.

No.

"The crawl door?"

No.

"In back?"

Yes. He must have stashed it between the packing panel and the push-out blade.

Johnny called Diane and asked her where the car was parked. He hung up abruptly, squeezed his uncle's hand, and kissed his forehead. "I love you," he said. "Don't worry. I'll take care of you."

Outside, on Park Avenue, he hailed a cab to Brooklyn. He found the Chrysler and headed for Jersey City.

"Where's No. 7?" he asked the foreman.

"Round back, end of the line. She's dead. Differential went about a week, ten days ago."

Johnny found and unlocked her, got in the cab, started her, and engaged the clutch. He pressed the power take-off switch, jumped out, and ran round just as the packing panel lifted. Out tumbled five liquor cases wrapped tight with wide black tape. Each weighed about forty pounds. He hauled them one at a time to the trunk of the Chrysler, then drove off toward the Holland Tunnel, grinning like a fool.

As he carried the last of the cases into the apartment on Sixty-seventh Street, the phone rang.

"How is he?" Louie asked.

"The same," Johnny said.

"And how are we?"

Johnny did not answer, and evil drifted through his mind. Then he said, as if saying nothing, "I've got your money."

As soon as he hung up the phone, he realized he had made a mistake. Now that he didn't have Joe to answer to, what was to prevent Louie from showing up, killing him, and taking it all?

Louie, as he traveled uptown, realized he was walking dead-on into a setup. There was no money. He couldn't say anything to Frankie Blue, who was driving him, because Frankie Blue was Joe's man, and Joe's man was Johnny's man. Instead of ringing Johnny's bell, Louie tele-phoned from the corner, asked Johnny to come down. But Johnny was not about to walk full face into a gunsight. For all he knew, Louie could be calling from Staten Island.

"Don't you trust me?" Johnny said.

"I trust you. I don't think you trust me."

"Well, you're the one seems short on trust these days, pal. Guy has a fuckin' stroke, you figure he's sold you out."

"And you didn't figure the same."

"No."

"So you fuckin' got a hard-on for me. Maybe you got somethin' else for me too."

"And maybe you got somethin' for me, sport. Maybe you got somethin' for me."

"Look. I know I'm in Dutch for shootin' my mouth off before. But that's over."

"So come on up."

Three, four months ago, Louie would have feared nothing from this kid. But now Johnny had tasted blood. He knew what Louie knew: that it was easy.

"Show me you got the scratch. Throw a bundle out the window. I see it, I'll come up."

"This is fuckin' ridiculous."

"Humor me."

"When I see you, I'll throw it down." He hung up the phone.

Each case was filled with bricks of a thousand hundred-dollar bills each. What if the fall broke the rubber band and the hundred grand blew all over the street? He rummaged through the cabinet under the kitchen sink, found what he was looking for: a five-by-ten-inch zippered leather pouch full of power drill bits and chuck keys. He dumped its contents, stuffed the hundred-grand bundle into it, zipped it, and carried it to the big Palladian windows. He looked. Louie was standing there, looking up. Johnny dropped the bundle. A moment later, his bell rang. He was waiting at the apartment door when Louie reached the landing. Each man regarded the other with the cold, wary gaze of strangers in a dark place.

Not long ago, after the explosion at sea, Johnny had asked Louie if he felt all right. It wasn't the sort of question you'd ask a tough guy, he had thought, but then again, he had thought, they weren't tough guys anymore, they were friends. Was friendship so tenuous, was trust so frail? Or was greed so great?

"I'm sorry about today," Louie said.

Would he have been sorry if a hundred grand had not fallen at his feet? Johnny thought. "Yeah," he said. "You look the same way when you're happy."

"Look. Let's spit this out right now."

A malevolent grin crept across Johnny's lips. Louie was still wearing that eight-hundred-dollar shirt. Louie mistook the grin for one of friendliness, which, in fact, it slowly became.

"You know," he said, smiling now himself, "the last time somebody used that tone of voice to tell me to go fuck myself, like you did today, I left them coughin' blood." His smiled widened. "Granted, it was a broad."

"Fuck today."

"I'm with you."

The two men slowly warmed to each other again. What greed could sunder, riches could heal. They talked awhile about Giuseppe's stroke. If Frankie Blue hadn't been at his apartment when it happened, it could have been the end.

"Sometimes I wonder if a slow count ain't worse. A guy like your uncle, God never meant him to end up in a diaper."

Johnny said he would have the old man moved in here, uptown, where he could take care of him.

"I told ya before, I'll tell ya again," Louie said. "You got what it takes. Things like this, that's when ya tell what somebody's made of."

Johnny inhaled, shook away the prospect of nursing his uncle: of spoon-feeding him and wiping his ass, dressing him and washing him, and seeing those eyes, day after day, until a merciful wind took him. Maybe there was a God of right and wrong. Maybe this was their punishment. Maybe this was their fate.

"So what do we do with all this?" he said, gesturing with a sweeping arm at the big money-filled boxes on the floor.

"We better get it downtown, into the vault. We got billin' to do anyway. We'll wash part of it through Lupino, like your uncle said." Louie reached into one of the boxes, counted out twenty hundred-thousand-dollar bricks into four piles of five bricks each. He passed half to Johnny, took half himself. "This should get us through the week-end."

Johnny sat there with the million in his lap and lighted a cigarette.

"What's your cut, anyway?" Louie asked him.

"Five hundred million. That was before we lost half."

"Shit. If you didn't split those containers up, we woulda lost it all. Five hundred it is."

"What about my uncle's share?"

"That's up to you. I say, as long as he lives, we don't touch it. It's his. After that, we do what's right."

After that, we do what's right. The word *right* seemed absurd here, in this room, with them and this money. It was not that Johnny felt them to be wrong by nature, or to have committed themselves irrevocably to wrong. No. He still felt within him the sense of right and wrong, pure of any law of god or man, that he had always known. But the weight of this money, these treasure chests of illimitableness, crushed every impalpable abstraction and all the endless words by which men sought solace from their lives.

He went to the kitchen to get another pack of smokes. There it was on the wall: Saint George on his white steed, his lance piercing the winged dragon beneath him, the Virgin Mary kneeling in prayerful observance nearby. Johnny remembered the first time he had looked at the faded picture's rearing, wild-eyed horse, remembered how he had thought of the story that the old man had told him about the horse on Cornelia Street, the *equus mundi* that his uncle wanted to ride. S. GIOR-GIO, PROTEGGI LA NOSTRA CASA DALL'INSIDIA DEL MALE. Was it protection that had been delivered to this house, or was it divine retribution? Maybe these notions were not so abstract, not so far removed from the palpable and real, for the weight in the other room had not crushed or effaced them.

Black horse, white horse. Which was it that had thrown old Joe?

That night, as Johnny sat alone with his million dollars and his ciga-rettes, he thought of Homer's garden of Alkinoös, where no season was without fruit or bloom or abundance. This sort of money, that's what it was: the garden of Alkinoös. Suddenly, he recalled the tableau in the Museo delle Marionette in Palermo. Il Giardino di Alcina. Alkinoös. Alcina. Of course. But there was no devil, no serpent, no winged dragon in the garden of Homer's Phaecian king. Johnny, who had never read Ariosto, had it all wrong. But it did not matter, for there was no devil, no serpent, no winged dragon in the garden of Ariosto's enchantress, the true Alcina, either, and Johnny was right about one thing: in Sicily, myth took darker turns.

The telephone rang. He knocked over two hundred grand reaching for it. What he heard sent a shiver down his spine, for it was a demonic echo of the devious words that he had uttered to Diane:

"I think we should talk."

"Who is this?"

"An enemy. A friend. It's up to you."

"I don't know who you are. I don't know what you're talking about. Don't call here again."

He hung up. Immediately, the phone rang again. It was the same voice, a voice he had never heard.

"If you want to live happily ever after with your money and your heroin, you'd better listen."

"You got the wrong guy, pal. I don't know what your fuckin' racket is, but you're barkin' up the wrong tree."

"Let me put it like this. I want your fucking blood or your fucking money. Which would you rather give me?"

"Who are you?"

"I'm a guy who could be at your door with a federal warrant in forty-five minutes," Peter Wang said. "So I think you'd better invite me up for coffee now. Because once I pull that fucking warrant, there's no turning around. Not for me. Not for you."

"I have no idea what you're talking about, and I'm gonna hang up."

"One thing. About that forty-five minutes. I lied. It's in my pocket, and I'm right around the corner. See ya in a few."

"Wait. Where are you?"

"The joint with the French name on Madison."

Johnny hung up. Peter Wang left the bistro and looked down the block till he saw Johnny coming his way, then he went back inside and waited. When Johnny entered, he waved to him.

"Are you crazy, or what?" Johnny stood over him, talking down, trying to sound angry but not loud and certainly not fearful. "I oughta call the cops."

Wang tossed his credentials wallet on the table. "Use my name when you do."

Johnny opened the wallet, looked at the badge, the ID.

"What the hell do you want with me? I got nothin' to do with drugs. I got nothin' to do with anybody that does."

"Just sit down."

Johnny did so, glared at him with bravado.

"Ever since you went to Milan to meet with Ng Tai-hei, ever since then, I've had you clocked."

Johnny felt sick to his stomach. He had no way of knowing that Wang was bluffing.

"You killed my partner, too."

Maybe this Chink knew. Maybe he knew if that cocksucker really fucked Diane. Shit. Maybe the Chink fucked her too, for all he fucking knew. Maybe it was Diane who had led them to him in the first place.

Johnny ordered coffee, put on a subtle show of bewilderment.

"Give me half a million, I'll go away," said Wang, who had no idea of the enormity of what had gone down.

Half a million, thought Johnny; that's chump change. He had more than that in walking-around money up the house.

"Why should I give you a dime? The only reason I'm here is I got a sick sense of humor and nothin' to do." He sipped his coffee. "Let's see that fuckin' warrant."

Wang really had a warrant. It was partially blank. Only Johnny's name was missing.

"Pay or die," said Wang.

"What kinda cop are you?"

"I'm not a cop. I'm a federal Justice agent."

"And this is your idea of justice?"

"Yes, if you must know, it is. There's no stopping the shit in this world. I used to think there was, but not anymore. I don't suppose you've ever heard of Xunzi."

Johnny looked dead into his eyes: " 'Human nature is evil.' "

Wang was taken aback. This was no ordinary wop.

"I don't suppose you've ever heard of Louie the Lug," Johnny said. Wang looked dead into his eyes but said nothing.

" 'Any man who needs the words of a philosopher to rationalize his ways is no man at all.' Fuck Xunzi. You hide behind good to do bad. It's as simple as that. You're lower than shit in the street. Don't give me that justice shit. You're a cop. A fucking cop."

"And what are you?"

"Me?" Johnny smirked. "I'm proud to be a Teamster. That's what I am."

Wang shook his head and grinned in a dirty way.

"I tell you what," Johnny said. "I don't know anything about this dope shit you're talkin' about. But there is somethin' you could do for me, somethin' that would be worth the kind of money you're talkin' about."

Wang said nothing, and Johnny continued.

"I got a sick uncle who's got a bum rap against him. I don't want him goin' from the hospital to the joint. You're a federal agent. Give his lawyer some paper to the effect that you had my uncle under surveillance all day long last June 27. You vouch for him, that he did nothing wrong that day, that he did nothing wrong, period."

"Fabricate an affidavit? Lie under oath? That's perjury."

"No it ain't. It's justice. You want your money, you do somethin' for it. I'll give you half now, half when you come through. After that, you bother me again, you can tell your ancestors to make room."

Wang paid the check, and they left. At the apartment, Johnny gave him a quarter of a million dollars. Then he handed him a pen and paper.

"What's this?" Wang said.

"Make me a receipt. I want a receipt. Date it and sign it. You got somethin' on me, I want somethin' on you."

Wang did as he was told. Johnny asked him for his wallet. He checked the signature on the receipt against the signature on Wang's DEA card.

The phone rang. Johnny pocketed the receipt, handed back Wang's wallet, and answered it. A moment later, he hung up the receiver and just stood there.

"You can forget about that affidavit. We won't be needing it. He's dead."

"I'm sorry," Wang said, surprising himself with his own words.

Johnny looked at him as if his expression of condolence were an affront. He gave him another quarter of a million. "Now get out of here. I don't know you."

Wang asked him for a bag. Johnny stared at him a moment, then got him one from under the sink.

"Wait a second," Johnny said to his back. "I wanna ask you something."

Wang slowly turned to face him.

"That partner of yours. Did he break into the apartment in Brooklyn, or did my wife let him in?"

"I don't know," Wang said.

Johnny nodded, turned away, and heard the door close as the Chinaman departed.

At the restaurant after the funeral, Johnny stared at the glass of wine before him and flicked an ash from the cuff of his black Brioni suit. He perused the bill the undertaker had handed him.

FUNERAL HOME EXPENSES
Use of Funeral Home and Facilities . . . . $ 700.00
Professional Services of Funeral Director and Staff 1220.00
Bronze Finished Steel Casket as Selected 2980.00
Standard Concrete Vault 750.00
_____
Total Expenses $5650.00

CASH AND MISCELLANEOUS EXPENSES
Greenwood Cemetery—Opening of Grave . . . . $ 655.00
Religious Service—St. Anthony's 100.00
Pallbearers—6 @ $25.00 . . . . 150.00

Burial Permit and 24 Transcripts 360.00
Gratuities 20.00
Transfer of Remains 185.00
Use of Hearse to Cemetery 135.00
Prayer Cards, Acknowledgment Cards, Registers for
    Visitors, and Crucifix 146.00
3 Limousines . . . . N/C

Total Cash and Miscellaneous Expenses $1751.00

TOTAL FUNERAL EXPENSES $7401.00

"Forget the buck," the undertaker told him.

What a fucking sport. Johnny counted out seventy-four hundred-dollar bills.

Louie looked at him from across the long banquet table, where he sat with his wife, Medusa, freshly frosted and resplendent in mourning black. Diane sat at Johnny's side, as if beside a ticking bomb.

"It won't be the same without him," Louie said.

"It sure won't," Johnny said.

Louie's wife clicked her tongue and shook her head in commiseration, as one might express regret that a coffee had been spilled on a tablecloth.

"First Tonio, now him. Terrible," she said.

Louie raised his eyebrows. Johnny snorted.

"God works in strange ways," said another woman, who spoke these words whenever death descended or an unlikely couple married. To her, all couplings were unlikely.

Farther down the table, a group of old men were recalling with laughter the time in their youth when Giuseppe had sent lengths of broom handle eye-hooked together and wrapped in wax paper to an imprisoned man with a craving for sausage. The youngbloods—Guarino, Rosario, others whom Johnny barely knew—looked repeatedly at Johnny and Louie, as if awaiting cues. Watching them, Louie thought of the eyes of Judas on the refectory wall of Santa Maria delle Grazie. Willie Gloves sat among them, not as one who coveted but as one who prospered and counted his blessings. Odd, Johnny thought, that Willie, whose daily bread was leavened by murder, should possess a decency more enduring and profound than that of most men. Stanley Krauss and Bill Raymond of Novarca seemed ill at ease. Rose, dead Giuseppe's old *comare*, had the look of one who believed there was a will that bore the testament of an old man's remembrance.

Johnny paid the bill, handed out a few hundred extra to the waiters. His glass of wine still sat undrunk upon the table. On this day, he had no taste for it, or for oblivion either.

"'*A cummari secca*," Louie said as they rose to leave. For a moment, Johnny thought he was talking about Rose. "That's what your uncle always said when somebody died."

The old man had been right, Johnny thought. That's what death was: a dry mistress. She filled our minds and shadowed our days our whole lives through, and in the end she took us, giving nothing of herself.

Outside, in the warm September air, Diane went her way, Johnny his. He watched her as she walked away. Her legs were still lovely, her sway still as rivery as a poem. Years ago, they had talked about buying a video camera. Now Johnny regretted never having bought it. He could have had tapes of that sway, those eyes, those lithe legs wrapped around his back. In a way, then, he still would have had her. Instead, he had nothing. She turned the corner and was gone. Over the Hudson, the evening sky was iridescent, like mother-of-pearl. Mother of melancholy, mother of mourning, mother of men left alone in the world.

THIRTY-FOUR

Louie Bones looked forward to greater things. Asim Sau and Tuan Ching-kuo had escaped death, but their power was broken. Once again Sicily, the beautiful isle, would feed the world's veins. In Louie's domain, which was New York, Johnny was free to roam and choose among the seasonless fruit of bloom and abundance.

With the coming of autumn, when the city skies were clear and blue and sanguine, Johnny sat in the park and walked the streets for hours on end. He and Willie still once in a while journeyed uptown for squid on Fridays, but the old man was losing his touch, receding from this world in body and mind, dying slowly in the tomb of his tending.

"You sure ain't actin' like a single man," Willie told Johnny one day, pushing aside the squid, which possessed only a trace of its old sea-sweet flavor. "If I had your money and your looks, I'd be out there livin' it up ev'ry night."

"Who says I'm not?"

"I can tell by lookin' at ya. Ya got that monastery skin."

"You know what it is, Willie? I'll tell you what it is. Every broad I've ever met, I met through drinkin'."

"Then drink."

"I'd be my own executioner."

"I don't buy that. I don't believe you're that weak. Don't get me wrong. You're better off without it. But if your mind ain't tougher than your body, not drinkin' ain't gonna make you any stronger, it's just gonna feed your weakness."

"You think it's easy not to drink? I mean, for me not to drink?"

"No. I think it's hard. I used to see you. It was like watchin' a guy jumpin' the line to the boneyard. It must be tough, a guy like you, livin' without the shit. It must be like livin' without an arm. But what I think's harder, for a guy like you, is gettin' your fill and then puttin' the shit aside the next day. Doin' that would say somethin'."

"There's the rub. My fill. It's not a fifth. It's an ocean."

"I still think you're bigger than a fuckin' bottle."

Sometimes Johnny believed that. Sometimes he knew it.

"Hell," Willie went on. "One way or the other, it's mind over matter. Forget the shit, just go out there sober and do what you do drunk. Be obnoxious. Make a fool of yourself. Beat up a few cops. Insult your friends and sweet-talk strangers. Stick your fingers down your throat and puke on your shoes every now and then. If that's your secret to the art of love, it should work just as good sober as drunk."

"You still pickin' up broads in church?"

"Why not? It's as good a place as any."

Johnny shook his head and grinned. "You're somethin', boy. You go out there, you do what you do, then you hit the holy water."

"Hey, look." In an instant, Willie's look and tone went from light-hearted to earnest. "Since when was God not a god of destruction?"

"Is that what you tell those church-goin' mamas?"

"No." Just as quickly, his look and tone reverted. "I tell them they seem to walk in grace and peace."

Johnny laughed.

"And the funny part," Willie said, "is—"

"They buy it."

"No. The funny part is, I mean it."

One afternoon Johnny bought a bottle of Scotch and put it atop the refrigerator, and every morning he looked at it. Soon, he told himself. Soon.

He saw women in the street. Willie was right. Some had the bearing of grace and peace. He hungered to explore their souls, to make a gift, or unburden himself, of his own. Still, he was not cured of Diane, who in forsaking him—yes, he saw it that way—had seemed to speak and act not only for herself but for every woman besides. Their grace and peace, he felt, was not for him. But there must be one, or many, among them who could understand. Who could feel the breezes. Who could see how, in one errant spirit, a breath of poetry left to stifle might in darkness become murder. He would find her, and love would come again. Soon, he told himself. Soon.

Not long ago, though it seemed a different age, he had watched a junkie die so he could afford a new transmission for his car. Now, all things reckoned, he was worth more than a billion. He thought of buying a house. Maybe down the shore. Spring Lake, someplace like that. Shit, he could buy a castle in Italy, a mansion in Manhattan. Fuck the shore. He could have an island of his own, a jet to carry him back and forth. He thought of making investments, of traveling the world. He could do anything now. Soon, he told himself. Soon.

Sometimes it seemed that the breezes of the past season had brought no others in their wake. Sometimes it seemed those breezes and those moments thrived only in the stillnesses amid death and ful-mination. At such times, he thought of calling Louie. Soon, he told himself. Soon.

The bottle, his Beatrice, the dollar, the gun. These became the stations of his daily cross, as the self-cut jewels of his moments became the smooth obsidian beads of rosary biding.

When he had cleaned out his uncle's apartment, he had not found much worth keeping. Under the refrigerator were two large manila envelopes filled with the big currency notes from the twenties that his uncle called bedsheets. Their total face value was ten thousand dollars. On the collectors' market, Johnny figured, they would be worth far more. Also under the refrigerator—he almost missed them—were three rolls of twenty-dollar gold pieces. In a bedroom drawer, there were a few pieces of gold jewelry: a pair of cufflinks, a tie clasp, a money clip, a wedding band. There were no photographs, no written remnants, no objects beyond the jewelry and the old baseball bat by the door that spoke to Johnny as keepsakes of the man whose death had left him as the end of the Di Pietro line.

In a drawer, beneath a stack of yellowed shirts, tucked away as if it were a treasure of some kind, Johnny found a small cloth sack. Inside it were three concrete-crusted stones. Like the hermetic canister of "bad meat" in the freezer, these drab and commonplace stones had meant something. They were, in a way, the old man's true legacy. Johnny could only guess at the lethal powers of that canister, and yet there it sat, like a common domestic good, with the ice cubes and frozen peas. To Johnny, there was no more fitting memento of his uncle's inscrutable ways: peas for me, bad meat for the world. But it was the image of those baffling stones that remained with him. What meaning had they held for the man who so purposefully preserved them? Johnny would never know. To him, those worthless stones represented a mystery that was both grand and sublime, as only a true mystery, a mystery without an answer, can be. Men died, but the secrets of their souls, the riddles of their ways, were everlasting.

Johnny had used to believe in the great rule of Socrates: know thyself. But he had come to see such belief as arrogance. One could only pretend to know the unknowable, and in doing so, one ultimately fell to delusions and lies. In truly knowing oneself, one knew the impossibility of ever really knowing. There philosophy and logic and ethics ended. For there was a darkness, a divinity perhaps, a universe unto itself, beneath the skin of the soul, where man-made elements such as they could not exist, where other powers, other forces, governed.

Johnny had placed one of the stones upon his uncle's grave, pressing it deeply into the soft soil with the heel of his shoe. The other two he kept. He placed one of them on a shelf—a private icon of sorts, a reminder of his uncle and of death and, above all, of mystery. The other he kept, in its old cloth sack, away in a drawer.

The leaves turned bright with death. On a lovely day toward October's end, the time of the year that he loved best, he drew a deep, sweet breath, filled his left pocket with money, cracked the seal on the bottle, and went to the phone. It was time to find a breeze.